## INTOXICATING PASSION

"From now on, I shall think of you not as a thief, but as a modern Robin Hood," Abra said with a smile.

Dash stared at her, his eyes deep blue and searching. "I think you've done a bit of romanticizing. Perhaps of your father's past?" he suggested. "Or dare I hope of me?"

This time, when the thought came to him that she needed kissing, he made no attempt to fight it. He put his hand to her waist and drew her to him, his lips finding hers warm and willing.

Abra filled with delicious warmth as her arms lifted, her hand dropping the bunch of violets to the ground by her feet, reaching up to the hard wall of his shoulders, then sliding to the warmth of his neck, the immensely pleasurable contact with his skin and hair skittering through her fingers and down her arms. She felt his embrace tighten as he pulled her closer, and when she breathed it was his breath she inhaled, oddly sweet to her, and tinged with the taste of champagne. She wondered if it was possible to become drunk on a kiss. . . .

# ZEBRA'S GOT THE ROMANCE
# TO SET YOUR HEART AFIRE!

**RAGING DESIRE**                                    (2242, $3.75)
by Colleen Faulkner

A wealthy gentleman and officer in General Washington's army, Devon Marsh wasn't meant for the likes of Cassie O'Flynn, an immigrant bond servant. But from the moment their lips first met, Cassie knew she could love no other . . . even if it meant marching into the flames of war to make him hers!

**TEXAS TWILIGHT**                                   (2241, $3.75)
by Vivian Vaughan

When handsome Trace Garrett stepped onto the porch of the Santa Clara ranch, he wove a rapturous spell around Clara Ehler's heart. Though Clara planned to sell the spread and move back East, Trace was determined to keep her on the wild Western frontier where she belonged — to share with him the glory and the splendor of the passion-filled TEXAS TWILIGHT.

**RENEGADE HEART**                                   (2244, $3.75)
by Marjorie Price

Strong-willed Hannah Hatch resented her imprisonment by Captain Jake Farnsworth, even after the daring Yankee had rescued her from bloodthirsty marauders. And though Jake's rock-hard physique made Hannah tremble with desire, the spirited beauty was nevertheless resolved to exploit her femininity to the fullest and gain her independence from the virile bluecoat.

**LOVING CHALLENGE**                                 (2243, $3.75)
by Carol King

When the notorious Captain Dominic Warbrooke burst into Laurette Harker's eighteenth birthday ball, the accomplished beauty challenged the arrogant scoundrel to a duel. But when the captain named her innocence as his stakes, Laurette was terrified she'd not only lose the fight, but her heart as well!

*Available wherever paperbacks are sold, or order direct from the Publisher. Send cover price plus 50¢ per copy for mailing and handling to Zebra Books, Dept. 2613, 475 Park Avenue South, New York, N.Y. 10016. Residents of New York, New Jersey and Pennsylvania must include sales tax. DO NOT SEND CASH.*

# LAWLESS ECSTASY

## SUSAN SACKETT

**ZEBRA BOOKS**
**KENSINGTON PUBLISHING CORP.**

ZEBRA BOOKS

are published by

Kensington Publishing Corp.
475 Park Avenue South
New York, NY 10016

First printing: March, 1989

Printed in the United States of America

*Lovingly dedicated to Amanda—*
*that WON-DER-FUL child.*

# *Prologue*

He checked his watch. Eight minutes, he decided, was all he had until the guard returned to the hotel office. That meant he had eight minutes to open the vault, take what he had come for, and then make his way back to the ballroom upstairs without being seen. A tight schedule, even for him.

His fingers touched the dark hair of his moustache fleetingly as he considered the vault. Then, without the smallest hesitation, he brought them to the dial and began to work. He'd practiced with an exact twin of this very safe for the past five weeks. If he couldn't open it, he knew, no one could.

In the end, it proved far easier than he had hoped it would. There was a moment, but one only, when he heard the noise of someone approaching in the corridor, of footsteps stopping by the office door, and he froze, tasting the fear of discovery and listening to the beating sound of his heart as it filled him. Then the footsteps turned away and continued on down the hall. His calm returned, he started once again with the vault door, outwardly unruffled, calmly resuming his task as though nothing untoward had happened. He felt the tumblers as they fell into place, the small internal movements of the locks like welcome friends to his inordinately sensitive fingers. And then, finally, he realized he could swing the door open.

He knew, of course, exactly what he had come for, and he methodically searched for it, pulling out the small safe drawers until he found the one he wanted, lifting the necklace and holding it up to the light for a small second of appreciation, peering at the enormous central emerald ex-

7

pertly, with an appraiser's eye, then slipping the piece of jewelry into his breast pocket.

He was about to reclose the safe when the image of a woman came to him, a tall, slender woman with titian hair, wearing an emerald-green satin gown, very much the color of the stones safely warming in his pocket, and a choker of pearls. He'd only seen her for a few moments, but somehow he seemed to know her. He pulled the drawer open once more and extracted a bracelet, heavy with diamonds and platinum. None of the stones were so fine as the emerald, but they would fetch a decent price. The diamonds joined the other jewels in his pocket and he pushed the drawer shut, carefully wiping the drawer pulls with a fine linen handkerchief, then pushing the door to the safe closed and relocking it. Again he fastidiously dusted away any evidence of his passing, then moved silently to the door, listened intently for a moment before slipping into the corridor and stealing along it to the stairway to the ballroom.

Music drifted down to him, pleasantly melodic. He was in the mood for dancing, he decided as he entered the glittering, crowded room. He straightened his tie with a quick tug and took a glass of champagne from the tray a passing waiter carried. His eyes narrowed as he sipped the wine, scanning the crowd for the woman with the titian hair.

He smiled when he finally saw her, swallowed the remainder of the wine from his glass, and left it on a convenient table before he began to make his way through the crowd to where she stood. She put him in the mood for dancing, and with any luck at all the theft would not even be discovered for a week or more.

# Chapter One

Abra Beaumont's eyes narrowed and she peered at the large hat box that occupied the seat opposite her in the carriage. Her father seemed oblivious to her preoccupation, but that was most probably because he seemed transfixed by a preoccupation of his own, she decided, and not really from any lack of interest. And that, Abra had to admit, was the real reason for her own confused state of mind.

She bit her tongue to keep herself from asking, knowing he would tell her if he was of the mind, and that nothing could induce him to if he wasn't. But still she could not but help wonder how long it would be that she would have to wait for him. She was not a person possessed of an enormous store of patience, and there were times, she remembered, when he seemed to delight in provoking her lack of it.

Whatever it was, it seemed to agree with him, she thought. She'd not seen him look so animated in a long while, his expression pleased, the wrinkles on his forehead almost smoothed, and his grey moustache looking jauntily upward, as though in anticipation. Whatever it is, she thought fleetingly, perhaps she ought to let it be if it pleased him. But the undeniable feeling of alarm she'd sensed growing in her since the start of their expedition told her that would doubtless prove unwise.

Her control began to shatter when he ordered the driver to pull up at the wharf at Pike's Slip, and she found that even the pressure of her teeth to her tongue could hold it still no longer.

"Papa," she began, leaning toward him as he opened

the door of the carriage for her. "Just what are we do-ing?" she demanded curiously.

"Just a short stroll before lunch, Abra," he returned, lifting innocent eyes to hers. Then he unfolded his long legs and stepped down to the cobblestone walk, turned back to her, and extended his hand. He inhaled with a theatrical gesture, filling his chest and stretching his arms. "The sea air will be good for your appetite."

"My appetite is quite fine as it is," she told him drily, but she accepted the hand he offered and stepped down to the curb beside him. She looked at him critically, wonder-ing how someone so familiar could sometimes seem so totally a mystery to her.

But now was not to be the right moment for explana-tions after all, she realized. Vincent Beaumont pulled her arm through his, then set off to the edge of the wharf, guiding her genially along at his side, chatting easily about the trading vessels tied up at the wharf, and lapsing into an off-tune whistle when he realized the subject had not captured her.

Despite his obvious intentions, Abra knew his mind was not on the offloading of the stores of tin and crockery that littered their path, for his eyes seemed intent upon something still a good distance offshore. She kept her eyes glued to his expression, to the oddly purposeful glance that focused on the brightly glittering waves.

He stopped when they'd reached the edge of the wharf and stood staring silently out at the water, his free hand reaching up to touch the edge of his moustache in a habitual gesture Abra knew indicated thought.

"A beauty, isn't she?"

The words startled her, for she'd not noticed the stran-ger who had strolled up beside them. She turned to him, and saw he was staring out into the harbor just as Vincent did, the object of his glance apparently the same as her father's.

He was tall, taller even than Vincent, she realized, and much broader, with startling blue eyes, a prominent, well-proportioned jaw, and dark, curly hair that the wind blew freely, for he wore no hat. Other than that, he was impec-cably dressed, and there was no thought in her mind that he might be a laborer any more than her father might be, despite his current preoccupation with the workings of the docks. A decidedly handsome man, she mused, only a bit surprised at the objective ease with which she made the observation. Then she realized he'd turned his glance away from whatever it was in the harbor that had seemed so intriguing, and leveled it at her. He seemed to realize that she had been staring at him, despite the fact that she quickly turned her glance away. He bluntly returned her fixed gaze, a smile lighting and softening what might otherwise be thought of as overhard features.

"The yacht, I mean, of course," he said with a self-deprecating smile, then pointed to a large, seagoing yacht that floated at anchor in the center of the harbor like a toy boat upon a pond.

Abra found the vessel, its sides so white that the sunlight reflected from them seemed to hurt her eyes, and felt all the more uncomfortable because she felt the touch of a blush reddening her cheek. It grew more pronounced when she turned back to him and found he was now repaying her for her stare, smiling, and apparently perfectly content to stand there silently, gazing intently now at her.

Vincent, roused by his last comment, turned appraising eyes to the stranger. "Most handsome," he muttered, then tightened his grasp on Abra's hand. "Come, Abra. I did promise you lunch, didn't I?"

The stranger smiled once more, his eyes catching Abra's, and nodded as he stepped aside to allow them passage. Abra darted a quick last uncomfortable glance at him as she passed him, then turned a suspicious glance to her father.

"Do you know that man, Papa?" she demanded abruptly when they'd walked beyond his earshot.

"Certainly not, Abra," he replied with a smile. "And I must admit to feeling that he was an acquaintance of yours, or at least had the earnest desire to become one." His smile vanished as he stared at her. "Not that I blame him," he continued thoughtfully. "Especially as you look so fetching in your new bonnet."

Now Abra grimaced, wondering once more what had prompted him to suggest this unexpected outing that morning, and his sudden insistence that she acquire a new hat. Not that she had minded the trip to the milliner's shop, not even his rather intent insistence upon choosing the hat himself, for he'd settled on a perfectly beautiful specimen, dark green velvet to match her best coat, trimmed with satin flowers and a wide satin ribbon. But she'd really not needed a new hat, and the episode was causing her more and more to feel that he was up to something, something of which he knew she would not approve.

He ignored her expression. "I do think I shall have to keep you under lock and key, Abra, my dear, or some stranger like the one on the pier will do me the wrong of stealing you from me."

Abra laughed despite herself. "Papa! The very idea."

Vincent shrugged then, and patted her hand where it rode on his arm. They walked in silence back to the waiting carriage. As he handed her up the steps, he called out to the driver to take them to Delmonico's. When he'd settled himself beside her, the carriage moved falteringly into the bustling traffic that filled the cobblestone street.

When they were settled at their table and Vincent was apparently intent upon the menu, she finally decided she would have to ask, or die of curiosity.

"Just what was it we were about this morning, Papa?" she demanded.

He put down his menu, reached for his water glass and grinned at her. "Why, a new hat, Abra," he answered as he lifted the glass to his lips.

"Stop it, Papa. You are driving me mad. That was an excuse, and you know it."

He looked seraphic as he smiled at her. "You're right, Abra. I simply couldn't help myself. I'd just decided that I needed someone prettier to look at across the table this afternoon than my broker. And you immediately came to mind. The hat was simply a lure, so that you'd endure my company for lunch."

"Papa!" Abra was gripped with a tearing sense of exasperation. "Why did we go to the docks?"

Vincent looked around the room, conscious of the quick stares her raised voice had garnered them. Then he leaned forward, took her hand, and looked at her rather sheepishly.

"I'm afraid I found the need to indulge myself a bit, Abra," he confessed finally. "A bit of the old sense of adventure, I'm afraid."

Abra furrowed her brow. "I don't understand," she insisted.

He smiled as one does at a slow child. "That yacht your handsome admirer pointed out to you, Abra. It is owned by the Emir of Mukalla, Sheik Shahab Sharify, and apparently he's brought with him on his visit a fabulous ruby, the Tear of Allah."

Abra's confusion vanished, leaving a cold tingle of fear along her spine as it fled. "Papa, you aren't planning to do anything," she hesitated, "anything untoward, are you?" she asked softly.

He stared at her a moment, then shook his head slowly. "Alas, my dear, no. I just was in the mood to look, that's all. I'm afraid those days are long behind me."

Abra put her hand on his and squeezed it gently. His tone had grown sad suddenly, and almost tired, and the animation that had lightened his features when he'd been on the wharf was gone now, leaving him looking quite old.

A ruby, she thought, the Tear of Allah. He'd never even seen it, and yet it had somehow managed to reach out to him and infect him with a poison he was powerless to fight.


Abra turned away from the piano, the last notes of the waltz still lingering a moment in the air. She stared at the chair where Vincent sat, his eyes closed, and smiled tolerantly. He'd asked her to play for him, asked for that specific waltz, and now he was asleep. She looked at the clock. It was late, she realized, and the day had roused a score of memories in him that would have better remained asleep. Perhaps she ought to wake him and see him up to his bed.

But his eyes opened even as she approached his chair.

"I'm not really asleep, Abra," he told her with a grin. "Just thinking. Did you know I danced to that waltz with your mother the night we met?"

13

She smiled at him indulgently. "Yes, Papa," she said softly.

"I've told you this a hundred times before," he said, turning away. "I think I'm growing old, my dear."

She leaned forward and kissed him on the forehead. "Not you, Papa. Never."

But he raised his hand and touched her chin with his fingers. "Yes, I've grown old, and you've grown up. Soon you'll be leaving me for another man, I think."

She smiled at him, taking his hand in hers and hugging it against her cheek. "You're the only man in my life, Papa," she assured him.

"But there'll be another soon, I think. Young and handsome, like your admirer on the wharf this afternoon."

So he's been mulling over that all afternoon, she thought.

"Someone like Freddy?" she asked with a playful nod of her head.

"Bah! Protect us both from the Freddies of this world. I certainly hope he'll be more of a man than Freddy Westmore."

Abra giggled. "Well, as there seem to be only Freddies on the horizon just now, Papa, don't let yourself fret about it." She stood. "It's late. Time we were abed, I think."

He looked up at her and shook his head. "You go on up, Abra. I'll be along."

Then he reached to the table beside his chair and picked up the morning paper that had been left there. It was opened to the center page, which was littered with ads for Mrs. Abagail Fullerton's Cures for Catarrh and Sciatica and darkly meaningful urgings for men to purchase Dr. Solvini's syrup, which assured a strengthening of the manly aspects and promised to lead to complete satisfaction in matrimonial endeavors. For a moment Abra wondered idly if Freddy Westmore availed himself hopefully of the good Dr. Solvini's cures. Then her eyes strayed to the side of the page where the daily gossip column glared up at her, announcing in boldfaced letters the visit of Sheik Shahab Sharify to the city. This, she knew, was what had intrigued her father.

14

"Papa," she began tentatively, "do you really think you ought to—"

He cut her off with a wave of his hand. "Just an old man's folly, Abra, fantasizing. Nothing more," he assured her.

She sighed. There was really nothing more that she could do, nothing more she could say to him. She leaned down to him and kissed him once more, gently, on the cheek.

"Then goodnight, Papa," she said softly.

He only nodded before turning to stare at the paper in his hands.


Abra looked at her father critically as she straightened her long kid gloves. Perhaps this evening will amuse him, she thought, perhaps all he's needed is a bit of diversion. But she sincerely doubted it. Despite Vincent's laughingly oft-repeated comments, mentioned only in the strictest of privacy, of course, that he'd bought his way into society with the Five Hundred's own diamonds, she knew he really did not enjoy these parties and attended them only because he felt she should become a part of the loftier, moneyed circles. As far as she was concerned, she was ambivalent. She enjoyed the music and loved to dance, but she doubted that she would ever find any interest in any of the rich, spoiled young men she met at these parties. Freddies, all of them, she thought, and wondered fleetingly if her life was ever to offer anything more exciting.

"Well, Abra?" Vincent asked as he offered her his arm. "Ready to face the social lions?"

"More cubs than noble beasts, I think," she murmured in reply, putting her arm through his and thinking of Freddy Westmore.

He looked at her, seemed to read her thoughts, and laughed. Then he patted her arm and led her into the huge ballroom.

Their entrance did not go unnoticed. Dashiel Thorne had just asked Eleanor Dewitte if she would do him the honor of a dance, and, unsurprisingly, she had smiled toothily, nodded an enthusiastic acceptance, extended a

15

small, bony hand for him to grasp, and slid her beaded reticule onto her wrist in preparation for the exertion of the event. An event that was undoubtedly not common in her life, Dash thought as he put his arm to her waist and thankfully noticed nothing more seductive than the feeling of whalebone and canvas beneath his grasp. For a moment he pondered why such a bony, unpromising figure as Eleanor's needed the protection of corseting, but the mere contemplation of his partner's more womanly attributes numbed him and left him avoiding thought altogether. He told himself to keep in mind the far more appetizing prospect of putting his hands on the diamonds Mrs. Dewitte wore draped from a rather fleshy neck. It was the Dewitte diamonds that were, after all, his prize, not the Dewitte daughter, and they, at least, were of ample and desirable form.

He manfully lifted his glance above her head, not very hard to do, since even the exaggerated arrangement of her curls hardly reached to his shoulder, as he shuffled her less-than-graceful form around the floor. It was then he saw Abra enter, and he was stricken with the dismaying thought that perhaps the Dewitte diamonds were not all that important after all.

It was absolutely inconceivable to him that he would allow the opportunity to pass. He'd lost one chance with her, the week before, at the docks, and he had scarcely dared hope that there'd be another. He remembered the feeling that had come over him as he'd turned his glance away from the yacht to find her staring at him, her huge, heavily lashed green eyes staring up at his, her full lips just a shade disdainful, a finely chiseled nose, a shade too long, perhaps, but elegant. For a moment he'd almost run after them, thinking to demand her name, knowing only that he'd been left there silently praying that the man who accompanied her was a father and not a husband. And in the days since then he'd thought of her, even repeated her name in his mind, and told himself a dozen times that he was behaving like a fool, that most likely he'd never even see her again. But there she was, looking even more beautiful than he remembered her to be. This time, he told himself, he would not lose the chance.

He swirled Eleanor Dewitte around so that she was

16

facing the doorway, feeling her nearly stumble as he left the more mundane pattern of their waltz, and found himself forced to steady her with a firm hand to her waist.

"Who is that tall gentleman who just came in?" he asked, his tone light, and waited until she'd turned to see who it was of whom he spoke. "The grey-haired man with the moustache," he qualified, smiling down at her as she squinted a bit myopically, then turned back to him, and looked up with a hint of suspicion in her eyes. "I think I may have met him," he told her by way of explanation, "in Paris perhaps?"

That seemed to satisfy her, and Eleanor shook her head in negation. "Oh, I think not. Vincent Beaumont and his daughter never travel to the continent. Abra says her father insists it's because an ancestor of his was an aristo guillotined by the Revolution, but I don't believe a word of it. My father says," and she lowered her tone as she imparted this final bit of gossip, "that there was some scandal in Cannes over a jewel robbery some twenty years ago, and he dares not return." Now that she'd begun to warm to the subject, Eleanor's features took on an animation they ordinarily did not contain. In fact, the matter held some kind of fascination for her, for she failed to notice the look of surprise that passed over Dash's face at the mention of Vincent Beaumont's name, and blithely continued on with her tidbits of information. "Of course, no one knows for certain, and he was married to one of the Waverly daughters, an impeccable family, if a bit, well, eccentric, as Papa says. The best families do not receive them," she noted, her tone implying that hers was decidedly one of those notable scions of society. "But some people, you know, are always intrigued by the hint of something unsavory."

Dash felt his stomach heave at her prattle. He tried to concentrate on her mother's diamonds, but found that a glance in Abra's direction quite overshadowed them. He smiled warmly down at Eleanor.

"Vincent Beaumont, did you say?" He heaved a sigh of relief as he realized the music was ending. "Why, this is a surprise. I do know him. Not from Paris, certainly, but from Charleston. He's a cousin of my mother's cousin. I met him at a wedding, not two years ago." The last of the

17

music faded from the air and he stopped dancing, his hands dropping happily from their contact with Eleanor's waist and weak-wristed grip. "You will excuse me, won't you?" he asked as he walked her back to the unnecessary protection of her mother's company, oblivious of the shocked glance she cast at him, and of the small, strangled sound that managed to work its way from her throat. He was sure the sound meant she was in a rage, something otherwise hard to recognize, as Eleanor's face always seemed to bear odd splotches of color, and from his experience with her, apparently carried a perpetual frown, even in moments of what he had perceived as delight, such as that moment when he'd offered himself up to her with the request for a dance. He wondered what penance he would have to serve to convince her to forgive him and allow him to charm his way once more into the bosom of the eminently respectable Dewitte family. He found the thought totally revolted him, and he mentally bid a mournful farewell to the Dewitte diamonds. The price was far too high, he told himself philosophically, silently mourning all the work he had gone to to gain entry in the first place. "I really should reintroduce myself to him. I'm sure he'll be delighted with news of his cousin." And with a crooked smile and a tight little bow, he turned and left her staring numbly after him.

Dash was not happy to find Abra was no longer at her father's side when he reached the bar where Vincent waited for a drink to be poured for him, but he told himself the delay was merely temporary. And he did know Vincent Beaumont, or *of* him, at least, and the prospect of talking to him genuinely pleased him. He should have known, he said to himself, when he'd seen the man on the wharf. Doctor had once told him Beaumont had returned to New York.

"Mr. Beaumont," he began, his hand extended cordially and a smile tugging at the corners of his lips as Vincent turned to him, the smallest flicker of recognition passing across his otherwise implacable expression as he recognized Dash as the man from the wharf. "Please allow me to introduce myself. My name is Dashiel Thorne, and we have a mutual friend, I believe, James Sutton." He waited, smiling as Vincent absorbed this information and finally extended a hand to take his.

"Doctor Sutton," he said softly. "It's been a great number of years, but I was still quite distressed to hear of his death."

Dash nodded. "A great loss, to us all."

The bartender deposited a crystal glass containing a single malt and soda on the bar with a flourish. Vincent, still examining Dash with steely blue eyes, nodded toward it. "Will you join me?" he asked. "In tribute to Doctor."

Relieved that he had apparently passed some test, at least provisionally, Dash nodded. "The same," he told the barman, and both waited silently as the drink was poured, then took their glasses away from the bar to a secluded spot near a marble pillar and a cluster of potted palms.

Vincent sipped the scotch meditatively. "Did you know Doctor well?" he asked.

Dash nodded. "He was sick the last few years, and unable to get about much. I visited him a good deal, filling him in on the local gossip. The comings and goings in Philadelphia were pretty much bread to him."

For the first time since he'd turned to find Dash at his side, Vincent smiled. "That was kind of you," he said, remembering how the old man had thrived on the happenings of other people's lives. That was how he'd come to be called Doctor, not from any medical training, certainly, but simply because he always seemed privy to absolutely everything about everyone in whatever city he took up residence—everything; and in the kind of sordid detail only a trusted friend or family physician usually heard.

Dash shook his head. "Not kindness, really, except on Doctor's part. I dare say he gave me a good deal more than I gave him. He shared a lifetime of experiences with me, not to mention imparting a good deal that I can only imagine would have been, to say the least, painfully learned had I been forced to discover it on my own."

Vincent lifted a brow. "Then you continue in Doctor's tradition?" he asked, but he already knew the answer. Dash's introduction and his presence at the wharf that afternoon the week before had been proof enough.

Dash nodded. "In my own poor way."

Vincent shrugged. "I doubt that Doctor would have taken on an untalented apprentice," he noted. "I abhor undue modesty."

Dash grinned. "Very well. I've had a bit of success."

Vincent took in the impeccably tailored evening clothes, the heavy gold signet ring on Dash's finger. "You're here," he said slowly. "That denotes a certain amount of success in itself. Perhaps you could come round to dinner one night and we could talk about it."

"There is nothing that would please me more," Dash replied quickly as he lifted his glass to his lips and stared out to the dance floor, finally catching a glimpse of Abra as she danced with a tallish blond-haired man who looked at her with what could only be termed total adoration. She seemed far less enthralled, he noticed with a feeling of satisfaction.

"If I may offer a word of advice . . ." Vincent murmured after a long moment of silence between them.

Dash turned to him. "Please."

"The diamonds around Mrs. Dewitte's neck, while genuinely worthy of your admiration, are, I feel obliged to warn you, nearly unapproachable." He looked thoughtfully off into the distance. "Damned shame, too. If ever a greedy, thieving man deserved a bit of fleecing, that man is Charles Dewitte."

Dash raised a brow. "Mrs. Dewitte's diamonds?" he asked innocently.

Vincent only shrugged at his pretence. "You were dancing with the formidable Miss Dewitte, weren't you?" he asked, as though that could be the only reason he could fathom why a man would put himself through such torture. "When not around the good woman's ample neck, where they are under the constant scrutiny of Dewitte's vigilant gaze, they are stored safely away in the man's private vault at his bank, an absolute fortress, if you will take my considered evaluation. When in transit, they are accompanied by two heavily armed guards. As I said, the jewels are unapproachable."

Dash had listened to him with strict attention, then he lifted his glass once more to his lips. "I was under the impression that you'd retired, sir," he said when he'd taken a swallow.

"And so I am. I occasionally indulge in a bit of mental exertion, and those stones you had your eye on were, of course, a natural target of my curiosity."

Dash waved a hand noncommittally. "They are tempting, though," he muttered.

"Decidedly," Vincent admitted. "But not half so tempting as the Tear." He stared at Dash, his gaze searching.

Dash thought of the huge yacht lying in regal state in the middle of New York harbor and of the treasure she held. He nodded slightly and sipped his drink once more.

"Now that would be a prize," he said finally, a small smile working its way to his lips.

"Abra, there's a place for sale on Gramercy Park, only a block away from your father's house. It has a lovely big parlor, perfect for parties, and a glassed conservatory. You could grow flowers all year round."

Abra stared at Freddy Westmore ingenuously, wide-eyed. "I really don't think it would be quite proper for me to come to your house to tend to your flowers, Freddy. People might talk."

"They wouldn't talk if you lived there, too," he insisted.

Abra smiled wickedly. "Really, Freddy, I'm shocked. And I do think that would make for a good piece of gossip. If I were you, I shouldn't let Papa hear you say such things. He'd absolutely ban you from coming to call." On second thought, Abra mused, that might not be such a bad idea. Freddy's insistence was becoming quite wearing. She looked away from him, humming softly to herself as she moved in time to the music.

"Dash it all, Abra," he sputtered. "You know I didn't mean anything like that. You know that I'm absolutely mad for you. Why won't you say you'll marry me?"

"We've been through all of this before, Freddy," Abra told him, turning back so that her eyes found his. "If you insist upon continuing with this, I shan't dance with you anymore this evening." She smiled at him once more. "And that would be a shame, for you are such a good dancer," she added as he swirled her expertly across the floor.

He was, too, she thought. A good dancer, good looking, even occasionally amusing. And unfortunately, nothing more. If only there were something behind all those words of passion that flowed so glibly from him, something that could convince her a real heart lurked somewhere beneath his perfectly tailored suits, his always immaculate linen. But all he ever pressed on her were his words, and she'd gotten the odd impression that were he to shed his jacket and shirt, she'd find nothing beneath, nothing at all, just empty space with that pleasant head floating above, eyes pleading as they were now, and lips perpetually smiling. Freddy Westmore was certainly not what she'd define as a man of passion.

The music stopped and she found herself standing with him on the dance floor, her hand still firmly clasped in his.

"Another dance, Abra," he pleaded softly. "I promise not to talk about anything that you'd disapprove of."

Abra considered his request solemnly. She really did enjoy dancing with him, but somehow his presence had begun to disconcert her lately, and she'd begun to be afraid that if she allowed him to continue pressing her, she might eventually say yes simply out of sheer exhaustion. Before she'd had a chance to reach a decision about his request, however, she was startled to hear a strange voice close by, obviously addressed to her.

"Miss Beaumont, Abra. You haven't forgotten that you promised me this dance, have you?"

She turned, a bit relieved and decidedly puzzled. She'd promised no dances. The tall stranger's features were vaguely familiar to her, but she could not place them. He obviously knew her, however, for he'd addressed her by name. And this was a way to rid herself of Freddy without hurting his feelings.

She smiled up at him. "Why, of course not," she murmured to him, casting a sideways glance in Freddy's direction, one that said she apologized, but what was she to do?

It was the smile, Dash thought, the wide green eyes shining and the lips that said to him, yes, it would be a pleasure to spend some time with you, to have your arms enfold me. He took her hand as the music started once more and they began to dance.

Abra soon discovered that Freddy was not the only accomplished dancer attending the party that evening. His hand held her waist firmly and seemed entirely at home there. There was not even an initial instant of strangeness, no moment of awkwardness or fumbling as they found each other's pace. It was an odd sensation, and Abra was not at all sure she trusted it.

"You seem to have me at a disadvantage, sir," she began as soon as they were well away from Freddy.

He offered her a wry grin. "Why, Abra, don't tell me you don't remember me?" he asked, his tone jocular, but his blue eyes taunting.

She nearly stopped then, thinking to drop his hand and simply walk away from him, sure she didn't like the way he stared so knowingly down at her. But the pressure of his hand to her waist was, somehow, irresistible, and she felt as though she were being pressed on by the music.

He seemed perfectly content to leave their conversation where it had stopped, for he made no effort to continue it. Instead, he let his blue eyes find and hold hers, realizing himself slightly mesmerized by the contact, as he swirled her expertly in time to the music, an enigmatic smile curling the edges of his lips.

Her curiosity whetted, Abra stared back up at him, contemplating the roughly handsome features, trying to remember. He did seem familiar, she had to admit, but try as she would, she could not place him.

Dash decided he was enjoying himself. For one thing, the hand he held to her waist told him quite distinctly that warm flesh lived beneath the covering of silk that so temptingly caressed it, a far different feeling from the sensation he'd had dancing with Eleanor Dewitte, and decidedly far more pleasurable. But to compare Abra with any other woman was comparing the sun to a distant star, he decided, and to compare her to Eleanor was simply beyond his powers completely. Aside from the decidedly ungentlemanly thoughts that crept into his mind at the realization of what lay just beneath the silk that separated his hand from the tempting warmth of her body, there was the simple pleasure of looking down at her, at her slightly perplexed expression, at those phenomenally beautiful green eyes and the thick cloud of reddish gold

23

hair. For a moment he was transfixed by the thought of what it would be like simply to put his hand to her hair and feel it, wondering if it were as soft as it appeared to be, wondering, too, what made it flash golden as they moved beneath the dazzling light of the room's crystal chandeliers. And then he was struck with the thought of what a pleasure it would be to remove the pins that constrained it, and watch those golden locks fall free.

This is foolish, he found himself thinking, for he'd never had quite the same reaction to a woman, at least not since he'd been a boy and first realized that there might be something curious lurking beneath the covering camouflage creatures of the opposite sex wore. And since then he'd certainly had more than ample opportunity to discover just how correct that inkling of the possibility of feminine mysteries had been. But still, here he was, staring into those eyes and wondering, and filled with a pleasantly elating sense of anticipation.

Added to that was the realization that he'd completely lost any interest that might have lingered over the Dewitte diamonds during the few moments he'd been in her company. The mere thought of wasting his time in the dreary Dewitte parlor totally repelled him, especially when there was the decidedly more appetizing prospect of addressing himself to the challenge of Abra Beaumont.

And the perfect vehicle for approaching that citadel, he realized, was within his grasp, as the thought came to him that Vincent Beaumont had suggested more than the scholarly interest he'd pretended when he'd mentioned the Tear. What had seemed the week before only an idle conjecture suddenly seemed to grow into something more pressing, and decidedly more within the realm of reality. If he could enlist a master like Beaumont, he mused, perhaps he could end up with two prizes—the jewel, and the woman who had so suddenly and so completely disturbed what he ordinarily regarded as a rock-steady equanimity.

Abra was more than a bit puzzled. This man, with his arrogant stare, surely ought to repel her. And the knowing look he leveled at her certainly aroused a certain store of anger. But still she could not deny the admission that she decidedly enjoyed the sensation of dancing with him, the firmly assured way he held her, the unfaltering way he led her around the floor. Aside from that, there was the sheer curiosity that bit at her, wondering who he was and why she'd never met him before, at least not that she could remember. The fact that he'd been invited to the party could mean only that he was a part of the socially prominent circle that felt itself to rule New York, or, perhaps, a visiting distant cousin. That fact depressed her more than not, she found. Despite appearances to the contrary, it could only mean that he was yet another spoiled, self-indulged young man with too much money, another Freddy Westmore. Still, she told herself, as long as she didn't know for sure, she could always imagine him something more, at least for the time being. And so for the time being she honored his silence, and simply smiled up at him as they moved in time to the music.

"All pleasant things must, alas, end," he murmured as the waltz music died. But then he smiled. "It is warm in here, isn't it? Perhaps a breath of fresh air?"

And then his hand was propelling her toward the open french doors that led to the veranda just behind them. It wasn't until she felt the cool evening breeze on her cheek that Abra realized he'd allowed her no chance to protest. More than anything else, her quiet acquiescence surprised her.

"Now," he said as they stared off into a crisp darkness, "we come to the thoughtless manner in which you've forgotten me, Abra."

She turned and stared up at him thoughtfully, more perplexed now than angered by his manners.

"Abra," he went on thoughtfully. "An odd name." He waved his hands in a theatrical imitation of a magician waving a magic wand. "Abra Cadabra." He smiled. "Your father was once a magician, then?"

She laughed despite herself and shook her head. Her laughter was deep and throaty, and the sound of it, he found, more than amply repaid him for the effort he'd taken with his gesture.

"No," she told him, "no magicians. Papa's simply a bit whimsical, that's all." She stared at him intently. "We haven't met, have we?" she asked him softly.

He moved as though to put his hand to her waist, and

25

Abra moved a step backward. There was something about his smile, about the way he seemed to assume she would be willing to have him hold her, that told her she ought not to be alone with him any longer. Then the breeze lifted a dark curl from his forehead and ruffled it rakishly across his brow. It was that more than the memory of his features—the wind-rumpled hair and the way he stood simply staring at her—that brought it back to her.

"The man on the pier," she murmured softly.

He smiled at her wryly. "So I made some impression on you, after all, Abra."

She backed away from him one step more. "Yes, you did," she replied. "One of boorish mannerlessness. If you will excuse me, sir, we have not been introduced." She began to turn away to the door.

But very suddenly there was a hand to her arm, pulling her back to face him.

"A situation that ought to be immediately remedied," he replied softly.

"I think not," she told him, staring pointedly to where his hand held her arm. "I have no intention of standing out here alone in the darkness with a man I do not know."

She pushed his hand away with her free one, realizing she was blushing and that the flush was doubtless all the more apparent because of the chill she felt from the breeze.

Not only did Dash notice the blush, he was extremely pleased by it, thinking how completely imperturbable she had seemed with Freddy. It flattered him to know that he could at least ruffle her enough to disturb her coolly aloof mien. This time he gave her no time to turn away from him. He put one hand to either of her arms and drew her to him, then pressed his lips to hers.

For a moment Abra was quite simply shocked. Freddy always begged plaintively for a kiss and waited obediently until she took pity on him and allowed him the honor of a chaste peck. Never would he have treated her this way. And then the pressure of Dash's lips seemed to flood through her, filling her with an odd warmth. It was that that surprised her, the realization that she no longer felt the cold of the evening air, that he was doing something

26

to her that seemed to crowd away such unimportant trivia as the cold or the thought that someone within the ballroom might venture out and find them there. There was simply the pleasantly tingling warmth that worked its way through her, a shockingly invasive feeling that was, somehow, quite pleasant.

For an instant when his lips left hers, she simply stood, dazed, staring up at him. But the instant passed, and as she saw the complacent smile that crept to his lips as he stared down at her, she felt her hand push against his chest until he released her. Then she raised her hand and slapped him on the cheek.

"You, sir, are no gentleman," she told him angrily.

Her revelation left him unmoved. "I dare say, I'm not," he replied, the smile still nudging the corners of his lips, and rankling her even more, all the more so because he gave no indication that he had even felt the biting contact of her hand to his cheek.

She threw him an icy stare, then stalked to the door. But before she left him entirely, she turned back for just an instant and saw him watching her. He was still smiling, she realized, and she had to force herself to keep the answering smile that itched at her mouth from appearing.

"*A bientôt*, fair Abra," he murmured softly, his blue eyes sparkling brightly at her in the darkness.

Abra felt a ghost of the warmth he had wakened in her when he'd kissed her. She stared at him soberly for an instant, and then turned to the door.

He certainly was not, she thought abruptly, a Freddy.

## Chapter Two

"Abra, I thought Freddy was taking you to the ballet tonight."

Vincent eyed his daughter's dress, a simple dinner dress, not at all the sort of gown she'd wear if she were going out for the evening.

"No, Papa," she told him absently as she went to the liquor cabinet at the side of the room and opened it. "I sent him a note that I can't go tonight. Nor any other night. I really think it's time he found some other, more appreciative recipient for his affections."

Vincent lifted an interested brow. "And what precipitated this rather abrupt action, Abra?" he asked as she lifted a glass and a decanter of scotch whiskey.

"Oh, the way he acted at the Brinksons' party the other night," she replied as she poured out the amber liquid into the glass, then seemed to stare at the reflection it made through the pattern of the cut crystal. "He asked me to marry him four times."

This information hardly seemed to surprise Vincent. "He's asked you before, Abra," he reminded her.

Abra shrugged. "Yes," she replied, returning the decanter to the cabinet and lifting a siphon, "but never so tiresomely nor so insistently. I've decided that the only way to prove to him that I'm serious is simply not to see him at all." She topped off the glass with soda and filled another entirely with soda for herself, then set the siphon down. She lifted the glasses and turned to him. "I'm afraid you will be forced to endure my presence this evening," she told him with a grin as she crossed the room to his chair.

Vincent frowned slightly as he reached up for his customary predinner whiskey and soda. "I'm sorry to hear that," he said as she settled herself on the couch across from him.

"Why, Papa!"

He smiled. "Not that you'll be home to dinner this evening, nor even about Freddy, Abra. But I'm afraid I've invited a friend of an old friend of mine to dinner this evening. You'll doubtless be bored to tears."

Abra sipped her soda water, unperturbed. "Couldn't be any worse than spending the evening with Freddy," she murmured and she found her thoughts drifting to another man, one who entirely lacked Freddy's reticence and reserve. Then she looked up sharply at her father. "What old friend, Papa?" she asked.

Vincent looked down to the glass in his hand. "Someone I knew before you were born, Abra," he replied softly.

"Oh."

Vincent silently cursed that he'd not known of her change of plans earlier. It was too late now to postpone the invitation he'd extended to Dashiel Thorne. And he had no doubt but that Abra would not approve. Her softly murmured "oh" had told him that more plainly than a far more fulsome response could have, for she was not one to loose her tongue, except under extreme duress. Her mother had been like that, he remembered, and her response to any mention of the vocation he'd abandoned some twenty years previously had often been of that very terse variety.

He was saved from any further discomfort from the resounding silence in the room by the shrill sound of the front doorbell, soon followed by the sound of approaching footsteps in the marble entrance hall before the door to his library was opened. Hemmings entered and announced, "Mr. Thorne, sir," in his brittle voiced Boston accent.

Vincent stood and moved to the door, hand extended to Dash who had appeared there.

"Glad to see you," he said, hoping there was a note of joviality in his tone, as he felt none at the moment. He led Dash forward, to the couch where Abra sat staring at them.

"Abra, my dear, I'd like you to meet Mr. Dashiel Thorne. Dashiel, my daughter, Abra."

But the silence that followed his introduction was even

29

more deafening than the one that had preceded Dash's entry. Vincent turned to Abra, perplexed to see her wide-eyed and staring at his guest.

"You," she mouthed silently.

Dash smiled roguishly. "Your daughter did me the honor of allowing me a dance the other evening at the Brinksons'," he told Vincent easily, then he bowed slightly and reached down for the hand she had not yet extended.

For a moment Abra felt gripped by the feeling that she ought to leave, to let her father have his dinner with his old friend's friend, and let it end there. After all, she told herself, she could well imagine what that shared acquaintanceship meant about Mr. Dashiel Thorne and she wanted nothing at all to do with any of it. It might have been a part of her father's past, but that was where it ought to lie, still and buried, in the past.

But the desire to flee dissipated quickly as she remembered the interest her father had shown in the newspaper article and, most especially, in the yacht that had floated that afternoon out in the harbor. He'd been tainted by thoughts of the jewel that lay aboard that yacht, of that she had no doubt. She'd seen him scour every article in the gossip columns, absorbing the sheik's social appearances, his comings and goings ever since that afternoon. And the sudden appearance of this "friend of an old friend" seemed entirely too precipitous to her for his good. She would stay and keep an eye on the two of them, she decided.

And trailing that thought, but not far behind, was the remembrance of the feeling that had come over her when he'd kissed her. She tried, unsuccessfully, to force it away.

She flashed him a dazzling smile and extended her hand to him. "Yes, Papa," she said, keeping her eyes to Dash's, "Mr. Thorne and I did dance, but I don't think we were ever properly introduced that evening."

Dash took her hand and raised it to his lips, kissing it quickly. "A situation that has haunted me ever since," he said softly before releasing her hand, something he did with obvious reluctance.

Vincent stared at his daughter, not quite sure what it was that was happening between her and Dash, more than a little surprised at her apparently delighted smile, and not at all sure he liked any of it.

"Can I offer you a drink, Mr. Thorne?" he asked as Hemmings returned to the room bearing a tray with glasses, cooler, and bottle. "Whiskey, or a bit of champagne?"

"Oh, champagne, of course, Papa," Abra interjected quickly, before Dash could reply. "One must celebrate old friendships."

She watched as Hemmings set the tray on the table in front of her, lifted the bottle, and began to pry off the cork. She was aware of the vague aura of discomposure that seemed to emanate from her father, but she tried to ignore it. "Isn't that the case, Mr. Thorne?" she asked when the bottle had finally been breached. "You are the friend of an old friend of Papa's?" She stared at him a moment, wide-eyed and innocent, expecting him to mirror her father's discomposure but unable to sense anything of that nature in him. A bit unsettled, she turned and accepted the glass Hemmings offered her.

Dash seated himself in the comfortable chair facing her and waited until he'd been handed a glass of wine before answering her. "Yes, Miss Beaumont. I was a good friend of James Sutton's. And I would not dream of forgoing an opportunity to celebrate his memory." He raised his glass. "To James Sutton."

"To James Sutton," Vincent echoed.

Then the three of them silently drank, Dash emptying his glass. When Hemmings had left them, Abra stood, lifted the bottle of champagne, and approached Dash.

"A refill, Mr. Thorne?" she asked, then, without waiting for his accepting nod, refilled his glass. "Another toast to the memory of Doctor Sutton, perhaps?"

Dash lifted his eyebrow. He was surprised at her apparent acquaintance with Doctor's name.

"Papa never mentioned Doctor had taken on a protégé," she went on blithely as she resettled herself on the couch and raised her own glass to her lips.

Dash's eyes narrowed as he contemplated his new awareness that Vincent Beaumont's daughter was a good deal more than simply a pretty, a very pretty, face.

"I never thought of myself as Doctor's protégé, Miss Beaumont," he replied softly. "Friends, occasionally associates, perhaps."

Abra returned his stare unflinchingly. "Then may I assume you follow him in his vocation, Mr. Thorne?" she continued, unperturbed.

He smiled wryly. "Yes, Miss Beaumont, you may."

"I see," she said softly. "You, then, are a thief."

"Abra!"

Actually, Abra was rather surprised Vincent had let her go on as long as she had with her rudely probing questions. After all, he'd always insisted that the niceties of human behavior were the basis of the sensitive soul, what separated man from the lower beasts. "There is no breeding without real manners, Abra," he'd told her a hundred times when she was a child. And here she'd managed to transgress all boundaries of good manners after only a few moments with Dashiel Thorne.

But the gentleman in question seemed more surprised than put off. He lifted a brow rakishly.

"Yes, Miss Beaumont," he replied without hesitation. "I am a thief."

"I'm appalled, Abra," Vincent hissed angrily at her.

She shifted her gaze to him when she heard the real anger in his voice, almost surprised when she found her eyes did not seem to want to leave their contact with Dashiel Thorne's. But once she saw the slight flush his ire and embarrassment had brought to her father's cheeks, she wished she could call it all back.

"I'm sorry, Papa," she said softly. She turned back to Dash. "My apologies, Mr. Thorne," she murmured as she put her glass down on the table. "Perhaps it would be best if I excused myself."

She started to rise. But Dash stood as she did, reaching out to her arm with his hand. The contact sent a pleasant tingling warmth through her arm.

"There's really no need, Miss Beaumont," he told her softly. "I've been looking forward to this evening. It would be ruined for me if I were the cause of your leaving."

"I've behaved badly, Mr. Thorne," she told him, but there was something about her tone that told him she was not really all that contrite. "My concern for my father exceeded my manners, I'm afraid."

"If I were to ask for penance, would that induce you to stay?" he asked.

32

"Penance?" she asked, suspicious.

He nodded. "I'm new to New York, and not very well acquainted with the city yet. Perhaps an afternoon of your time as my guide might even the tally?"

Abra was confused now, and she turned her gaze to her father. But Vincent seemed determined to let her settle the matter on her own, justifying his indifference by noting that she'd managed to get herself into the situation quite well by herself. He simply shrugged and turned away.

Abra nodded, "Very well, Mr. Thorne. An afternoon."

"Tomorrow?" he pressed.

"If you like," she agreed, albeit reluctantly. He'd seemed quite able to find his way about that afternoon at the wharf, she recalled.

But her acquiescence seemed to push him. "Oh, and one more thing," he continued, with a crooked smile.

"Mr. Thorne?"

"Dash," he said. "You must call me Dash, Abra. All my friends do."

"Are we friends, then, Mr. Thorne?" she demanded.

"Decidedly, Miss Beaumont. You just haven't realized it yet," he told her.

What's wrong with me, she asked herself as she heard herself meekly murmuring, "As you like, Mr. Thorne. Dash." And when his hand left her arm, she found it decidedly cold, bereft at the loss of the small contact.

But he seemed entirely satisfied with the situation. He leaned forward and lifted her glass from where she'd placed it on the table.

"To friendship," he said as he handed it to her, then smiled and raised his own. "To new and lasting friendships."

And when Abra turned to her father, she found his expression showing a good deal of surprise, but also a decided satisfaction that he made no attempt to hide. He looked up at her, his eyes laughingly telling her that she'd been bested.

He raised his glass in response to Dash's. "To new and lasting friendships," he repeated with a smile.

Abra had no choice but to follow. "To friendship," she murmured before bringing her glass to her lips.

A gentleman, Abra fumed silently, would have come to the house to fetch her rather than insisting she meet him at his hotel. But then the man was no gentleman, she told herself, remembering that he had admitted as much himself. That memory led her to thoughts of the way he had kissed her that evening at the Brinksons' party. Although she had to admit that dinner the evening before had certainly been pleasant enough once the stiffness following her own lapse had been gotten through. And her father had actually been quite lively, really enjoying himself as he and Dash traded stories about Doctor Sutton, stories that had, she had been forced to accede, however grudgingly, been more than a little amusing. Had she not known that those stories recalled to Vincent things he should not dwell on, things he should forget of his past, she would have quite enjoyed herself. But as it was, the stories had only made her worry, and all of it, she'd decided in the end, was Dashiel Thorne's fault.

She was sure he had come to New York with the intention of maneuvering her father into joining him in some illegal venture. As far as she was concerned, he could spend the rest of his life in some filthy jail. But her father, well, that was an entirely different matter. With his weak heart, the last thing he needed was Dashiel Thorne elbowing his way into his life and destroying what time there was left.

She'd slept badly that night, and that, too, she blamed on Thorne, but she stopped short of admitting to herself that the reason for her troubled sleep was her anticipation of this afternoon that she'd condemned herself to spend alone in his company. I'll tell him at the outset, she fumed, that this matter is simply one of honor, of penance for my ill manners. And she would suggest, most politely, of course, but firmly, that in the future he leave her father in peace.

"Four, please," she snapped a bit waspishly as she stepped onto the lift.

The porter who tended the mechanism seemed surprised at the sound of her voice, he but nodded smilingly as he pushed the gate closed.

Abra ignored him, biting her lower lip contemplatively.

34

There will be no repetition of what happened the other evening at the party, she told herself. Whatever his intentions, I shall make that quite clear.

"Four, miss."

The gate glided open in front of her. Abra nodded her thanks and stepped out into the heavily carpeted hall. It seemed unnaturally silent to her, and the swish of the elevator as it traveled back downward seemed the only evidence that anything lived in this sumptuous bastion of money.

He must be quite a successful thief, if he can afford to live at the Saint Pierre, she mused, then started off along the hall, glancing at the gilt room numbers on the heavy mahogany doors.

She found his, suite 404, and stood hesitating a moment before the door. This is foolish, she told herself firmly, and raised her hand to knock. But she found that in spite of her determination, her hand was shaking just a bit.

There was no immediate response to her knock and she was about to try once more when the door opened. He was in his shirtsleeves, his cravat around his neck, but as yet untied.

"Miss Beaumont, this is a surprise." His expression seemed entirely ingenuous. "There was no need for you to come up yourself. You ought to have sent a porter."

Abra felt a bit foolish, for she'd not thought of that. And now she began to feel guilty about her thoughts, her suspicions of what she'd assumed he'd expected of her that afternoon.

"Good afternoon, Mr. Thorne," she murmured.

"Dash," he reminded her with a smile. "Well, as you are here, come in. I'm a bit late, I'm afraid. And you are quite prompt, I see. I'd assumed all New York ladies were habitually late."

He put his hand to her waist and ushered her into the room, closing the door behind them with a quick kick.

"Only the truly fashionable ladies," she replied offhandedly.

"I can hardly imagine a woman more fashionable than yourself, Miss Beaumont," he told her as he made a slowly appraising survey of her outfit—the green velvet coat with gold braid trim, and the new bonnet her father had chosen for her.

Abra could not understand why, but the outcome of that appraisal seemed irrationally important to her. She found she was holding her breath until he smiled at her, apparently pleased with what he saw. Then she told herself she was behaving like a fool, and she swore at herself silently, and once at him, too.

"Please, make yourself comfortable," he said as he motioned her toward a small puffily cushioned couch.

Abra sat, noticing the opened door to the bedroom beyond, the large, rumpled bed. It flitted through her mind to wonder if he was a restless sleeper, or if he'd had some help the night before in disarranging the bedclothes so completely. She turned away quickly, hoping he had not seen the sudden blush that came to her cheeks at the thought.

His fingers worked quickly at the tie, and as he finished with it he moved to a mirror to assure himself it was straight. That task completed, he turned to her and smiled rakishly.

"As you are here," he said, motioning to the table by the window with its burden of glasses, ice bucket, and bottle, "you are partial to champagne, aren't you? I took the liberty of ordering a bottle, hoping you'd have a glass." He moved quickly, lifting the bottle and beginning to pry up the cork.

Abra gritted her teeth. So he'd expected her to come to his room after all, she realized, and she wondered what ruse he would have employed had she sent a porter to fetch him as he had suggested.

"Please don't," she protested. "At least not for me. It's far too early in the afternoon."

"Nonsense," he replied as the cork was freed with a loud pop. "It's never too early in the day for champagne." He poured two glasses and brought them to her, pressing one into her hand. "To friendship," he murmured, just as he had the evening before.

Obediently, she raised her glass and brought it to her lips, but did not drink. She put the glass down firmly on the table beside her.

He half emptied his own glass and stared at her still full one, but said nothing as he turned to retrieve his suit jacket from the back of a chair at the far side of the room.

"Mr. Thorne," she began awkwardly as she watched him pull on the jacket.

"Dash," he corrected her quickly.

She looked up to find him staring at her. "Dash," she acceded, then hastily continued. "I believe we ought to make something clear between us, from the start."

"By all means, Abra," he agreed, returning to her and seating himself on the couch beside her. She felt the air between them stir, then settle, warm with his presence. He sat then, staring at her expectantly.

"I don't know quite how to begin," she admitted softly after a long moment of silence she found extremely uncomfortable.

"Perhaps I can make it easier for you," he suggested. "Let's see. Perhaps what you're struggling to say politely, because you've sworn to your father to maintain politeness at all costs this afternoon, is that you don't like me, that you certainly don't approve of me, and you want me to keep away from Vincent before I get him involved in something unsavory." He thought meditatively for a moment, then, when she made no response, went on. "Have I about covered everything, Abra?" he asked her softly.

"Yes, I suppose you have," she replied after a short but pregnant silence.

He smiled. "Good. I think we should always be honest with each other, Abra. Honesty, I'm told, is the foundation of all strong friendships."

Abra gritted her teeth, decidedly disliking his smile, and even more, the way he spoke, the way he seemed so sure of himself, and the way he showed her that he was amused by her anger.

"Ours is an acquaintance, Mr. Thorne, and not likely to become anything more," she told him acidly.

He leaned back into the cushions behind him and laughed. "The most unlikely things do occur in life, Abra," he told her. Then he sat forward, his body leaning toward hers, his arm moving to the back of the couch behind her. "And some things," he continued, his voice low and husky, "are fated, and useless to rail against."

His face was inches from hers, and Abra felt stiff with panic, sure he was going to put his hands to her arms and

37

hold her, as he had at the party, and then kiss her. She felt a sudden, fluttering thrill of anticipation within herself, remembering the odd reaction she'd had to that first kiss, and not quite so sure now that the opportunity presented itself that her determination to remain coolly aloof with him and entirely indifferent was really what she wanted to do. She felt a dull thud in her chest, realized it was the thumping of her heart, and she waited, unmoving, anticipating the warmth of the contact of his hand to her arm, the press of his lips to hers.

But instead, after what seemed to Abra an interminable time, he leaned back once more to the cushions of the couch. She felt an angry rush of heat to her cheeks as she saw the look of amusement on his face and knew he realized what it was she had been thinking. She hated him, she told herself. She hated his arrogance and his smug assurance.

"First, Abra," he said very slowly, "I think we ought to discuss the injustice you are doing to your father."

She was shocked at his accusation. "I'm quite sure I don't know what you are referring to, Mr. Thorne," she told him archly.

He smiled benignly. "Dash," he corrected. "An oversight, I'm sure," he smiled.

"Dash," she sputtered. "What are you talking about?"

He lifted his glass of champagne and sipped it. "You are stifling him with your concern, Abra, making him old before his time."

"How dare you?" she demanded as she began to rise, but his hand reached out to her arm, pulling her back down to the couch.

"I dare, Abra, because however difficult it may be for you to believe me, I find that even on short acquaintance I feel quite close to Vincent. Perhaps it's our mutual affection for Doctor Sutton, perhaps simply the kinship our vocation forces upon us, but whatever, it pains me to see him as he is, and it pains me even more to know you are the cause, all the more so because your intent is one of misguided concern."

"You are arrogant, Mr. Thorne, and presumptuous," she burst out, unable to contain herself, but then she stopped. There was more than a grain of truth in what he said, and

38

no matter how much she wanted to pretend it was not there, she could not ignore it. She recalled the look of animated interest that had filled Vincent's features the week before when he'd stood on the wharf looking out at the yacht, the youthful enthusiasm he'd shown as he and Dash had spoken of Doctor Sutton the evening before. She could not deny the accusation that she was trying to keep him from those very things, nor could she ignore the fact that the life they represented seemed to fill him with excitement and an interest in life that was otherwise missing in him.

She looked down, to where his hand still held hers. "Whatever your intention, I can't help but think you will drag him into something that will only end in misery for him. Or worse."

"Surely you can't think that is my intent, Abra?" he asked, his hand releasing hers and reaching up to her chin, pushing her face upward until she was facing him once more.

"Intent or not, it is what I fear." She sighed. "He's no longer a young man, no longer has a young man's heart. I can't help but fear for him."

He stared at her in silence for an instant, then his hand dropped away from her chin and he stood. "There is no resolution to this matter, Abra. Will you at least accept my word if I promise you that I will do nothing that could possibly harm him?"

She struggled with herself for a while, not quite sure why, but aware that she wanted to believe him. "I'll accept your word," she said finally. "It seems I have little choice."

He smiled at her, his expression telling her that he felt he had, at least partially, achieved some goal. "Good." He reached forward to the table, lifted her glass and held it out to her. "As for the matter of your not liking me, I'd intended this afternoon to prove to you the error of your hastily reached opinion." He smiled again, this time a bit rakishly. "You do owe me the opportunity to show myself to you as an entirely trustworthy and likable fellow. I assure you, there is some honor among thieves."

Abra could not help but laugh. "You can try, Mr. Thorne," she replied, then she grimaced. "Dash," she corrected before he had the chance to do it for her. "But I must warn you, it will be a decided battle." But she smiled and took the offered glass.

"Oh, I'm a very resourceful man, Abra," he told her, "and not easily given to accepting defeat."

She had not a thought but that he was, she decided. She sipped the wine, and found that it was very good.


He'd ordered an excellent and decidedly extravagant lunch for them in the hotel dining room, oysters and more champagne, roast quail and wild rice, a chocolate soufflé for dessert.

"This is unfair, Dash," Abra said as she drained the remaining champagne from her glass. "After so sumptuous a meal, it would be absolutely unforgivably ungrateful of me to cling to any feeling of animus toward you that I may have harbored."

He grinned at her as he signaled to the waiter for the tab. "Exactly as I had planned, Abra. It's true, you know." He smiled at her conspiratorially. "The way to a woman's heart is through her stomach."

Abra gazed at him thoughtfully, apparently contemplating that possibility. She was aware of a slight light-headedness, a dimly buzzing sensation, which she realized came from the quantity of champagne she'd drunk. It was not strong enough to make her feel unwell. In fact, she'd decided it was quite pleasant. But still there was the nagging suspicion that she ought not to allow herself to relax with him, that however charming he could be when he chose, he was still untrustworthy and doubtless a scoundrel.

"I assume you've made a great study of the matter?" she asked a trifle archly. "Oysters and soufflés as a direct means to a woman's affections, I mean."

"I'd hardly call it a great study," he replied noncommitally. Then he grinned. "Modesty prevents."

"You, sir, are a swine," she told him.

"I plead nolo contendere, Abra," he replied easily.

She laced her fingers together, rested her elbows on the edge of the table, and cradled her chin on her hands. "Who are you?" she asked him, her expression suddenly turned very intent. "Where do you come from?"

He seemed startled by her questions, by the serious look

40

she wore as she stared at him. "Now questions such as those ought to be answered with only Mother Nature as a witness, Abra," he replied. Then he waved over the waiter, who presented him with the check. He signed it with a flourish. "Shall we take an amble through the park, Abra?" he asked as he rose and offered her his arm.

She dropped her hands to her lap and stared up at him. "I'd thought you'd enlisted my services as guide this afternoon, Mr. Thorne, to show you about the city." She saw his brow rise with her use of Mr. Thorne, but she made no attempt to correct herself.

He shrugged. "Actually, I find myself quite well directed. Surely you saw through my ruse to spend an afternoon alone with you?"

"I suppose I did," she replied with a grin.

"And yet you came anyway?"

She nodded. "In the interest of protecting my father."

"And nothing more?" he pressed her softly.

She looked down at her clasped hands.

"You needn't answer," he told her cheerfully. "As to the walk, with only Mother Nature to hear my answers to your questions?"

She returned her gaze to his face, found it suddenly quite serious. "Are the answers so dire as that?" she asked softly.

He shrugged. "I'll leave the judgments to you," he replied. "I'm not very good at making them."

She stood, and he tucked her hand firmly into the crook of his arm.


Abra's head cleared immediately as they walked down the front steps and onto the street. A cool, brisk breeze tugged, unheeded, at the curls that showed from beneath her hat. She inhaled it, feeling the refreshing bite on her lips and cheeks, and grateful that it seemed to clear her head of the bit of befuddlement that remained.

She turned to Dash and saw that the wind had rumpled his hair as it had that afternoon at the wharf. She realized his eschewal of hats was habitual, and she wondered if it was intentional, if he realized that wind-ruffled hair, especially the single unruly lock that seemed determined to lean forward over his brow when given the slightest encourage-

41

ment of freedom, made him look even more handsome, somehow boyish, and far more approachable than he was when perfectly groomed. She decided abruptly that he did know, that such a calculating man as she had determined him to be would know everything about himself and leave nothing to chance, unstudied or unexploited.

As it happened, Abra was doing Dash a disservice in her cynical appraisal. If he had a certain assured manner, an awareness of his powers both professional and social — specifically his not unimportant ability to charm members of the opposite sex, this last skill sometimes rather mystified him. At that moment he was considering Abra, wondering how best to proceed, whether a direct attack as he had attempted the evening of the party would melt her or disgust her entirely, and quite unsure of what he ought to do next. His indecision was well hidden, however, as he guided her down the block and across the avenue. He bought her a bouquet of violets from an old woman at the curb, and felt inclined to buy her the whole cartload as he watched her bring them to her nose, inhale, and smile in appreciation. Once again he tucked her hand into the crook of his arm.

"Forward, to nature," he admonished, and turned onto the brick path into Central Park.

They walked in silence for a while, their feet kicking up the fallen brown and yellowed leaves, the intense sunshine skittering off those that still clung tenaciously to the trees. Finally the path brought them to a small pond where a half-dozen swans floated with regal imperviousness.

Abra found a stone bench and sat, leaving the other half empty for him to join her.

"I think we're alone now," she told him as she looked up at him, squinting a bit from the sunlight that outlined him, making him look somehow larger and more prepossessing than she was prepared to think of him. "No one but Mother Nature to overhear your dreadful secrets." She cocked her head. "Are they really all that dreadful?"

He laughed as he seated himself beside her. "Hardly," he replied. "In fact, the whole thing is rather dull. Are you sure you want to hear?"

She sniffed thoughtfully at the bunch of violets, then nodded her head. "I'm prepared for the worst," she assured

42

him.

He laughed once more, this time a bit self-deprecatingly. "I've no intention of revealing anything incriminating, Abra, if that's what you have in mind."

"How did you became a, a . . ."

"A thief?" he prompted. "You had no difficulty saying the word last evening, Abra," he reminded her.

She nodded. "So I didn't. I suppose it was easier because last evening I knew I didn't like you."

"And now?" he pressed, taking her hand in his.

She looked down to his fingers as they wove themselves together with hers, but made no move to withdraw. "Now," she admitted slowly, "I'm not quite so certain."

He grinned. "That's a start."

He was tempted to kiss her then, wanting to as much as he had sensed her wanting him to earlier, when they'd still been in his hotel suite. But there was a new feeling of ease between them, and he was loath to disturb that, regardless of the provocation he felt. Instead, he raised the hand he held to his lips, brushing it gently, his eyes on hers. It seemed to him that he had chosen well, for a slight blush colored her cheeks and she looked down to the bunch of violets she grasped in her free hand.

"Now," he asked, "What was it you wanted to know?"

She smiled then. "It seems to me, sir," she told him, "that my father has become fond of you. Who are you? Where do you come from? And, most important, what are your intentions?"

He laughed at her tone, one of a protective parent grilling a prospective suitor.

"Who am I?" he mused. "Actually, a rather middle-class person, born and raised in Philadelphia, father a lawyer, mother churchgoing and entirely proper. In fact, I even read law for several years in my misguided youth."

"You?" she demanded with a quick laugh. "A lawyer?"

He nodded solemnly. "I'd intended to spend my life upholding the virtues of law and order," he replied.

She sobered. "What happened? Why did you change?"

He stared at her, wondering how much or how little he ought to tell her, finally deciding she was truly interested. He shrugged. "Have you heard much of the riots in the mines in Pennsylvania, Abra, of the killings and the beatings by thugs the mine owners sent in to keep the workers from unionizing?"

"Yes, of course, I've heard some of it. It was horrible," she replied, surprised at his question and thoroughly sobered.

"More horrible than you could ever imagine. And, when I found myself a law clerk defending the mine owners, even when I knew I should be out with the miners, defending their rights, I knew I could never be a lawyer, not for a system that makes right the sole province of those with enough money to buy it."

She was silent for a moment, as though it took time for her to digest what he had told her. Finally, she turned to him, her expression thoughtful.

"So you turned a kind of Robin Hood?" she suggested softly.

His lips curled into a wry grin. "Hardly. I take from the rich, but I only occasionally give it to the poor, Abra. I'm afraid I'm not nearly so noble as I would once have wanted myself to be."

She seemed to accept that. "And then you met Doctor Sutton?" she asked.

"Actually, that was not until a few years later, in London. There was a certain lady of our mutual acquaintance. A lady with a capital L, actually. She introduced us quite unknowingly, however, it was fortuitous for us both. It seems she had been party to a few, shall we say, indiscretions, and having hint of Doctor's estimable connections, went to ask a favor. Apparently she had bestowed her favors rather excessively, and none too wisely. One of her lovers was threatening to go to her husband unless she placated him with some much needed funds. None of this came to Doctor's ears, at least not just then. All he knew was that she asked him to introduce her to a jewel broker, one who was not too fussy about ownership. She intended to sell him a rather extravagant necklace, then claim it had been stolen. Doctor, who had also enjoyed the largess of her affections, felt inclined to oblige. Unfortunately, she'd decided to make a rather slow but exceedingly handsome upstairs maid whom she suspected of entertaining his lordship when she was about business of her own the unsuspecting target of the police when she reported the heinous

44

crime. In the end, when Doctor heard of this rather un-ladylike action, he was quite shocked. He bought back the necklace from the broker and had it appear under rather compromising circumstances. The maid was freed, and then, mysteriously, the lady's jewels, including the troublesome necklace, quite suddenly disappeared."

Abra laughed. "And I take it you and Doctor had something to do with the contrivance of that mystery?"

He nodded. "The maid now runs a small but quite cozy little inn at Brighton, all nicely paid for."

She laughed once more. "And you said you never played Robin Hood."

He fixed her with a seraphic smile. "Oh, the inn was Doctor's idea entirely. He thought placing a large amount of money at the woman's disposal would surely bring her to a dissolute life. I suppose he was right. Anyway, having her mysteriously inherit the house, however, seemed to be the right sort of challenge for her housekeeping skills." He smiled again. "It seems she rose nobly to the challenge."

"And the lady?" Abra asked, entranced.

"She endures, squandering her husband's ill-gotten money in a most ladylike flurry of excess."

Abra's eyes narrowed. "Is any of this true?" she demanded suspiciously.

He raised his right hand. "All of it. Gospel."

"Then from now on, I shall think of you not as a thief, but as a modern Robin Hood, after all," she told him.

He stared at her, his eyes deep blue and searching. "I think, Abra, you've done a bit of romanticizing. Perhaps of your father's past?" he suggested. "Or, dare I hope, of me?"

This time, when the thought came to him that she needed kissing, he made no attempt to fight it. He put his hand to her waist and drew her to him, his lips finding hers, warm and willing.

Abra was surprised at herself. If she'd thought earlier that afternoon of the surprising reaction she'd had to that first kiss at the Brinksons', she realized now that her willing acceptance of his touch was more than mere curiosity, more than an idle query, if a repeat performance of the act would produce the same reaction in her. It did, she realized as she felt herself filling with the remembered warmth, but

45

she realized, too, that she felt an unexpected delight in simply being close to him, that the preceding hours had muted her feelings of trepidation about him and replaced them with an active and entirely unprecedented contentment just being in his company. If she'd had the fixity of thought to pursue the matter, she'd have realized that he'd somehow managed to make her completely reverse her opinion of him.

But thought quickly evaded her as she filled with the pleasant warmth, as her arms lifted, of their own accord, it seemed, her hand, unheeding, dropping the bunch of violets to the ground by her feet, reaching up to the hard wall of his shoulders, then sliding to the warmth of his neck, the oddly pleasurable contact with his skin and hair skittering through her fingers and down her arms. She felt his arms tighten at her waist as he pulled her closer, and when she breathed it was his breath she inhaled, oddly sweet to her, and tinged with the taste of champagne. It seemed to make her dizzy as the wine had done at lunch. She wondered if it was possible to become drunk on a kiss.

The gentle probe of his tongue was at first a surprise, but not an unpleasant one. She welcomed the advance with a willing enthusiasm mixed with curiosity, wondering where this new contact would take her, and found herself rewarded with the answering sharp thud of her heart as it filled her ears and shook her chest. She could only wonder that he did not feel it, too, then realized that he must, for she could sense an answering beat of his heart close to hers.

The contact was a pleasure Dash would have prolonged, even indefinitely, had not a loud squawking and the flapping of wings warned him of an interested audience in the form of a pair of young boys at the far side of the pond who'd begun to chuck small stones at the swans. He released Abra and sat, mute for a moment, gazing down at her. Then, collecting his thoughts somewhat, he bent forward to the ground and retrieved her lost bunch of flowers, returning them to her hand with a small flourish. She took them, tearing her gaze from his eyes, looking down at the small bouquet as she felt the warmth of a blush beginning to creep to her cheek. He put his hand to her chin, however, and forced her eyes back to his.

46

"You're thinking that was exceedingly ungentlemanly of me," he told her, although there was no indication that he regretted his action in the least.

"No," she admitted slowly. "Actually, I was thinking that it was not at all an unpleasant experience."

He grinned lopsidedly. "One that might not grow odious upon repetetion?" he asked.

She felt the flush increase, and she pulled away from him, to stare pointedly at the two boys at the far side of the pond.

"Well, then," he said evenly, "I've still to answer your last question, Abra."

She turned back to face him, surprised at the sudden seriousness of his tone.

"My intentions are, of course, quite honorable," he told her as he lifted his hand to her cheek once more, this time to stroke it softly with his finger.

Abra felt the heat grow at the contact, and this time she realized it was not from a ladylike blush, but caused by the softly sensuous touch.

He grinned at her then, a shade lecherously. "At least in so far as your father is concerned," he told her.

This time, when he pressed his lips to hers, when his hands stole to her waist and then to her back, pulling her close to him, neither of them were at all concerned about the young and extremely interested voyeurs at the far side of the pond.

## Chapter Three

"Well, Beaumont, I've good news for you."

Vincent put his paper down slowly and stared at the beefy man in the nubbly brown suit who slowly lowered himself into the leather armchair beside his own.

"I'd thought this club only for gentlemen," he murmured archly. "I shall have to speak to the screening committee about the shocking laxity being allowed in granting admission."

"No need to bother," his newly arrived companion replied jovially. "I'm not a member. Couldn't afford the dues even on the slim chance that they'd admit me. I simply told that stiff-necked darky at the door that I was your guest, that you were expecting me to join you for lunch."

Vincent offered a disgusted look in return for the slur. He held his tongue, however, not really voicing his anger, knowing it would do no good and thinking it best to be, at least a bit, cautious of his unwelcome visitor.

"I can't believe Walter," here he stressed the name, causing the bearer of the nubbly brown suit to turn bilious eyes to him, "would believe such an outright fabrication. He's far too good a judge of character to think that I would lunch with a policeman," Vincent finished evenly. "Especially one so scruffily dressed."

There was no rancor in his expression as he smiled then, and his unexpected visitor withdrew any suggestion of affront from his own. Returning smile for smile, the policeman's tone took on a bantering note when he replied.

"Actually, you're quite right. I was forced, I'm afraid, to show my badge and demand entry." He smiled again, this time quite sincerely. "I hope that won't in any way cause you embarrassment," he added hopefully.

Vincent shrugged disinterestedly. "There's been a shocking display of ineptitude by members of your brotherhood of late, Inspector McErlaine. I shouldn't think that anyone would think twice of it, even were you to come here and demand an audience with the queen of England. They'd assume it part of some professional depravity and dismiss the matter."

McErlaine laughed at that, a heavy rumbling sound emerging from deep within his barrel of a chest. "I'd no idea that the public took my fellows for such fools," he said when his laughter had died, only now the hint of amusement was gone from his voice. "I'd thought we retained that right for ourselves."

Vincent stared at him intently. "Not the public in general, inspector," he assured his visitor. "Just those who have suffered the misfortune of having been forced to endure such unwelcome company as yours."

McErlaine sneered. "And that includes that darky by the door, I suppose?"

Vincent stiffened. "That is the second time you have used that expression, inspector. I expect there won't be a third." His eyes narrowed and he surveyed McErlaine with now open hostility. "You said you had news for me. I presume that is why you are here, and not simply for the amusement of exchanging witty conversation?"

McErlaine seemed delighted at Vincent's reaction, as though he had been waiting for some outward sign of annoyance or hostility.

"Ah, yes," he replied, genially pleasant once again. "My news. I've come to tell you that I'll be retiring next month, Beaumont."

Vincent accepted that bit of news without obvious interest. "Retiring? Has it really been so long as that? Why it seems only yesterday the first time you pounded on my door and accused me of some unspeakable crime or another, inspector."

"Of jewel robbery, Beaumont," McErlaine hissed.

"Ah, yes," Vincent replied, smiling once more. "I remember now. And I also remember your boasting that you'd be chief inspector one day. It seems you were wrong on both counts."

49

"There was no mistake about you." McErlaine told him heatedly. "And I would have been chief inspector, but for you." An unhealthy red splotch had appeared on both of his dark veined cheeks.

"I'm honored, of course, inspector, but I really think you put far too much credit to my account." Vincent smiled as he spoke, watching as McErlaine thrust a hand into a bulging jacket pocket and pulled out a scruffy-looking tin, which he proceeded to open and from which he withdrew two large green tablets. The inspector suffered from a nervous stomach and poor digestion, a fact of which Vincent had become only too well apprised over the years. It delighted him to see that his conversation had discommoded the man enough to merit not one, but two of the odious-looking tablets. "In any case," he went on as McErlaine placed the tablets into his mouth and began to chew energetically at them, "I assume you've come to tell me this news so that I might offer you my heartiest congratulations. Which I sincerely do, inspector." He beamed a seraphic smile. "I most sincerely do."

McErlaine swallowed the chalky mess in his mouth and wiped the back of his hand across his lips. "It wasn't your congratulations I come looking for, Beaumont, or anything else, for that matter. I just thought you'd like to know that once I've retired, I'll have much more time for my hobby." He smiled unpleasantly, displaying teeth coated with a scum of greenish chalk. "You."

"Me?" Vincent seemed on the edge of laughter.

"Yes, you, Beaumont," McErlaine replied, once again baring the odious display of his teeth. "You're my hobby. I'm going to prove you did that job. It may be too late for chief inspectorship, but the satisfaction will more than do, if I can see you finally where you belong, behind bars."

"Really, inspector, I do think this preoccupation you have is becoming unhealthy for you. An unsolved crime, some twenty-five years old. Surely you ought to be able to forget it and take up something else as a hobby." Vincent offered him a concerned look. "Have you thought of gardening, perhaps? I'm told it's quite soothing for distraught nerves."

"You'd like that, wouldn't you? If I forgot all about you and let you end your days as if you were a pillar of society.

50

Well, I'm not going to do that. Instead, I'm going to dog your footsteps, make sure that every time you turn around, you see me behind you."

He smiled malignantly, and the sight of it made Vincent shudder inwardly. McErlaine's face, despite its beefiness, had an unpleasant resemblance then to a death's head, a grotesque apparition grown malignly corpulent. Vincent chased away the thought and ventured a humorless grin.

"I'm sure I'll look forward to knowing I'm so well guarded, inspector." He lifted the paper from his lap. "And now, if there's nothing else . . ."

"No, nothing else," McErlaine replied, his tone gone oddly flat, as though he'd expected something more and was disappointed not to have found it.

"Good," Vincent told him, turning his eyes firmly to the paper, the gesture one of dismissal. "I'm sure you can find your own way out."

The inspector stayed where he was a moment longer, but when he found Vincent was apparently now completely unaware of his presence, he heaved himself wordlessly from his chair and made his way from the room.


The wind came as a brusque surprise to Abra as she walked through the doors the guard held open for them. It had been quite warm inside, if a bit damp and musty, and the clean bite of the autumn breeze was a big enough contrast to seem almost a surprise. She pulled her coat hastily closed and worked at the buttons with intent industry.

When she'd done, Dash firmly took her arm and placed it comfortably in the crook of his own. He looked out at the dimming evening sky.

"It's getting dark," he mused aloud. "I had no idea it had grown so late. I don't suppose you'd allow me to buy you a tea or a glass of fizz, would you? Or has your penance been done and set you free?"

Abra looked at his expression cautiously. "Well, actually I think my honor demands full retribution to you. Another half an hour at least," she told him gamely.

"Have you ever considered making a career out of tour guiding?" Dash asked as they descended the long flight of steps that fronted the museum. "I'm quite impressed with the afternoon you've given me. I'd be more than willing to make an unsolicited testimonial to that fact."

"Really?" Abra inquired with a raised brow. "And I thought you a bit bored by the museum."

"Me?" There was the hint of hurt in his tone. "Can you think me the soulless sort of man who has no appreciation for art, Abra?" he asked.

"Most certainly not," she replied with a hasty laugh. "But for some reason I thought your thoughts were wandering, especially in that last gallery."

He nodded his head gravely. "Perhaps." he replied. "The sight of virgins being martyred always baffled me as a subject for art. Seems like a waste of perfectly good canvas and pigment. Not to mention the odd virgin." He turned to Abra and his eyes narrowed in concentration. "Besides, I found a far more worthy subject for my inspection in that gallery, a true work of art."

She returned his stare. "I think I would blush if I thought you meant what you say, Mr. Thorne." She smiled warmly. "Dash," she amended.

"You have blushed several times this afternoon, Abra. So you must believe at least part of what I've told you."

She turned away, feeling the habitual warmth creeping into her cheeks. "It's a curse," she told him as they started for the curb to hail a hansom cab. "Not at all fitting to my temperament, either," she added with a laugh.

He stopped then, and, her hand tight in his arm, she was forced to do the same. "On the contrary, I think I find it most becoming, Abra," he told her softly.

It was while they stood together, involved in each other rather than in the passersby who crowded the sidewalk, that a large man in a disreputable-looking brown suit, one that had the appearance of not having seen a proper brushing in far too long, marched breathily up to them and settled himself at Abra's side.

"Miss Beaumont? Miss Abra Beaumont?"

His inquiry was direct, without apparent notice of Dash's presence. Abra turned to answer him, puzzled at this sudden, entirely unlikely apparition.

"Excuse me?"

"You are Miss Beaumont, aren't you?" he asked. She

nodded as he put his hand into his breast pocket and removed a small leather case. This he opened and held out for her inspection. "Inspector McErlaine, Metropolitan Police." He smiled unpleasantly at her and allowed his glance to stray quickly to Dash before returning it to her.

"What is it?" Abra demanded, a sick feeling beginning to blossom in the pit of her stomach.

"Just a word of caution I hope you'll have the good sense to relay to your father, Miss Beaumont."

"What are you talking about?" Abra demanded, her voice beginning to shake.

"Just tell your father," McErlaine replied. "Tell him we're watching."

Dash put a hand to McErlaine's arm. "I don't know who you are or what you think you're doing . . ."

But McErlaine shook him off roughly, turning to look at Dash as though he'd only really just come to his notice. "Don't go handling officers of the law, if you know what's good for you," he snarled. "And if you know what you're about, you'll stay away from Beaumont and his family." He smiled once more, the same unpleasant smile he'd bestowed on Abra. "Unless your own good name means nothing to you." With that, he turned and moved into the flow of pedestrians on the sidewalk.

Abra stared after him until he'd melted into the flow of humanity, leaving nothing but the unpleasant residue of his presence, the knotted feeling he'd caused in her stomach.

"Abra," Dash ventured softly, putting his hand to her arm gently.

She pulled away angrily, finally turning her attention back to him.

"You said you'd not get him involved in anything," she accused angrily. "You gave me your word."

"I haven't, Abra," he replied, as bewildered by what had happened as was she. "I've done nothing in which he could be involved."

"Then how do you explain what just happened?" she snapped at him.

"I can't," he replied.

She started to turn away and he reached for her arm, holding it firmly until she turned back to him.

53

"Look, Abra. Be sensible. That policeman didn't even know who I was. Whatever his interest in Vincent, it has nothing to do with me."

She stared at him for a long moment, slowly realizing that what he said made sense. But that left her with the alternative that her father had in some way come to the attention of the authorities on his own, and that made no sense to her at all.

"I think I should go home now, Mr. Thorne," she said, each word pronounced slowly and quite distinctly. "You needn't bother yourself to accompany me. I can take a cab alone."

Dash gritted his teeth, aware that nothing he could say to her would in any way alleviate the suspicions she had suddenly acquired of him. He held up his arm to hail a passing cab.

"No need, Miss Beaumont," he told her through a clenched jaw. "I wouldn't dream of leaving you unescorted after dark."

A cab pulled up to the curb and Dash handed her in, called the address up to the driver and then climbed in after her, preparing himself to face the ride in stony silence.

Inspector First Class Patrick Daniel Francis McErlaine — Patty Mac to his friends, or more precisely, to those of his subordinates who wished to keep themselves clear of the long list of individuals McErlaine classed as thieving, godless, stinking bastards and to whom he made no effort to hide his hatred, or the fact that he deliberately made life miserable for them whenever the occasion presented itself — had quite enjoyed his lunch. Surprisingly, this was not an altogether common occurrence, despite his corpulence. On the contrary, his subordinates often felt that he compensated for his lack of enjoyment of what was served him by demanding a second and often third plateful, ostensibly with the presumption that it would please him better on second, or third, try.

That afternoon, however, he'd ordered his meal jovially, quite disconcerting the waiter at McFeeley's Tavern, who often wished the good inspector would take his customary business elsewhere. The heaped plate of boiled beef and potatoes and the quart mug of Porter were laid before him as a sacrificial lamb before an altar, and the waiter withdrew immediately to a safe distance, not prepared at his busiest hour for the expected diatribe.

Despite this poor beginning, McErlaine attacked the heap with relish, slathering a good deal of sharp mustard on the greyish meat, then forking up immense bites and chewing them contemplatively. When the plate was emptied, he drained his mug, asked for his tab, and counted out the coins, even adding a nickel to his customary miserly four-percent tip. This was a true outpouring of good will, also attested to by the fact that he did not grumble about the fact that honest workers were content with what they were paid and did not go about with hand out, always expecting something extra, his ordinary modus operandi.

As he returned to his office, his sergeant, one Cecil Breadon by name, a small man who accepted his superior's semiconstant harassment with the silent stoicism of a man who counts the days until the promised release of freedom, was in the act of crossing out the date on a small calendar and contemplating beatifically the day at the end of the month, which he'd circled with glowing red ink, the day of the inspector's scheduled departure. He looked up with the furtive expression of a man found out inopportunely, and shoved the innocent calendar into his desk drawer with a vehemence the inanimate object hardly deserved.

"Chief inspector wants to see you," he said hastily as McErlaine removed his jacket in preparation for a diligent half hour scanning the afternoon newspapers.

McErlaine pursed his lips. "Did he say what it was about?" he demanded suspiciously, peering down at Breadon with the sort of expression one offers a hapless mouse who makes the mistake of running across a room into the waiting claws of a hungry cat.

Breadon could only shake his head. "But he had his steam up," he offered, and the pleasure he felt at the possibility that McErlaine just might be in trouble drifted into his voice despite the earnest endeavor he made to hide it.

McErlaine frowned. "You might have told me before I took off my jacket," he snapped dispetically. He was aware of the growing feeling that his lunch was not agreeing with him, after all. He thrust his hand into his pocket in search of his tin of medication as he pulled open the office door, then pulled it shut again with an angry slam behind him.

Sergeant Breadon turned and smiled at the sound, watching impassively as the slight shimmer of the door window the slam had caused slowly settled itself into inertia.

McErlaine ambled the length of the corridor with a deliberate leisureliness the situation hardly required. When he'd reached the proper door he stopped, knocked, and waited stolidly, his stomach heaving, until he heard the word "Come" called out, dimly recognizable through the chief inspector's solid mahogany door. *I* ought to have had a solid mahogany door, he fumed silently, just as he always did when he contemplated the portal to the chief inspector's office and contrasted it with the more plebian glass-windowed affair the lesser offices boasted, the implication being that the chief inspector's actions required privacy, while less lofty mortals deserved to have their activities within plain view lest they be tempted to shirk during hours for which they were paid. "Come." The single word of admittance, too, irked McErlaine, as it was all the chief inspector ever called, as though the mere addition of "in" were more effort than his subordinates deserved.

McErlaine opened the door and marched through heavily, feeling the boiled beef and beer beginning to set up a holy row in his stomach. He silently cursed the tavern's cook, the waiter, the hapless Sergeant Breadon, and most especially, Chief Inspector Flynt, whom he hated for many reasons, but most especially because the man had the nerve to hold a position McErlaine felt rightfully should have been his own.

Once inside the office, however, with the mahogany door quietly closed behind him, he found another target at which to aim his silent invectives. Vincent Beaumont sat comfortably on a heavy leather-upholstered chair, legs crossed lazily and a newly lit cigar in hand, at the side of the chief inspector's own enormous leather-covered wing chair.

"Ah, Patty Mac," Flynt called out to him, motioning

56

him to take a seat as he held a match to the cigar in his hand, his indifference no greater an insult than the hard wooden chair that had been pulled up across from him at the outer side of the desk.

McErlaine inwardly cringed as he sat. Flynt only called him Patty Mac when he had something unusually unpleasant for him to do or when he intended to suggest, in a more than moderate way, that he had not performed his duties in the best tradition of the force. From the absent look of contentment he saw on Vincent Beaumont's face, McErlaine decided this was to be one of the latter occasions.

"You sent for me, chief inspector," McErlaine said, pretending indifference to and total obliviousness of Vincent's presence.

Flynt looked up at him, then down to the cigar he'd just lit, and deposited the spent match in a large cut glass ashtray on the desk.

McErlaine gritted his teeth, knowing Beaumont had received the honor of one of the chief's precious hoard of cigars, knowing that no such offer would be tendered him.

"You do know Mr. Beaumont, I believe?" Flynt asked, his tone arch.

Here's for it, McErlaine thought, and once more he leveled his mental curses at Flynt, and wondered at the fates that could allow so stupid and unworthy a person into a position of superiority over him.

"I know him," McErlaine responded. "He pulled the Caverleigh jewel job some twenty-five years ago, and some day I intend to prove it."

"Enough of this, McErlaine," Flynt fumed, flaring into one of his sudden tempers. He leaned forward, over his desk, his eyes darting angry daggers, apparently preparing himself to level a mighty blow.

Vincent, however, seemed entirely calm, despite the provocation. "You see, chief inspector, the man seems to have fixed himself, for some reason that I can only admit baffles me, on my guilt for some trifle that happened a quarter of a century ago."

"Trifle?" McErlaine shouted back. "Half a million and he calls it a trifle?"

"Quiet, inspector. I think I've heard quite enough from

you. Mr. Beaumont has come to me with a story that you have been harassing him all these years, something that would seem fantastic were it any other of my men but you."

Vincent waved the hand that held his cigar, a small cloud of bluish smoke rising to the ceiling in its wake. "In the past I've looked upon the inspector more as an object of pity than anything else. And as he came on his monthly visits either to my home or to my club, reserving his fantasies for my ears only, I felt it only Christian charity to humor him a bit and let him go on with whatever it was he did, with no great harm done. But yesterday he accosted my daughter. Not only did he disturb and alarm her, he also insulted the gentleman with her." Vincent leveled steely eyes on McErlaine. "When it comes to my daughter's peace of mind, it seems my pity for the man has evaporated. What he did yesterday is one thing I will not countenance."

"Set off the swell with her, did I?" McErlaine sneered, apparently quite pleased at the prospect.

"Inspector!" This time Flynt's anger was entirely uncontrolled. "You have only a matter of weeks until your retirement. If you wish to reach it without censure and impairment to your pension, I suggest you offer your apologies to Mr. Beaumont."

McErlaine's already splotchy cheeks began to glow with irate color.

"Apologize?" he sputtered, spraying a good deal of hops-scented saliva on the chief inspector's desktop in his rage.

Vincent stood then. "Frankly, chief inspector," he said, turning away from McErlaine as if he intended no further recognition of the man, "I am disinterested in anything the inspector might say, including his apologies. I came to you for some assurance that what occurred yesterday will not be repeated. I trust I can assume that it is offered?"

"Certainly, Mr. Beaumont," Flynt replied, hastily standing as well, darting an I'll-deal-with-you-later look at McErlaine before offering his hand to Vincent.

"Well, then, I'll consider the matter settled," Vincent replied, taking the offered hand and shaking it, his expression plainly pained but making an effort at affability. "It pains me to have been forced to bother you over so inconsequential a matter. I'm sure you have far greater matters with which to deal."

"Whatever the occasion, Mr. Beaumont, the force is always grateful for the chance to be of service to a prominent citizen such as yourself."

Flynt's smile, saccharine and placating, was almost more than Vincent could stomach. He thought he almost preferred McErlaine's honest and open hostility.

"Well, then, I'll leave you to your duties. Thank you once again," he finished with as sincere a smile as he could muster, then he picked up his hat and walking stick and strode to the door without so much as a look in McErlaine's direction.

The hatred with which McErlaine stared at his retreating back only began to dim when he realized that Beaumont had given him a tool, a wedge to get at him. After all the years of looking, he finally knew how he could trap the man. It was so simple, McErlaine thought. He felt himself a fool not to have seen it before, as it had been there all along for him to recognize. The way to Vincent Beaumont was through his daughter he mused happily. It cheered him enough to begin to tamp down the fires in his stomach, and allowed him, once Vincent had disappeared and the door closed behind him, to turn back to face Chief Inspector Flynt and his dressing down without any real feelings of renewed distress.

The man who sat across the desk from Dashiel Thorne was small and spare, and his wrinkled shirtsleeves gave evidence to the hours he'd spent cubbyholed in the overcrowded room that day, pouring over the heaps of reports that littered his desk. Papers seemed to flutter tentatively in a breeze of their own, an observation that mystified Dash, as the tiny office was close and practically airless. They hovered in disorderly stacks, great piles of papers staring down at him from the rows of shelves that covered three of the four walls, taunting him with the secrets of the superior knowledge they surely held.

"The man's a nuisance, not a menace, Dash. He was the investigating officer on the Caverleigh heist, God only knows how many years ago." He grinned at Dash conspiratorially, then returned his gaze to the file in his hands. "No clues, nothing to trace, it was done real neat. But this McErlaine got it into his head that your man Beaumont had done the job, and wouldn't let go. He haunted every one of his superiors with the thing until they finally threatened to dismiss him unless he let it lie and got on with his job." He put down the folder and looked at Dash once more. "I guess he didn't quite follow their orders."

Dash considered this news thoughtfully. "The statute of limitations has to have expired years ago," he said.

"Precisely," his companion replied with a nod. "Insurance nicely paid and all parties apparently satisfied." He tapped the folder quickly with his fingers. "Except for this fool inspector, that is."

"His turning up like that rather startled Miss Beaumont," Dash mused aloud.

Once again his companion smiled. "It seems to me, Dash, your concern for Miss Beaumont's upset is a bit more than mere professional interest."

Dash raised an eyebrow sharply. "You know as well as I do that we will need her," he replied, then his face softened and he smiled. "Perhaps it is," he conceded slowly. "Just perhaps it is."

A fleeting smile passed over the other man's face, only this time he chased it away quickly, as though he were ashamed it had gotten there in the first place.

"Do you think that's wise, Dash?" he demanded softly as he removed the spectacles he wore and began to polish them with what could only be described as excessive care.

"Damn it, Charles," Dash retorted, "I know what I'm about."

"No one would dream of suggesting anything to the contrary, Dash. Just that you stop and think about it before you do anything rash." He stood up and looked as if he wanted to pace, but found the confines of the room entirely excluded any such activity. Instead, he replaced his spectacles and stood staring down at Dash quizzically. He was silent for a moment, then his eyes narrowed speculatively.

"I don't suppose, Dash," he asked softly, "that you've had any second thoughts? Like backing out on our little arrangement? Perhaps taking the Tear, then disappearing with it, Beaumont, and his lovely daughter?"

The look Dash threw at him more than answered his questions, and this time when he removed his spectacles and began once more to rub at the invisible spot that had somehow gotten on them in the previous few seconds, it was done vigorously, as a means to cover his discomfort.

"I thought you knew me better than that, Charles," Dash told him softly, his tone cold and hard-edged. "Although now that you've mentioned the possibility, I might just consider it."

"I meant no offense, Dash." The reply was offered placatingly, the tone softly gentling. "It's just that were I to ignore the possibility, my, uh, employers would make life highly unpleasant, for me as well as you."

Dash could not help but hear the hint of threat in the words, but he chose to ignore it. Instead, he sat silently a moment, apparently considering. Then he turned to where the other man stood.

"For God's sake, Charles, will you sit down? I can't stand you peering down at me." He grinned crookedly as he measured the smaller man's size visually. "It's unnatural." He waited patiently until the man he called Charles reseated himself, then he leaned forward, ignoring the papers that littered the desktop, resting his arms among the clutter. "Look, Charles. You want the stone. I told you I could get it for you, but that I couldn't do it alone. And we agreed on Vincent Beaumont. If you want me to back out of it, say so now. Otherwise, I do it my way. And Abra Beaumont is none of your business."

He stared at the smaller man, measuring the eyes that stared back myopically at him through the thickness of the glass lenses, aware that he knew what it was he would say before the words had been spoken.

Charles Nevin blinked, then turned his gaze away from Dash's expectant stare, back to the heaps of papers on his desk.

"No one's doubting your ability, Dash, or even your intentions. It's just that an entanglement right now can only make things far more difficult."

"Entanglement or not, Abra Beaumont is part of it, even if she isn't aware of the fact. So, if you've quite done with the subject . . ."

"As you like, Dash," came the unenthusiastic reply.

Dash heard the hesitation in Nevin's voice and decided it was time to change the subject. "And this McErlaine? You're sure he's nothing to worry about?"

Nevin brightened visibly. "The man's unhinged, Dash, but I honestly can't see how he could make any real difficulties for you. I suppose if he got it into his head to embarrass Beaumont, he could, but I doubt it would amount to much. As you mentioned, the statute of limitations is long past on the Caverleigh heist, and even were it otherwise, Beaumont's work was far too professional for McErlaine ever to get anything on him. I don't think there's anything to worry about there."

"That's all I wanted to know, Charles," Dash said as he rose and took the single step that brought him to the door.

Nevin's eyes followed him and for an instant the man felt a nearly physical disinclination to speak. But he overcame it as Dash's hand reached for the knob.

"I have a query for you, Dash. What happens when Beaumont comes to the inevitable conclusion that you've used him to get the jewel and then left him with nothing for his pains? And, what may be more to the point under the circumstances, what happens when Miss Beaumont realizes it?"

Dash turned back and faced him for a moment. A pained expression crossed his face.

"I don't know, Charles," he said thoughtfully. "I suppose that's something I'll have to face when it happens."

He didn't have to say that the prospect was something he could only consider with a good deal less than thrilled anticipation.

## Chapter Four

The large private dining room at the Saint Pierre Hotel could only inadequately be termed elegant and sumptuous, for all such descriptives were only thin echoes of the grandeur of the place. It had been decorated in boiserie taken from a castle on the Loire, with gilded puttis and wreaths of flowers rampant at every turn. Huge Irish crystal chandeliers offered sparkling light that more than compensated for the lack of any sunlight that was filtered out by the heavy folds of silk that swathed the tall, elegant windows. In fact, the room fairly glowed with silver and vermeil, ormolu, and the reflected light dispersed by literally millions of facets of crystal. With the patron's comfort always in mind, thickly upholstered chairs and settees invited him to take his ease, the warmth of scarlet silken velvet beckoning. The room was an environment that reminded him that for some, money was no object.

The half-dozen men who sat around the table in the center of the room seemed nearly lost among the grandeur of a room intended to pamper the whims of some five hundred without the unseemly sensation of being crowded, but they seemed oblivious as they sipped their postluncheon brandies and ritually lit their cigars. Of the six, five seemed less interested in their brandy than was their usual wont, doubtless because they wanted to keep their heads clear and unbefuddled, and the sixth eschewed it altogether, a religious dictum that he secretly dispensed with when in his own company, but found useful to adhere to rigidly when in public, especially when in the company of foreigners. Other than that, there was little to differentiate him from his companions, as all six were impeccably and conservatively dressed in dark grey or blue, except perhaps his manner, which seemed just a shade superior as he listened to their talk, when a small smile edged to his lips and his dark eyes considered them with precision and concentration.

Had he known of the meeting, the mayor would have been greatly hurt that it had not been held in City Hall or Gracie Mansion, and the governor, come all the way from Albany expressly to meet the guest of honor, more than a bit put out that he had not been invited to host the affair. Such trivialities, however, seemed to matter very little to the assembled group who'd carefully and secretly arranged the meeting. Their affairs were those of the country's well-being, and they had little time or interest in the parochial concerns of even the leaders of so great a constituency as New York.

The leader of this group was undoubtedly the tallest of the five, although his height was of little consequence as he sat at the table. Grey hair edged his temples, a symbol of the image of sagacity and reserve he fostered, and his long aquiline nose spoke to all who cared to look of the fine breeding of which he was the current shining product.

"If you will consider our offer, Your Excellency," he was saying, his tone very grave as he considered the ash on his cigar, "I'm sure you'll realize it's the most felicitous arrangement for us all."

The others nodded encouragingly, then turned to the man referred to so deferentially as "your excellency," hoping that he, too, would agree.

But Sheik Shahab Sharify, emir of Mukalla, seemed less than completely convinced. "Felicitous for your people, Mr. Atwood," he replied in an impeccably haughty British accent, "but I am not entirely convinced the same is true of mine." He returned his patient stare to the man who had addressed him, the slightly amused smile returning to the corners of his lips. "And although I appreciate the effort you've gone to, and of course this fine meal, I fear I must remind you that I have undertaken this trip for pleasure alone. Matters of state are best left for more thoughtful moments, when one's mind cannot be dulled by the lavishness of one's host's hospitality." The smile returned fleetingly. "After all, there is more to be considered than my own humble inclinations. The well-being of my people

64

must rule my decision, not my own softhearted sympathies for you Americans, my dearest friends, all."

The others at the table absorbed this small speech with the unemotional response of practiced cynics, unaccepting, as they were well aware that the emir's concern for his people was dispensed with as easily as the heads of those of his countrymen who opposed him. But the final tone for the meeting had been set by this unbreachable wall of emotional sentimentality, something they could not easily argue against. The emir would hold out for better terms for his oil, and nothing they could do could persuade him to do otherwise.

"But you will consider, Your Excellency?" Atwood pressed, not wanting to lose completely, wanting to be able to report to President McKinley that he had won at least this small point for all the pains he had taken.

"Most certainly," came the expansive reply. "I will offer your terms to my advisors as soon as I've returned home, and will ask them to ponder this grave matter with all appropriate concern, I can assure you."

Atwood shrugged, then motioned to an apparently empty wall at the far side of the room. As if the wave of his hand held magic powers, the room was suddenly alive with the flurry of waiters as they removed the remaining sweets from the table. Four silent, burly men surrounded the emir. The latter were darkly silent, their broodily untrusting eyes leveled at the small group of Americans. They affected no concession to western garb, as their master chose to do. Instead, they wore dark grey- or brown-striped burnooses. They were apparently unconcerned with the eyes their presence drew, and they returned the curious and questioning looks with silent suspicion.

The emir rose, as did the others at the table, and offered his hand to each of the Americans in turn, his manner distantly friendly, but not the least bit obsequious. Then the four guards closed ranks around him and escorted him to the door. Atwood and the remaining officials watched him leave with looks of grim determination.

Once they were in the hotel's front lobby, Sharify and his guards aroused the open interest of practically every eye in the expansive space. Open interest, that is, of almost all eyes. Those of a tall, handsomely dressed man sitting near

65

an ornate marble pillar flanked by drooping palm fronds did not even rise. He seemed too much interested in the amber liquid in the glass in his hand, and the precise circles he blew with the smoke of the cigar he gave every appearance of enjoying completely, to bother wasting his attention on anything so trivial as the group of strangely dressed men who walked across the far side of the lobby. But his eyes strayed to them once they'd passed him, and it seemed then that he was more than superficially interested.

When they'd left the hotel, Dash put his untouched whiskey down on a table and stood. He considered the cigar in his hand for a quick moment, then decided that it was a worthy prop, after all, and did not warrant wasting. He knocked off the ash into a nearby brass ashtray, then made his way to the large front doors.

"What's this, Papa?"

Vincent looked up idly and then took the heavy envelope Abra held out to him from her hand.

"Invitation," he replied in a judgmental tone. "Engraved." He fingered the tiny impressed letters on the envelope's flap. "Tiffany's," he added without bothering to look down at the tiny seal. "But that's only to be expected. Felicia Westmore observes all the niceties, at least those she could be socially faulted for ignoring."

With that, Vincent dropped the envelope carelessly to the table beside his chair and prepared to take up his evening paper once more.

Abra snatched up the discarded missive. "This reception is in honor of one Sheik Shahab Sharify, emir of Mukalla," she read, pronouncing the honorific slowly.

Vincent reached for the gold-embossed card, seemed to scan it carelessly, then released it back into Abra's grasp.

"So it would seem," he replied offhandedly.

"Well, we shan't go," Abra retorted.

Vincent finally looked up at her, his expression seraphically innocent. "Now that would be rude, Abra, as I've already sent along a note to the estimable good Mrs. Westmore saying we'd attend."

Abra exhaled audibly, making no effort to hide her vexation. "Papa, you're planning something with that horrible

66

Mr. Thorne, something concerning that Arab whatever-he-is, and that something has to do with his ruby." The accusation in her tone was sharply biting.

Vincent regarded her for a long moment in silence. "Why, Abra, I'm quite dismayed," he said slowly, and there was hurt in his tone. "How could you even think such a thing, when I gave my word to your mother twenty-five years ago to live an exemplary, law-abiding existence, a solemn oath I have never even considered breaking."

Abra drew back, suddenly ashamed. He seemed entirely genuine, and it pained her to think she had hurt his feelings. She felt guilty for the injury she saw in his expression.

"I'm sorry, Papa. It's just that since that horrible policeman. . . ."

"Abra, I told you," Vincent interrupted, "that was simply a stupid mistake. I've spoken to the chief inspector and had the matter tended to. It's not worth thinking about."

Abra dropped into the chair opposite him and sat staring at him. He was her father and she loved him dearly, she told herself. Surely she owed him the small courtesy of believing what he said.

"I saw him this morning, Papa," she told him softly.

Vincent's brow furrowed. "Him?" he demanded. "Who?"

"That McErlaine, that policeman. I saw him on the street this morning." For a second she wondered why she had not told him that first, why the fright of seeing the man a second time had somehow robbed her of the ability to think of him with any objective clarity, let alone talk to Vincent of him.

Vincent leaned forward to her, his expression entirely serious. "Did he approach you, Abra?" he asked. "Did he speak to you?"

She shook her head. "No," she told him. "He stayed on the opposite side of the street. But he was there, staring at me." She paused for a second, calling up the image of the jowly face with its burden of darkly probing eyes. "He just looked at me, and then he disappeared."

Vincent leaned back in the chair once more and the distress disappeared from his eyes.

"Perhaps it was simply a chance happenstance that he was there, Abra," he told her thoughtfully. Then he smiled

67

at her. "Or perhaps it wasn't really him, just someone that resembled him. On a street, in a crowd, it wouldn't be a unique mistake."

Abra stared at him, at the hopeful way he tried to comfort her. "Yes, Papa," she said slowly, although there was no thought in her mind that she had been mistaken, nor that the policeman had simply been there, a chance meeting in a busy, crowded city street. She smiled at Vincent gently. "Perhaps I was mistaken. Things have happened very strangely lately. And I can't help worrying about you. Ever since that Dashiel Thorne showed up, things seem odd around here."

"Odd, Abra? Don't be silly. And as for Dash, I thought you'd decided he wasn't really all that bad, after all?"

"No, Papa. You decided. We both know what he is, and the fact is, quite simply, he can only bring trouble with him. I'd be perfectly happy never to see him again, and even happier if you wouldn't either."

The last came out a bit tartly, even to her own ears, and Abra wondered if that wasn't because she wasn't quite convinced of her words.

"Abra, I've always allowed you to choose your friends as you like. I'd appreciate it if you gave me the same courtesy."

That ended her thoughts of protest, at least for the time being, with respect to Dashiel Thorne. But she was not ready to give up the fight completely. "I really don't think it would be quite politic, Papa, if I were to go to Freddy's mother's party. I was rude to him, even if my motives were for his own good, and it might be unpleasant for him if I were to appear. I really don't think we ought to go at all." She stared at him thoughtfully, hoping he'd agree.

She was to be disappointed.

"Not at all, Abra," Vincent told her blandly. "I saw Freddy only yesterday afternoon. He told me that he thought you were quite right, that he has been pressing you unreasonably and takes the responsibility for your small disagreement entirely upon himself." Abra groaned and Vincent smiled. "He's told me he intends to make it all up to you at his mother's reception, and begged me to smooth the way, to convince you he's entirely serious when he promises to behave as you would have him."

Abra was hardly comforted by his words. "Papa, I can't go."

Vincent held up a hand. "I don't see how you can refuse, Abra, as it would absolutely crush poor Freddy if you don't at least appear and give him the opportunity to make his little speech to you." He grinned delightedly, then quickly forced it from his face and tried to look properly parental.

"You're terrible, Papa," Abra laughed.

"And besides, my dear. Have you no curiosity with regard to this sheik? I should think you'd be as intrigued as every other female in New York. Even my club is filled with a flurry of jealous whispers about him."

Abra suddenly lost all desire to laugh. The sheik and his jewel, that was where her father's interests lay. And it occurred to her that she would be a fool to allow him to go without her.

Vincent peered at her slyly, apparently reading her thoughts. "But if you're quite determined to avoid Freddy entirely, although I really think you should take pity on the poor sod and at least appear, then I'll simply go without you."

Abra realized he was simply reinforcing her decision, and she wanted to fool him, to agree to his going alone if only for his apparent sureness that he'd convinced her, but she knew she would not.

"No, Papa, we'll go. But only on the condition that you don't leave me alone with Freddy," she told him with wry resignation.


The bookshop had been unusually crowded when she entered, and Abra edged her way to the table that offered the newest arrivals. She lifted a copy of Whitman's *Leaves of Grass* and began to browse through it, intrigued by the disparaging comments she'd heard about the poet and wanting to see for herself what could possibly have provoked such condemning appraisal. She lifted the volume and started to skim through the pages, oblivious of the crush around her.

She looked up only when her arm was so strongly jostled she nearly dropped the volume. There was a murmur of apology at her side, but Abra heard none of it. Instead, her eyes were glued to a heavy, rumpled-looking man who stood at the opposite side of the table staring blandly at her. When her eyes met his, she realized he had been there, watching her, for a while, because he smiled slowly at her, nodded his head and tipped his hat, then turned away and ambled to the door with the air of a man who had accomplished what he had set out to do. Abra stared after him, silently frozen, still feeling his eyes on her even when the tinkle of the shop doorbell told her he'd left. There was no mistake, she told herself, not this time. That policeman had been there, and he had wanted her to know it.

"Abra!"

Abra returned to reality slowly, finally hearing her name through the haze of speculation that followed McErlaine's departure.

"Really, Abra, what is the matter?"

She turned, finally, at the familiar voice. "Oh, Louisa, what are you doing here?"

"I was about to apologize for bumping into you and explain that it really wasn't my fault, but the fault of the dotty little woman with the yellow birds on her hat," and here Louisa pointed to a small, dark figure moving through the store and leaving a path of bewildered destruction in her wake. "But I think, instead, I'll scold you for being here and not across the street at the tea shop. We were supposed to meet there, don't you remember?"

"Oh, I'm sorry, Louisa," Abra murmured.

But Louisa seemed to be oblivious of her interruption, going on as though there'd been not a word offered. "Although it really is my own fault. I should have known that you couldn't pass Mr. Nolletti's without coming in."

"I was early, Louisa, honestly. I really intended to just stop for a moment. I thought I'd be there on time," Abra apologized, but her eyes turned again to the door through which McErlaine had vanished. Then, almost as though she were doubting what she had seen, she turned to Louisa. "You did see him, didn't you Louisa, that big, unkempt man in the wrinkled brown suit?"

Louisa stared at her silently for a moment. "Whatever are you talking about, Abra?" she demanded as Abra returned her gaze to the door, which had just opened once

70

more, admitting a waft of cool air and allowing one of the occupants to escape into the roomier environment of the street.

Abra turned back to her friend. It was obvious from Louisa's expression that a sighting of the beefy inspector was not high on her list of important things to remember. "No, of course you didn't see him," she murmured absently. "Well, shall we have our lunch? I know you must be anxious to get about your shopping."

"I'm always anxious to be shopping," Louisa replied with a slightly self-deprecating smile. "That's why I insist you come along with me. You keep me from overindulging my natural inclination to buy everything I see." She smiled and pointed to the book in Abra's hand. "And what bit of naughtiness have you there, Mistress Abra?" she demanded, her tone officious as she scanned the title. "Walt Whitman? You are too bad, Abra," she finished with a breathy little laugh.

Abra chased McErlaine from her mind and forced her attention to return to the volume in her hand. She shook her head. "No, Louisa, listen." And she read: 'I depart as air, I shake my white locks at the runaway sun . . . I stop somewhere waiting for you.' It's quite beautiful, don't you think?" She tucked the book firmly beneath her arm and looked around at the close crush of bodies in the narrow aisles. "I shall buy it, if we can ever manage to work our way to the front of the store," she finished with determination.

Louisa's answering look and shrug stated more eloquently than words that she thought there were a great deal more worthy objects on which a young woman ought to squander her money, but she turned to the shop front and began to work her way forward, her breathily offered "Excuse mes" and an occasional dazzling smile more than ample ammunition to clear a path for the two of them.

The atmosphere in the tea room when they finally reached it was decidedly more refined than that of the bookstore, and Louisa seemed to expand in the easy elegance. Perched on a small gilt chair upholstered in maroon brocade, she put her fork tentatively into a ladylike serving of lobster salad that waited hopefully on the small plate in front of her.

Abra could only smile. Despite Louisa's never-ending verbal rhapsodies over the pleasures of male company, she really thought her friend was actually frightened by members of the opposite sex, especially in a crush such as the bookstore had offered. Although Abra really couldn't understand just why. Louisa Richards, dark-haired and fair-complected, had a beautiful face, with large brown eyes and a virtually ever-present pleasant expression. And of late, as Louisa traversed the path from girlhood to womanhood, her more womanly attributes had begun to flower perceptibly, rounding her figure to the point of voluptuousness.

"I'll wear my ecru silk, of course. You know, with the embroidered seed pearls on the bodice. I wanted to wear the flowered Chinese silk, from the last season, it was so becoming, but Mama was positively shocked when I tried it on yesterday. She says," and Louisa lowered her voice to a muted whisper, "that since I've begun to fill out it looks absolutely scandalous, and I must give it to Elizabeth, and that impudent little imp had the nerve to sit there and absolutely gloat." Here Louisa stabbed at a lump of lobster meat, apparently substituting it in her mind for her younger sister, lifted the fork, and took the piece into her mouth, then chewed vigorously. That act complete, she returned to the matter of the ecru silk. "If there were more time, I could have convinced Mama to order something new for me, but Saturday's only two days away, and so it will have to be the ecru silk." She looked thoughtful. "The embroidery is really quite nice. So I must get a new pair of gloves, my old ones have a tear on the right thumb and I refuse to wear a mended glove to meet this mysterious sheik, and Mama said I might have a strand of flowers and pearls I saw at Fortmason's last week, tiny little satin flowers and seed pearls, so precious, on the thinnest satin ribbons that you weave into a braid or wrap around a chignon, they were lovely." Apparently run out of either breath or words, Louisa paused and looked up at Abra. "Abra, are you listening?"

Her voice managed to work its way through Abra's daze, and she struggled quickly to pull her mind back to the tea room.

"Of course, I'm listening, Louisa. Gloves and ribbons

with flowers and pearls." She smiled. "Right?"

Louisa nodded and returned her attention to her plate of lobster salad. "What are you wearing?" she asked as she impaled a bit of cucumber flower and a small bouquet of watercress.

Abra shrugged and poked at her own untouched salad. "I hadn't thought about it, really," she said.

Louisa stared at her curiously across the small separation of the tiny table. "How can you be so cool, Abra? Mama says that Mrs. Douglas says he's marvelously handsome. Everyone's talking. I can't think of anything even half so exciting happening in ever so long."

"He's just a man," Abra replied offhandedly and lifted her fork to her mouth.

"But he's a sheik, Abra." Louisa closed her eyes and intoned, "Sheik Shahab Sharify, emir of Mukalla. It even sounds romantic."

Abra laughed softly and shook her head. She had an odd feeling that the afternoon round of the shops with Louisa would be more than usually wearing.


Hemmings greeted Abra at the door with his usual tight-lipped "Afternoon, miss," and directed her attention to a substantial gilt foil-wrapped box tied with a large blue satin ribbon.

"It came not an hour ago, miss."

Abra handed her coat and hat to him and lifted the box curiously, making her way with it to Vincent's library.

He was there, seated in his leather chair, apparently absorbed by some weighty tome, but he lifted his eyes as soon as she entered and smiled up at her.

"Well, Abra, have you ruined me this afternoon? What extravagance did Louisa persuade you to indulge yourself in?" He smiled at her tolerantly.

"Actually, I was quite good, Papa," she replied, neglecting to tell him that she had been a bit distracted as well, and that the face she'd seen across the counter in the bookstore had haunted her for the rest of the afternoon. "This was my only purchase," she told him, handing him the wrapped volume of Whitman from the bookstore.

He only glanced at it, his attention held by her other

73

burden, the one done in gilt and blue. "And that?" he asked, his brows raised questioningly.

Abra plopped down lazily on the couch and set the box on the table in front of her, staring at it cautiously. "I don't know. Hemmings said it arrived about an hour ago."

"Well, aren't you going to open it?"

Abra shrugged, then leaned forward to the box, her hands reaching out to pull the ends of the bow until the ribbon fell away and left the box undecorated, shimmering, pristine gilt. She looked up at Vincent once more before pulling away the top. The heady perfume of heavy chocolate and liqueur floated up to her. She lifted the small envelope from the top, then swept away the layer of white tissue.

"Chocolates," she said, unnecessarily. Her nose twitched contentedly. "They smell delicious."

She stared at the small envelope with her name neatly penned in an easy masculine script, then slipped her finger beneath the flap, opening it and pulling out a small card. She read the four words it bore: "Please accept my apologies," which only made her curiosity grow. Just the four words, no signature, and the handwriting didn't look like Freddy's, although she couldn't really be sure. She could think of only one other man who might send her a peace offering and that, she would have thought, would have been offered two days previous, immediately following the strange afternoon she had spent in his company, an afternoon that had started with anger, proceeded to a pleasant comradery and then something more, and finally ended as it had begun.

Now that she had gotten over her initial anger, she almost believed what he had told her, that he had not been the cause of McErlaine's odd behavior. And as the days passed and the inspector seemed to be carefully and purposefully haunting her, she felt a strange need to talk to him about it, to ask his advice. She was mystified, and although she hated to admit it, a bit frightened by the policeman's appearances, and he was the only person she could think of with whom she could talk of it.

But nothing had come from him, not on the day following their afternoon together, nor on the one after that. She had forced herself to assume him indifferent, and told herself that she was glad of it, that she wanted nothing more to do with him. She told herself the same thing once again now, forcing away the thought of him as she dropped the note to the table.

"It must be from Freddy," she said offhandedly to Vincent as she stood and he looked up at her and shrugged indifferently.

"Probably," he replied as he finally unwrapped the brown paper that covered her afternoon's purchase. "*Leaves of Grass,*" he read, and proceeded to open the volume, glancing at the first few pages. "I bought one of the first editions," he told her, "but I can't think where it's gotten to over the years. I wonder how much he altered the poetry with the later editions."

Abra brightened, relieved to turn her thoughts away from Dashiel Thorne. "Is it really so shocking, Papa?" she asked him.

He looked up at her, a half-smile on his lips. "To some, I suppose," he replied absently. "I'm often amazed at what some people find shocking: love, expressions of love."

His expression had grown very serious, and Abra had a feeling that he was telling her something he had waited a long time to say, something that was meant to convey to her the fact that he recognized her to be a woman now, no longer a child.

"Papa," she said softly, reaching out her hand to him, waiting for him to grasp it and press it gently.

He dropped it when the sound of Hemmings's knock at the door intruded on their silence. The door opened and the butler walked sedately in, his arms filled with a large white box.

"This just arrived, miss," he told Abra as he placed this second offering on the table beside the extravagant box of chocolates, then stood eyeing it as Abra lifted the top.

She gasped. Hemmings followed her glance down to the dozen sprays of tiny white orchids and two dozen stems of red roses.

"I'll bring a vase, miss," he told her practically, but his normally impassive tone slipped just a bit, telling her that he was not above being impressed. "A large vase," he added as he disappeared in search of a properly splendid receptacle and some water.

"It must be Freddy," Abra murmured as she read the second card, identical to the first, that huddled amongst the blooms. She looked up at Vincent, but he only shrugged.

She'd just finished arranging the flowers and sat considering them speculatively when Hemmings reappeared. This time, however, he bore nothing but information.

"You've a visitor, miss," he intoned. "Mr. Thorne."

Before she could ask that Mr. Thorne be shown in, he was there, handsome and smiling in his evening clothes.

"Vincent," he said heartily as he crossed the room and offered his hand. Then he turned to her, his eyes sparkling with good humor. "I see you've accepted my peace offerings," he said flatly, as though he had expected nothing else. "That must mean I'm forgiven."

He reached down for her hand. She offered it to him mutely, and he slid onto the couch beside her as he pressed it gently.

"Just what is it that you've done to require so extensive a mollifier?" Vincent asked, his tone soberly paternal but laughter in his eyes.

"Damned if I know," Dash replied easily. "But so logical a person as Abra would not take offense needlessly, so it must have been serious." He turned to Abra, his blue eyes finding and capturing hers. "I have been forgiven, haven't I?" he asked her softly.

"I'm not sure," she replied, but she could not help but feel the warmth in her hand where his fingers touched hers.

"I hope so, for if I haven't been, you'll miss a wonderful evening." He dropped her hand, then offered her a rakish smile. "That is, if you're free. I've tickets to a music hall, "Fanny's Wayward Aunt," harder to get than hen's teeth."

"What?" she asked, the smile she'd been suppressing finally making its way to the surface. A music hall, she thought. Freddy would never take her to a music hall. The ballet or the opera, if she were to insist on music, but never anything so crude as a music hall.

He seemed to read her mind. "I dare say your society beaux would spurn such entertainment, but I am not so proud that I can't admit I've no such reservations. And not just seats, mind you, but a box, a true feat of Herculean proportions to acquire. I nearly had to offer my firstborn

76

son, should there ever be one, in pledge." He smiled invitingly. "Can you come?"

"I'm not sure," she hedged.

But Vincent interjected. "Abra is quite free this evening, Dash," he said before she could dither any further.

"And you?"

Vincent shook his head. "Afraid not. But you two enjoy yourselves."

Abra furrowed her brow as she turned to her father, not aware he'd made plans for the evening. But he ignored her.

She turned back to Dash. "I'll have to change," she told him.

He leaned back and smiled easily. "I'll wait."

"I'll be a while," she warned.

"Not too long," he countered. "I'd hate to miss the opening number. I understand it's almost indecent."

She laughed and stood. "Well, then, I'll try to hurry," she said as she started for the door.

When she'd gone, Vincent motioned to the bar at the far side of the room. "Why don't you make us both a drink, Dash?" he suggested.

Dash nodded, and crossed the room. "Is it set for the reception?" he asked softly. "You'll both be going?"

Vincent nodded. "She's determined to keep me out of trouble," he said.

"Just as well," Dash told him as he lifted the bottle of single malt and poured out a tot in each of two glasses. "We'll need your expertise soon, and we all ought to keep an eye on you, just for good measure."

He smiled as he offered one glass to Vincent, then raised his own in salute.

"To the Tear," Vincent offered in toast.

Dash nodded. "To the Tear and its soon-to-be-acquirers. May it leave the sheik's hands without a whimper."

Vincent smiled in response, and both men quickly drained their glasses.

77

## *Chapter Five*

The travails of "Fanny's Wayward Aunt" proved to be everything Dash had promised, vulgar and rowdy, and hysterically funny. At the intermission he disappeared momentarily from the box, only to reappear a few moments later bearing a bottle of champagne and two glasses.

Abra looked up at him and smiled. "The proverbial Greek bearing gifts?"

He shrugged. "At least you've been forewarned," he told her as he handed the glasses to her and began to busy himself with the foil and cork.

A similar ritual was being repeated along most of the long row of boxes that surrounded the theater, and a chorus of sharp pops was added to the animated talk and laughter. Abra peeked out at the occupants of the other boxes, all as elegantly dressed in evening clothes as she and Dash, all apparently enjoying themselves enormously. She realized sharply that she knew several of the gentlemen, older men mostly, leaning anxiously close to their companions, but the ladies were, without exception, strangers, and decidedly not those men's wives. She turned quickly away, not really wanting to see more, feeling as though she had trespassed, somehow, where she ought not to have gone.

She thought of those men's wives, of the glimpses she'd had of their lives. Tied to men who were, at best, indifferent to them, and for whom they felt little more than a passing contempt, they immersed themselves in gossip, judging the successes of their existence by the number of invitations they received each week, and by who of importance accepted their invitations in return. Abra pushed the thought of such lives aside, revolted, and thought about the role of the mistress. That relationship, at least, bound people together by passion, a far more tenuous tie than that of marriage, perhaps, but far less false. Even though she had turned her eyes away, her mind refused to leave the subject, and images of the men, leaning toward the pretty, young, very young, women, most in finery that seemed to please them, but with which they seemed remotely uneasy, pressed close on her. The feeling of trespass turned to one of contamination. She wished fervently she'd never seen anything.

The cork exited the bottle in Dash's hand with a loud noise, pulling her away from her musings. Dash quickly poured wine into the glasses she held out for him before it overflowed. He settled himself then on the chair beside her.

"Are you enjoying yourself, Abra?" he asked as she handed him a glass.

She sipped the wine and nodded to him. Then she peered at him intently. "This is awfully risqué, isn't it? The sort of thing a man takes his mistress to, not his wife?"

His expression sobered and he looked around the hall, becoming aware of the large number of older men at the sides of young women in the other boxes. Abra realized he'd thought of none of that, that his intention had truly been only to amuse her.

"If you'd like to leave, Abra . . ."

She shook her head and smiled, realizing her sides had begun to ache from laughter during the last hour. She forgot those men in the other boxes, forgot everything but how much she'd grown to enjoy his company.

"Actually, I'm having a wonderful time, Dash. Nothing Freddy ever took me to was half so much fun." She brought her wine to her lips, staring at him as she drank. "Besides," she murmured softly. "I think I'd rather be a mistress than a wife."

His eyes held hers, and she thought she saw a gleam of interest in them, a flash of surprise.

"Be careful what you ask for, Abra," he told her, his voice very low, husky. "You may get it."

And then the lights began to dim for the second act.

After the play ended, he took her to his hotel dining room for a late supper. The room was brightly lit, full of the sound of people talking, the noise of heavy silver against fine porcelain.

Abra felt a swell of well-being as she sat across the small

79

table from Dash. She kept her eyes on him as he ordered their meal, realizing that she found him extremely handsome and not really sure why that awareness seemed to startle her. At first she thought her good spirits were a result of the aftereffects of the comedy she'd seen and the wine she'd drunk. But now she was starting to believe it was something else entirely, something to do with Dash's company, and that awareness bothered her more than she would have liked to admit. She told herself that she ought to hate him, that his reasons for entering her and her father's life were all the wrong ones. But even as she found herself wondering what she was doing there, why she had gone out with him at all that evening, she found herself wandering into the memory of how his kiss had made her feel, and then, quite suddenly, realized she wanted to feel that way once again.

"A penny for your thoughts, Abra."

She tilted her head and smiled at him. Dash felt something lurch inside himself. It was a smile of invitation, and at the same time, of challenge. One look at those wide green eyes, he realized as he drank them in, and there was no thought that it was a challenge he would not rise to meet.

"I was just thinking what an evil man you are," she told him, her eyes laughing at him. "Tit for tat?"

"And I was thinking that you are the most beautiful woman I've ever seen." He was thoughtful for a second, apparently just realizing what it was she had said. "Why evil?" he demanded abruptly.

"Because you've come here intending to harm my father. . . ."

"Abra," he interrupted her, "that is the last thing I ever intended or want."

"But you don't deny your intentions about the Tear?" she persisted.

"Please, Abra, we'll talk about that later if you like, in a more private place," he interposed quickly.

She nodded, realizing she had been indiscreet, that their conversation could be overheard by the people sitting at the nearby tables.

"The worse of it is, though, that despite all that, I'm still glad I'm here with you." She had almost whispered the

80

words, as though she were ashamed of them. "Can you tell my why that is?"

He reached across the table and took her hand in his. "Let's not quarrel now, Abra," he said softly.

She stared at him thoughtfully. "No. Let's save that for later." Then she smiled impishly. "I'm hungry now, and quarreling will ruin our dinner."

He laughed then, as the waiter approached bearing plates of venison steaks and a bottle of dark red wine. A comradely truce settled between them as they addressed their meal.


"Well, you said you wanted to talk."

Abra looked around the room. It was just as she remembered it from that first afternoon, the quiet opulence, and the impersonality that all hotel rooms have, no matter how elegant. There was little one could learn about a person from a hotel room, and that disturbed her. There was a great deal she would have liked to know about Dashiel Thorne.

She settled herself on the couch and watched him as he knelt to the fire, pushing the embers to the back and adding more coal from the scuttle left by the hearth. The maid had obviously made up the fire several hours before, and now it had died back and the room had taken on a dull chill. But a moment after Dash had stirred the coals to a bright, shining glow, the chill was gone and the heat radiated warm against her cheeks and the flesh of her bared shoulders.

He turned to her, watching as the pale skin took on a flash of pink from the warmth. Again he felt the heaving lurch inside himself, and Dash prayed quickly that her promise of an argument would be a false one. She seemed reluctant to begin, so he put down the poker, and settled himself beside her on the couch. He leaned forward, wanting to kiss her, until his face was inches from hers.

But she turned away from him and he did not press. When she turned back to him, there was a spark of anger in her eyes.

"That policeman," she burst out. "He's been following me."

His eyes narrowed as he stared at her. "You mean the man who approached you the other day?" She nodded mutely. "You're sure?" he asked slowly.

"Yes, I'm positive," she fairly shouted back at him. She sighed and composed herself. "I saw him on the street the day before yesterday, and then again this afternoon, in a bookshop. He didn't appear to be interested in literature."

That said, she sank back in silence. It was ridiculous, of course, to think that telling him would change matters, but still she realized that she suddenly felt better about McErlaine's sudden appearances, and that the feelings of panic they had caused had grown distant and seemingly childish.

"I'll see that it's stopped," he said softly, not doubting her, not suggesting, as Vincent had, that she had been mistaken.

"But how?" she asked, bewildered, surprised at his reaction.

He smiled mysteriously. "I know a few people," he told her evasively.

"But you mustn't. It might make them suspicious, you might place yourself in an awkward position in the event . . ."

She stopped and he finished her sentence for her. "In the event the Tear is stolen?" he asked softly.

She nodded.

"And would that disturb you, Abra, if I were placed in what you so obliquely call an awkward position?"

She looked up at him and felt a kind of melting inside. "Yes," she whispered, her voice sounding hoarse, as though the words were hard for her to say. "That would disturb me a great deal, I think."

And then his arms were around her, and his lips pressing hers, and she realized the melting she had begun to feel inside was only a hint of what was now happening to her. She put her hands to the back of his neck, letting her fingers lace themselves through his thick dark curls, savoring the melting warmth that flowed through her, the steamy liquid feeling that so suddenly seemed to seep into every pore of her body. She could feel his hands, warm on her back, the hard press of his arms as they pulled her close, the solid wall of his chest as she pressed against him.

At that moment she knew she had been a hypocrite,

lying to herself each time she had tried to tell herself that she didn't care what happened to him, that she only wanted him out of her and her father's life. All of it had been clumsy lies, and it was only too plain to her that what she had really wanted, from that first time he had kissed her, was to be alone with him like this, to feel the strange, pleasant awakening that flowed through her body when he touched her.

He lifted his lips from hers and looked down at her, at her reddened cheeks and flushed shoulders, at the filmy look that had come to those magnificent green eyes, and he could only think of what it would be like to have her, to feel her close beneath him, to love her. He pulled himself from her reluctantly, dropping his arms and standing, walking to the fire, finding its heat only a mild echo of the fire that she'd lit in his veins.

"Perhaps I should take you home now, Abra," he told her softly, trying not to look at her, to keep his eyes to the fire.

She stood and walked silently up to him, putting her hand to his shoulder, waiting for him to turn to face her before she spoke.

"Is that what you want to do, Dash?" she asked softly.

"Damn it, Abra, you're making it incredibly hard for me to behave like a gentleman," he told her softly.

As though it moved of its own volition, his hand slid to her waist and drew her nearer. He realized then that he would not offer twice to bring her home, that he'd begun something and there was little chance he could turn away from it.

But Abra seemed as little inclined as he to ignore what was growing between them.

"I thought we decided that first evening at the Brinksons' that you were no gentleman, Dash," she whispered. "Besides, I'm not at all sure that I want to go home just yet."

He accepted the words without comment, wondering vaguely what he would have done had they been entirely different, if she'd demanded to leave then, wondering if he'd have the strength to accede to her wishes. But at that moment he realized that the fire she'd ignited in him had

83

caught within her, too, and waited now, smoldering, needing only his touch to be fanned into flames. He put his arms around her and drew her to him, and as he felt the heat of her body close to his, all thought of restraint left him.

He pressed his lips to hers, hard and seeking. His tongue quickly parted her lips, seeking the sweet, moist haven, in the first step on the ancient journey of discovery and pleasure.

For a moment Abra felt a flash of disbelief, wondering why she was there, how it had all happened so suddenly. And then she simply didn't care.

His fingers stole to the piled curls on her head, moving sinuously, freeing them of the pins that held them until the long strands fell loose and unfettered in his hands. There was the momentary memory of his wondering how her hair would feel, and then the exultant realization that it was even softer than he'd imagined, like thick ropes of fine, heavy silk beneath his fingers.

She lifted her hands to his shoulders, pressing herself close to him, bathed in a heady, narcotic warmth. When he swept her up into his arms, his lips still pressed to hers, she almost thought it was his kiss that had lifted her. Her body had grown buoyant with the strange flood of pleasure that encompassed her, and she only knew that it surprised and pleased her beyond measure, all the more so because she had never thought such things possible, certainly never expected them.

He carried her to the bedroom, laying her on the satin coverlet and following her. Then he brought his lips to the pale warm flesh of her neck, then, slowly, trailed downward to the tempting valley of her cleavage, leaving a swath of tingling, blushing warmth wherever he touched her.

He pulled himself from her then and looked at her face, at the expression of disbelieving pleasure. Then he stood by the bed, looking down at her, offering her his hand.

"Come here, Abra," he told her softly.

Bewildered, she accepted his offered hand, letting him pull her until she stood before him, unsure of what it was he expected but offering herself quietly to his wishes.

Then he put his arms around her, kissing her neck softly, whispering in her ear, "Let's not ruin that lovely gown."

The words came to her through a soft haze of pleasure, and she was only dimly aware of his fingers unfastening the buttons at her back, of the warmth of his hands as they brushed against her flesh. And then he stood back from her and she found herself, somehow, standing, staring at him, the heavy silken folds of her gown fallen to a shimmering circle at her feet.

He smiled, pleased at the picture of her, naked save for the thin silken shift she wore, her hair a reddish golden mane, loose around her shoulders, one long, heavy lock trailing across her shoulder to her breast. He put his hand to the long shimmering curl, pushing it back, his fingers brushing against the soft smoothness of her skin. Then, very quickly, he swept away the shift as she stood, quietly acquiescent, and lowered his head to the milky whiteness of her breast.

His touch sent a thrill of unexpected pleasure through Abra, and she stood, her hands to the back of his neck, filled with the heady feeling of the warmth of his lips and tongue against her flesh. She let her head fall back, and she trembled, awash with the heat of the liquid fire that he had ignited within her.

He looked at her face then, and he smiled. She smiled back, then tentatively brought her fingers to the buttons of his shirt. As obvious as it had been to her that he was no stranger to the intricacies of woman's clothing, it suddenly became abundantly apparent to her just how ignorant she was with respect to his. Her fingers trembled, brushing briefly against the growing vee of dark-haired, muscled flesh her efforts revealed.

For Dash, it was a painstaking advance, most especially the touch of her fingers against his skin, a sweet torture of anticipation, and somehow more potent, much more provocative to him than a knowledgeable display could possibly have been. By the time she'd done, he felt the rush of his blood pounding through him, heard it throbbing, thick and hot, in his ears.

He lifted her hands and brought them to the muscled wall of his chest, then wrapped his arms around her and pulled her close, pressing searing kiss upon kiss to her lips and neck and breasts. Then he lifted her, brought her once more to his bed, and stood over her, staring at her naked

85

beauty as he quickly removed the remainder of his clothing, then lowered himself to her.

This time he brought his hands to her naked flesh, unhindered by her clothing, his body hot and hard against hers. And as he brought his lips to her breasts once more and heard the intake of her breath, the heady heat of her pleasure filled him. Slowly, he made a careful and pleasurable journey with his hands and lips and tongue, breathing the fire within her to new life, kissing and caressing her breasts and belly and thighs and then, finally, the sweet moist warmth of her, until he heard her moan softly with the throbbing of her pleasure.

Then he raised himself to her, his legs parting hers as he kissed her lips and slid inside her.

Abra floated on a sea of pleasure. When she thought at all, it was with a shocked surprise that her body could have this capacity, hidden so completely, unsuspected, apparently waiting, asleep, for this one man to bring it to life. It was as though her body was awake for the first time in her life, and it was a mystery to her how it had come about. For a moment she thought that it was wrong, that he ought not to have the power to do such things to her, and then he began to move inside her and she knew she didn't care, wrong or right, she wanted nothing more but to feel his weight upon her, the heat of his flesh against hers, the sweet, hot fire of him inside her.

He moved slowly, and she allowed his hands to guide her, moving her hips as his fingers hinted until her body quickly learned the dance and instinctively rose to the tidal swell that he had released within her. She wrapped her arms around him, pressing herself close to him, accepting the warm thrust of his tongue, the heady narcotic taste of his lips against hers. She was adrift, helpless in a whirlwind of passion that possessed her, willing herself to it, and, at the same time, remotely aware that in some way she did not understand, she was frightened by it. But as the waves of pleasure rolled over her, as she felt them breaking against her, each time higher and higher, the fear disappeared, lost in the press of the heat that filled her.

Dash held himself taut, aware that more than anything he wanted her to know pleasure from him, more than anything else, more than any time he'd been with a woman before, he wanted to know he had pleased her.

It was not until he felt her breath against his neck come in short, ragged gasps, not until her body arched trembling to his, that he allowed himself to find the release of his own passion. And then it came, filling him, an explosion that ran through his blood like burning quicksilver, flashing hot and fast. More than anything else, the intensity of it surprised him. He'd never felt such pleasure ever before in his life.

For a moment then he held himself over her, wrapping her in his arms, cradling her as her body slowly relaxed and fell, limp and breathless. He kissed her gently, on the lips and then on each eye, his breath soft and warm against her cheek. Then he looked down at her, smiling, as she peered up at him, almost as bewildered as she seemed to be by what had happened between them.

She put her hands to the back of his neck and pulled him back down to her, kissing him once more, a kiss filled with the completeness of her passion. He moved himself so that he was beside her, and drew her close, her head against his chest, her hair, glowing softly in the lamplight, intertwined with the dark wiry curls of his chest. He pressed a soft kiss against the top of her head, and hugged her close. She lay willingly in the hammock of his arms, spent and satisfied, and let her eyelids drift slowly closed.


Abra dozed for half an hour, then woke with a start. Confusion settled over her as she opened her eyes to the strange room, to the strange realization that a hard masculine body lay close to hers.

"Abra? Are you awake?"

The whispered words settled her confusion and she felt herself heat with the memory of what they had done, what they had shared. She turned her face up to his, smiling, waiting for him to kiss her. When he'd willingly obliged, she snuggled back down into the warmth of his arms.

She sniffed contentedly, almost surprised at the simple pleasure she took from the warmth of his body close to hers, at the realization that his body smelled pleasantly of spice, uniquely his, sure she could recognize him from that alone. Intimacy, she realized, once begun, had many faces, some homely and uncomplicated, but no less pleasant for that.

"Dash," she said softly.

He looked down at her and brought his fingers to her face, gently tracing the line of her jaw and her lips.

"Yes, love?"

"Is that the way it ought to be? The way it always is?"

She seemed genuinely curious, and the innocence of her question surprised him. He smiled wryly.

"The way it ought to be, most decidedly."

"Then I didn't do anything wrong?" she asked, suddenly aware that she would be mortified if he'd thought her a clumsy fool, if she'd performed badly. Her need for assurance surprised her, for she'd never really thought in that way, never really thought of being in bed with a man at all, except occasionally in a remote, academic way. Surely the thought of Freddy had never aroused any mental wanderings in that direction.

"You," he replied in a laughingly tolerant, reassuring tone, "are a most decidedly talented beginner."

The assurance seemed to please her, for she smiled smugly up at him, and he laughed at her expression, a pleasantly basso, rumbling, amused sound that emanated deep in his chest.

"A lesson or two more and you are apt to have me groveling hopelessly at your feet."

There was laughter in his words, and she ignored the slightly superior way he voiced them, turning over to face him, resting her elbows on his chest. She smiled at him slyly.

"Then you would do anything for me?" she asked playfully.

He nodded. "Your every request, mademoiselle, is my humble command."

She hadn't really planned for the words to come out as they did, hadn't really planned any of it, actually, but suddenly the thought of one single request came to her, and she spoke it before she thought.

"Then will you forget this thing about the sheik's jewel?" she asked him, suddenly serious.

All the humor drained from his eyes and she could feel him stiffen beneath her.

"Is that what this was all about, Abra? Some bargain you'd decided to make, offering up your maidenhead for my word? Is that what really happened between us?"

She reached out to him, putting her fingers to his lips to stop the flow of words.

"You know it's not, Dash," she said. "You must believe me, it's not."

He couldn't doubt her tone. The anger that had flared within him ebbed away quickly.

"I can't Abra. I can't forget it."

"Why? I don't understand. Papa certainly has no need of money." She motioned quickly to the room. "And it would appear that you don't, either. Why take the risk, when you could be killed or spend the rest of your life in prison?"

"There are reasons," he told her, his tone firm, almost cold.

She drew back from him. "What reasons?" she demanded.

"Things I can't explain to you now," he replied.

"When?" she pressed. "When will you be able to explain?"

"Not until it's done," he whispered, watching her eyes grow distant as he spoke the words.

She sat back on her knees, her eyes trapped by his, a cold misery and regret beginning to fill her. All she could think was that she had somehow fallen in love with him. She certainly hadn't wanted to, but somehow it had happened. And he was racing toward something, pursuing it with such intentness, that there was nothing left in him for her, nothing left but the need to take what he'd intended, regardless of the cost to them both. She thought then that she could not bear to watch him ruin himself, that it would kill her if she were to see him die.

She bit her lip, aware of the dull lump that had formed in her throat, then turned away from him, getting out of the bed, feeling the room turn suddenly cold around her.

"You'd better take me home now, Dash," she said softly as she reached for her clothing. "Papa will be worried."

# Chapter Six

Inspector Patrick Daniel Francis McErlaine gritted his teeth and counted, very slowly, to twenty. He stared at Chief Inspector Flynt's face, his expression rapt, but he was not paying attention to what it was his superior said, nor would he have been able to repeat a single word of the lecture if he'd been called on to do so.

Instead, his mind wandered to its own thoughts, and he sat wondering who it was that Beaumont had gotten to, the mayor, perhaps, or the chief of police. Because Flynt had made it entirely clear that it was no longer a "family" matter, as he termed it, no longer simply within the confines of his precinct. Word had come down to him from his superiors, and Flynt's superiors, he was quick to observe, were far less charitable in the expression of their displeasure.

Flynt having run out of words temporarily and having grown fitfully quiet, McErlaine took the opportunity to offer a word or two in his own defense.

"I didn't say a word to her," he said stubbornly. "And don't it seem strange to you such a fuss being made? If there's nothing to hide, why all the to do?"

"What you think, Patty Mac, and most certainly, *if* you think," and here the chief inspector's voice grew heavy with sarcasm, "are of little concern to me. I warned you once, you are to stay away from Beaumont and his daughter. This is your last warning. You are to sit at your desk until the end of the month, filling out old reports if you like, keeping your nose buried in the pages of the *Policeman's Gazette* if there's nothing more important going on in that empty skull of yours, but you are to make no further

90

trouble for me, or so help me, McErlaine, I will make so much trouble for you, you'll wish you'd never left your mother's back yard. Do I make myself clear?"

McErlaine heaved himself clumsily out of the leather chair he'd taken before Flynt could motion him elsewhere, sorry now that he'd taken the effort, because the small groan he'd made on rising seemed to amuse his superior, and Flynt's amusement with him only fed his own anger.

"Quite clear, chief inspector," he muttered through clenched teeth, and then he turned away, ambling, with a purposeful swagger that ill fit his huge body, to the door.

Once back in his own sparse little office, however, his response was quickly forgotten. Beaumont had some powerful friends, he mused, that was certain. But what intrigued him the most was the possibility that those powerful friends might have something to hide of their own, or why the bother over Beaumont and his daughter? Something was in the wind, he decided, something big, and Beaumont was in the center of it.

And the very fact that they all seemed to want him to stay away from the daughter was just enough spur to him to determine to stay close to her. Not in the way he had been, of course, not so she'd be aware of him. Because if they were so determined to keep him away from her, then she must be some sort of key to whatever they were about, Beaumont and his powerful friends. And wouldn't that be a nice parting gift for him, he thought, to see them all skewered on their own shafts after the way he'd been put down all those years? McErlaine actually rubbed his hands together, warming them with his anticipation.

Someone in the city government, he thought, someone conspiring with Beaumont on something that would have to be big, very big. That was why word had come down to that fool Flynt, it was a plain as the nose on his face. And if Flynt thought he was going to sit around in his office and forget about it, he had even less brains than McErlaine gave him credit for having, and that was not much.

He'd get that superior bastard Beaumont finally, he decided. He'd have him on a spike. And he didn't care who else came down with him. In fact, the idea gave him the first real feeling of pleasure he'd had in days.

* * *

"He doesn't look like a sheik, does he?"

"And just how is a sheik supposed to look?" Vincent whispered back, humor in his tone.

"Oh, I don't know," Abra responded. "Louisa had me prepared to find someone swathed in flowing white robes and armed with a jeweled scimitar. Instead, he looks like almost anyone else."

She paused and stared at the tall, darkly muscular man at the other side of the room. His eyes, roaming away from Felicia Westmore, who stood talking volubly at his side, caught hers in one of those odd happenstances that sometimes occur, and he smiled, apparently delighted for the respite before Felicia took his arm and prepared to display him to her guests.

"Just like anyone else," Abra repeated as she sipped from her glass of champagne, "but handsomer."

This last seemed to disturb Freddy a bit, but he struggled manfully with the emotion and smiled. "It appears Mother's headed this way, so it seems you won't have to wait long to meet him."

Abra swallowed a smile. Except for a moment when she and Vincent had entered the ballroom to find Freddy waiting at the door, tensed and ready to spring, he'd been as good as his word, making no mention of honeymoon cottages, curbing his natural bent for rapturous speeches, and in general avoiding the subject of marriage altogether, much to her relief.

She looked around the room vacantly, only half aware that it was Dash she looked for, half hoping to find him there, half hoping not. He'd sent her a note the day before, the afternoon after their lovemaking, a letter of apology, she'd thought as she'd torn the envelope open, for the cold way they'd parted. She'd even dared to hope that he'd changed his mind, that he'd decided to give up the madness about the jewel. But the words he'd written had not been any of that, had not suggested in any way that he would give up anything, change any part of his life for her. She'd told herself she was a fool to think he'd relinquish his past, abandon it in exchange for her. It struck her bluntly that that was what she wanted from him, and it hurt her to know he would not give it to her. She had crumpled the letter in her hand in sudden anger, then thrown it into the fire, watching the flames bite at the white of the paper and blacken it, and only when it was gone did she regret its loss, did she remember that he'd written he cared for her and asked for her trust.

She gave up her search and turned back to Freddy, telling herself he loved her, that she should be happy with what he offered her, accept it, and be done with the matter, let her life settle into some kind of certainty. She felt herself turn leaden inside at the thought. Better to sleep alone all her life than to consign herself to a Freddy, she thought.

Just as he had predicted, Felicia Westmore, living up to her role as dowager empress of the city's elite, bore down upon them with her prize specimen of the season.

"May I introduce Vincent Beaumont and his daughter Abra, Your Excellency," she intoned proudly. "And you remember my son, Freddy," she added quickly, almost as an afterthought.

The sheik nodded absently in Freddy's direction, then apparently chose to forget his presence entirely. He offered his hand to Vincent.

"A great pleasure, Your Excellency," Vincent said.

"For me, as well," the sheik replied as they shook hands, his accent decidedly upper class British. Then he turned to Abra and lifted her hand to his lips.""But the greatest pleasure for a man can only be the moment he first gazes upon a beautiful woman," he whispered before he pressed a kiss to her hand.

"I must admit you are a bit of a surprise, Your Excellency," Abra murmured as he released her hand.

He raised a dark, arched brow. "A surprise, Miss Beaumont?"

"The popular press, which has found little else to print of late except news of your visit, leads one to believe your accent and person would appear, well, more," she waved her hand and smiled, "more exotic, Your Excellency."

He smiled. "I fear they would like me more had I not attended Eton and Cambridge. But alas, not all of us can tend sheep and goats in the hills," he told her with a crooked smile.

Abra laughed. "Now that I've met you, I think I could

93

never picture you in the company of either goats or sheep."

He returned her smile, this time with no hint of condescension. "That is well, Miss Beaumont, for the thought of such beasts fills me with shuddering revulsion."

"And I've always thought lambs such adorable little creatures," she returned.

"And so they are," he agreed, "except for the unfortunate habit they have of growing into mutton unless turned into a cutlet early in life." He sighed. "But if I thought it would please you, I might take a few lambs on to nurture."

"A great sacrifice, Your Excellency, to have gamey little beasts befoul your magnificent yacht," Freddy offered.

The sheik turned to him as though just discovering he was there. "You've seen it?"

Here Vincent smiled. "It fills half the harbor, Your Excellency," he said. "It would be hard to miss."

"And besides," Freddy interjected, "as Abra mentioned, the press is full of you, your yacht, and the Tear of Allah."

"Ah, the Tear."

"Yes, Your Excellency, you're terribly brave to bring it with you," Felicia added. "Aren't you afraid it will be stolen?"

"It is a matter of honor, madam," the sheik returned. "The emir is never without the Tear. It is believed by my people that the jewel guards him, and thus his people."

The mention of the Tear, and the suggestion that it might be stolen, sent a shiver through Abra. The fact that it had come up in conversation really should not have surprised her, for, indeed, it had been more than hinted at in the many articles in the papers that chronicled the sheik's comings and goings. Actually, in the last few days, it seemed as though there had been no other news in the whole of the city except for the visits the sheik had made, the tours with the mayor and the governor, his attendance at parties and concerts. But to have the mention of the Tear's theft brought up so casually filled her with fear for her father, and, almost a bewilderment to her, for Dash as well.

She wanted to turn to her father, to see his reaction, to see if the odd animation came to his face at the mention of the Tear, but found she could not for fear of seeing it there. Instead, she kept her eyes on the sheik's face, pretending interest only in his words, wishing that they had not come to the party at all.

"It is reported that the ruby is flawless and as large as an egg. It must be quite beautiful."

Vincent's voice came to her as though from the distance, through a fog, but the sheik's response was quite clear, as he addressed it to her, his eyes once again turned to meet hers.

"Yes," he said slowly. "Quite beautiful. But there are some beauties that pale those of mere stone. I hope you will give me the opportunity to make that comparison face to face, Miss Beaumont, before I leave," he finished, bowing slightly and taking her hand once more, smiling as he brought it to his lips.

Abra felt herself in a dimly remote daze as Felicia Westmore bore him off once more, and for the remainder of the evening she was oddly withdrawn, enough so that even Freddy made mention of her lack of attention. But somehow the evening did end, and she breathed a sigh of relief when she found herself snugly wrapped in her evening cloak and sitting in the darkness of their carriage beside Vincent on their way home.

"You seemed awfully quiet this evening, Abra," her father told her gently. "I hope nothing's wrong."

She brought her eyes slowly to his, trying to measure his mood, what it was she could expect him to tell her.

"I suppose you know that more than I, Papa," she said slowly.

He returned her look for a moment, then turned away, out to the dark shadows they passed in the quiet streets.

"You sometimes bewilder me, Abra," he told her softly.

Abra sighed emptily. Something was going to happen, something that could hurt him and Dash, and it would be of their own making. And there was nothing that she could do to stop them.

"No, Papa. It's you who bewilder me," she replied with a feeling of dull resignation.


When she came down to breakfast the next morning she found her father already at table, and, surprisingly, he was not alone. Dashiel Thorne turned and stared up at her with a wide smile that showed genuine pleasure at the sight of her as she entered the room, momentarily ignoring the remains of ham and scrambled eggs that littered his plate.

"A bit early for social calls, isn't it, Dash?" she asked, pretending indifference, hoping he could not see just how unindifferent she really was.

"Your father was just telling me about the conquest you made last evening, Abra," he told her, his tone cool, as he stood and held her chair for her.

She settled herself and reached for the pot of hot tea that had been left at her place, pouring the liquid with exaggerated care.

"I'd hardly call it a conquest. He only spoke to me for a few moments." She sipped her tea, then looked up at Dash. "It was the sheik you were speaking of, wasn't it?" she asked with a quiet, wide-eyed innocence.

"Oh, I think Dash may be right, Abra," Vincent agreed brightly as Dash resettled himself in the chair beside her and reached for the tray of rolls to offer her. "You do have an odd habit of disturbing young men when you look into their eyes and smile. I've seen it happen quite often of late," and here Vincent stared meaningfully in Dash's direction.

Dash returned the look for a moment, then turned sharply away.

"Where better men have found themselves crushed, I can not think the sheik will prove himself immune," he murmured with an odd vehemence that he did not quite understand himself as he directed his attention back to the contents of his plate.

He thought, miserably, of what Charles Nevin had told him regarding the sheik's reported insatiable taste for women, especially his interest in blondes and redheads. He had no doubt that Abra, beautiful, striking Abra, with her reddish gold hair, had not failed to draw his attention, however short the time he had spent in her company the evening before. She would receive word from him, he knew, and the thought was a bitter one, despite the fact that it was what he told himself he wanted.

Abra offered him a penetrating stare. "And why should you consider the man's interest in me with such relish, Dash?" she asked him softly, the anger she felt well hidden

96

from her tone. She considered him for a moment. "Do you think it will make it easier for you and Papa to steal the Tear?" she finally demanded, her words filled with a fierceness that surprised her. She was conscious of Vincent staring at her, his expression suddenly become less amused by what was happening between his daughter and his guest, but she ignored him, staring instead at Dash, at the probing glance he turned in her direction. "Well, is that it?" she pressed. "Are you somehow using me to get to the jewel?"

Dash felt his teeth grinding against each other, his jaw aching from the pressure with which he worked it. His first thought was to lie to her, to slough it off as a joke. For this was the last thing he wanted, for her to know, for her to see him using her and think he had wanted her for nothing else from the start. He could see it, read the accusation in her eyes, and yet there was no way for him to refute it.

"Yes," he said finally, his tone cold and empty. "It's the easiest way to find out what defenses he has for the protection of the jewel without arousing any undue suspicion." In a way, he was glad when it was said. At least now he did not have to feel the sting of his own conscience when he thought of how callously he was using her.

Abra sat and stared at him. For a moment, the anger was intense, but that slowly ebbed, leaving her feeling numbed and empty. How could she have fallen in love with him, she wondered. How could she have deluded herself into believing he was anything but callous, selfish, and indifferent to everything and everyone but his own wants? He'd made love to her, as he'd quite obviously made love to many women, and now could think of her only as a means to get to the jewel.

"Abra, you make it sound much worse than it actually is," Vincent interposed, but she darted an angry look at him and he sank into silence, aware that what was happening was between the two of them, that it was more than he understood, that somehow their relationship had progressed much further than he had realized. He, too, felt guilt, that he had encouraged Dash to pursue her, that what had been begun in innocence had somehow become intense and hurtful.

Abra lifted her tea cup, but saw her hand shake and quickly returned it to the saucer. She glued her eyes to it, not wanting to let them wander to Dash's, not wanting to see something in his look that she knew now could not be there.

"I'll help you," she said finally, very quietly. "I'll do whatever it is you want, but on one condition, that once you have what you came for, you leave and we never see you again." She swallowed hard, and finally could not keep herself from looking up to the deep blue ice of his eyes.

"Abra," he said softly, reaching his hand to hers, but she shook her head violently and pulled her hand away.

"Say it," she demanded, her tone turned brittle and louder.

He stared at her silently for a second, then shrugged.

"As you like," he said softly, his tone firm and indifferent. "Once I have what I want, I'll leave."

Abra turned away from him, to the food on the table, and felt her stomach heave. She couldn't sit there any longer, she realized, couldn't stay in the same room with him. She stood, her body feeling strangely stiff and foreign to her, as though she'd lost control of it, as though she were simply visiting it while someone else gave her leave.

"I'll accept your word," she told him as she dropped her napkin to the table. "I assume there really is some honor amongst thieves."

With that she stalked to the door, not daring to turn and face him again, hating the bite of tears she felt rising within her throat, and knowing there was nothing she could do to force them away.

"One thing more," she managed to say without bothering to turn to face him as she reached the door. She felt herself shaking, but knew she would say these words or they would choke her. "My father must not in any way be connected with this madness. Whatever happens, no stain must come to him." She turned slowly then, finally finding the strength in her anger, her eyes attesting to the immediacy of what it was she felt. "If he is, I promise you, I won't rest until I see you dead."

Dash glanced at her, at the sudden sharp hatred he saw in her eyes as she stared at him. He realized now how completely she thought he had betrayed her. He felt a stabbing, near physical pain as he answered her.

"I give you my word, Abra. There will be nothing to tie

Vincent to the theft."

Then he watched as she turned away from him, apparently satisfied, and disappeared through the door, closing it sharply in her wake. The sound echoed through the still dining room. Dash found himself staring numbly at the blank space of dark mahogany, wondering how it had happened.

"When it's done," Vincent told him calmly, "she'll forget all of this nonsense, Dash."

Dash looked up at the older man and nodded, apparently ready to dismiss the moment of anger, the words. But he knew that it would not be so simple as that, that what they'd shared when she'd come to his bed had complicated everything until none of it would ever be simple again.

"When it's done," he repeated in an empty, dark tone, and he wondered if anything would ever be right between them again.


Abra wondered what sense of satisfaction her father had when he showed her the invitation, the short note begging him and his daughter to do the honor to Sheik Shahab Sharify of granting him their company for luncheon aboard his yacht the following afternoon. She scanned it quickly, then dropped it to his desk.

"This is what you wanted?" she asked him coldly, letting him feel the bite of her anger and not caring, indifferent to the discomfort she saw it bring to his eyes, yet hating herself for her indifference.

Vincent decided to let her have her anger, that there was no use to try to talk her out of it, at least not just yet.

"Yes," he told her evenly. "That's what we wanted. An invitation, lunch, conversation. And then it's all over as far as we're concerned."

Abra dropped herself into the chair beside his desk, her concentration on him intent.

"Is it, Papa? Can it really be so simple as that?"

He looked up at her, suddenly finding himself completely bewildered by her, realizing that she was no longer a child he could know completely, that she'd turned into a woman, something apart from him, and in many ways secret and mysterious.

"Yes, Abra, as simple as that. We hopefully convince him to show us the Tear, and when he does, I simply observe the type of vault, whatever safeguards are employed. And that's all."

She returned his look thoughtfully. "And then, forearmed with this knowledge, Dash goes in and steals the thing." She snapped her fingers. "Abracadabra. Just like that. And no one the wiser."

"Abra, it's ten times easier and much less risky to rob a safe you're familiar with, and better yet if you know if there are guards and what their routines might be."

"Oh, I don't doubt you, Papa. After all, you were a master at that sort of thing, robbing vaults, relieving the unworthy rich of their excess jewels."

Vincent felt himself coloring, hearing the disapproval in her voice. "That was a long time ago, Abra. And I hardly think it necessary to defend myself to you."

"No, Papa. Certainly you don't. But you did tell me about it, over the years, how you could open any vault invented, how you could walk in, take what you wanted and leave, and no one the wiser."

Vincent considered her words. She was telling him that she had understood the reasons he had told her those stories, the need to appear larger and more important to her than he felt himself to be, the need for her to think of him as smarter and craftier and wilier than those men who had stolen their wealth from the labor of the men they employed in their mills and mines. At least he'd been an honest thief, he'd told himself, not pretending morality while he stole men's youths and ambitions and buried them in the poverty of unfair wages and cavalier disregard for health and safety.

"You've lived all your life off what I stole, Abra. Just as Freddy lived all his life off the thievery his father did, sending men into coal mines that collapsed and killed them, or choked them with fumes or gassed them if they couldn't get out in time from an unexpectedly exposed pocket. Just as your friend Louisa lives on the money old man Richards stole, paying men a pittance to work themselves to death laying railroad track so that he could make a fortune from Freddy's father, using his railroads to haul coal. I'm no better, but certainly no worse, than the rest of them."

Abra felt cowed by his vehemence. She had not really meant to attack him, she realized. It was that she was so filled with anger, with Dash, with herself, that she didn't really know which way to turn.

"I'm sorry, Papa," she whispered, turning away, wishing she'd said nothing to him. "I just wish none of this had happened." She sat thinking quietly, then added, "That policeman, McErlaine, he frightened me."

"You've not seen him again, have you, Abra?" he asked, his tone intent.

She shook her head. "No, not the last few days."

She could not help but wonder what it was that Dash had done, how he'd managed to have McErlaine stop following her, appearing that way and frightening her. Still, the thought of him sent shivers down her spine. The man was after something, and although she hadn't seen him, she was not at all convinced that he had given up.

"Well, Papa. I suppose you'll want to send Dash word that he was right," she said, feeling empty as she mouthed the words and rose, wandering idly to the door. "It seems he does know what he's about, after all."


They were met at the wharf by a huge tender, manned by four burly seamen clothed entirely in pristine white that contrasted sharply with their swarthy complexions and the bright red cummerbunds they wore around their waists. As though added for effect, a large-hilted dagger was tucked into the folds of red at each man's side.

Abra shivered when she saw them, and she felt an icy finger of cold run through her, despite the unseasonable warmth of the brightly sunny afternoon, as she allowed one of them to take her hand and help her on board.

Once she and Vincent were settled in the small cabin, away from their hearing, she felt some of the unease pass.

"Well, his minions certainly look the part, even if he doesn't," she remarked offhandedly, thinking how entirely normal the sheik had seemed the evening of the reception, and how sinisterly exotic these men who had been sent to fetch them seemed in contrast.

"Do you think it might seem a game to him, Abra? After

all, you told him you expected something different when you met him. Perhaps he's decided to give it to you."

She laughed. "Do you really think he'll appear like some prince out of Scheherazade?" she demanded, not really believing it, but intrigued by the possibility. Somehow, she thought, that would suit him better than black tie and tails. But she dismissed the thought. After all, it was, if at all, how he might appear in the desert. The middle of New York harbor was something else again.

But Sharify, it seemed, was determined to humor her imagination, for when the tender drew up to the yacht, there he stood on the deck, staring down at her with those intent, dark eyes as she was handed up to meet him. Like his men, he, too, was dressed in pristine white, only the splash of color at his waist was purple silk, and over it all he wore a long loose white coat. There was a large brilliant cut amethyst hung from a heavy rope of gold around his neck, another flashed from a thick ring on his finger. Abra realized that this was precisely how she had imagined he would look. In fact, beside all his glowing white, she felt herself a bit dowdy, demurely dressed in a pale blue-grey silk with lace at the high, stiff neck and cuffs, her mother's fine old cameo pinned neatly at her throat.

He took her hand in his immediately, his full-lipped smile revealing white, even teeth.

"Your presence honors and delights me, Miss Beaumont," he told her very solemnly before he raised her hand to his lips.

"On the contrary, Your Excellency, your invitation came as an unexpected pleasure."

He waved his hand. "Enough of this Your Excellency. Friends call each other by name," he told her with a smile. "And I insist that we be friends." He extended his smile to include Vincent. "You must both call me Shahab," he directed. "And extend to me the honor of calling you both by your given names, too, I hope." He seemed full of expansiveness as he put one hand to Vincent's shoulder, and with the other took Abra's arm. "May I welcome you both to a small bit of my country?" He turned to Abra, his eyes full of laughter. "I hope it pleases you and meets your expectations."

"Quite exotic, Shahab," she laughed in response as he

led them into the large salon of the yacht, for, like the sheik and his men, it was draped in all the trappings she had imagined, bright silk-covered pillows, thick, intricately woven carpets layered haphazardly on the floor. The windows gave a view of the harbor and lower Manhattan, shiny and brightly sharp in the crisp afternoon sunshine, seeming entirely out of place and strange when viewed from the confines of the cabin.

"I thought, as the day is mild and fair, a short cruise while we dine might amuse you, Abra," he suggested.

She nodded, delighted at the prospect. "That sounds lovely," she replied, shedding her coat and hat and leaving them to the care of yet another white-attired servant, then sinking onto the pillowed couch to which the sheik led her.

"Excellent," he replied as he waited until Vincent sat beside her, then lowered himself to a chair facing them. "Up the Hudson it will be, and then a leisurely float back down. I find your scenery incredible, nature so gloriously excessive, and you Americans so intently industrious with all your steeples and spires, as though you were reaching up to accost some god and show him your powers."

Abra stared at him, at the languid way he sat, mentally likening him to a powerful coiled snake, apparently at rest, but possessing strong, hidden reserves that waited for provocation to be unleashed. The thought surprised her, for he'd certainly shown her no indication that there was anything remotely dangerous about him, and yet she could not shake the feeling, and the image stayed with her, tantalizing her somewhat.

The servant who had taken her coat appeared once more, this time bearing a silver tray with three tall glasses, the golden bubbles of the champagne rising merrily. Abra took a glass, then waited as Vincent and the sheik were also served.

Sharify raised his glass in toast. "To my most welcome guests," he said. "And to the most beautiful," he added, with a nod in Abra's direction, before he drank.

"If you will forgive me, Shahab," Vincent ventured. "I'd thought alcohol was forbidden you."

The sheik smiled. "It is. It seems that despite the clothing, I am in many fundamental ways as western as you, Vincent." He smiled wryly. "Too many years in English

103

schools. One can not avoid the stuff, much to my shame. I'm afraid I developed rather a taste for it."

The yacht lurched slightly as the anchor was drawn up in preparation for the cruise upriver. He raised an arch brow. "I've come to the point where I take what I wish of my father's culture, and leave those portions of it that do not please me. For instance, the matter of wives. My father's culture allows me as many as I like, and so I oblige," he smiled benignly. "I now have fourteen."

"Fourteen," Abra exclaimed. "But how do you remember all their birthdays?" She sipped her champagne primly and regarded him with very wide-eyed attention.

He leaned forward. "You surprise me, my dear Abra. Most American ladies act quite shocked when they learn of my harem."

"If your situation pleases your wives, Shahab," she replied, "what right have I to be shocked or to disapprove?"

He laughed then, and leaned back into the pillows behind him.

"But how do you remember their birthdays?" Abra pressed, this time with a smile.

He laughed again. "Faultless and painstaking accounting. Actually, it's the children that are the most worrisome. Twenty-two, no twenty-three at last count." Then, with some pride, he added, "Fourteen sons."

"And your sons, will they be educated in the West, as you were?" she asked.

He turned thoughtful. "That is a difficult matter to decide. You see, so much of my people's lives is ruled by ancient customs, ancient superstition. The matter of the Tear, for example. It is believed that when Allah died he cried tears of blood for the poor mortals who remained to mourn him, and one of those tears turned into the ruby. My people believe the gem is holy, that without its protection an emir cannot rule. In fact, each spring there is a procession through the countryside, and the emir must show the stone to the people. Each flock his sight touches while he touches the stone thereby becomes fertile. It's all nonsense, of course, absolute superstition, but the people believe, and therefore the superstition carries the strength of being real for them. My sons must understand this, understand the ancient powers that govern their people."

104

"But they must also understand the world they live in, the modern world, as you do."

"Precisely. And therein lies the quandary," he told her with a smile and a shrug. "That world is much harder to understand, in many respects."

Abra looked thoughtful as she returned his gaze. "I see," she mused aloud. "A difficult choice." She cocked her head. "But is the jewel so important as that?" she asked, her expression naive, apparently artless. "Can so simple a thing as a bit of stone really have so much significance?"

"If enough men believe something, my dear Abra, then the truth has little consequence, only what they believe to be true. And something as rare as the Tear inspires superstition among the ignorant, those who thirst for something in which to believe." He leaned forward to her and offered her his hand. "Come. I'll show it to you, and you will begin to understand, I think."

With that he stood with an easy, fluid motion. Abra and Vincent followed. He guided them through the long salon and down a narrow flight of stairs. A long corridor greeted them, pristine white, except for the dark wood of the floor and the polished mahogany of the doors.

Beside the second of those doors along the corridor stood two of the white-clad seamen, their expressions fixed, the knives at their waists looking somehow more prominent than those worn by the servants on the deck above.

Abra could sense a second of discomposure in her father as Vincent took note of these two men. If the servant above had seemed burlier, physically more impressive than one would expect from a steward, he was, like the men who had brought them from the wharf in the tender, completely obsequious in his attentions. These two men who guarded the door to which Sharify led them gave off an aura of trained combatants. They held themselves with the control of warriors. Their presence was totally unexpected, and more than a little frightening to Abra.

But as their emir approached, the two stepped aside with a deferential bow, and the sheik opened the door, ushering both Abra and Vincent inside.

"You see now why I have no fear of theft." Sharify smiled at Vincent. "There are more than thirty men aboard this yacht, all armed and skilled in the use of the weapons they carry. This ship is a little piece of my country, and here I rule as I do in my own land." He smiled wryly. "I have no fear of loss. No thief would live to come even so far as this."

He guided them through a huge and opulently furnished stateroom, a stark contrast to the white corridor outside the door, for here everything was boldly-colored, the heavy, ornately woven rugs on the floor, the pillow strewn divans, and, most conspicuously, a huge, dark maroon satin-covered bed.

The sight of the bed could not help but remind Abra of all those boastfully mentioned wives and the score of children, and that thought all too predictably brought the hint of a blush to her cheeks.

The sheik smiled when he saw it. "I fear I have erred, Abra, in bringing you to my bedroom," he told her, but there was no visible contrition in either his tone or his expression.

"Not at all," she replied, a bit too quickly. "It simply surprises me that you keep the stone so close to you. After all, you just told us that you do not believe the superstitions that surround it."

He grinned then knowingly. "One never ignores a well-founded superstition, Abra," he told her softly as he strode to the far wall beside the bed and pushed aside a heavy wall hanging.

There, set into the wall, was a very western-appearing vault. Abra turned to her father, not surprised to see him watching intently as the sheik opened the safe and withdrew a small leather pouch. He looked at Abra as his fingers loosened the drawstrings, reached into the bag, and drew out what appeared to be a large, blood-red egg.

Abra could not take her eyes from it. It seemed to glow with its own light, as though a small fire burned within the cold confines of its center, a tiny flame imprisoned in stone. And when he put it into her hand, she found it seemed to carry its own warmth, its inner fire, which, while not strong enough to escape the confines of its cell, was still strong enough to generate this mysterious heat. She wrapped her fingers around its sides, marveling at the smooth warmth of the stone, more intrigued by its strange glow than by its phenomenal size.

"It's incredible," she breathed softly, quite at a loss for other words as she passed the stone to Vincent, only remotely aware of the intensity of his interest as he took it onto his palm.

"It is truly an unbelievable ruby, Shahab," Vincent said softly, his tone seemingly muted in respect for the magic he held in his hand.

The sheik smiled at them both. "You see now, Abra," he said, his tone, too, softened in the presence of the jewel, "why it elicits such strong beliefs."

She could only nod her agreement, her eyes still tied to the hypnotizing stone as Vincent held it up to the light, then slowly, with only the slightest visible reluctance, returned it to the sheik's waiting hand.

Once he held it, Shahab, too, held the ruby up to the light. "It's beautiful," he said, his tone almost reluctant, his eyes on hers, "but I still believe yours is a finer beauty, my lovely Abra."

Abra smiled, and once again felt the warmth of a blush flooding to her cheeks.

"But a woman's beauty is fleeting, Shahab, while the ruby's is forever," she protested.

The sheik quickly put the stone into its leather pouch. "It is because it is fleeting that a woman's beauty is so wonderful, Abra," he told her, putting a finger to her cheek. His expression grew suddenly hungry and intent. "It is the knowledge that soon it will be dust that makes it so incredible. To touch the immutable is one thing, but to touch what exists only a moment in time, that is something different and far rarer."

Vincent cleared his throat awkwardly, wondering what the sheik would dare if he were alone with Abra, as his words were so provocative in her father's presence. But his host seemed not to notice his discomfort, turning away to return the stone to its place in the vault.

"Shahab is right, Abra," Vincent said, his discomfort hidden by the easy flow of his words, "a beautiful woman stirs something in a man that nothing else can reach." Then he put his hand to her arm, not quite sure why he felt she needed his protection, but suddenly wishing Abra had not been a part of his and Dash's plan.

But when Sharify turned to face them, the vault duly locked and hidden by its wall hanging, his face showed nothing more sinister than simply good humor.

"But now to lunch, my friends. Not even beauty can live long without sustenance."

As they climbed back up to the parlor, to a table lavishly set beside a large window offering spectacular views of the cliffs along the Hudson, Abra could only think that it was done, that now Dash had what he wanted, that she and her father had done what they had promised him they would do. Despite the trepidations Vincent felt when he watched the sheik look at her, Abra was only distantly aware of the dark-eyed glances, the intent looks. Instead, she ate her lunch with as much enthusiasm as she could muster, forcing herself to keep her attention on the conversation, to answer appropriately when the necessity arose, to behave as she ought.

And then the meal was somehow, mercifully, over, and her suggestion of a walk around the deck gallantly accepted. For a while she stood with the two men as they lit their cigars and talked of politics and finance. But their conversation held little interest for her, and she wandered along the side of the huge yacht, staring up at the magnificent peaks of Bear Mountain, bright in the warm autumn sunshine.

She was really enjoying herself, she realized abruptly. As long as she could lose herself, her thoughts, in contemplation of the beauty around her, she was satisfied and content within herself. As long, she amended, when a blue-eyed image crept into her mind, as she did not think of Dashiel Thorne.

She had little chance to consider the unpleasant prospect of his complete and imminent departure from her life, however, for she soon found a tall figure standing at the rail close beside her. She looked up at him and smiled.

"This is a lovely way to spend the afternoon, Shahab," she told him pleasantly. "Thank you."

She raised her hand to a stray lock the breeze had managed to free from the confines of its pin, intending to push it away from her cheek. But his hand caught hers.

"Let it stay, Abra. It gives me some small hints of the beauties you keep hidden from the casual observer."

108

Then he released her hand and brought his fingers to the shining lock and rubbed it softly between them, savoring the satiny feel of it. His voice was low when he spoke again, and with a surprised feeling of shock, Abra stood still beside him, trying to make sense of his words.

"When a man in my country finds a woman who sets his blood on fire," Shahab began, "he simply goes to her father and arrangements are made. Unfortunately, it is not so simple here."

"And the woman," she asked softly, "what if she does not feel the same way he does?"

He shrugged. "A good daughter grows quickly to love the husband her father chooses for her."

She backed away a step, suddenly unsure of herself, wondering fleetingly where Vincent had gone.

"Chooses for her?" she asked, her tone rigid. "Or sells her to? I've heard women in your country are sold."

His eyes narrowed as he stared at her. "Yes, a bride portion is paid. But that is a business arrangement, a sum to compensate a father for the loss of his daughter. The matter between man and wife is different."

His calm tone did nothing to mollify her, however. "And if she does not come to love this man despite her father's injunction?" she demanded. "What if she cannot be quite so obedient a daughter as that?"

He smiled wryly. "Then I suppose she makes his life a misery. A woman has a great deal of power over a man who loves her."

His tone was so doleful, so totally and unexpectedly steeped in melancholy at the prospect, that Abra found she could not help but laugh.

"I am glad, then, that I was born here," she confided. "I do not think I could ever be quite so fine a daughter as to love a man simply because my father bade it, nor would I wish to destroy a man's life so callously as you describe."

"I dare say you have already unknowingly destroyed more hearts than you realize, Abra. Some women were simply born to drive men to madness. If Allah did not wish it to be so, he would not fashion them with such care, would not give them charms that can trap a man's soul."

Abra felt the warmth creeping to her cheeks as she looked up at him. He was gazing at her intently now, and

109

she found she could not mistake what it was she saw in his eyes. She tried to turn away from him, tried not to look into the searing, knowing gaze.

"I don't think you should be saying these things to me, Shahab," she told him softly.

"Why not, Abra?" he demanded. He moved closer to her, taking her hand in his, holding her eyes with his. "My intentions are honorable. I can offer you a life of ease, surrounded by beauty, a life of absolute pleasure."

Abra felt numb. Her first thought was that it was a joke, that he was trying to shock her, perhaps, or unsettle her. After all, she hardly knew this man, and it would be madness to think he could actually mean any of what he'd said. But when she stared into the molten coals of his eyes, she somehow knew he was completely serious.

"I, I hardly know what to say," she stammered.

"Say you will come back with me," he told her with a smile.

She came to herself, suddenly aware that he had already decided he'd won. She could see it in his smile. More than that came the realization that such a commitment meant little to him. He'd seen her and determined he would have her, just as he would any other object that caught his fancy. Fourteen wives or fifteen, or even twenty, what difference would it make to him?

She smiled at him playfully. "But I could never share a man with other women," she told him. "Certainly not fourteen other women."

He put his hand to her cheek. "I would make you happy, Abra," he told her, dismissing her objection, his voice very low, very convincing.

And for a moment she felt almost hypnotized by his dark eyes, by the handsome, assured smile. She felt as though she were sinking into thick, heavy mud, unable to work herself free.

"My father," she objected weakly. "I'm all he has. I could not think to go so far away."

This objection, too, seemed unimportant to him. "My palace is large, Abra. Certainly large enough to find place for him."

And with that, he slowly began to lower his face to hers. Still she felt frozen, unable to move. All she could see

110

were his eyes, dark and mesmerizing. He was trying to seduce her, and somehow she felt powerless to keep it from happening. But when he was close, close enough for her to feel the warmth of his breath on her cheek, his lips only a few inches from hers, Dash's face seemed to float before her. She turned away abruptly.

"You quite take my breath away, Shahab," she told him, offering him just the hint of a smile. "And to think, the evening we met, I thought you not unlike all the other men I've always known." She moved back, away from him, and felt far more comfortable with the distance.

A hint of his anger passed across his features, but he hid it quickly, then smiled at her words.

"I think you will find I am not at all like your American men, Abra," he said softly, without a trace of humor. "I am not only wealthy and powerful, I also have an uncanny ability to get whatever I want."

His words, his direct stare, sent a shiver of fear through Abra. And as muddled as her thoughts had been a moment before, they became abruptly crystal clear. This man would not be a pleasant enemy, she thought. Suddenly she could think only of her father and Dash. She turned away from Sharify, forcing her eyes back to the swelling cliffs that edged the river.

"Papa must be wondering where I've gotten to," she said softly, and began to walk back to the stern, to the door to the salon.

He moved quickly to her side, offering her his arm. But as she took it, his voice floated down to her, and his words, she would find, would haunt her for days to come.

"I always get what I want, Abra, and what I have, I hold on to."

111

## Chapter Seven

"The vault is nothing, easy enough for a child to take, a McCulleagh, simple tumbler. Abra could open it. I'll have the same model delivered here tomorrow for you to practice with. It won't require a week to teach you enough so that you can open it in the dark." Vincent sat quiet and thoughtful for a moment before he continued. "The yacht itself, however, is a different matter. It's an armed camp, more than thirty men, and those I saw appeared all too competent."

Vincent's words seemed to fill the silent room. Abra sat quite still, not even bothering to sip the sherry from the glass she held, simply watching the faces of the two men as they spoke. They both seemed so matter-of-fact, so entirely businesslike. Suddenly the previous afternoon seemed very distant and unreal. Images of the giant ruby, of the white-clad men with knives at their waists, and most of all, of the sheik, all seemed incredibly improbable, as though it had been some sort of a dream.

"Then the problem, once I've mastered the safe, is to get into the stateroom unseen," Dash was saying, his tone pensive as he looked down at the large blueprint of the yacht spread out on Vincent's desk. The sheik's stateroom had been circled in red, the position of the vault precisely noted.

Abra stared at them, unbelieving.

"What is the matter with the two of you? Don't you understand? If you try to get into that stateroom, if you even try to get onto the yacht uninvited, they'll kill you. Give it up now, before any harm's been done."

She was surprised to hear her own voice. After all, she'd sworn to herself that she wouldn't interfere, as long as

112

Vincent was out of it, she wouldn't let herself care. But she did, violently, and the realization was not one she accepted happily. He'd be out of her life soon enough, one way or another, and if she had an ounce of sense, she'd forget about Dashiel Thorne now.

Dash turned to her, looking at her as though he'd only just noticed her there. "Would that bother you, Abra?" he asked her slowly. "If I were killed?"

She stared at him in silence and thought of the last time he had asked her almost that same question, alone, in his hotel suite, and of where her answer, her admission that she did care, had finally led them. He'd used her then, she told herself, just as he had used her to get the information he wanted about the yacht and the safe. And she had allowed herself to be used, she reminded herself, even helped him in the matter. She stood with an abrupt movement.

"No," she said, turning away from him, to the garden window. "Why should I care what happens to you?"

"Then why the fuss? This is as far as Vincent is involved. He teaches me how to open the same kind of safe, helps me learn the layout of the yacht, and then I leave your lives, just as you wanted. Why should you care what happens to me after it's done?"

Abra thought of the feel of his kisses, the way she had felt when she'd lain in his arms. And now, his coldness, the way he was treating her with apparent indifference, made it all too clear to her that none of it had meant anything to him at all.

"Because," she shouted back at him, aware of the anger rising inside her, "because you'll ruin it for me, that's why. He's asked me to go back with him, and if he catches you stealing his jewel, if he ties you to me and my father, it will be over." She glared at him with a shaking anger, feeling at that moment as though she hated him, sure that she hated him.

"Abra!"

Vincent was standing, crossing the room to her. But she hardly saw him, for her eyes were on Dash, on the look of bewilderment and pain that crossed his face as her words slowly sank into him. For a second it occurred to her that she'd hurt him, that he was not as indifferent as he'd seemed. Then the look was gone and she could think only that she'd been mistaken, for it was replaced by one of complete impassivity.

"I don't believe you," he said softly. "You've met the man only twice."

"He seems to be a man of quick decisions," she spat back at him. Then she pushed her hand into the pocket of her skirt and removed a slightly rumpled envelope and a small black velvet box. These she held out to him, as though daring him to come and take them from her.

"Abra, what is this?"

She'd almost forgotten her father was in the room with them, but now his words reminded her. She didn't turn away from Dash, however, just moved her arm, allowing the envelope and the box to fall into Vincent's hands.

"It came this morning," she said absently.

Vincent stared at his daughter for an instant and then at Dash as they gazed at each other, he with emotionless fixidity, she with obvious wrath. He found himself wondering why his cool, level-headed daughter seemed so easily churned to anger when in Dash's presence, but his curiosity about that, he realized, would have to wait until other matters were explained. He opened the letter first and read aloud:

My dearest Abra,
   You mentioned the other evening that you found these creatures appealing, so I send you a small member of my flock as a token of my deepest regard. Perhaps it will make you think of me, and consider sympathetically joining it?

                                        Shahab

Vincent opened the box, then, revealing a brooch fashioned into the shape of a lamb, gold heavily encrusted over the body with diamonds, and sporting two small sapphires for eyes and a ruby for a tiny mouth.

"When did you receive this?" he demanded anxiously as he handed both note and jewel box to Dash.

"I told you, this morning," Abra replied as she watched Dash first scan the note, then glance quickly at the brooch.

He glanced up at her when he'd completed his cursory

inspection.

"Lambs have brown eyes, not blue," he said absently, then he brought his eyes to meet hers. "You don't mean to tell me you actually would consider becoming part of this man's harem, do you?"

He asked the question almost abstractly, as though the whole matter were nothing more than a jest and hardly worth his contemplation. Abra wanted to scream at him, to do something, anything, that would shake him from his complacency.

"Would that bother you, Dash?" she asked, mimicking his tone when he'd asked her the same question. But then the veneer of indifference broke and her eyes flashed at him in anger. "Besides, what difference would it make to you? Why should it matter to you if I choose to become a part of his harem, or if I decide to marry Freddy Westmore? A philanderer like you, what do you care about any woman's life, let alone one who has made it abundantly clear to you that she considers you despicable and worthless?"

Then she turned on her heel and stalked from the room.

Abra was in the front hall when the bell rang, and so it was she who opened the door, not Hemmings as Dash had expected. He stood for a moment on the front steps and stared at her, thinking only that she seemed to grow prettier each time he saw her and unable to explain to himself just why that was so.

"Papa's at his club. If you want him, you'll have to look for him there."

Her voice sounded cold to him, ice that moderated the warmth that had begun to fill him at the sight of her. She moved back, turning away from him and starting to close the door.

"Aren't you at least going to ask me in?" he demanded, putting his hand to the knob and pushing, ignoring her startled reluctance.

"I told you, Papa's not here," she said tartly, but she backed away into the hall and allowed him to enter.

Hemmings, answering the summons of the bell, appeared behind her.

"Afternoon, Hemmings," Dash offered, reasonably jo-

115

vially.

"Mr. Thorne," Hemmings responded, then turned to Abra. "Will there be anything, miss?"

"Mr. Thorne won't be staying," she told him without turning to him.

Dash stood and watched silently until the butler had disappeared and he was once more alone with her.

"I didn't come to see Vincent, Abra," he told her softly. He moved close to her, surprised that she did not back away from him, but not really pleased, for he felt no softening in her, not even as he put his hand to her waist and pulled her close to him. "I came to talk to you."

She looked up at him, unmoved. "Is that what you want?" she demanded. "Talk?"

He felt the warmth of her body, saw the challenge in her eyes.

"No," he replied as he wrapped his other arm around her and pressed his lips to hers.

Abra felt a small thrill of triumph, the knowledge that, despite everything, he was not so completely indifferent to her as he had pretended. The sheik's words drifted through her mind, that a woman holds a great deal of power over a man who loves her. Then words, thoughts, everything disappeared as the heat of his kiss kindled a fire within her.

For a moment she let herself melt against him, let the resistance seep away and felt nothing but the yearning. She brought her hand to his cheek and gazed up into his eyes.

"Then you'll end this madness, Dash?" she asked softly, elated, feeling her heart beating in anticipation.

He'd known it was too easy, that a kiss would not end the battle that had begun between them.

"I can't, Abra. As much as I want to, I can't."

For a moment she didn't move, as though it took time for the words to make their way, to have some meaning for her. Then she drew back from him, putting her hands to his chest and pushing with angry, sharp thrusts.

"Let go of me," she told him, and reluctantly, he let his hands fall. "You said you came to talk. Say what you came to say and be done with it."

Her expression had grown suddenly hard, and he felt his own responding in kind.

"Very well, Abra. Vincent told me you've seen the Sheik twice in the last three days since I've seen you."

116

She shrugged her shoulders absently. "And what if I have? What business is that of yours?"

"The man is dangerous, Abra. Stay away from him."

She began to turn away, dismissing him, but he grabbed her arm and swung her to face him.

"I mean it. You have no idea of what you're doing."

She shrugged her arm angrily from his grasp. "I have a very good idea of what I'm doing," she retorted. "I'm enjoying the company of a very handsome, attractive, charming man. One who seems to find my company pleasant, one who goes to a great deal of effort to please me."

She stopped there, only thinking the words "unlike you," but Dash could almost hear them in the challenging glare she leveled at him.

"You're behaving like a fool," he told her, his voice coldly venomous. "He's not a man you can play with, · Abra. When he gets tired of the game, he'll simply take what he wants."

"The way you did?" she snarled back at him, hating him for reminding her.

"No, damn it, not the way I did."

Then his anger seemed finally to boil over, and when he grabbed her, his grasp was like a metal vise. She stood no chance of simply shrugging away from him this time. She seemed to be struggling with him, he realized, but he ignored it, telling himself he would teach her a lesson, show her just how vulnerable she was, but realizing that more than anything else he wanted to feel her body against his, to hold her close to him in his arms. He pressed his lips to hers, demanding, hard and seeking, making no game of what he was doing, letting his touch tell her what he intended, what he could do if he so chose.

She pushed against him, straining, but the harder she struggled, the tighter he held her, until, finally, the struggling ceased and she stood, meekly pliant in his arms. He kissed her again, his tongue darting, insistent, seeking what he remembered to be so sweet of her, hungry for the taste. Then he put his hands to her hair, pulling her head back, and pressed his lips to her neck, feeling the heat of her skin rise, the throb of her pulse grow sharper.

"Please stop, Dash," she begged softly. "Please. Please stop."

He could hear the catch of tears in her voice, and he

hated himself for what he'd done to her. He lifted his head and pulled her close, letting her cheek rest against his chest, his fingers still entwined in her hair. His heart pounded wildly, and he breathed deeply for a moment to silence it.

"He wouldn't be stopped with a few words, Abra. Not words or tears. He'd take what he wanted without a thought."

She felt rather than heard his words; rumbling softly upward from his chest, they filled her. She knew they were true.

"Give it up," she begged him softly. "Just give it up."

"I can't, Abra. I wish I could, but I can't."

There was a hint of pain in his words. She could hear it even if she did not understand its cause. But still she could not let it die.

"Why?" she cried.

He dropped his hands from her, letting her stand away, staring up at him.

"Can't you simply trust me?" he asked her softly, wondering why it couldn't be so, why she asked more of him than he could give her then.

She heard the hurt in his tone, the unasked questions, but she couldn't help herself. She backed away from him slowly, her eyes bright with tears, the golden flecks sparked with regret.

"I can't," she whispered softly.

Then she stood silent a moment, staring hopelessly at him before she turned and ran up the stairs, leaving him alone to stare numbly after her. He breathed deeply twice, then turned to the door and let himself out.


The letters beside the door read Inspector First Class Patrick Daniel Francis McErlaine. The person described by that rather impressively long stretch of gold letters stood and stared at them for an extended moment before putting his hand to the knob and letting himself into his office.

He walked heavily, his footfalls sounding hollowly against the bare wooden floor as he crossed to his desk. He stood for some moments staring down at the litter of papers that covered it, somehow sure that the answer was there for him to see, if only he could recognize it.

Then he lowered himself into his chair, closing his eyes as he sat, putting his hands to his temples and rubbing them, hoping for a ray of inspiration. That ritual completed, he cleared his mind and reached for the papers, determined to go over the whole series again.

He took out a fresh sheet of paper from the desk drawer and began to write in a cramped, small-lettered script that seemed entirely out of character with his large, clumsy-looking fingers, noting dates, times, events, all meticulously, in neat, even rows. That task finished, he sat and stared at his chart, aware now of something he had missed before.

He'd followed Beaumont's daughter for nearly a week and a half now, carefully assuring himself that he was not seen by her, trailing after her when she went shopping or met with other women of her own age in stuffy little tea rooms, chafing for something more precipitous to happen than the normal dull activities of a rich young woman's life. When she'd gone to the Lower East Side he'd been sure he was onto something, for it seemed to him an unlikely destination for one of her social position. But that time, too, he'd been disappointed to find her entering the settlement house. After she'd left, he'd made inquiries and found she taught a class in English to immigrant women there. It had rankled that he'd gone to the trouble for nothing, even more when he contemplated the dull, flat faces of the women she taught, Poles and Russkies and Guineas, all of whom he hated instinctively. There'd been no settlement house for him forty years before when he'd arrived in New York, no one with any offer of help, and he'd done well enough by himself. Her act of charity took on an ominous aspect for him, as he decided the rich had no real interest in the poor, that there must be something to be had from the effort.

As he sat at his desk remembering the afternoon, he grew once more angry, although he wasn't quite sure where he ought to direct that anger. He lifted his pen and crossed out the entries from the list that seemed frivolous to him, the shopping, the visits to galleries and museums, the tea parties. He hesitated for a moment, then crossed out the entries that related to the settlement house as well, and then he considered what was left.

What he saw stunned him. First, there was the trip to the wharf where she and her father were met by a tender, a tender that took them out to the large yacht anchored in the harbor, the yacht that belonged to that Arab beggar he'd read about in all the papers lately. And since then, she'd been in the foreigner's company no less than four times. Four times in less than two weeks, he mused. That was a good deal, he decided, for a simple expression of friendship to a visiting foreigner. Something stronger than courtesy motivated her, he decided, and a glimmer of what that might be was starting to nudge at the edge of his mind.

Even as he discounted the fact that the filthy Arab was reported to be immensely wealthy, there was no doubt in McErlaine's mind that no decent white, Christian woman would lower herself to consorting with such a heathen.

He scanned the list. There were only two other men who'd enjoyed her company on more than one occasion during that time, the Westmore whelp and the swell who'd been with her that first afternoon in front of the museum. Westmore had called at the house twice, the other one, three times, the last of those times looking like fury when he left. He ought to find out who the second man was, McErlaine mused as he considered the list. Then he wondered what kind of a shock it might cause Freddy Westmore, or even more his mother, were they to discover that the object of young Westmore's affections was involved in the kind of scandal a robbery would bring down. He thought of Felicia Westmore, that pinch-faced scion of society, of the stiff, snob-nosed pictures he saw of her in the newspaper society pages. Wouldn't that be pretty now, he laughed to himself, wouldn't that bring her down a peg?

But there really wasn't much time to waste on these others. The really interesting one was the Arab, he decided. She'd seen him four times in the past ten days. And that meant only one thing, he decided. Beaumont's plan concerned the Arab. That was why he'd objected so strenuously when his daughter had first realized she was being followed. Beaumont did not want the police to know that he was having his daughter get to know his target. And if the Arab was the target, then there could be only one thing Beaumont would consider worth his efforts, and that, of

120

course, was the ruby.

McErlaine felt suddenly like laughing. It all seemed so clear, so obvious, that he wondered how he could have taken so long finding it. He'd go to see the damn Arab, he decided. Not that he really cared if the filthy beggar had his damned precious ruby stolen from him. But he had no intention of letting Beaumont get away with outwitting him yet again. Yes, he'd go to see the Arab and then he'd simply stand aside and enjoy the spectacle as Beaumont stood there when it all hit the fan.

"These past days, your father seems not to want to let you out of his sight, my dear Abra."

Abra smiled up at the sheik as he settled himself on the couch at her side.

"I think he's decided I've the need of an attentive chaperone of late, Shahab," she told him playfully.

He took her hand in his own and brought it to his lips, brushing it quickly while he peered at her, then dropping it, but not releasing it from his hold.

"Am I to interpret that to mean he does not trust your safety when you are in my company?" he asked her.

Abra shrugged. "Should he?"

Sharify laughed. "Perhaps not," he conceded. "But I cannot help but think that if I could get you alone for a while, I might convince you to agree to come with me when I return home."

"Shahab," she began.

He put a finger to her lips. "I know. I've promised not to press you in return for your promise to consider my offer, not to reject it outright." He smiled at her. "Have you kept your promise, my dear Abra?"

She looked down at the hand that held hers. It was large, the fingers long and thick. Not an idler's hands, not weak or vacillating.

She felt herself wavering internally, not understanding what had happened and not quite sure what she was going to do about it. She'd begun the thing with him a little out of spite, perhaps, because she had wanted to hurt Dash, but mostly because she had hoped it would force him to forget about the Tear. She'd never really thought it would become a problem, had assumed that all she would have to

121

do to rid herself of the sheik would be to return his trinket, express her thanks for his attentions, and plead the impossibility of her leaving her own life. But more and more she had come to realize that Dash had been right when he'd told her that Sharify was not a man she could play with, and most certainly not one who would accept anything less than what he wanted. It had all become far too complicated, and harder for her to cope with, especially with her thoughts of Dash churning away, making her feel more and more unsettled with each passing day.

"Well, Abra?"

She looked back up to him, startled, almost surprised to realize she was still sitting there with him.

"I have considered, Shahab," she told him. "Surely you can understand how difficult it would be, how impossible . . ."

Once again he put his finger to her lips, stilling the words. "No. Nothing is impossible. You have only to realize that, Abra, to consider what I could give you that none of these other men could."

He made a vague gesture toward the crowd in the room, and Abra looked up, wondering how he could be saying these things to her amidst the hubbub of a party, with all those people milling about. But no one seemed to be paying attention to them; everyone was busy with their own priorities, their own lives, and she realized that despite the crowd in the room, they were effectively alone. He was still talking, she realized, and she forced her attention back to him.

"You are different from these women, Abra. I knew it the first moment I saw you. You are unique." His glance settled on Eleanor Dewitte where she sat primly conversing with a solemn-faced, hawk-nosed young man. "That unappealing creature," he said, nodding toward Eleanor, "she is suited for this brittle, passionless society. Her husband will come to her bed as a duty, not as a joy, and she will receive as little as she gives. But that kind of life is not for you." His fingers moved to her wrist, and she could feel the pressure of them against the beat of her pulse. "There," he told her, "there is life and passion throbbing within you. Embrace it, or you will lose it forever."

He spoke with such vehemence, such force, that Abra found herself believing him. It had happened before, this feeling of being swept up by his words, the force of his presence, the oddly disconcerting pressure of his dark glance. She cocked her head, staring at him, wondering how she could escape.

"You frighten me sometimes, Shahab," she told him. "When you talk that way, you frighten me."

He leaned back, smiling at her, apparently not displeased with the possibility. "I have no wish to do so, Abra," he told her. "And you must realize I would never hurt you. I only speak as I do because I want you to realize what your choices are, what you risk losing. And I'm afraid I cannot give you very much more time."

She offered him a curious glance.

"I must leave in a week," he explained. "Not that the prospect pleases me. But I have already stayed longer than I had intended, and there are matters to which I must attend in my own country."

"A week?" she repeated dully.

He nodded. "One week more." He smiled wryly. "I will have a party, I think, aboard my yacht, to thank all these pasty-faced women and their dull little husbands for the unwanted attentions they have shown me while I have been here. After all, I owe them my thanks, for without them I would not have met you." He smiled again. "And you must give me your answer then, so consider well. There's little time."

Abra felt a swell of relief fill her. A week. Only one more week. Not much time to plan a robbery. Hopefully, not enough. And then the Tear and Sharify would be gone from her life forever. She found she could even manage an honest smile when he lifted her hand and kissed it once more.

# Chapter Eight

Abra had dressed carefully. Cream-colored satin hugged her waist, bared her shoulders, and cascaded luxuriantly to the tip of her matching satin dancing pumps. Her mother's pearl choker made her neck look longer, more delicate, as did the tendrils of red-gold curls that framed her face. And pinned into the satin folds at her waist was the brooch, the small lamb face peering out quizzically from the sea of silk that surrounded it.

She'd watched Vincent's eyes as she'd descended the stairs, the way he'd studied her appearance and smiled with apparent pleasure, then turned away.

"This is the end of it, then," she'd said, and he'd nodded, ready to agree.

"Yes, the end."

But he'd said no more, offered her none of the assurance she'd wanted that there would be no attempt to take the ruby that night, that it was all, indeed, over, and she found she could not press, afraid of what he might answer. She'd wanted to ask him why Dash hadn't been to the house in the previous few days, but that question, too, died unvoiced. Instead, they'd ridden to the wharf in near silence.

When they'd boarded the tender, Vincent had seemed relieved at the presence of the dozen other partygoers already there, as though her mute presence was an uncomfortable weight for him to bear. She'd pretended not to notice, but the awareness of his discomfort pressed down on her, bothering her, for the only reason of which she could think to attribute it was the possibility of his doing something at the party of which he knew she would strongly disapprove.

She determined to keep her eye on him, not to let him out of her sight for the whole of the evening. And then it would be done, and she wouldn't have to think of any of it, not ever again.

The tender finally reached the yacht where it floated at anchor, and Abra allowed herself to be helped aboard, one of the seamen daring a small smile at her in recognition as he took her arm. She returned it warmly, secretly amused when the man seemed startled and even a bit embarrassed as he turned abruptly away from her. Sharify's intentions were apparently known among his crew, she thought, and there was no question but that the seaman would not dare show too overt friendship to the woman his master intended to add to his harem.

For a second she pondered what havoc a western woman, a strong-willed western woman at that, might wreak upon the gentility and peacefulness of the seraglio of even so powerful a man as Sharify. The prospect seemed to offer intriguing possibilities.

But she had not long to consider, for the sheik was on deck, himself greeting his guests and shepherding them to the parlor and out of the brisk wind that tore along the outer deck.

He smiled when he saw her, abruptly dropping the hand of Charles Dewitte and leaving him and his wife to find their own way.

"Vincent", he said, nodding, then turned to Abra. "My lovely Abra," he said as he put his arm to her waist. "How angelic you look tonight. You need but a pair of wings and you could, I think, fly to heaven and leave us lesser mortals."

Vincent, standing at Abra's side, laughed. "No one has ever accused my daughter of being remotely seraphic, Shahab," he said. "Perhaps she should dress in white more often. There's always the possibility that the resemblance might grow to be more than skin deep."

"A woman becomes what a man believes her to be," the sheik told him solemnly. "That has been my experience."

"Perhaps the women with whom you've had such experience are more malleable than Abra might prove to be," Vincent replied, his tone a bit strained, as though with a hint of warning.

But the sheik seemed to notice none of it, and he

clapped a hand to Vincent's shoulder as he guided the two of them to the shelter of his lavishly exotic salon.

Abra thought drily that the remainder of the arriving guests would be forced, it seemed, to find their way unaided.

There were many admiring gasps from the newly arrived guests. Abra and Vincent, who had seen the room before, drank in the exoticism added by the yellow light offered by ornate brass lanterns and the slightest scent of incense that perfumed the air. The others, however, encountering it all for the first time, seemed quite bewildered and not a little taken aback. There were muted sounds of surprise, and Abra could not help but notice the intrigued looks of more than one woman turned toward the sheik.

"You've quite conquered every lady you've invited this evening, Shahab," Abra told him with an impish smile as she motioned to the room's trappings.

"Ah, but there is only one woman whose conquest at all intrigues me this evening, Abra," he replied. He stared at her until Abra could feel the warmth of red in her cheeks, then turned to the crowd. "This is nothing to what they have in store for them this evening," he confided to her softly. "These women all think me a savage. . . ."

"Surely not," she objected, interrupting him, but she knew he was right, remembering the whispered comments she'd heard in the preceding weeks when the subject of the handsome foreigner arose. They did think him a savage, and that only served to tantalize them all the more.

"Oh, yes, my dear Abra," he insisted. "These fine people think me a total barbarian. Anyone not completely like them, as a matter of course, must belong to a lower level of human." He smiled at her wickedly, his dark eyes shining ominously at her. "And I'm not really sure they aren't right. At least in so far as their petty values are concerned." He paused and raked her with his eyes.

Abra felt a shiver of illogical shame pass over her, especially as his glance lingered thoughtfully over the decolletage of her gown. I'll be happy when he's gone, she thought, and told herself there was just this one last evening to be gotten through.

"In any case," Sharify went on, "I intend to give them a taste of what they expect. Something to give them ample subject for gossip for a few days to come."

He was as good as his word. When a goodly quantity of champagne had been disposed of by the guests, something he disdained to touch in their company, Abra noticed, a deep gong sounded. Abra had supposed that, since no dinner table was in sight, it would be brought in at the appropriate moment, set with the extravagant silver and crystal she and Vincent had dined from on their previous visit. Instead, Sharify motioned his guests to the couches, urging her to the place beside him. As bewildered as the rest of the guests she complied, staring at him in confusion.

And then the doors at the far side of the room burst open and two dozen of the white-clad servants emerged. The first four carried long, curved scimitars, and they ran to the center of the room while behind them two musicians played a wild melody on a stringed instrument and a flute. There were small shrieks of disbelief from several of the ladies, but Abra watched, fascinated, as the four dancers in the center of the room twirled, ran, and jumped, all the time brandishing their swords wildly, even throwing them into the air and catching them without apparent concern for the injury a miscalculation of timing or distance might cause them. As this was going on, others deftly skirted them, carrying large brass trays laden with food, which they distributed among the guests who sat, stiff and unprepared, on the couches that surrounded the room.

When the frenzy of the dance ended and the room grew suddenly quiet, Abra turned to the sheik, wide-eyed with pleasure. She found him staring at her, apparently waiting for her response.

"Does all this please you, Abra?" he asked in a whisper. "If it does, I will be amply rewarded for the effort."

"Oh, it's wonderful," she cried, completely willing to show him what seemed to him an almost childlike enthusiasm.

Her reaction seemed to please him, for he smiled, apparently satisfied.

"Is this, then, what dinner parties are like in your country, Sheik Sharify?" came a questioning voice from the far side of the room.

"Oh, hardly," Sharify replied amiably as he lifted a small, flat bread from a pile of them on the tray between him and Abra, tore it in two, and handed her one of the

127

pieces. "In my country women do not dine with men in company. They might serve, or dance, or provide music, perhaps." He paused a moment, turning thoughtful. "Unfortunately I could not offer you the pleasure of seeing a belly dance, but there are no women among my company, I'm afraid."

There were several gasps from various parts of the room, but the sheik pretended not to notice, instead busying himself with the food, using the flat piece of bread to scoop up some of the steaming mixture of lamb and rice from one of the bowls.

"*Marka hlouwa*," he said to Abra, motioning to the mixture of lamb, rice, raisins, and prunes. He motioned to her and Vincent to follow his example, and Abra complied, eager for something to do to cover the laughter that threatened to erupt from her at the displays of shock from her countrywomen. She took a bite of the mixture, found the sweetly spicy taste exotically strange, but good. She looked up to Sharify, not at all surprised to find him staring down at her, smiling encouragement to her as she sampled the food, pleased when she returned his smile and ventured a less tentative bite. He dipped his bread into the bowl they shared between them, eating with obvious relish as he watched her. Then he turned his attention back to the universally dismayed looks on the faces of his other female guests. He smiled in anticipation as he cleared his throat and returned to the conversation he'd not quite completed.

"It is truly a shame I did not think to bring with me two or three of my wives who are skilled in the art," he continued, aware he had the attention of the whole room. "The female anatomy is a wonder to men. Sinuous and provocative, to see it move beneath the near-transparent camouflage of a gauzy veil, that is enough to set a man's blood to boiling." He paused thoughtfully for an instant, then continued. "It is a shame it is so cold here. You American men must deny yourselves of a great deal, with your women so heavily padded." He stared directly at Mrs. Dewitte as he finished. "But perhaps that is just as well. Your customs allow your women much freedom, and were it otherwise your ladies would prove a decided snare to any passing man who might lay eyes on them."

Again there were the shocked murmurs, and Abra was

128

aware that Mrs. Dewitte had turned an impossible shade of near purple. She looked up at Sharify, surprised that he seemed to be taking such delight in scandalizing these women. She looked around the room then, and noticed that several of the men seemed thoughtfully considering. She wondered how many of them would have been pleased had the sheik been able to provide the entertainment he had described.

After a moment it became obvious that Charles Dewitte was hastily calming his wife, who seemed on the verge of getting up and demanding to be taken home. But then the music started once again, and the dancers returned to their efforts. Whatever argument had been triggered between the banker and his wife was drowned in the general melee.

Abra turned back to Sharify. "Aren't you afraid of outraging these ladies' fine sense of morality, Shahab?" she asked him. "Certainly they have never been subjected to such talk in their lives."

"Have I shocked you, my dear Abra?" he asked her. "I think not."

She shook her head. "But that's probably only because I knew that's what you were about," she replied. She nodded to where Eleanor Dewitte huddled in the lee of her mother's shimmering wrath. "I think you were about to be denounced by the banking community," she added with a small laugh.

Sharify only shrugged. "The good Mr. Dewitte would hardly have allowed that, I think. I made a very lucrative business arrangement with him yesterday afternoon. He would not allow his wife's prudish hysterics to ruin a profitable venture for him, I think. In fact, I had the distinct impression that were I to ask it, he'd gladly offer up his stick of a daughter, if the profit seemed great enough." His gaze grew intense, and she realized he was telling her many things now, things that needed no words to say. "Like the rest of the men in this room, he will not dare offend me."

Abra mused on his words. She found that none of them pleased her very much. She realized she had sobered completely, that much of her amusement was gone. Whatever she might think of Mrs. Dewitte's inflexible morality, the obvious discomfort of the woman she could only find pitiable. And the sheik's enjoyment of it, on the other hand, grew steadily more unpleasant to her, as did his apparent nonchalant acceptance of the fact that no one would dare offend him for fear of losing a financial advantage. She remembered her father's calling these men thieves, all in thrall to their power and wealth, and the realization that he was right settled into her as a dull, unpleasant reality.

She turned away from Sharify and addressed herself to the food, trying to concentrate on the strangely spiced mixtures in the bowls that covered the tray, trying not to think of anything beyond the unfamiliar tastes and the need to pay attention to what she was about or she would hopelessly ruin her gown, eating as she was without benefit of fork or spoon.

But she quickly realized she had little appetite. The man really is a barbarian, she thought suddenly, and realized the awareness had little to do with his suggestive remarks or even the casual way he discussed the role of women in his country. He took a barbarian's delight in exercising power, she mused, and in showing others just what it was he could do.

She wiped her fingers on her napkin furiously, then put it down and forced her attention once more to the dancers. They had abandoned their scimitars and replaced them with burning torches. The room shimmered with an eerie light as they weaved and twirled, the flames trailing behind them like bright, pursuing ghosts.

"Have you done, Abra?"

Sharify was once more staring at her with those disturbing dark eyes. She nodded, and he put his hand to her arm. He nodded to the dancers.

"No one will notice if we slip away for a moment," he whispered as he stood.

She found she had little choice but to do likewise. Offering Vincent a single, concerned glance, she allowed Sharify to lead her out to the deck.

The wind had died away and the sky was filled with a brilliant yellow moon floating on a field of jewel-bedecked velvet.

"Here we can talk, Abra," Sharify said as he led her to the rail.

"Yes," she replied quickly, her fingers moving to the gold-and-diamond-excrusted pin she'd placed at her waist, hastily working the clasp as she removed it from the folds of satin.

130

Sharify stared at her as she took the brooch from the fabric and held it out to him. Then he put his hand to hers, folding her fingers firmly over the pin.

"I can only assume you mean this as a rejection, Abra," he said slowly.

"I've tried to tell you before," she replied softly. "You wouldn't allow me to."

"Has this decision anything to do with either of the two men you've been seeing lately, Abra?" he demanded abruptly.

She felt herself flush. He'd taken the liberty of discovering that there were other men in her life. At first all she felt was a numb anger at his presumption, but then her thoughts drifted quickly to Dash and Freddy. Freddy could be dismissed immediately, for despite his passive expectations that she would eventually come round, she could no more contemplate a life with him than she could joining a nunnery. And, as painful as it was to accept, even the feelings she had begun to harbor for Dash were not enough to make her believe there could ever be anything more between them.

"I'm sorry, Abra," he told her softly as he read the disapproval in her eyes. "But a good businessman considers his competition as a matter of course. I consider myself a good businessman."

"I'd not thought this a matter of business," she snapped. Then she turned away, and stared at the city lights, brilliant in the darkness, beautiful from where they stood in the harbor. "No," she told him decisively. "Neither of those men has any claim on my life. Nor is it likely that either ever will have."

He put his hand to her arm and his voice gentled. "I'd hoped that the idea might grow more appealing to you given some chance for thought," he told her.

She shook her head slowly. "It is appealing," she admitted reluctantly, aware that she was not lying, that there was more than gentle refusal in her words, for he was compelling, despite the things about him that repelled her, and he still held a kind of fascination for her. "But I can't change my life to become the sort of woman you would have me be, Shahab. I wouldn't fit into your life, and even were you to humor me, there is little possibility that I could survive leading the sort of life a woman must in your country."

131

He did not refute her words so much as dismiss them. "I could make you happy, Abra," he insisted.

"I have little doubt but that you could," she replied.

But once she'd said the words, she knew they were a lie. However many times in the past weeks she'd found his words and his manners hypnotizing, however much she had thought him romantically exotic, she knew there were facets of his personality that were totally repugnant to her, all the more so because he seemed to pride himself on them—his arrogance, his complete self-absorption, his willing ease in abusing the power he held over others. He could never make her happy, she knew. However handsome, however generous he might be to her, there was no possibility that she could endure a life with a man of his temperament.

He stood silent a moment, staring at her, his dark eyes searing into her. And then he moved quickly to her, his arms enfolding her, his lips finding hers with a harshly possessive determination.

Abra grew numb, remembering Dash's warning that the sheik would not be put off with words, that he would take what he wanted when he'd tired of waiting for it to be offered to him. A chill finger of fear crept along her spine. She wanted to cry out, to run. But she could not. The arms that surrounded her held her, as unmalleable as steel bands. The fear turned the numbness to panic.

But through the panic seeped the dim awareness that his kiss answered many questions for her. It generated no heat in her as Dash's kisses did, no fingers of liquid fire stole through her body at this man's touch. What little power he had over her lay in those piercing dark eyes, not in his lips, not the press of his body close to hers. That magic, it seemed, was reserved for another man's touch, another man with whom it was as impossible for her to consider a life and a future as with the sheik. That realization seemed to intensify her fear of him, and she forced herself to fight it.

By the time he'd lifted his lips from hers, she'd managed to calm herself. They were, after all, only a dozen feet from the crowded lounge from which more than fifty people had access to the deck where she stood with Sharify. His kiss was intended as inducement, she realized, not as a preamble to rape.

132

He stood silent for a moment, staring down at her. Her apparent indifference to him seemed to puzzle him more than anything else.

That fact sent a glimmer of amusement through Abra. It seemed incredible to her that no woman had ever said no to him before, but it was obvious that that was the case. She returned his stare defiantly.

Finally he released her, and she backed away a step from him, once again holding up the jeweled brooch she still held in her hand.

"I can't accept so extravagant a gift from you, Shahab," she told him evenly.

His expression grew openly perplexed. "I'd thought, Abra, that women accepted such baubles as deserved tribute," he said.

Abra shrugged. "Some do, I suppose. But I consider it a symbol of a pledge, a pledge I cannot make to you."

He stood and considered her wide-eyed, intense expression, realizing she was entirely serious. There was nothing he could do to change her mind, at least not then, not with the yacht crowded as it was, not with her father only a few feet away. He mused for a moment about what it might have been like with her had circumstances been different, had he had more time to waste on the effort. But that, it seemed, was not to be.

He grinned at her unexpectedly. "Keep it, my dear Abra," he said softly. "It will please me to know that a small member of my flock is close to you when I am far away."

"Shahab . . ." she began to protest, but he put his hands to hers, forcing her fingers once more to close around the brooch.

"I refuse to accept its return. If you would think of it as a pledge, then let it be a pledge of friendship. Surely you would not deny me that?"

For a second she seemed dazed by his words, the pressure of his eyes on her, and then she smiled.

"I shall try to become a good shepherd," she told him with a small laugh.

She was filled with relief. After having dreaded for days the final words she must have with him, she realized suddenly that it had all happened far more easily than she would have thought possible. It's done, she told herself.

133

Tomorrow he leaves and there is nothing more to think of, no choices to make, no thoughts of the damned jewel.

She noticed him smiling as she returned the little lamb to its place at her waist.

"My little lamb is a very lucky creature indeed to be granted the pleasure of dwelling so close to you, Abra," he told her with a smile. "I am, if not content, at least resigned. Perhaps you will sometimes look at it and think of what might have been."

That seemed to Abra an odd thing for him to say, but she had little time to contemplate his words. He put his hand to her waist and drew her back to the lounge and the rest of the party.

After the dim glow of the moonlight, the bright light in the lounge was momentarily blinding, and it took Abra several seconds to adjust. The music continued in a slightly more conservative bent now, and the dancers had disappeared. The large trays had been cleared away and servants were passing among the guests bearing plates of sticky-looking pastries dripping with honey and nuts and tiny cups of very dark, very pungently bouqueted coffee. Abra took a cup, found its taste intensely sweet but still biting. An odd combination, she thought as she sipped, very much like the sheik, overt charm cloaking what she now thought of as an uncompromisingly determined personality.

Apparently the sheik had been forgiven for his previous lack of decorum with the ladies, for at his reappearance he was accosted by one after another, all more than willing to talk to him, to express their delight at his hospitality, with the display and taste of his land. Abra used the opportunity to slip away from him, to scan the room for her father, wondering where he had gotten to in the few moments she'd been out on the deck with Sharify.

Her search was begun with only mild curiosity, but as the moments passed, as she worked her way through the small milling groups of men and women and still there was no sign of Vincent, she grew more and more disturbed. When she'd finally reached the far side of the long lounge and had not found her father, she was struck by a new panic, much stronger and far more pressing than the one

134

she'd felt when she'd been alone on the deck with Sharify. Vincent had left the party and was somewhere below, she thought. And there was only one place she could think of that would have drawn him, only one thing that he would find irresistible. Dash had been unable to manage to find a way onto the yacht, she decided. And her father had determined to take the stone himself. To a man who felt the press of age growing ever stronger, stealing the jewel would seem a fitting swan song, a fitting proclamation that said, "You see, I still am a man." She understood that, just as she understood the reasons for his originally joining into the venture with Dash so enthusiastically. What she could not understand was why he refused to let himself see the risks he took, or the fear she felt when she thought of his being caught.

He was below, she told herself, opening the sheik's safe on some foolish search for his own self-approbation, ignoring what the consequences of that search might be for him. And she had but one thought, and that was to stop him before it was too late.

She darted a quick glance around to be sure that no one was watching her, and then she quickly slipped through the door that led to the stairs below.

Once she entered the corridor on the lower deck, the sounds of the party in the lounge receded entirely, until there was simply a soft, dull drone in the background that hardly intruded on her thoughts. And those thoughts were seriously confused, for the corridor was completely empty. No evidence of the presence of the guards she'd seen on her last visit to the yacht was apparent. Surprisingly, the realization that the guards were gone was almost more distressing to Abra than their presence in the corridor would have been. She could only think that her father had done something desperate, and desperate actions could only lead in the end to disaster.

She approached the door with a numb feeling of dread filling her. Perhaps it was not too late, she told herself. Perhaps she could convince him to replace the stone, return it to the vault, before its absence was discovered. She forced her hand to stop shaking, then placed it on the knob and turned it.

The door opened silently inward. Abra darted a glance into the dimness of the room, then entered quickly, closing

135

the door behind her.

"Papa?" she whispered into the silence, peering intently toward the place where she knew the vault to be. The only light was from a small pierced brass lantern, turned very low. It threw grotesque shadows along the walls and the floor, filling the void with a terrifying horde of phantoms.

"Papa?" Abra whispered once more, this time a bit more loudly, but there was no response.

Her eyes adjusted finally to the darkness and she moved carefully, crossing the room, reaching the bed and the far wall where she knew the vault was hidden. She brushed the wall hanging that covered the vault aside, perplexed, not understanding what had happened, what Vincent had done. Perhaps she'd been wrong, she thought hopefully, and then the thought came to her even more acutely, or, more likely, too late. She felt herself fill with a dull, numbing dread.

"Ah, Miss Beaumont. Come for the jewel, have you?"

Abra froze at the sound of the voice, the silence causing it to echo unmercifully in the room. She could not help but recognize it. After all, the specter of Inspector Patrick Daniel Francis McErlaine had haunted her unremittingly during the past weeks. But this time, she knew, the phantom would not simply turn and disappear.

## Chapter Nine

"I knew he couldn't keep his hands off it. I knew he hadn't changed. But I must admit I really hadn't expected you to do the snatch for him."

Abra felt her heart beat with strangely aware senses as she watched the lamplight grow steadily stronger and the policeman appear out of the dimness of the room.

"So much for the fine gentleman, sending his own daughter to do the deed," McErlaine finished as he heaved himself across the room to where Abra stood.

"I'm sure I don't know what you're talking about," Abra retorted, her tone as stalwartly haughty as she could make it. Hoping he could not see she was trembling inside, she turned and began to walk toward the door.

But McErlaine's hand caught her arm, his beefy fingers surprisingly strong, the pressure of them biting into her flesh.

"I'll thank you to release me," Abra told him, her glance filling with disdain even as the terror inside her grew unimpeded. Pretend innocence, a voice inside her counseled, and she clung to the thought. Pretend innocence and he can only offer his word against yours.

"Oh, no, my dear young lady," McErlaine responded with a satisfied smirk. His fingers grew even tighter. "You came down here to steal that damned ruby, and I've no intention of letting you walk away from the fact."

"Don't be absurd," Abra retorted.

"Absurd is it? If not that, then why are you here? Not to warm that Arab beggar's bed?" The prospect seemed to amuse him.

"You are coarse and disgusting," Abra snarled at him.

But McErlaine was paying her no attention. His laughter

137

began with a low rumble and grew steadily louder as she struggled to get away from him, pushing against his hand with her fingers, balling her hands into fists and directing them at his arm, all to no avail. He simply stared at her, obviously amused by her anger and her fruitless efforts.

"I've caught you in the act, and now you and your father will pay for the years I've spent being laughed at, being the brunt of jokes. Look at old Patty Mac, they'd say, chasing after ghosts. Well, I'll show them the ghosts were real, after all. I even think it's been worth it, just to see Vincent Beaumont behind bars."

He wasn't even talking to her, Abra realized. He was saying the words for himself. And she felt a dull, panicked dread. It was all terribly clear to her now. McErlaine had somehow managed to convince the sheik that she and her father would make an attempt on the jewel, and the trap had been set for them to try to take it, with McErlaine lying in wait, guarding the bait. That was why the guards had not been posted by the doorway, to make it seem easy. And she'd been fool enough to fall into the snare, giving McErlaine what he wanted, a hold on her father.

"Shall we go see what that Arab beggar thinks of you now, eh, missy?" McErlaine asked as he began to push her toward the door. "Him, and the whole of New York society, all ready and waiting to watch you be shown up as a petty thief, you, and that damned superior father of yours?" The prospect obviously gave him a great deal of pleasure, and he grinned in delighted anticipation.

"I shouldn't say petty."

The words had been whispered, the voice was low and gruff. And the confusion Abra felt as she heard them was paltry compared to the disbelief that followed as a dark figure emerged from the shadows and something fell against the back of McErlaine's head. The policeman's grasp on Abra's arm loosened, and then his hand fell away altogether as he crumbled into a huge, ungainly heap at her feet. She stood staring down at him numbly, not knowing what to do.

"Well, don't just stand there. Get the hell out of here and back up to that party, Abra, where people can see you."

"Dash?" she asked, still dazed.

"Were you expecting someone else, perhaps?" he countered, a note of exasperation creeping into his tone.

"But Papa . . ." Her words trailed off in her confusion.

"He's at the party, making himself seen, just as you ought to be doing."

"But he's not," she protested weakly. "When I came in with Shahab . . ." She paused once more, her words sinking away into a weak whisper as she saw the look Dash leveled at her.

"An amble in the moonlight with the sheik, was it Abra?" he demanded, anger leaking into his words.

"What business is that of yours?" she snapped back at him, surprised at the ire he'd managed to raise in her, but still finding herself irrationally hoping he'd say it was his business because he loved her.

Instead he leveled a cool glance at her, and then turned away.

"None," he told her softly. "No business of mine at all. And now that you've managed to ruin our little escapade, why don't you run along to his waiting arms?"

"Ruin it?" she asked weakly, feeling the confusion seeping back into her.

"For God's sake, Abra, use some common sense. I can't take the jewel now. This fool of a policeman has seen you down here. When he wakes up, don't you think he'll race up and point a finger at you and Vincent? If the jewel isn't safely in the vault, you'll be the perfect suspect, now, won't you?"

"What, what shall I do?" she asked him, cowed now by his manner and his obvious disgust with her.

"What you should have done in the first place. Stayed up at the party, insuring an alibi for yourself. And pretending complete innocence."

"And you?" she ventured softly.

He turned back to her, his look no longer angry, just disappointed. "It seems you get your way after all, Abra. Your precious sheik gets to keep his stone, and I get to slip by the sheik's men, slide into the filthy, cold water of the harbor for a pleasant little swim, and nothing to show for it." He took her arm and propelled her toward the door.

"I'm sorry, Dash," she murmured. "I didn't mean to ruin anything, just protect Papa."

"Your father is a professional, Abra, and he's doing just what he's supposed to be doing. And we both should have known better than let you get involved in any of this,

139

should have known it would just lead to disaster." His hold on her arm loosened as they neared the door, and he opened it a few inches and peered out. "No one there," he whispered. "Get going."

But she stayed where she was. "You'll be all right?" she asked softly.

"If you get the hell out of here before one of the sheik's friendly little minions happens along," he told her impatiently. Then his expression softened. "Don't look so worried. Just get up there, and remember, whatever happens, you and Vincent are lily white innocent."

She nodded mutely, and he moved to open the door for her, then paused.

"Abra," he whispered.

She turned her face to his, and suddenly found his arm around her, pulling her close, and his lips pressed to hers. For a few seconds she forgot where she was, and was aware only of the feel of him close to her, and the frantically irregular beating of her heart. Then he dropped his arm and she drew back from him.

"I love you, Abra," he whispered.

If the beating of her heart had felt pressingly immediate when he'd kissed her, it seemed absolutely deafening to her at that moment as those three words filled her with a euphoria she'd never felt before. But before she could say anything, before she could tell him that she loved him, too, there was a low moan behind them from the heap of flesh that was McErlaine.

"Hurry," Dash whispered to her, then pulled the door open and pushed her through.

She stared at him, numbed, seeing only his face as the door silently closed. Then, she turned to the long, empty corridor and the stairs that led up to the lounge above. He loves me, she mused, feeling slightly foolish as she silently sang the words over and over to herself, but nonetheless content. She didn't need the sheik, not his riches or his power. All she really needed was Dash. Somehow they'd work things out between the two of them. And nothing else mattered.

She ran the length of the corridor without even realizing it, and sped up the stairs, all the while listening to the words repeating themselves in her mind, he loves me. However irrational the thought, however impossible she knew it to be, she could not force away the feeling of elation and hope. Nor had she any desire to do so.


Dash turned from the closed door to the less-than-appetizing form of the policeman on the floor. McErlaine's head lay beside the heavy leg of the sheik's bed. Dash realized that the policeman must have hit his head when he fell, for there was a small puddle of blood leaking from his nose to the floor. Dash stared at him dispassionately, realizing he felt absolutely no remorse for whatever damage he'd done to the man. He'd managed to ruin a month's work, and Dash could only feel he deserved whatever he'd gotten.

McErlaine stirred, moving his head and groaning loudly. He'd have to leave quickly, Dash realized, or not only would he have nothing to show for his efforts, he might have the unpleasant experience of finding himself inspecting the conditions of the New York jail from the inside, as well.

He moved quickly, back to the far corner of the room, and hoisted himself up to the ventilation shaft, heaving himself up quickly and then pulling up the carved fretwork cover and securing it. He realized he was none too soon. In the room behind him were the sounds of McErlaine returning to consciousness, rolling over and moving clumsily to his knees.

Silently, Dash edged himself along the darkened shaft, his hearing sensitive to the sounds in the room he'd left behind him, as McErlaine swore volubly, and with a good deal of scuffling noise, staggered to his feet. There'll be all hell to pay when he gets to the sheik, Dash thought, and prayed silently that Abra would have the good sense to do as he had told her and pretend complete innocence.

But he had little time to waste on worry, and he knew that Vincent would take care of her. He had to get himself off the yacht and away before the sheik decided to have the vessel searched, just in case the policeman's story had some grain of truth in it. He silently cursed Charles Nevin for his graphic descriptions of what would probably be done to him if Sharify were to catch him in the act on the yacht, which he undoubtedly considered as legally a small finger of Mukalla sitting in the middle of New York harbor, and therefore being under no law but his own. Dash could have done very well without knowing the more bizarre and protracted methods of killing a man that could be devised with deep thought and time, hundreds of generations of time.

He inched his way through the shaft, trying to balance silent caution with the need to hurry, until he finally managed to pull himself to the grilled opening far to the fore of the yacht's upper deck. He peered out into the darkness, eased himself through the opening he'd cut in the grill, and then quickly pushed it back so that the hole could not be seen on casual inspection. Then he hunkered down into the shadows, his eyes roving the deck, looking for the guard he'd seen when he'd climbed aboard.

He stayed where he was, a shadow among other shadows, until the guard had passed him by on his tour, and then he whispered a quick prayer that the doryman that Charles Nevin had found for him had not lost his nerve and was still waiting for him, and that he would find the small boat tied to the freighter some fifty yards from the yacht. As it was, it would be a cold, unpleasant swim. He had not thought that he'd like to make it all the way to shore. He thought about the man's barely controlled fear as they'd neared the yacht earlier in the evening and Dash had pulled himself up the shadow-darkened side. The possibility that his boat would be missing when he reached the rendezvous seemed more and more likely.

When the deck before him was clear and the guard far to the stern, he edged himself out of the safety of the darkness and onto the open deck, making directly for the rail. He climbed over it with a stealthy silence, finding the anchor line and slipping his feet to its support, remembering to brace himself against its wet slipperiness. Then he lowered himself quickly, just as the sounds of a shrill female voice stabbed through the night from the confines of the salon above.

Eleanor Dewitte, he thought with a dull awareness, realizing that distance hardly served to improve her brittle, high-pitched tone. Then he felt the cold bite of the water as he lowered himself into it, swore silently as the chill filled him, and set out with as much determination as he could muster, moving with a solidly workmanlike stroke through the cold, murky water.

When she'd returned to the party, Abra had quickly found that Dash had been right, and Vincent had been sitting on a couch along the far wall talking to, of all people, Charles Dewitte, in what was undoubtedly the first overtly friendly exchange between the two that she could ever remember. She'd probably walked right by them, she realized, peering at the milling crowd and never thinking to look to the couches. He'd certainly found the ideal alibi, she mused, spending his time with the most stalwartly pompous and upright of those assembled in the huge room. She wondered what pangs of self-disgust her father suffered as he smiled and nodded at Dewitte's dull drone. And it was all for nothing, she mused, with not the slightest sense of guilt.

It's over, she thought. Dash hadn't stolen the stone and they were all safe. And he loved her, she heard a voice remind her, and she smiled at the memory of his words.

"You seem quite pleased, Abra. Can I assume you're enjoying yourself?"

Abra caught her breath at the sound of the now familiar voice. For an instant she felt a dull finger of fear nudge her as she thought that Sharify had somehow discovered what had happened below. But then she heard Dash's voice telling her to pretend innocence, and she turned to the sheik with a ravishing smile.

"Yes, it's a lovely party, Shahab," she replied.

His eyes narrowed for a moment as he returned her wide-eyed stare, and the thought that there still might be a chance crept into his mind.

"I wonder if you might not join me on deck, Abra, for a more private farewell? After all, I leave tomorrow. I must admit that now, knowing that you are not coming with me, my departure has grown exceedingly unpleasant to me."

He put his hand to her waist and began to edge her toward the door.

Abra felt the panic that had begun with the first of his words grow, and this time it refused to be forced away. Dash's words repeated themselves in her mind for the second time that evening, that the sheik would take what he wanted when he became tired of waiting for it.

"I don't think, Shahab . . ." she began, filled with confusion, not really knowing what to say.

But then she found herself suddenly relieved of the need.

Eleanor Dewitte's frantic, sharp cry pierced the air, reaching above the other sounds in the salon. All conversation stopped, all eyes turned to her and then followed the direction in which she stared with obvious shock.

A large, rumpled man had staggered into the lounge from the door at the far end of the room. He looked wild and disheveled, and there was blood on the handkerchief he held to his nose, and a good bit more was spotting the front of his not terribly neat shirtfront. He stood less than steadily on his feet as he made a concentrated survey of the occupants of the room.

His search came to an abrupt stop as his glance fell on Abra. He raised a thick hand and pointed a stubby finger.

"I warned you," he shouted at Sharify, his voice loud in the sudden silence of the room. "That woman is a thief!"

Abra darted a quick look in the sheik's direction, saw him stare at McErlaine with obvious distaste, and knew that Dash had given her good advice. The look heartened her, and she turned quickly back to the policeman, her expression wide-eyed with shocked innocence.

"The man's mad," she said softly, so that only Sharify could hear her.

He nodded to her. "Quite possibly," he agreed, and put his hand to her arm, leading her forward to the mottled, sputtering face of her accuser. "But perhaps we should listen."

Vincent had leaped to his feet, pushing his way through the crowd that had closed in around the policeman.

"How dare you speak of my daughter that way?" he bellowed, his outrage evident.

McErlaine's eyes turned slowly from Abra to Vincent. He seemed almost pleased by Vincent's response.

"And you planned it all," he continued without making any effort to subdue his tone.

By now Abra and Sharify were directly in front of the policeman, the sheik eyeing him with a distant interest.

"You managed to convince me that an attempt would be made this evening on the Tear of Allah," he said, his voice low and hard, but without any great show of concern, "and I honored your whim, allowing you to remain here and play whatever games it pleased you to play. But I will not have you accusing my guests without proof."

McErlaine took the bloodstained handkerchief he held

to his nose and waved it furiously. "I have proof. Look at this," he cried, pointing to the red clots. "I was struck from behind as I was about to bring her up to you, caught redhanded." McErlaine looked around wildly, then pointed at Vincent. "It was him, I tell you, and they stole your precious ruby."

Sharify turned his glance to Abra, his arched brow only hinting at curiosity, but his hold on her arm tightening.

She shrugged her shoulders. "If you were struck on the nose, why is it you didn't see your attacker?" she asked McErlaine mildly.

His cheeks reddened. "I said I was struck from behind. I must have hit my nose when I fell," he growled back at her.

"The man's obviously fallen, hit his head, and become deranged," she suggested mildly, turning to Sharify. "But if you think I have the jewel, I'm willing to allow you to search me." She offered him a challenging smile.

He stifled a grin. "A pleasure that manners require I forgo, my dear Abra," he replied. Several gasps of dismay from the ladies in the crowd followed his words.

"This is all nonsense," Vincent interrupted, his manner vexed, but hardly that of a cornered man. "I was here, all evening, and for the last twenty minutes I've been in the company of Charles Dewitte." He turned to the banker for confirmation, which was duly rendered.

"It's true," Dewitte muttered, obviously bewildered by the fact that fate now required him to provide an alibi for a man he'd slurred quite often in the past.

Vincent smiled at the words, and turned back to McErlaine, his brows raised expectantly. "I suggest you offer my daughter and myself an apology, McErlaine. Immediately."

But the policeman would not be cowed. He turned to the sheik.

"Shall we have a look in that vault of yours before you dismiss me as a madman, then?" he suggested. "Or does the woman mean more to you than the ruby?"

There was a protracted silence as every eye turned first to Sharify and then to the challenging visage of the policeman. Finally, the sheik shrugged.

"I regret, Abra, Vincent," he nodded at them each in turn. Then he moved to the door and held it for McErlaine. "We are in your thrall, inspector," he said with mock servility as he motioned to the stairs.

145

McErlaine scowled, but moved to the opened door, reaching for the railing as he approached the stairs. Abra nodded quickly to Vincent, her look meant to allay the fear she saw creeping into his expression, and then she turned quickly to the sheik. Sharify offered her his arm and she took it, not daring to look into his eyes. She held herself stiffly as she descended the stairs behind McErlaine, watching his large form as it seemed to roll from side to side, wondering how it had managed to go so far.

Vincent took Abra's hand and squeezed it encouragingly, then turned his attention to where Sharify stood in front of them, busying himself with the safe. Behind them, spilled into the corridor, were the other guests, silent in their curiosity, caught up in the drama as though they were witnesses to something they imagined could only touch their lives from the distance of their morning newspapers or via the delicious savoring of gossip. And McErlaine stood staring at Abra and Vincent, his eyes filled with the satisfaction he knew he would feel when the safe was opened, when he'd be proved, after all those years, right, after all.

As the door of the safe swung open and Sharify reached in, Abra could feel the tense expectancy of the people standing behind her, and she knew that many of them would be secretly as pleased as McErlaine were the jewel to be missing. After all, they'd whispered about Vincent for years. They would savor being proved right. But when the sheik turned to face them, the leather pouch was in his hand. He slowly approached Abra as he opened it, taking her hand in his and turning the pouch over, emptying it into her upturned palm.

For a second time Abra felt the odd warmth of the stone, and she stared at it as curiously as she had the first time she'd held it, wondering at the mysterious force it enclosed. But she only had a moment to hold it now before the sheik's fingers reached out and enclosed the stone. He held it up to the sight of those behind.

"The Tear," he said loudly, so that they would realize what it was he held. Then he turned to McErlaine who stood still and dazed, staring at him with disbelief.

"I couldn't have been wrong," the policeman muttered angrily.

"But it seems you were, inspector. Not only wrong, but insulting to my guests."

With that Sharify returned the Tear to the pouch, drew it quickly closed, and replaced it in the safe, which he proceeded to close with a swift motion. Then he turned back to his guests.

"The excitement seems to be over," he said, smiling benignly at their curious faces. Then he turned to McErlaine. "I think we won't be needing your services any further, inspector. Please get your things together and leave immediately."

He turned away, dismissing the man as he motioned to the crowd to move back up to the lounge.

He took Abra's arm once more, this time more gently, as he leaned close to her. "Forgive this, Abra. But I could not ignore the man."

"Would it have pleased you if what he had claimed was true, Shahab?" she asked him softly.

He stared down into her eyes. "Perhaps," he admitted softly. "It would, at least, have given me a hold on you."

"And the consequences of so heinous a crime?" she pressed.

"The act of such sacrilege earns the retribution of beheading in my country, Abra," he told her softly.

"Then it is indeed fortunate for my father and myself to be innocent of such a crime."

"Perhaps in your case I might have tempered the punishment to one I found more personally satisfying," he suggested.

She stared at him a moment, then drew back from him. "In any case, it is not a matter worth contemplation."

He darted a quick look at the sumptuous bed. "And our more private farewell?"

"I think it best that our farewell be conducted in public, Shahab," she told him firmly, moving away from him to the door.

He moved after her quickly, holding the door for her and allowing her to precede him.

"Perhaps in another lifetime, my dear Abra," he whispered softly as she passed him.

McErlaine stood by the filthy window, hunched over the

147

beer that had been set before him on the bar.

This was not an entirely healthy place for him, he knew. Dock hands and sailors were not usually overfond of the police. But he persisted, refusing to move from his place, ignoring the unfriendly, suspicious glances the other patrons cast in his direction and keeping his eyes strained through the small hole he'd made in the dirt that caked the window.

Outside, on the far edge of the wharf, the tender was being docked, and the sheik's guests would soon climb into their carriages and make their way into far more elaborate beds than any of the men in the dirty bar had ever even imagined.

He lifted his beer and drank slowly, trying to ignore the sour smell of unwashed bodies and the slight tinge of vomit that clung to the still, smoky air of the saloon. He'd been in worse places, he told himself, but he could not remember how long ago that had been, or, for that matter, where.

He swallowed the liquid in his mouth as the first of the ladies was handed up to the wharf, eyeing the group in their evening finery, the flash of silk and diamonds in the dark clarity of the night oddly out of place amidst the dank disorder of the wharf. He picked out Vincent Beaumont and his daughter easily, Vincent's tall figure recognizable amidst the men, Abra's halo of reddish gold hair unique among the women. And when he saw them, McErlaine smiled.

They won't be so grand in a few more hours, he thought as he lifted the dirty tankard and swallowed the remainder of the beer. The thought mellowed the stale taste and he pushed the container forward as the bartender neared him.

"One more," he suggested, feeling effusive. After all, he mused, this is just the start of a celebration. A long, long celebration.

He'd finished his second watching the carriages depart and was contemplating a third tankard when he saw the second tender reach the wharf. This time there were no partygoers on board, only the distinctive-looking members of the sheik's crew in their white and crimson.

He took some coins absently from his pocket and dropped them hastily onto the bar, not even stopping to count them out in his haste, an unprecedented extravagance. But he was in a hurry, he told himself as he moved quickly to the door and stepped out into the night. After all, it would not do to have the foreigners forced to go looking for an officer of the law when they'd been the victims of a crime. That would reflect badly on the New York City Police Force, not something he would ever want to occur.

He moved to the wharf with a certain step, unmarked by the consumption of the two quarts of beer.

"Excuse me, gentlemen," he said jauntily as he neared the men who were just making the tender fast to the dock. "Would you be needin' a policeman, now?" he asked with a wide smile.

Hemmings seemed to have lost a trace of his eternal sangfroid. Perhaps it was simply that he had been roused from his bed and forced to attend the door in the informal attire of his dressing gown, perhaps it was the unlikely and decidedly unpleasant experience of greeting a large number of policemen at three in the morning. Whatever the reason, his face showed the distinct presence of emotion, none of it pleasant, as he announced to the still bleary-eyed Vincent that his presence and that of Miss Abra were required by some insistent callers in the front hall below. With that information conveyed, he ventured once more down the stairs to do his best to hold the invading horde at bay until his employer could take responsibility himself.

But in the few minutes it took Vincent to rouse Abra and then to descend, Hemmings managed to force back some of his usual control over his countenance, and he stood a stern-eyed guard, obviously unimpressed by anyone, regardless of his office, who would dare invade the sanctity of a home at so unholy an hour. He cast a jaundiced eye at McErlaine and Chief Inspector Flynt before turning to face Vincent.

"These gentlemen insisted upon seeing you immediately, sir," he intoned, and there was something about the way he said the word gentlemen that made everyone within hearing understand quite distinctly that he held grave doubts as to the credibility of the title as applied to the men involved.

"It's all right, Hemmings," Vincent assured him, his hands busy tying the silk belt of his dressing gown as he turned to Flynt. He completely ignored the fact of McEr-

149

laine's presence. "To what doubtful honor may I credit this unprecedented visit, Inspector Flynt?" he demanded.

Flynt cleared his throat uneasily. He'd not enjoyed being dragged from his own bed, and he sympathized with Vincent's displeasure. Under any other circumstance, he'd have dismissed the matter as yet another of McErlaine's ravings, returned to his bed, and then brought the matter before a board of internal affairs in the morning, suggesting the inspector's immediate dismissal, something of which he'd daydreamed with pleasure on several occasions in the past. But somehow the man had convinced the sheik, and even a chief inspector dared not dismiss the demands of so powerful a man. And so, here he stood, hat in hand, wondering how he should address Vincent Beaumont and tell him he intended to have his house searched in the middle of the night. It was not an appetizing prospect.

"What is it, Papa?"

Flynt was not the only member of his party who was pleasantly surprised by the appearance of the tall, slender, reddish golden haired young woman dressed in pale turquoise silk at the stair landing. He looked up and smiled at her, musing at the number of years it had been since he'd last seen a pretty young woman in her dressing gown, and realized that he'd never had the pleasure of seeing one nearly so beautiful.

"I'm afraid, sir," he said, his voice filled with a genuine regret as he nodded first to Vincent, then to Abra, "miss, that there's been an unfortunate misunderstanding. It seems there's been a theft, and I'm forced to make inquiries."

Abra moved slowly down the last of the stairs and stood with her hand on the ornate newel post. "A theft, sir?" she demanded, staring directly into Flynt's eyes.

"The missing object is the, uh, property of Sheik Sharify," Flynt replied, aware that his cheeks were becoming ruddy as he stared at her. "And it has come to our attention that you and your father were present on the sheik's yacht this evening."

"And are all the other guests who attended the sheik's party to be questioned, as well?" she demanded tartly. She stared pointedly at McErlaine. "Or is this honor being reserved only for us?"

But Vincent moved to her side and took her hand in his.

"We've nothing to hide, Abra," he told her quickly before turning to Flynt. "How can we help you, inspector?"

Flynt cleared his throat once more, trying vainly to find his composure.

"I'm afraid I must ask you if you have any immediate knowledge of the whereabouts of the Tear of Allah, Mr. Beaumont."

Vincent lifted a brow curiously. "Only that it was, the last time I saw it, earlier in the evening, in the possession of Sheik Sharify."

"Enough of this pussyfootin'," McErlaine burst out. "We've come to search for the stone, Beaumont. That is, unless you'd rather just surrender it and be done with it."

Vincent smiled crookedly. "How droll, McErlaine." He turned back to Flynt. "If you've determined upon a search, I will make no effort to impede you, inspector." He looked thoughtfully at McErlaine. "But on the condition that you personally accompany McErlaine. I would not be terribly surprised if the man stole the stone himself and plans to plant it in my home. As I've told you before, he is decidedly deranged."

McErlaine sputtered in rage, but his superior waved him to silence. He repressed his anger, aware that there was nothing he could do but accept the condition as he watched Flynt nod acceptance to Vincent.

"Under the circumstances, Mr. Beaumont, I find your request quite reasonable," Flynt replied easily. He'd expected far greater resistance, and was more than happy to accommodate, especially as he quite agreed with the evaluation of McErlaine's mental state.

He turned then to the half dozen of his men who waited mutely behind him, and issued terse orders. Then, as the men fanned out, starting for the stairs and the interior of the house, he offered Abra a weak smile.

"We'll try to be done quickly, miss, with as little fuss as possible. If you and your father will wait here with Sergeant Breadon?"

Abra nodded and watched as Flynt motioned to McErlaine and the two moved off toward the dining room and parlor.

This can't be happening, she told herself. The stone was never taken. Dash promised. None of this can be happening.

151

"Well, sergeant."

Vincent's voice interrupted her thoughts and she turned to him.

"I think I could use a small brandy and soda. I don't suppose you're allowed to drink on duty?"

The sergeant shook his head with obvious regret.

"Well, why don't we retire to the library to await the chief inspector's return from this fruitless endeavor? Abra, my dear, I don't suppose I could bother you to fix me that drink?"

Then he ushered her and the sergeant into the library.

"I had a dozen men besides McErlaine and myself. We spent more than three hours searching the house. The stone is not there."

Sharify turned steely eyes to Flynt and nodded. The man was obviously not pleased with the way things had turned out, but that hardly surprised him. He was less than pleased himself.

"Perhaps a mistake was made, Inspector Flynt," he said carefully.

"No mistake was made," McErlaine burst out, his beefy cheeks red with emotion.

Sharify moved his glance with slow deliberation to McErlaine. That man knows more than he's saying, he mused, but he paused at that thought. He was probably right about Vincent Beaumont and his daughter, though. The things he'd learned about Beaumont in the last two days had convinced him about that.

"I appreciate your efforts," he said and stood, wanting to be done with these men and get about things in his own way. "But you've done all you can. I will handle the matter by myself now."

"But, but the ruby," McErlaine stammered.

Sharify smiled as he would at a simple child. "Ah, inspector, certainly I did not leave you with the impression that the stone was the real Tear of Allah? How careless of me. Certainly I would not take so precious and holy an object from my own country. The stone that was stolen was a copy, paste." He looked thoughtful. "An excellent copy, of course, and valuable, worth close to five hundred pounds. But the real Tear is priceless. Far too valuable to be left so carelessly to the hands of chance." And once more he smiled the complacent, reassuring smile.

"You're lying," McErlaine snarled.

There was a moment of tense silence before Sharify spoke. "I do not think I like your tone, inspector," he said with dull anger.

"You don't want it known that your precious relic was stolen," McErlaine countered. "It would make things difficult for you in your country, now, wouldn't it? But it was the real ruby."

"Whatever your misguided ideas, inspector," Sharify replied, his tone turned cutting, distinctly threatening, "I suggest you keep them to yourself."

Flynt seemed to flounder in the open hostility the two men generated around him. "I'm sure it's simply the inspector's overzealousness, sir, that leads him to such extravagance of speech. On behalf of the New York Police Department, please accept my apologies."

McErlaine stood tight-jawed and indignant, but remained silent.

"I suggest you both leave," Sharify told them with a nod toward the door, then he turned away, done with them apparently, and angry with himself for having allowed them to enter into the matter at all. Safeguarding the Tear was his duty. He'd been a fool to allow the foreigners to meddle.

He didn't even notice they were gone until he looked up and found the lounge empty save for one of his own men. He sat, silent and unmoving, and simply thought. Then he turned abruptly to the white-clad servant.

"Amad. Bring me note paper, pen, and ink. Then find two others. I've a task for you to do, and when it is done, I want you to deliver the letter."

Amad bowed and disappeared silently, intent upon his task. And Sharify sat mulling over his decision. It was by far the best way, he decided. He'd get back the Tear and have the woman into the bargain.

# Chapter Ten

It was well after eleven the next morning when Abra descended the stairs and entered the front hall. It all seemed so quiet, so entirely normal. It was hard for her to believe that only a few hours before the police had been storming through the house, pawing through every drawer and shelf, invading every closet. As Flynt had promised, they'd made some effort to leave things as little disturbed as possible, but still her surroundings seemed violated to her, and the sensation made her shudder.

Hemmings met her in the hall and offered her an uncharacteristic heartening smile. Apparently the evening before had changed his attitude toward her. Despite the years in Vincent's employ, he'd never once made any personal gesture. But now he seemed to feel as though there was some new bond between them, of having faced a more powerful foe and overcome him, and he obviously took some pleasure in that recollection.

"Will you be wanting any breakfast, Miss Abra?" he asked, his tone solicitous.

She shook her head. Her head hurt and she still felt slightly befuddled from lack of sleep. It had already been morning when the police had finally left, and she'd had little enough sleep, especially considering that despite her exhaustion, she'd been unable to rest even after they'd gone. Her thoughts came back to her, as disturbing as they had been while she'd lain, completely awake, in her bed. How had she ever been so stupid, so childishly naive, to trust a man like Dashiel Thorne? she demanded of herself. More to the point, how could she have allowed herself to believe him when he'd told her he loved her? How could she admit to herself that she loved him?

154

"Just some coffee in the library, please, Hemmings," she replied wearily as she crossed the hall. "My father?" she queried as she put her hand to the knob.

"He left about an hour ago, miss. Said he was going to his club," Hemmings replied before he turned away, directing himself toward the pantry and the preparation of the requested coffee.

Abra scowled. Club, my foot, she mused. He's gone to see his partner in crime. Damn them, damn them both. How could they have been so stupid as to ignore the consequences of the theft? How could Dash have lied to her, and taken the stone after he'd promised her he wouldn't touch it?

She realized she was still shaken from the late-night search, the evident police interest. They'd be watching her and Vincent now, she felt sure. If that horror, McErlaine, had haunted her before the stone had been stolen, he'd certainly not leave them a moment's peace now that it was missing.

She stalked into the library and threw herself disconsolately onto the couch. She would not see Dashiel Thorne again, she decided. She would somehow convince her father to reject whatever portion of the proceeds he'd agreed to. They certainly didn't need the money, and besides, McErlaine would somehow find out if it came into their possession, of that she was doggedly certain. She cringed at the thought of his beefy hands pawing through her belongings as he had the night before, just as he would soon be pawing through their finances, their lives, and she grew sick at the prospect.

And it was all Dash's fault. If only he'd not taken the stone, if only he'd not lied to her when he told her he loved her. If only, if only. The words echoed in her mind like relentless little harpies, pleased with the misery they caused her.

But despite it all, despite the logic that told her she was a fool, she knew the part that hurt the most was not the police scrutiny, not the demeaning social stigma that would surely follow, but the simple fact that she must now rid her life of Dashiel Thorne. She knew him to be a thief and a liar, a blackguard and completely unscrupulous, but still it pained her unbearably to know that she must never let him touch her life again. For that was, she knew, the

155

only way, the only means she had to protect Vincent from the police. Because if there continued to be any relationship between them, McErlaine would eventually figure it all out, he'd realize that it had been Dash who had taken the Tear. And then it would be prison for them all. McErlaine was a bulldog. She knew instinctively that he'd never let it go.

She was still deep in thought when Hemmings brought in the tray with her coffee, but the sight of the envelope on the tray pulled her back to reality. It looked outwardly completely innocent, but for some reason it sent a shiver through her.

"This just arrived by messenger, miss," Hemmings told her as he handed her the letter, then turned his attention to pouring her coffee.

Abra took the envelope gingerly in her fingers and stared at it numbly. "A messenger dressed in white?" she asked. "With a dark crimson sash?"

Hemmings nodded. "Yes, miss. A foreign brute."

He handed her the cup and then turned away, leaving her in the silent library to stare at the dull beige envelope in her hand.

She realized her hand was shaking, that the coffee was sloshing out of the cup and onto the saucer. She put it down carefully, concentrating her attention on the task as though it were of supreme importance. When the coffee was safely returned to the tray, she found she had no choice but to open the envelope and read the note inside, despite her irrational desire to toss it into the fire and watch it burn.

Her fingers shook as she tore open the flap and pulled out the single sheet of paper, so much so that she had trouble deciphering the words. And when she'd done, she reread it, sure she hadn't understood properly, sure it was too impossible to be true. But the second reading didn't change a word, and she leaned back into the couch, staring with unseeing eyes at the ceiling, unaware that a low moan of pain had escaped from her lips.

This was all Dash's fault, she thought suddenly. She pulled herself together, standing abruptly and running toward the door. It was all Dash's fault, and, like it or not, he would help her repair the damage he'd done, now, before it was too late.

"Hemmings," she called distractedly. "Bring my coat, and have the carriage brought round. Immediately."


"Abra. What a pleasant surprise."

Dash's obvious delight at the sight of her faded quickly, however, when he recognized her expression. He stood aside and allowed her to enter, watching the stiff way she held herself, the tight shoulders and the quick, measured steps.

She waited until he'd closed the door behind her, then turned to face him, her expression pale, barely managing to control the anger surging within her.

"Damn you, Dashiel Thorne," she told him through tight lips. "Damn you for a liar and a thief."

And then her hand shot out, striking his cheek with a loud, fleshy-sounding impact.

She could see the surprise leave his face and quickly be replaced by an anger he fought to control. She could see his jaw clench rigidly, and she knew that had she been a man he would have responded quickly and with decisive force. She didn't care. She almost wished he would strike her back. Then she could tell herself that he was without honor as well as devoid of scruples.

But he didn't. He stood staring at her, his hand slowly unclenching, and then he reached to the suddenly reddened splotch on his cheek.

"To what do I owe this unexpected honor, Miss Beaumont?" he asked her with pained control.

Her only response to his anger was disgust. She wanted to ball her hands into fists and strike at him, to beat them against his chest, to hurt him in any way she could.

"How can you dare stand there, pretending innocence? How can you, after what you've done?" she shouted at him.

He took her elbow firmly in his hand and led her into the room, pushing her to the couch without any attempt at niceties.

"Now," he said when she was seated and staring up at him with dagger-filled eyes, "if you'll kindly extend the courtesy of explaining what has gotten into you, Abra? And while you're explaining, you might include the reason why Vincent didn't meet me this morning at his club, as he promised."

"Damn you," she fumed, almost speechless in the presence of his calmly pretended innocence.

"I've no doubt but that will be tended to in due time," he responded drily. "In the meanwhile, I'd like an explanation."

He stood, staring down at her with steely eyes. She looked up at them, then turned away before she could allow herself to wonder at how they could unsettle her so.

She replied to his questions by shoving her hand into her pocket and pulling out the letter.

"Here," she said as she thrust it toward him, "this is what your damned greed has done."

His eyes lingered for a moment on her angry expression before he tore them away, taking the crumpled sheet of paper she held out to him and scanning the words quickly.

"You had to take it, didn't you?" she went on, accusing him, filled with anger. "Even after you promised, even when you knew that Papa and I would be suspect. Well, you'll have to give it back. I won't let you buy yourself a life of ease with my father's blood."

She started to rise, but he put his hand to her shoulder, forcing her back to the couch.

"Abra, will you please be quiet?"

He darted a perturbed glance in her direction and then returned to the letter, reading the words once more, slowly:

My dearest Abra,

It pains me to realize that you have, indeed, taken my Tear, after all. And so, in return, I have taken your father. I reluctantly remind you of our conversation of last evening, that the punishment for such sacrilege is beheading. My regard for you is such that I deny custom, deny reason even. I will delay execution until the first day of Ramadan, February 3, giving you the opportunity to redeem Vincent by returning the Tear.

I honestly regret the necessity that has forced me to this extreme. And, as much as I will regret that, too, I will part Vincent from his head if you do not return to me what is mine. I swear to you this is true.

There was no signature, not that one was needed. No

158

wonder Vincent had not met him at the club, Dash thought. They'd probably abducted him as soon as he'd left his house.

"Listen to me, Abra," he said, turning his attention back to the anger he could see seething within her. "I know you think I took the ruby, but I swear to you, I didn't. I left the yacht as soon as I sent you back up to the party."

She shook her head. "I don't believe you," she told him. "If not you, then who?"

He seated himself beside her. "Why would I lie to you?" he asked her softly.

She inched away from him. "Why did you lie to me last night?" she demanded.

He knew immediately what it was she spoke of. His eyes caught and held hers even as he reached out and put his hand to her arm, holding her fast.

"I didn't lie to you last night. I didn't say a word that wasn't absolutely true."

She stared at him silently for a moment, feeling the anger begin to ease as it became edged with doubt. She wanted to believe him, she realized. More than anything else, she wanted that.

"But it had to be you," she insisted, but her voice had grown steadily less strident. "The police came. They searched the house."

"Last night?"

She nodded then, and began, haltingly, to relate the events of the previous night.

"You've got to return it to him, Dash. Don't you see? If you don't, he'll kill Papa," she finished, her voice grown unsteady as she looked up to him, her eyes pleading and starting to fill with tears. "He means it when he says he'll kill Papa."

He put his arm around her shoulder and drew her to him as the tears began to stream down her cheeks.

"I swear, Abra, if I had the damn ruby I'd give it to you. If I knew where it was, I'd steal it for you. But I don't."

This time she believed him. And the misery that filled her as she realized he could not provide her with Vincent's ransom was overpowering. She lay with her face against his chest and sobbed, feeling defeated and overwhelmed, and powerless to fight back.

Dash let her cry, not moving, just holding her gently

until the sobs began to ease.

"We could try to reason with him," he suggested softly when he thought she had composed herself enough to hear his words. "We could go to the yacht and try to make him believe we didn't take it."

She pulled herself away from him abruptly, drawing the back of her hand across her cheek. He smiled at her gesture and pulled out his handkerchief and offered it to her.

She took it from him absently and used it to rub away the moisture from her cheeks. "Yes," she said slowly, determination starting to work its way back into her. "We'll go to him. He'll have to believe us." She looked up at the clock on the mantel and stood. "He was to leave this afternoon, Dash," she told him, urgency now filling her voice. "We'll have to hurry." She started for the door.

Dash stood, wondering why he had made the suggestion, knowing it would be fruitless. Even if the sheik's yacht had not already sailed, there was little possibility that Sharify would believe them. It was simply that he could not stand to see her look so defeated, he decided as he strode to the door and opened it for her. Any action at all was better for her than doing nothing and expecting the worst.

Abra stood on the empty wharf and stared out at the expanse of the harbor. Despite the rush of traffic that moved along the water, pushed by brisk autumn breezes, the panorama seemed bleak and empty to her. The sheik's yacht had sailed and taken her father with it as an unwilling passenger. She felt herself shiver with cold and an unbearable weight of emptiness, yet realized herself incapable of movement. She was too numbed to recognize anything beyond the fact that Vincent was gone.

Dash took her arm gently. She seemed not to be aware of his presence, and he stared at her a moment, watched the lock of hair the wind tore from its pins and whipped across her cheek. He oughtn't to have brought her there, he thought. He had known that Sharify would not simply lie waiting, that he would sail with the noon tide.

He pressed his fingers where they held her arm, pulling her away from the wharf's edge and back to Water Street where their carriage waited.

"We can't stay here mourning, Abra, not before we've some good reason to mourn," he told her, his voice crisp and businesslike. "We've work to do."

She looked up at him, her expression surprised at his tone, and he felt a stab of conscience that he'd spoken to her that way, with so little feeling. But he realized that if he did what he wanted to do, if he let her give into her misery and merely offered her comfort, she'd be lost. She needed the distraction of doing something, anything, if she was to manage to work her way through the events of the last day with any kind of sanity.

He pressed her toward the carriage at a brisk pace, and she had little choice but to keep up with him. She maintained her numbed silence as he handed her up to the carriage, and it was not until he'd given the driver her address and settled himself beside her that she spoke.

"Work?" she demanded, as though he'd just spoken a few seconds before.

He was forced to muse on that a bit, trying to remember what he'd last said to her.

"We have to find the ruby and get it back to Sharify," he told her. "He's given us three months' time. It ought to be sufficient."

She turned and stared at him as though he'd gone completely mad.

"But we have no idea who took it, or where it is," she protested weakly.

But Dash was not about to let her give up. "You and Vincent saw the stone shortly after our little debacle with McErlaine, didn't you?" He barely waited for her answering nod before he continued. "You are certain it was the same stone he'd shown you the previous time?"

She nodded once more. "Yes," she replied, her voice tight.

He could see she was forcing a precise control on herself, and was thankful for her slowly returning composure.

"I felt the same strange heat from the stone as that first afternoon, the odd feeling that it contained some inner fire of its own. It was the same stone," she finished decisively.

"And we know the police were at your door some four hours later," Dash went on, almost more to himself than to her. "It would have taken at least an hour and a half, more likely two, to organize the search party, even assuming

161

McErlaine had no problem rousing his superior and convincing him of the likelihood that you or Vincent had lifted the stone. That leaves only about two hours for our unknown thief to have made his way onto the yacht, located and broken into the safe, removed the ruby, and made a completely undiscovered escape. And all that while there were still some fifty guests on board." He looked at her and grinned crookedly. "No mean feat," he told her. "I know. I tried it."

He saw her make an effort to return the smile, and despite the fact that the expression that emerged was hardly amused, he appreciated her try.

"Now, I want you to think. Did you see or hear anything in the last few hours you were on the yacht? Did any of the other guests act differently, out of character from the way you'd have expected them to behave? Can you remember anything, anything at all, that might help us?"

Mental images of the other guests passed through Abra's mind.

"You really don't think it might have been one of the others?" she murmured, obviously not receptive to the thought.

"Anything is possible, Abra," he told her. "Don't dismiss anything simply because it seems unlikely on the surface. Now think."

Obediently she did as he bid her, musing silently, replaying the events of the previous evening in her mind as the carriage rumbled through the late-afternoon traffic and finally drew to a stop. Dash stepped out wordlessly, reaching up and helping her down and walking her to the door without any attempt to interrupt her.

"There's nothing," she said emptily as he knocked at the door.

He turned to face her. "There is, Abra. There has to be. Maybe it's there, but you simply don't know how to interpret it," he told her as Hemmings opened the door to admit them.

The butler stood aside silently as they entered, his bemusement at Abra's pained expression obvious.

"Is there something I can bring you, miss?" he asked solicitously, daring an accusing glance in Dash's direction.

"Miss Beaumont could stand a bit of brandy just now, Hemmings," Dash told him without showing notice of the

162

glance. "And something to eat. In the library."

Then he marshaled Abra through the hall and into the mahogany and leather room that had been Vincent's domain.

Abra unfastened the buttons of her coat with unfeeling fingers, looking around the room as a stranger might, a stranger with an intimate knowledge of the man who had spent so many hours there. She stared at the empty desk, at the small collection of Italian bronzes that decorated the table behind it. He's never coming back, she thought in mute misery as she sank into a chair.

Dash saw the signs, the damp swell of tears in her eyes and the trembling fingers, and he moved to her quickly, helping her off with her coat, then holding out the snifter of brandy Hemmings brought for her.

"We'll find it, Abra," he whispered to her gently as he pushed the glass into her hands. "And we'll get Vincent back."

He helped her to hold the glass steady as she took a tentative sip, and watched the color slowly begin to seep back into her cheeks as the alcohol worked its numbing path through her. He drew up a chair to face hers, seated himself, and stared directly at her.

"Now, start from the moment Sharify opened the safe last night, Abra," he told her evenly. "Tell me all of it, no matter how insignificant. Just tell me everything you remember happening."

She took one more swallow of the brandy, this one far larger than the first, apparently needing the strength it gave her. Then she began to talk, her voice flat and emotionless as she began once again, this time aloud, to replay the events of the preceding evening.

She'd just reached the point where Flynt had proposed his search of the house and Vincent's conditional acceptance when Hemmings returned, bearing a tray of sandwiches, a pot of strong tea for Abra, and a whiskey and soda for Dash, as well as a plate of dark spice cake. Dash interrupted her as she paused for breath, and she turned startled eyes to him at the sound of his voice, for he'd not said a word since she'd begun.

But it was to the butler that he spoke, turning to where Hemmings placed the tray on a table beside them and bent to pour Abra's tea.

"Hemmings," he said abruptly, without preamble or explanation, "please tell me what you remember of the police visit last evening."

Hemmings's brow furrowed at the request and he turned to Abra, apparently for leave to ignore the request. But she only nodded to him, and he returned his glance to Dash's expectant one.

"They arrived about three forty-five in the morning, sir, making a good deal of noise at the door. When I finally got there, I was surprised they hadn't roused the neighbors and was quite put out."

He went on, his monotone somehow managing to convey his distaste at being forced to repeat so unpleasant an episode, but obedient to the request. He seemed to be making an effort to recall it all precisely.

When he'd finished, Dash thanked him, and obviously relieved to be done with the matter, Hemmings left the room. Dash leaned to the table with the food, lifted the plate of sandwiches, and brought it to Abra, his expression thoughtful.

"Is there something there?" she asked him hopefully, her expression tentative.

When she made no move toward the food, he lifted one of the sandwiches and held it out to her.

"Have you eaten anything at all today, Abra?" he asked. "You look pale."

She pushed his hand away. "I'm not hungry," she told him, her tone grown sharp.

"Take it," he told her, his voice firm. "And tell me once more, what happened when Flynt mentioned the search."

She scowled as she took the sandwich he held to her, and repeated it all once more, keeping her eyes on his.

"Hemmings's version is almost identical," he murmured thoughtfully as he reached for a sandwich and began to chew at it with a distracted hunger.

"Of course it is," she snapped at him. "That's how it happened."

He looked at the sandwich that she held, untouched, in her hand.

"Eat it, Abra," he directed.

She stared at him in defiance for a long moment, her eyes telling him that he could not make her do anything she didn't want to do, until it became apparent to her that he had no intention of going on until she'd complied and done as he directed. She took an angry bite, and chewed it with exaggerated force.

"There," she muttered angrily, "does that satisfy you?"

He smiled, apparently placated. He took another sandwich, and as he ate, he spoke slowly.

"Think what Vincent said, Abra. About McErlaine. You and Hemmings recall the words almost identically, so it must be close to verbatim."

She stared at him thoughtfully, not quite understanding.

"What if Vincent wasn't simply baiting the inspector," Dash went on. "What if he had a suspicion that McErlaine had really taken the Tear and intended to magically find it here, thereby proving his long-held contention that your father was a jewel thief?"

Abra's eyes grew round as she considered his words.

"You mean you think it was McErlaine who took the stone, meaning to use it to implicate Papa. And when he couldn't do as he intended, because Papa had Flynt accompany him, he simply kept it?"

"Well, it makes sense, doesn't it?" he asked. "More sense, at least, than anything else I can come up with."

She nodded and took another bite of her sandwich, realizing as she ate that she really was quite hungry.

"What do we do?" she asked.

He smiled, and this time was rewarded with an answering smile from her. "We go to the inspector and pay him a pleasant little visit, I think," he suggested.

"Now?" Abra asked.

He shrugged. "No time like the present."

Abra jumped to her feet.

"Aren't you forgetting something, Miss Beaumont?" he called after her as she moved toward the door.

She turned around to face him, her head cocked to one side.

He replied by pointing to the chair where her coat lay, and to the half-eaten sandwich still in her hand. She moved back to the chair, retrieved her coat, and donned it, transferring the sandwich from hand to hand as she thrust her arms into the sleeves.

"Well," she demanded when she had done. "Surely you don't intend to simply sit there?"

He grinned at her with tolerant good humor.

"No," he replied. "Surely that would be unthinkable."

It was not as easy as they thought it would be. The desk sergeant they addressed at the precinct house informed them that the inspector was not at work that afternoon, and he refused to deliver up McErlaine's home address. He directed them upstairs, to Flynt's office, when they made the inquiry, and they had little option but to oblige. They turned to the stairs, aware of the sergeant's contemplative stare.

When they entered Flynt's office, they found the man distracted and obviously harassed. He seemed quite startled to see Abra.

"Miss Beaumont," he said, moving out from behind his cluttered desk to greet her. He looked at Dash expectantly.

"This is Mr. Thorne," she murmured, then paused in confusion.

But Dash seemed unshaken. He offered Flynt his hand. "Dashiel Thorne," he said easily, completing the introduction, "a friend of both Mr. Beaumont and his daughter, as well as their legal representative." He stared steely-eyed at Flynt, who seemed completely flustered at this last bit of information.

Flynt took the offered hand warily. "I hope this has nothing to do with the unfortunate occurrence last evening," he ventured.

"I'm under the impression that the unfortunate occurrence, as you call it, sir, took place in the early hours of this morning," Dash responded, pleased, as his attack seemed to further unsettle Flynt. "A most uncivilized hour," he finished, his tone terse.

"Yes, yes, it was unpleasant. But our apologies were given Mr. Beaumont. It was all, as I told him, an unfortunate mistake." Flynt looked at Dash, evaluating. "I hope Mr. Beaumont is contemplating no action. That would indeed be unpleasant."

Abra stared at Dash, surprised at his fabrication, wondering what he hoped to obtain by lying, by trying to bully the policeman. But she didn't interfere.

"Yes, I suppose that it would be unpleasant, especially for your department," Dash mused aloud. "The courts, I believe, take a dim view of foundationless searches."

166

"I assure you, Mr. Thorne, Mr. Beaumont quite agreed—"

Dash waved a hand, cutting him off. "As matters stand, sir, I have not come to address the matter of last evening. Miss Beaumont and I have need to speak with Inspector McErlaine. We came here to find him or, if he's not here, to obtain his address."

Flynt heaved a sigh of obvious relief and chanced a weak smile. "I don't mind telling you both that this matter has been one of great embarrassment to me personally. I've spent a long and very tedious day trying to explain the matter to my superiors." He looked at Abra, his expression pleading, telling her that he'd paid for his mistake by having been forced to remain at his desk well beyond his usual hour, and that after a night of very little sleep.

She believed his distress was real. There were dark circles beneath his eyes, and his skin had an unwholesomely greyish hue.

"I assure you that I commiserate with your distress, inspector," she told him softly. "But as to Mr. McErlaine . . ."

Flynt seemed to cringe at the continued use of McErlaine's name. "That man has been no end of trouble to me. I told him, if he didn't quit with his nonsense in regard to your father, Miss Beaumont, he'd find himself before a board of inquiry and dismissed before he knew what happened to him. And that's just what happened this morning. Not that he wasn't aware that it was coming. I always knew the man had no courage. He didn't even appear at the hearing. I suppose I didn't expect much else from him." He frowned, then brightened quickly. "But he was summarily dismissed, in any event." He smiled weakly at Abra. "I hope that is some small satisfaction to you, Miss Beaumont, for the distress you've suffered."

Abra turned to Dash, feeling steadily more perplexed, but he kept his attention on Flynt.

"Under the circumstances, I hope it will not transgress any of your regulations for you to give us his home address," Dash said, as though the information Flynt had given them was received with absolutely no surprise. "I'm sure Mr. Beaumont will be thankful for whatever aid you offer us in this matter," he added, implying that lack of cooperation might incur unpleasant repercussions.

167

But Flynt was only too happy to comply. He hastened back to his desk, pulled a file folder from an open drawer, and leafed through it quickly.

"I'm sure such a small matter is perfectly within your rights under the circumstances, Mr. Thorne," he said as he reached for a piece of paper to scribble down the address. "And please convey my personal apologies once more to Mr. Beaumont," he finished as he handed the slip to Dash and ventured a hopeful smile in Abra's direction.

"I don't understand," Abra murmured to Dash as they hurried along the hall away from Flynt's office. "He acted as if the whole thing were a regrettable mistake, as if a robbery had never happened."

"Sharify, it would seem, is not anxious to broadcast the news that his symbol of power has been stolen, Abra," Dash told her as he took her arm. "It makes one wonder how important it is to him, after all."


It was an ill-kept house on Horatio Street to which Flynt's address brought them. It was a large structure that had doubtless seen better times, but they were long past now. The house had a seriously ill-used look about it, the brick in need of pointing, the window frames looking as though they welcomed winter winds rather than repulsing them, the door in dire need of paint. But it might have maintained some tinge of its former haughtiness had not the final indignity been done to it. It had been broken into single-room divisions, in which lonely people with not much money lived out the free hours of their existences in solitude, clinging desperately to their feeble hold on respectability. The house seemed to mourn for them.

Abra felt a bit awed by it, in a way she had not been by the rather more impressive presence of the city's arm of law enforcement. She shivered slightly as she looked out of the coach at it, wishing she had not had to come.

"What shall we do, Dash?" she asked, her voice a near whisper. "What can we say to him?"

Dash took her hand and held it for a moment, then leaned toward her and kissed her gently on the lips. He felt her lips tremble beneath the pressure of his, and wished there were time, wished the circumstances were different. He pulled away from her abruptly.

168

"Whatever comes to mind at the moment, Abra," he told her calmly. Then he grinned. "It seemed to work well enough with the police."

"It did at that," she agreed, and she mused on the ease with which he'd been able to bully Inspector Flynt. "But then, I suppose you've had a good deal more experience dealing with them than I have."

He ignored the note of accusation in her tone and helped her down from the carriage, then up to the front door where he made use of a tarnished brass knocker.

The landlady who greeted them was grey, a pasty-faced woman sporting a dingy gingham apron with voluminous pockets. She stared out at them with a suspicion that was quickly tempered as she noticed their clothing and the carriage that stood waiting for them at the curb. If nothing else, she was obviously a woman who respected the trappings of wealth. The suspicion, however, once again replaced the respect when Dash asked for McErlaine.

"The copper?" she asked, making no attempt to hide her distaste. "What'll you be wantin' him for?"

"A small private matter," Dash replied evasively with a smile as his hand moved forward to hers, offering the expected tip for her cooperation.

She pocketed the bill in her apron with a display of surprising professionalism, not even bothering to inspect its denomination, as though she knew she could not be cheated in the exchange. She smiled benignly as she stood back allowing them to enter.

"Well, if it's Patty Mac you'll be seekin', you might follow me up to his room," she told them when they stood inside the dim entry hall.

She turned to the stairs without looking to see if they followed, took the front of her skirt in hand in a manner that implied the act was an intrusion on her time, and began to climb.

Abra mounted the stairs directly behind her, trying not to show her curiosity at the dark-painted, stained, green walls, at the thick smells of cabbage and onions and fish that lingered in the still air, mementoes of meals consumed long past. She followed the woman to the end of the corridor on the second floor, her own footsteps and those of Dash behind her seeming terribly loud in her ears.

"Well, here 'tis," the landlady announced as she pulled a

169

large key ring from her pocket.

"Shouldn't we knock?" Abra asked tentatively.

But the woman only smirked at her, as though delighted with her own, superior, knowledge. She waited for a moment before answering, as though for the simple effect, then fitted the key into the lock as she spoke.

"Don't matter none," she told them as she turned the key in the lock with a solid click. "Ye've come just a wee bit too late." She pushed open the door. "He packed up his belongin's and was gone early this mornin'."

Abra stared in at a small, virtually bare furnished room. It was obvious no one lived there any longer. McErlaine, it seemed, had flown, and there was not a doubt in her mind that he'd taken the Tear with him.

## Chapter Eleven

The landlady seemed entirely satisfied with Abra's numbed reaction to the sight of the bare-looking room. She grinned pleasantly.

"I guess I'll be needin' to find a new tenant now. You folks wouldn't be interested, now, would ye?"

Dash ignored her, moving past both her and Abra, entering the room and staring at the bare table, the single straight chair, and the bare mattress and single, thin pillow. He walked across the room, pulling open the closet door to stare at the spotted back wall, the few empty hangers that were its sole occupants. He turned back to the landlady, then pointed to a sealed, bolted trunk that stood in temporary grandeur by the empty wall behind the door.

Apparently the woman decided his dollar had earned something, because she relented. "It's his," she told them. "It's to be sent on to him."

Dash grinned slightly as he moved to the trunk, kneeling to inspect the label stuck conspicuously to the top. Then he straightened, and putting his hand to his pocket, retrieved another bill, which he slipped neatly into the waiting hand of the landlady.

"It was very kind of you to be so cooperative, ma'am," he told her as he crossed the room and took Abra's arm. He propelled her through the door.

The woman smiled once more, this time with genuine warmth. "If there's anythin' else I can do for you, sir?" she suggested hopefully, pulling the door closed behind her as she followed them along the length of the hall to the stairs.

* * *

"A trunk with a shipping label," Abra mused when they were once more settled in the moving carriage. "That tells us where he's gone."

Dash nodded. "More than that," he replied. "It also tells us he definitely has the ruby."

Abra offered him a confused expression in return for that bit of news, and he obliged.

"Why else would he run, Abra?"

She nodded agreement, then turned away from him, staring out the window of the carriage at the evening darkness. "Knowing that he's gone to France doesn't feel like it's bringing us any closer to getting Papa back," she murmured.

Her voice had grown hoarse, she realized, and she knew the numbness was leaving her. The startling and unpleasant realities the day had brought were closing in on her, and she wasn't sure she knew how she was going to face them.

Dash put his arm to her shoulders and pulled her close to him. At first she thought to resist, but then realized she didn't want to, nor did she have the strength. She let him draw her to him and put her head against his chest, needing the comfort of his body beside her more desperately than she knew.

"We'll find McErlaine," he told her, his words confident. "And we'll get Vincent back. The only thing we can't do is to give up now."

The words came to her in a rumble, reverberating in his chest, the sound low and steady. Cling to him, a voice inside her told her. If you don't you'll lose yourself.

She stayed as she was, silent and unmoving, grateful for the warmth that flowed from him, until she felt the carriage draw to a halt.

"You're home, Abra," he whispered gently, and she sat up, hating to pull herself away from him.

She looked into his eyes and knew she could not face returning to the house alone. "Stay here, Dash," she whispered. "At least a little while. I can't face it without him."

He answered with a nod, then climbed out and helped her, putting his hand to her waist to keep her from falling, seeming to sense the fragility she felt within herself and honoring it with the care with which he held her.

172

Hemmings, too, could sense her unease as he took her coat. His eyes grew sympathetic.

"Shall I hold dinner for Mr. Beaumont, miss?" he asked her, unaware of the sudden, sharp pain his words brought her until he saw it mirrored in her expression and then becoming bewildered as to the cause.

"No," Dash broke in firmly, answering for her. "Mr. Beaumont has been forced to take a short trip, Hemmings. He'll be away for a few weeks."

Hemmings seemed a bit put out by Dash's manner, by the way he seemed to be taking control, but a glance at Abra convinced him something was indeed wrong.

"I suppose we might just as well have dinner now, Hemmings," she murmured softly, barely able to force the words out. "Mr. Thorne will be staying."

Then she turned away, and he had the feeling she was hiding her tears from him.

But when she turned back to face Dash, Abra seemed to have once more regained control.

"A drink before dinner?" she asked him, and she gestured towards the library, pretending that it had been just another day, that nothing out of the ordinary had occurred. She managed to smile, a hard, brittle little smile that seemed to hurt her lips.

Dash stared at her silently rather than answering. Then he took her arm firmly with his hand. "I think you need some food, Abra," he told her softly as he led her to the dining room.

She'd watched as he ate, only picking at her own food. Then, when he'd suggested he leave her for the night, she had offered him a brandy in an obvious effort to keep him there, to keep from being alone. And now he sat sipping brandy and watching her as she prowled around the room, touching the objects on Vincent's desk fleetingly, then moving to his bookshelves and reading titles, but backing away a bit too quickly, as though any continued contact with her father's belongings might prove painful.

"Abra, sit down," he told her firmly.

She turned to face him, a look of surprise passing quickly on her features and then disappearing.

He tried to look reassuring. "What you're doing looks

173

suspiciously like mourning to me. You've no time for that, and while we're discussing the matter, no one to mourn. Vincent is alive, and I intend to make sure he stays that way."

"Can you?" she demanded softly.

He stood, leaving the glass of brandy on a table as he crossed the room to her. "Yes, damn it, I can. It's my fault the two of you were involved in any of this in the first place. Do you really think I could live with myself if I didn't see him back here?"

She stared at him mutely, thinking how much she had wanted to put the blame all on him that morning, how she'd been so sure he'd taken the stone. She'd been wrong, terribly wrong. And it suddenly occurred to her that Dash was wrong, as well.

"You just happened along," she whispered to him, not wanting to say the words, not wanting to admit it, not even to herself. "But he would probably have tried anyway, even without you. I saw it coming. I just didn't know what it was at the time."

With the words came the thought that she should have known, that she should somehow have stopped him, should have kept it all from happening. The press of her own responsibility seemed more than she could bear.

She fell into his arms and began to sob softly, not really caring now why or how things had happened as they had, just feeling terribly lost and knowing only that she needed him.

He held her gently, putting his fingers to her hair and stroking it, wanting to soothe her, to comfort her. But then, when she lifted her face to his, he realized he wanted something far more.

He put his hands to her cheeks, wiping away the dampness with his thumbs, lowering his face to hers with a deliberate slowness, stretching the feeling of expectancy until he knew he could no longer bear it. He wanted her, wanted to feel the magic he'd felt when he'd made love to her, wanted to possess her, make her understand that he would protect her, that he'd walk through hell for her, if only she'd trust and accept him. And then he kissed her, his lips pressing hers hungrily, his hands snaking around her waist, holding her close to him.

All Abra knew was that she wanted him, that she needed

174

him to make her forget everything, at least for a little while, except that she could lose herself to him. She parted her lips to him, tasting the brandy he'd drunk on his lips, then his darting tongue, and feeling the melting fire begin within her.

He released her suddenly and drew back. "This isn't the wisest thing for me to do, Abra," he said softly, hating every word, but knowing he had to say them. "You're vulnerable right now. Later, you may think I've taken advantage of you." He stared at her, wondering if she'd agree, not quite sure what he'd do if she did.

But she shook her head slowly. "Don't leave me tonight, Dash," she whispered, her throat catching with the thought that he might. "I couldn't face being alone tonight."

He needed nothing more. He wrapped his arms around her waist and pulled her close, felt the lithe pliancy of her body beneath his fingers, the growing warmth that surged through her. He moved his hands to her hair, releasing the pins that held it, letting the glowing red-tinged gold fall to her shoulders and down her back. Then he pressed his lips to hers.

He lifted her, and she allowed that, wrapping her arms around his neck, not really caring that one of the servants might see them as they emerged from the library into the hall, aware only that he was climbing the stairs with her in his arms, that he was taking her to her bed. The only thought that seemed real to her was that he would share it with her, that she would not have to face the horrors of the night alone.

"Which room is yours, Abra?" he asked as he reached the top of the stairs.

She directed him, feeling a tinge of guilt about what it was that she was about to do, there, in her very proper, very ladylike bedroom. But then he opened the door and walked through, and kissed her once more with an ardent urgency that made her forget those thoughts, forget everything but the feel of his arms and his lips. He kicked the door closed behind them, then crossed the room and lay her on her bed.

He stood back and stared at her for a moment. "You are the most beautiful woman I've ever known, Abra," he told her, his voice husky.

She smiled in reply, then sat up and began, quite determinedly, to unfasten her buttons.

Her clothes lay on the floor in a discarded heap. He'd watched her shed them, unmoving, unblinking, and she had felt his eyes on her as though they could touch her. She'd felt her naked flesh heat beneath the nearly palpable touch of his eyes. And now she lay on the bed and watched him as he had watched her.

Somehow, although she did not quite understand why, the sight of his body, of the hard, rounded muscles of his chest and shoulders, the taut hardness of his belly, had aroused the liquid fire in her. It was a mystery to ponder, that the sight of his body could bring about this change in her, just as his touch, his kisses did. But she left that mystery for another time, not wanting to think, refusing even that thought lest it lead her to others, less pleasant.

He came to her, moving naked to her across the room, his arousal yet another unponderable secret, one that filled her with a heady expectancy.

When he bent to kiss her, she reached up to him, pulling him down to her. She surprised him with her insistency, but it was a welcome surprise, for he smiled as he brought his hands to touch her, and then pressed his lips to the warm flesh of her neck and her ear. She felt the darting probe of his tongue on the concavity of her ear, and shivered with the suddenness of her longing, pressing herself to him, eager for his touch. She spread herself beneath him, wondering even as she moved what power within her directed her movements, what sudden creature had sprung up to govern her with such authority.

She cried out softly as he surged into her, and she dug her fingers into his back as she moved herself to him. She had wanted him to stay with her that evening for all the wrong reasons, for comfort, to allay her fear and her loneliness, but that was past. She loved him, she realized, and nothing was more important than this simple act, this losing of herself to him, this pained, startling urgency that swept through her. She loved him, and nothing that could happen would ever change that fact.

She let the knowledgeable creature that had come to life within her sweep through her and control her, the creature

176

who apparently had a certain, instinctual knowledge of how to please him, her belly to his, her lips and tongue softly wet and warm against the warmth of his neck. She could feel the thick, hard thud of his pulse beneath her tongue, and knew only that it matched her own, hot and strong, reverberating in her own ears as his filled her touch. She gave herself up to the tide of it, letting it rise within her, not caring where it led her as long as it took him with her. Like a tidal wave, pushing everything in its course aside, the anger and the pain, the uncertainties and the suspicions that had seemed to rule her since that horrible moment when she'd first taken Sharify's note in her hand were gone, swept aside in the heady ebb and flow of her body's tides. Thought gave way to far more primitive, more primal needs, and she gave herself over to them, the creature inside her knowing that only there could she mute the hurt, overcome the uncertainties, and find some strength to survive what was to come. For that moment she was lost, adrift in the tiny world that was enclosed by his embrace, and needing nothing more.

She felt her body straining to his, her flesh melding to his, as though trying to make him feel the same need, the same urgent pressure to lose himself in her that she felt to find herself in him. The flow grew ever headier, the force ever stronger, until it seemed to shatter within her, and the creature that governed her tremblingly arched her body to his as the release swept through her, leaving her somehow lost and feeling exposed in a way she'd never felt before.

For a few moments neither of them moved. They lay, still and silent, not wanting to lose the feeling, not yet willing to relinquish the shattering intimacy. Abra was conscious of the slowly abating thud of her heart as she looked up into his eyes. He was still, staring down at her, his breath warm against her cheek. With his arms holding hers, he slowly lowered his head, his lips finding hers with a gentleness that surprised him. She freed her hand and moved it to the dark lock that had fallen across his brow, pushing it aside before softly caressing his jaw, then running her finger along the long, straight plane of his nose. He moved himself to her side, taking her hand in his and pressing it to his lips.

There were a hundred things he wanted to say to her, he realized, but he knew the most important ones could not

177

yet be told, however much he wanted to say them. And so he smiled down at her, then lay back against the lace-edged pillows, pulling her close in his arms, contenting himself with the feel of her body beside his, the weight of her head pillowed on his shoulder, the silken shimmer of her hair in the dim lamplight.

She pressed her cheek against the dark mat of his chest and inhaled with a weary contentedness.

"You smell like spice," she told him softly as she kissed the damp hair and tasted the warmth of his flesh.

He ran his hand lazily along the side of her hip and down her thigh.

"And you taste like heaven," he replied.

She smiled at that, and let her eyes drift closed.

"I think I love you, Dashiel Thorne," she told him softly as she began to drift toward sleep.

He hugged her close and pressed his lips to the fiery golden halo of her hair, waiting until the steady, even cadence of her breathing told him she was asleep.

"And I know I love you, Abra Beaumont," he murmured softly, knowing she did not hear the words, but feeling the need to say them, nonetheless. They were, he realized, painful for him. Because he had little doubt that, when she learned how he had used her and Vincent, she would not want to hear them, or anything else, from him. He'd used them, and now, because of what he'd done, Vincent's life was in danger. No, he had no illusions that she would welcome him to her bed once she knew the whole of it.

He moved his lips once more to her head, inhaling the sweet fragrance of her hair as he brushed it with them, thinking painful thoughts. She needed him now, he realized, and he would have her, at least temporarily, until that need had been filled.

And after it was over, he mused, he'd have the pleasure and the pain of the memory.


Abra was alone when she awoke.

Her head felt as though she were moving it through a heavy mist, as though she had been drugged the night before and the effects were still not quite worn off. She slowly peered around the room, its emptiness making her

178

feel empty, too. The fact that Dash was not there felt like desertion to her.

She turned her head into the pillow, burying her face into the white linen, telling herself not to think.

But it wouldn't do, and she turned back to face the frilly white lace of the bedding and the curtains, the pale, flowered wallpaper, the small mirrored dressing table with its slight burden of tiny covered porcelain boxes, her silver-handled combs and brushes, a crystal bottle of her perfume. With the exception of the porcelain patch boxes, a collection that had been her mother's, she had chosen everything in the room, had been pleased with it all.

Until that moment, she'd been pleased with it all. It was a virginal room, she told herself dully, fussy and perfect. A man would find no place in it. And, suddenly, neither did she.

Hardly a virgin any longer, she told herself as she threw back the covers and swung her feet to the floor. There was a bitterness to the thought that surprised her, and then she realized what she had done the night before, how she'd begged him to stay with her, to make love to her. No wonder he'd gone. What would he want with a woman who forced herself on him, who begged him to lie with her?

She thought what it was he must now think of her, and the realization left a bitterness on her tongue that would not subside. She'd demeaned herself to him, lowered herself in his eyes to a point where he would rather steal silently from her room in the morning rather than remain and face her.

Everything she touched, everything she did, had been disastrously wrong. And now she was left alone, without her father and without Dash. She felt the bitterness grow in her until it seemed it would overwhelm her.

She drew a bath that was far too hot, nearly scalding herself as she entered, ignoring the hurt as she scrubbed furiously at her reddened skin. Despite the effort, however, the stain seemed not to fade. It was there, irreparably there, something she would never be able to hide from or ignore.

She dressed with an empty resignation, going down to the dining room feeling as though she were about to face a firing squad. She endured Hemmings's mute stare as she seated herself, telling herself she deserved nothing better. She kept her eyes on the tea he poured for her, not daring to look up and face him with the question that burned her tongue, instead trying to hide it under a mask of apparent indifference. Finally, she found she could hold it in no longer.

"Did Mr. Thorne leave any message for me?"

It came as a surprise to her that her voice sounded entirely normal to her ears, even a bit distracted, as though the answer held nothing for her. But her heart knew, and she could feel it thumping loudly in dreaded preparation for an answer that would confirm what she'd thought when she'd wakened and found him gone, that there was no message, that he'd left her as wordlessly, as indifferently, as he'd leave a whore. After all, she told herself, he had paid for his night with her. Her interference had cost him the stone. Indeed, he'd paid highly for the privilege of her bed.

She was concentrating on the contents of her cup, and so did not notice Hemmings's bewildered stare.

"Yes, miss. He asked that I tell you he had several errands to do this morning, and that he'd return sometime this afternoon. He hoped you'd be here then."

Well, there was something at least, a voice within her said hopefully. But she could only respond to it by thinking how cold it seemed, how businesslike. And the last, the request that she remain in the house, seemed suspiciously like a command. It didn't make her feel very much better.

She waved away the offer of breakfast, ignoring Hemmings's reminder that she'd eaten almost no dinner the previous evening, and watched him as he cleared away the trays of food that littered the sideboard. When he'd completed the task and left her alone, she sat staring down into the amber liquid in her cup, thinking miserable thoughts.

What happened last night must not happen again, she told herself firmly. I will not give him any further reason to disdain me. She thought briefly of what he'd said the previous evening about his feeling of responsibility for Sharify's abduction of her father. That's all that interests him, she told herself, the easing of his conscience. When this business is done, when we've gotten Papa back, he'll be freed of whatever guilt he feels and he'll simply leave. Not that she would be able to blame him when it happened. She'd called him a thief and a liar, thought him even worse. And when the time came, he would leave, and she would have no way to hold him, no desire to hold him, if it was against his will. At least, she told herself, I can behave with dignity and some sense of pride until he's decided he's free.

Dignity and pride. The words sounded hollow and meaningless to her. What did she care for dignity or pride when her heart was breaking?


"Under the circumstances, your not gaining possession of the Tear for them, I'm afraid my employers feel a strong disinclination to stand the rather exorbitant cost of your expenses for this little fiasco, Dash."

"Expenses be damned." Dash was leaning forward on his chair, his body angled toward the eternally disorganized desk. "What about Beaumont?"

Charles Nevin cleared his throat. "On that matter, too, they feel they have no culpability and therefore no responsibility.

"I don't think you or they understand, Charles." Dash could almost taste the bitterness of his words on his tongue. "Sharify has taken Vincent Beaumont. And he intends to have his head on a plate." He paused for emphasis for a second. "Quite literally."

Charles Nevin ventured a benign, commiserating smile. "A situation I find as painful as do you, I can assure you, Dash."

"Spare me."

Nevin shrugged. "As you like," he replied, his tone complacent. "All I can say to you is, my superiors are not totally pleased with the outcome of the venture. They are no longer willing to expend any more time or energy, and most decidedly, any more money on it. Your expenses have been quite substantial, I'm sure I hardly need remind you."

"Your superiors be damned," Dash retorted caustically. "It was with their blessing that I approached Beaumont in the first place. They agreed he was the only man available who had the resources, the skills, and social position which this little venture required. Without him, I'd never have been able to lay my hands on plans of the yacht, never have been able to find a fairly risk-free way to get in and get out. And without his apparent friendship with Sharify, we'd never have found the damned vault, even if we'd known where every nail and bolt in the damned boat was located."

Nevin cleared his throat. He was a bit disturbed by Dash's use of profanity, but apparently decided it politic not to mention it.

"You mean his and his daughter's friendship with Sharify, don't you, Dash?" he asked, then sat forward, adjusting his glasses, waiting for some reaction.

Dash leaned back into the chair, none of the tenseness leaving his face, the anger he felt growing more and more personal. "Yes, damn it. His and his daughter's," he muttered with intense ire.

"And for all the skill and information with which Beaumont provided you, you still let the stone slip through your fingers."

Dash colored. "I had no other choice."

"You had a choice. You simply made the wrong one. You chose to keep the woman and lose the Tear," Nevin went on, his voice softly vicious. "As I said, my superiors are not happy. But they are willing to let matters ride. They would have preferred to have the Tear at their disposal, but they will satisfy themselves that Sharify no longer has it. What they will not do, my dear Dash, is help you steal it and see it returned to a power-hungry man who openly flaunts his disdain for them. They are not happy, but they will live with matters as they stand. And if Vincent Beaumont's head is the price, they will regretfully pay it."

"*They* will pay it?" Dash roared.

Nevin only nodded emotionlessly.

Dash pushed himself to his feet. "Your superiors and I got that man into this. If they can wash their hands of their responsibility for that, I can't." He moved toward the door.

"Dash."

Dash stopped with his hand on the knob and turned. Nevin's brow was lifted and the expression made him look like an inquisitive owl.

"I feel it only fair to warn you that my superiors will not appreciate any attempts you might take that might upset the status quo. And believe me, you will find that they can make your life quite miserable if they so chose. My advice to you, as an old friend, is to go about your life and forget all this has ever happened."

"And Vincent Beaumont and his daughter?" Dash asked pointedly.

Nevin shrugged. "The victims of unfortunate circumstance. It's not exactly pleasant, but it can't be helped."

Dash stared at the other man, and he felt sickened at what he saw.

"I have only a few words for you and your superiors, old friend." He managed to make the last two words sound like profanity. Nevin winced as he heard them spoken. "The lot of you," Dash finished, "can rot in hell."

## *Chapter Twelve*

Dash merely glanced at the sign beside the dark mahogany doors at number twenty-two Broadway. White Star Passenger Line, the brass letters proclaimed with admirable distinction, the letters not too large, the brass brightly shiny. Very British, very proper.

The liveried doorman sped past him and held the door for him to enter, his white gloves leaving the polished brass surface of the elaborate knobs unmarred and brilliant in the morning sunshine.

The portly man behind the screening desk looked up and inspected him for a moment, then seemed satisfied with what he saw, for he stood quickly and moved to the low mahogany rail that divided the large office into a sitting area where the less fortunate humbly waited some notice from the carpeted, official-looking office area where large desks surrounded by comfortable chairs accommodated the well-to-do passengers as they booked their staterooms and sipped a very British afternoon whiskey and soda.

"Mr. Grandin will help you, sir," the portly man confided as he led Dash to one of those islands of propriety and respectful service. He held the chair as Dash seated himself. "Might I offer you some refreshment, sir?"

Dash waved him away absently.

"Ah, here's Mr. Grandin now," the receptionist said as he moved away, apparently summoning forth the object of their need by the sheer will of his thoughts.

Mr. Grandin had suspiciously red, round little cheeks, and a bulbous nose to match. In fact, all of him was fairly bulbous, and he gave the impression of a genial gnome who'd gotten lost one evening on his way back to the forest and had resigned himself to life in the service of the White Star Passenger Line, in return for an occasional bottle of decent brandy.

"And how may I have the pleasure of serving you, sir?" he asked Dash breathily as he seated himself in front of the large desk whose proportions only served to make him seem even smaller and more elfin.

Dash allowed him an absent smile. "Passage to the continent. Two staterooms, please. To sail as soon as possible."

The amiable Mr. Grandin took out a thick folder and flipped through the papers inside.

"Let me see, now. I can give you two lovely staterooms on the *Aurora,* sailing two weeks from tomorrow," he said hopefully.

Dash shook his head. "I'm afraid that's too late, Mr. Grandin. There must be something sooner."

Grandin again consulted his ream of papers. He hummed softly under his breath. "I do have a late cancelation on the *Arcadia,*" he mused half aloud. "But no, that won't do, it's only one stateroom, and you need two."

Dash leaned forward. "When does the *Arcadia* sail?" he demanded.

Grandin pointed to a large board on the far wall that indicated the arrivals and departures of all the line's ships. "Day after tomorrow," he replied without looking, repeating the itinerary like a catechism. "Stopping at Southampton and Lisbon. But you did mention two staterooms, Mr. . . ."

"Thorne," Dash told him. "And if there is only one available, it seems that it will have to do."

"Yes, sir, of course," the small man dithered as he lifted his pen with a flourish and dipped the point into a crystal inkpot. "If I might have the passengers' names?"

Dash smiled for the first time that day. "Mr. and Mrs. Dashiel Thorne," he said slowly.

Grandin lifted a brow, remembering that the original request had been for two, not one, staterooms.

"Mr. and Mrs. Dashiel Thorne," he repeated as he penned the names on a form, then looked back at Dash with the same questioning stare. Dash met it without so much as a movement of the eye, and he turned back to the papers in front of him, while Dash's attention wandered to the arrivals and departures board. "And will Mrs. Thorne be needing accommodation for a servant, a lady's maid?" he asked.

Once more Dash smiled, and this time there was genuine amusement in his eyes. "No. This is to be a honeymoon voyage," he replied, his voice low and conspiratorial. "A man doesn't want a lady's maid along on his honeymoon."

The elfin smile returned to Grandin's face. "Most certainly, Mr. Thorne. I'll see to the arrangements."

He asked a few more questions, noting down Dash's hotel address on the place indicated on his forms with his busy little pen, while Dash contented himself with a further inspection of the neatly lettered list of recent departures on the board on the far wall.

"There is one more thing," he said when Grandin passed the forms and a sizable bank draft to him for his signature.

Grandin tilted his head. "I'm most willing to help if I can, sir," he replied.

Dash smiled amiably and wondered if it could really be so easy to find any trace of McErlaine. "I'm looking for a bit of information about a passenger who left yesterday on the *Mauritania*," he said evenly, staring at the entry on the board. "A Mr. Patrick McErlaine."

Grandin grew doubtful. "It's not our policy to give out any information in regard to our passengers," he replied. "We must, of course, respect their privacy."

"Certainly," Dash agreed willingly. "I wouldn't dream of asking you to do anything indiscreet," he said mildly. "It's just that I was to meet Mr. McErlaine in Marseille at the end of the month. He had some matters to finalize in London first, then was to go on to France. I just wondered if he left as scheduled. Our business, you see, must be concluded before the New Year."

"Combining a bit of business with pleasure?" Grandin asked with a grin that said he entirely understood the inclination. "Well, let me see, I don't suppose that would be considered a real transgression." He removed yet another thick folder from his desk drawer, and once more began to leaf through the papers. "Yes, here it is. Mr. McErlaine took first-class passage on the *Mauritania*, a lucky last-minute booking." He paused. "But, now, this is odd. He's had us arrange direct transfer to the Lisbon,

Marseille packet from Southampton. If he had business in London, why would he do that?"

Dash smiled, satisfied with what he'd learned, not quite believing he'd been so lucky as to stumble onto McErlaine's trail so easily. No wonder the man hadn't appeared at his hearing the previous morning. He'd already boarded the *Mauritania,* taking first class, at that, and been well under way before he'd been dismissed from the service of New York's finest. He obviously had some idea as to what he would do with the ruby, but that was not surprising, for the man was, after all, a policeman. He would know where to market the stone. And he'd obviously determined to begin his new life of wealth with his passage.

"That matter must have gone more smoothly than either of us expected," Dash said easily to Grandin, sweeping away the man's doubts by his manner.

"Of course," Grandin nodded. "Assuming you take the first packet from Lisbon to Marseilles you should arrive only a day or two behind him," he mused, eager to be helpful. "If you wish, I could make the arrangements for you so you won't be bothered with the details in Lisbon."

Dash smiled thankfully. "If you'd be so kind," he agreed, then quickly signed the passage forms as well as the bank draft for the fare. The amount of it was a good deal more than he had expected, and he made some quick mental calculations, considering the hotel and other expenses he'd incurred since he'd come to New York and for which he would now receive no reimbursement, and realizing that the passage would nearly exhaust his current resources. He told himself not to think about that now, that it was one thing he'd have plenty of time to worry about later.

His signatures duly completed, he passed the forms across the desk. Grandin took them, carefully clipping a note to the top to remind him to arrange for the packet, and fussily neatening the edges so that they matched exactly.

"Papers specifying the arrangements for the packet will be waiting for you when you disembark in Lisbon," he said.

"You're most efficient," Dash told him as he rose.

"It's my personal pleasure, as well as that of the White Star Lines," Grandin replied with his rosy elfin grin. He stood, offering his hand. "And may I offer you my sincerest congratulations?" He noticed Dash's questioning look. "On your imminent marriage, I mean," he explained quickly.

Dash reminded himself of what he'd told the man regarding a honeymoon. "Thank you," he replied as Grandin reached across his desk, offering his hand. When Dash took it, he felt some real warmth in the response. "Good day," he said as he turned quickly away.

Grandin called out "Good day," but Dash didn't really hear him. He was too busy contemplating what his new bride would say when she learned of their imminent marriage and impending honeymoon.

In the end, he didn't tell her any of it

The reception he found to greet him when he returned to the house later that afternoon was a good deal cooler than he had anticipated. She was sitting in the front parlor, a formal, elegant room, her head bent over what appeared to him, even from the far side of the room, as a much maltreated piece of needlework.

"Good afternoon," she said evenly, not even lifting her eyes from the needle she was in the midst of threading.

"It seems odd to see you alone in here," he told her. "I went to the library first."

He regretted the words as soon as he'd uttered them. He saw her shoulders tremble a bit, then stiffen. Her fingers had trouble pushing the wool through the eye of the needle, and she was forced to try it twice before she had any success.

"I couldn't face it there," she said, her tone a near whisper. "Not alone."

He took a stop forward, seeing the hurt in her and wanting to comfort it, but stopped when she began again to speak.

"Have you had a pleasant morning?" she asked, her tone once more controlled, her attention now firmly riveted on the task of forcing the needle through the canvas.

He shrugged and started to approach her once more, but paused when he was still several feet away. She was angry with him, he realized, and the only reason he could think of was that he had been right the night before when

188

he'd told her that she might have regrets, that she might feel he had abused her misery and taken advantage of her when she'd been least able to determine what it was she really wanted.

His first instinct was to say something about it, to apologize to her, but then he drew back, angry. Damn it, he told himself, what had happened had certainly been as much of her making as his. She had no right to blame him.

"It was more a fruitful morning than a pleasant one," he replied, his tone as cold as hers.

She looked up, her expression interested now, but fixed. "Fruitful?"

"McErlaine's gone to Marseilles."

She shrugged indifferently. "We already knew that," she said, turning back to the needlework. "From the sticker on the trunk."

He seated himself across from her, staring at her evenly, watching the way she stabbed with her needle, forcing the wool with a vehemence it hardly deserved.

"But now we know when he'll arrive."

She looked toward him once more, this time dropping the canvas and yarn to her lap. "How?" she asked.

"I found a copy of yesterday's papers and looked up the list of sailings. There were only three. And while I was at the White Star Lines booking our passage, I took the chance of inquiring about him. He's smart. He took the *Mauritania* to Southampton rather than either direct ship to Marseilles."

She scowled, puzzled, and he explained.

"The *Mauritania*'s faster. Even with the longer packet ride, from Southampton, he'll still make Marseilles before either of the other two boats."

"Then we'll never catch him," Abra said softly, her shoulders sagging in resignation and defeat.

Dash smiled. "I didn't say that. I've booked us passage on the *Arcadia,* day after tomorrow. Direct to Lisbon. We'll be one, at the most two, days behind him."

Her expression grew sharp. "And then what?"

He didn't seem concerned. "I'll see when we arrive." Her puzzled look begged an explanation, and he obliged. "Look," he told her, "there are only so many places you can dispose of a stone, especially a stone as unique as the

189

Tear. We'll simply find some track of McErlaine, figure out where he took it, and from that we'll know whom he intends to sell to. It's not that difficult."

His manner infuriated her, so offhand, so indifferent. "Yes," she told him, "I forgot you can deal with things so easily as they arise." Is that what the night before had been to him, she wondered, just an odd occasion that had arisen to be taken advantage of? "But that's what a thief does, doesn't he? Use circumstances to his advantage?"

His eyes grew hard. "Yes, I suppose it is, Abra," he replied through tight lips.

"And I'm afraid my abilities in that area are not quite enough to be terribly helpful to you."

She said the words very precisely, as though she had to force herself to utter them. He almost heard the thought behind them, that he was a thief, that the whole business was repugnant to her. And the thought came to him that she shouldn't care what he was, that if she felt anything at all for him, she ought to trust him, to accept him as he was.

"You're as much a part of this as am I," he told her. He realized that he sounded cold, but he didn't care.

She looked at him sharply. "More. He's my father."

There it is, he thought. The accusation. That it's my fault, that it wouldn't have happened but for me. The unspoken words rang in his ears, tearing through the silence between them, filling him with anger at her lack of understanding. But in the end, he told himself, she's right. It *is* my fault.

He stood abruptly. "I'll be here to collect you first thing Tuesday morning. See that you're packed and ready." Then he made his way to the door without offering her a backward glance.

Abra watched him leave, and she felt as though he were striking her with each step he took. She'd been right, she thought. She meant nothing to him, nothing more than a warm body the night before, nothing more than a way to the ruby before that. And what he'd told her, all that had been nothing more than a lie. He didn't care about her. All he cared about was relieving his conscience with regard to her father, living up to whatever code of honor thieves subscribed.

She put her head into her hands and told herself to cry,

for there'd be no time for tears later. Later she would have to face him, be with him, do whatever she could to help him find the ruby. But somehow there were no tears within her and she sat dry-eyed, unable to find comfort from the hard ball of hurt that seemed to have lodged itself inside her.

Dash let himself out, slamming the door behind him. It seemed impossible to him that she could be so close-minded, so generous with her blame, as though she had had nothing to do with anything that had happened, as if he were the only one who ought to feel responsibility. He'd been a fool to allow himself to care about so opinionated, so righteous a woman, he told himself. Especially one who thought him to be nothing better than a common thief.

When the business with Sharify and Vincent was done, he promised himself, he'd be glad to leave, to be rid of her. And his conscience, at least, would be clear. But at the back of his mind was the nagging realization that he really didn't want to forget about her.

His mood was such that he didn't even notice the man approaching the front stoop until they'd brushed shoulders. He darted an angry glance at the other, vaguely recognizing him as Freddy Westmore, and finding the sight of Freddy's pleasant features decidedly unlikable.

"For God's sake, can't you look where you're going?" he snarled as he strode past, leaving Freddy, bewildered, to stare after him for a moment before he turned back to the stairs that led to Abra's front door.

Abra was staring numbly at her empty hands when Hemmings entered.

"Excuse me, miss. Mr. Westmore is here to see you."

"Freddy?" she asked, not at all pleased.

But she nodded and stood, letting the forgotten needlework fall to the floor, and wandered to the far window. When she looked out, she could just see Dash disappearing around the corner, his walk determined and quick, as though he could hardly wait to get away from her.

"Abra."

She turned to face Freddy, and realized that talking to him was the very last thing she wanted to do at that moment.

"How nice of you to call, Freddy," she told him drily. "Is there something you wanted?"

He began to move toward her but stopped when he saw the look she leveled at him.

"I'd thought that you might need someone just now, Abra," he told her slowly.

"And just what is that supposed to mean?" she demanded tartly, turning all her anger with herself and Dash to him, for he was, after all, an easy target.

He seemed bewildered by her ire, but determined, as though he'd made a promise to himself and would not allow it to go unfulfilled.

"There's been a good deal of talk about you and Vincent, Abra," he told her bluntly. "And the sheik."

"Talk? What kind of talk? That Papa and I are jewel thieves? That we've stolen the sheik's damned ruby?" She stared at him unblinkingly, feeling the angry flush that colored her cheeks, but ignoring it.

He seemed unable to stand the weight of her stare and looked down to the polished tips of his shoes.

"Yes, it is pretty much like that," he admitted. He lowered his voice. "And that you allowed the Arab to seduce you."

"Then why have you come here, Freddy?" she demanded. "Aren't you afraid you'll be contaminated? Don't tell me your mother didn't remind you that she'd been right about me all along? Didn't she warn you about me?"

"Abra, please!"

"Didn't she, Freddy?" she insisted. "Didn't she remind you that she had reservations about me and Papa from the start, that rumors must be founded on fact, or they wouldn't be started at all?" She was hurting him and she knew it, and she hated the awareness. He was so totally defenseless, and she was disgusted with herself. But then she told herself that perhaps, in the end, that might just be the kindest thing she could do for him.

He returned his glance to hers. "Yes," he replied, obviously reluctant. "She told me to stay away from you. But I don't care what they're saying about you, Abra. None of it matters. I want you to know that I intend to stand by you. That I still want you to be my wife."

For a moment a feeling of hysteria gripped her and all she could think of was that she wanted to laugh. She couldn't count the number of times she'd thought that if he could only stand on his own, if he'd only act like a

# ---- FREE ----

# BOOK CERTIFICATE

## ZEBRA HOME SUBSCRIPTION SERVICE, INC.

**YES!** Please start my subscription to Zebra Historical Romances and send me my free Zebra Novel along with my first month's Romances. I understand that I may preview these four new Zebra Historical Romances Free for 10 days. If I'm not satisfied with them I may return the four books within 10 days and owe nothing. Otherwise I will pay just $3.50 each, a total of $14.00 (a $15.80 value—I save $1.80). Then each month I will receive the 4 newest titles as soon as they come off the press for the same 10 day Free preview and low price. I may return any shipment and I may cancel this arrangement at any time. There is no minimum number of books to buy and there are no shipping, handling or postage charges. Regardless of what I do, the FREE book is mine to keep.

Name _____
(Please Print)

Address _____ Apt. # _____

City _____ State _____ Zip _____

Telephone ( ) _____

Signature _____
(if under 18, parent or guardian must sign)

Terms and offer subject to change without notice.

---

## MAIL IN THE COUPON
## BELOW TODAY

To get your Free ZEBRA HISTORICAL ROMANCE fill out the coupon below and send it in today. As soon as we receive the coupon, we'll send your first month's books to preview Free for 10 days along with your FREE NOVEL.

GET YOUR FREE GIFT

# ACCEPT YOUR FREE GIFT
# AND EXPERIENCE MORE OF
# THE PASSION AND ADVENTURE
# YOU LIKE IN A
# HISTORICAL ROMANCE

Zebra Romances are the finest novels of their kind and are written with the adult woman in mind. All of our books are written by authors who really know how to weave tales of romantic adventure in the historical settings you love.

Because our readers tell us these books sell out very fast in the stores, Zebra has made arrangements for you to receive at home the four newest titles published each month. You'll never miss a title and home delivery is so convenient. With your first shipment we'll even send you a FREE Zebra Historical Romance as our gift just for trying our home subscription service. No obligation.

## BIG SAVINGS
## AND FREE HOME DELIVERY

Each month, the Zebra Home Subscription Service will send you the four newest titles as soon as they are published. (We ship these books to our subscribers even before we send them to the stores.) You may preview them *Free for 10 days*. If you like them as much as we think you will, you'll pay just $3.50 each and *save $1.80 each month off the cover price. AND* you'll *also get FREE HOME DELIVERY.* There is never a charge for shipping, handling or postage and there is no minimum you must buy. If you decide not to keep any shipment, simply return it within 10 days, no questions asked, and owe nothing.

man, she might possibly fall in love with him. And now he was doing just that, defying his mother, chancing social ostracism for her. Now that it was all too late.

She allowed a hollow little laugh to escape her lips. "Even if I'm a thief, Freddy?" she asked. "Even if what they're saying is true?"

He finally seemed to have worked up the courage to approach her, and he moved quickly, taking her hand before she could pull it away from his grasp.

"It's not true, Abra. I know none of it's true."

"And if it were?" she taunted him. "What then?"

He looked as though she'd struck him. "Please, Abra, don't."

"I need an answer, Freddy. You asked me to marry you. How am I to decide if you don't answer me?" she insisted relentlessly.

He dropped her hand and backed away from her. "It wouldn't matter," he replied after a long, empty silence. "I'd still want you."

His response shocked her, for she'd never given him the credit for any real strength, never given him any credit at all, she realized. She wished she hadn't treated him so cruelly.

She moved to him and put her hand to his arm. "You say so now, Freddy," she told him, her tone grown soft now, and understanding, with none of the strident taunting with which she'd spoken before. "But you'd come to regret it. You know it as well as I."

He took her hand in his, pressing it hard, then lifting his eyes to hers once more. "No, Abra. I swear to you."

She smiled sadly. "I couldn't do that to you, Freddy," she said softly. "I'm not so bad as that."

She looked away, unable to face the crumbling hurt she saw in his eyes. "Besides, there's something I must do now, something I can't tell you about."

He continued to stare at her, but his eyes grew harder. "It's that Thorne person, isn't it? You've fallen in love with him. You plan to marry him."

And now she felt as though he'd struck her. "No, Freddy. I know I'll never marry him."

Her tone was soft and filled with an empty reluctance, a hurt he'd not expected ever to hear from her. And it told him that whatever possibilities there might once have been

193

for him, they existed no longer. But somehow he could not let go.

"If not him, Abra, then what?" he prodded. "If we pretend we'd decided a month ago, then people couldn't believe any of this nonsense about Sharify. It'll be forgotten."

"It's not so simple as that, Freddy," she told him. Her throat felt tight, and she could barely get the words out. "I have to leave New York for a while. There's something I must do."

"You can't be serious. If you and Vincent leave now, people will believe the worst, that it wasn't just a foolish mistake, but that you actually had something to do with Sharify and his jewel. It's the worst thing you can do, surely you can understand that?"

She turned away from him, back to the window, her eyes turning to the place where she'd watched Dash vanish from her sight.

"I know, Freddy. But that's not important now. None of that matters."

"Then what does?" he demanded harshly.

"Please, Freddy . . ."

Her words faded away. There seemed nothing left for her to say. She turned back to him, letting her eyes explain, not understanding why she felt the desire to have him at least not hate her.

"It is Thorne," he said, and the words were no longer a question, but a statement of fact. "If it's true, what you say, Abra, that you won't marry him . . ."

This time she cut him off. "For God's sake, Freddy."

He heaved a thick sigh. "Where are you going?" he demanded, as though it was his right to know.

"It doesn't matter, does it?" she asked.

She turned away again, wishing now that he'd simply leave. Surprisingly, he seemed to understand her for once.

"I'll wait for you, Abra," he told her back softly. "When you return, I'll be here for you."

He stood then, apparently waiting for her to respond, to turn back to him and say something, anything. But she didn't, she just stood with her head bowed, her back to him. After a few moments, he simply turned and left.

Abra hardly even noticed when he'd gone.

# Chapter Thirteen

They rode to the wharf in a brittle silence. Once there,
Abra waited, standing aside, as Dash directed the porters
with their bags. Then he went to her, taking her elbow in
his hand and leading her with an uncompromising grip to
the deck of the *Arcadia*. There they were greeted by the
purser, and once again she stood mutely aside, letting him
attend to the business of their passage.

She felt bewildered and lost, and the sensation was not
one that sat well with her. She was leaving on a voyage
with a man who seemed at that moment intent upon
making it perfectly clear to her that he held her in the
lowest regard, on a task of which she had only the dim-
mest understanding and an even poorer hope of success.
And yet she had no choice in the matter. To do otherwise
would be to condemn her father to certain death. For the
first time in her life, she realized, she was afraid, completely terrified of what was to come. She had been
pushed by circumstance, without any control of what was
happening to her. Somehow her pleasantly ordered life
had taken on an amorphousness, an undirected quality
that left her feeling like a child, alone and unprotected,
lost in some menacing forest, with no hope of finding her
way home ever again. She wondered if she would ever
again feel as though she directed her own actions, as if
her life belonged to her and was not part of some other,
more powerful being's play.

Dash took her arm once more and this time they followed a steward. The decks, the hallways, everywhere she
looked there were people who seemed to be in a festive

mood, as if their departure were some part of a great, pleasing adventure. She felt none of that, and when she dared dart a glance at Dash, his grim expression told her he felt none of it, either. There was no prospect of pleasure for either of them, she decided, and the adventure that loomed promised to be harrowing, if anything at all.

The steward opened the door for her and she passed into her stateroom, letting Dash tend to the details of keys and the like. But when the steward left and she turned to find Dash closing the door behind him, she realized something was not quite as she had expected it to be.

"Is your stateroom next door?" she asked absently as she removed her coat and gloves and dropped them to a chair.

He didn't answer her and in the dull silence that surrounded them she looked at the neat row of luggage that had been left by the far wall near the closet, waiting for the room steward to come and unpack.

"There's been some mistake," she said absently. "They left your things here, too."

"No mistake," he replied without emotion.

She turned to him and found he was smiling grimly at her. "What do you mean, no mistake?"

"Just what I said. This was the only stateroom available. The alternative was to wait for two weeks for the next sailing. That was out of the question, so it seems we'll simply have to make do and share."

She stared at him as if he'd suddenly gone mad. "But how could you? What will people think?"

He shrugged, and dropped himself lazily into a chair. "Not much, I should think. We are traveling as Mr. and Mrs. Dashiel Thorne."

He stared complacently at her, obviously expecting some response. She was only too happy to oblige.

"How could you be so low?" she snarled at him, stamping her foot in impotent fury.

"I didn't have much choice, Abra," he replied, his tone growing cold. "You can either stay in New York or resign yourself to the circumstances."

"Stay in New York?" she retorted. "And leave my father's fate to you?"

196

"That would be unthinkable, wouldn't it?" he replied. "A thief. How could you trust me? I might just find McErlaine and take the jewel for myself, Vincent be damned. We both know you can't trust a thief."

There was a vehement anger in his words, an anger she couldn't ignore, and she knew it was directed at her. But she didn't care.

"He's my father. I intend to go. Who or what you are is of absolutely no concern to me," she told him primly.

He offered her another grim smile. "Well, then, it seems to me you have two choices. You share the state-room with me, answering dutifully to the name of Mrs. Thorne when required while on this vessel, or you go alone."

She crumbled. She knew she could do nothing alone. She needed him, desperately, and he knew it.

She stared dully at the single, large bed. She needed him in more ways than one, she realized, now that she felt so lost and alone. She needed him more than she wanted to think about, more than she would ever admit.

"Very well," she answered him finally, defeated. But when she lifted her eyes to his face and saw him smiling, she could feel the anger well up in her, anger that he could think he'd won so easily as that. She scowled at him.

"I'll sleep there," she said, pointing to the small couch that flanked the far wall of the room. "You can have the bed."

His face colored slightly and he stared at her in silence for a moment. He had something to say to her, but apparently thought better of it, because he stood and ambled to the door.

"Suit yourself, Miss Beaumont," he said. He put his hand to the knob.

"Where are you going?" she demanded, wishing she could take back the unpleasant words, hating the thought of being alone with the new dread that had settled into her since Vincent's disappearance.

"As my presence is quite obviously unpleasant to you," he told her, "I will take it to the gentlemen's bar where I feel sure some decent bourbon will manage to abide me."

197

With that, he opened the door, strode through, and pulled it shut with a decidedly untimorous bang.

Abra stood where she was, watching the motionless door, listening to the silence. He has no right to be angry with me, she told herself righteously. After all, I wasn't the one who got us all involved in this mess.

She marched to the armchair he'd vacated and threw herself into it. It enveloped her in a surprising warmth, and she realized it was his warmth, the heat of his body that lingered. It felt comforting and friendly to her. And it started to melt some of her anger.

Perhaps, she thought it would be wisest to come to some terms with him. After all, they were to be forced to spend the next ten or more days in very close proximity with each other. And a constant war would not improve their situation. Not, of course, that she intended to change her decision with regard to her relationship with him, or allow him to think of her as an available, willing body to warm his bed. They might be traveling as man and wife, but she had no intention of becoming too far immersed in that role. But a quiet truce, she mused, that didn't seem to be unreasonable under the circumstances.

She left the stateroom, making her way toward the public sections of the ship, asking a harried porter directions to the gentleman's salon. He offered them, along with a bewildered stare, which she ignored.

The gentlemen's salon was sumptuous, with a brass-edged, dark mahogany, and burgundy velvet masculinity. And it was lively with laughing groups of men, toasting the *Arcadia's* departure. Abra stood in the doorway, scanning the crowd. Her presence did not go unnoticed. The ordinarily boisterous atmosphere slowly hushed as pairs of eyes found the pleasant, if unexpected, sight of her, and used the opportunity of her entry to the all-male sanctuary as an excuse to stare outright at her.

She didn't notice. Her attention had been caught by a pair of curious eyes lifted to her from a card table at the far side of the room, a pair of blue eyes whose curiosity turned quite suddenly to vexation. It occurred to her that

198

coming after him in this way might not, after all, have been the wisest thing for her to do. But now that she was there, there was little for her to do but go on to him, despite the interest and amusement her presence seemed to have aroused.

She crossed the room quickly and stopped a few feet from the table where Dash sat. Cards, bills, and heavy crystal tumblers of liquor littered its surface, alerting her to the fact that she was interrupting a poker game. The size of the ante pile in the center of the table told her that the stakes were considerable.

"Dash," she murmured, not quite knowing what to say to him, surrounded as he was, and obviously in no mood to deal with her.

He looked up to her as if he'd not seen her standing in the doorway and forced a smile.

"Abra," he said, his tone falsely warm. "What are you doing here, my dear?"

Then he stood, his smile turned now to the other men at the table, apologizing. "It seems my bride has come to remind me that now that we've wed, I must begin to change my bachelor habits," he said.

There was a murmur of gentle laughter among the others, who turned, now, to look at her. Abra could feel her cheeks begin to burn with embarrassment.

An older, grey-haired, rather portly man stood and smiled at her. "As indeed she ought," he said to Dash. "For shame, Mr. Thorne, to leave such a lovely creature unaccompanied." He turned back to Abra. "I shall be more than happy, Mrs. Thorne, to thrash some manners into this young blackguard if the need arises."

There was a round of genial laughter, for Dash was a good deal taller than the speaker and much broader, all of him muscle, not at all like the older man. There was little question of who would thrash whom if the occasion were ever to arise.

"I'm sure that won't be necessary," Abra managed, embarrassment nearly choking the words from her.

"As am I," Dash concurred. Abra heard a bite of something that was not pleasant raillery in his tone, but the others seemed not to notice. "I wonder if you gentlemen would care to join Mrs. Thorne and myself in a glass of champagne and a last glance at the lady?" he asked as he gathered up the stack of bills at his place and slipped them into his pocket. "I'm afraid I shall have to bow out of the game."

"It would be ungentlemanly of us to intrude upon newlyweds, Mr. Thorne," the portly little man smiled, and the others nodded.

Dash excused himself and rounded the table to take Abra's arm. As they started for the door, a stage whisper followed them.

"I can't believe the fellow doesn't know what honeymoons are for."

A round of slightly lecherous laughter followed. Abra could feel Dash tense beside her.

He hustled her away, into the ship's main lounge. Now that the *Arcadia* was moving slowly out of New York harbor, it afforded the best view of the city. He silently directed her to a table by a window, and she sat at the chair he held for her, unprotesting. A waiter arrived immediately, and took Dash's order of champagne. When they were finally alone, he turned to her, his gaze accusing.

"I hope you realize you've just done me out of a healthy pot, Abra," he told her, his eyes coldly unforgiving.

She drew back at his manner. After all, she'd come to make peace with him, and all he seemed to want to do was to begin another argument.

"So you're a gambler as well as a thief?" she asked, her tone brittle, more accusing, perhaps, than she intended. "Don't you have any conscience about taking money from a nice little man like that?" she demanded, remembering his cheery little rounded cheeks and effusive gallantry.

Her words seemed to amuse Dash, for he smiled. "That nice little man is a professional gambler, Abra, out to fleece the wealthy men at that table, not that they probably didn't deserve the fleecing. I was planning only to take a small bit of his action."

She was mildly shocked at the information he had offered her, but chose to ignore it. "I'd no idea you had so

200

many talents," she told him, her tone showing less admiration than accusation.

He leaned across the table toward her. "I don't suppose it has occurred to you that I have been to a good deal of expense, Abra, and my funds are not limitless? To put it bluntly, we need the money." He sat back once more, and this time his stare was slightly condescending. "Unless, of course, you thought to bring along funds to finance this little expedition?"

She drew back. She hadn't even thought about money. And even if she had, there was no way she could have gotten very much. She had some personal funds, but they were not great. Her father, of course, had always provided her with whatever she had needed. His banker, however, would not be so obliging, she knew, without direct orders from Vincent.

"No," she told him, her manner cowed, "I have no money."

"And I don't suppose it ever occurred to you that we'd need some, a good deal, as a matter of fact?"

She shook her head mutely.

"But then, I'm a thief," he went on. "I could always just steal something, right? A diamond necklace from one of the dowagers on the ship, perhaps, or one of the rings off a finger of one of those men at the poker table with me?"

His voice was filled with venom, and the intensity of it surprised and frightened her. She thought she had understood him, but now his temper completely baffled her.

"I suppose I didn't think about it," she confessed softly, turning away from him as the waiter approached bearing a tray with bottle, bucket, and glasses.

She was relieved at the interruption, and the two of them sat silent as the man uncorked the bottle and filled their two glasses. All around them were the sounds of laughter, excited talk, the sounds of a festive sailing. None of it made any impression on her, however. All she could see was the anger in his eyes, the look that told her she was a great disappointment to him. She was not sure why, but that look bothered her terribly.

When the waiter had gone, the two of them sat in

silence for a few moments longer, and the pain of his disapproval seemed almost physical to Abra. Finally, she looked away from him, and stared down at her hands, which seemed suddenly foolishly ungainly to her. She clasped them firmly and deposited them into her lap.

Her discomposure surprised Dash. After a moment, he leaned once more toward her, pushing her glass of champagne closer to her as he did so.

"Drink your champagne, Abra," he directed her firmly. "After all, this is the start of our honeymoon voyage, and we've appearances to maintain."

At first she thought his words were intended to be teasing, but when she returned her glance to his, she saw that he was staring at her with an uncompromising firmness.

"Or have you forgotten that we've both acknowledged the fact that you need me along on this little venture?"

She swallowed the angry words that welled up in her at the superiorly smug smile that crept to his lips as he lifted her glass.

"With you ever willing to remind me," she retorted as she took the glass from him, "I'm sure forgetting will be quite impossible."

"To our honeymoon, and our future together," he said, his voice fairly loud now, enough to carry to the tables that surrounded them.

People turned to stare at them, to watch him smile with an exaggerated display of what she assumed was intended to be loving tenderness. He touched his glass to hers. Abra scowled at him, but when she saw the look of warning he directed at her, she changed her expression to include a simpering smile.

"To a mutually satisfying voyage, and the future we each desire and deserve," she countered with saccharine sweetness.

She saw his brow lift and a smile tug at the edge of his lips as he brought his glass to his mouth. But she felt little like laughter. She sipped the wine and stared at the receding form of the statue in the harbor, wondering what would happen before she saw it again.

Dash sat scowling at her.

"Aren't you ready yet?" he demanded. "I'm hungry."

Abra smiled to herself and continued to primp unnecessarily at her hair. She was quite enjoying his ill humor, she decided.

"Typical beast," she replied congenially. "Growling for your supper." She swiped at the curls that framed her face with her brush for the third or fourth time. "It seems you're not quite so content with married life as I thought you'd be, Mr. Thorne."

Dash stood and crossed the room in a half-dozen long strides. "Perhaps I can make it more to my liking," he suggested as he stood behind her chair, leaning down to her. "I could demand my conjugal rights," he said softly, his breath warm against the back of her neck. "If I can't satisfy one hunger, I can always substitute another."

She tried to draw away from him, but she was trapped in the small space between the chair and the dressing table.

"You're vile," she announced with a frigid sneer, then put her brush down on the tabletop.

He put his hand to hers before she released it. "I'm a thief," he taunted her. "What did you expect?"

She shrugged away from him and he moved back, allowing her to stand. He seemed thoroughly amused by her discomposure.

"Very well, you win. I'm ready for the social gauntlet," she told him as she lifted her gloves from the table and began to pull them on, keeping her attention firmly centered on the tiny pearl buttons and carefully away from his eyes.

Dash watched her, and realized she was decidedly ready for any inspection she was likely to encounter. She was wearing the gown she'd worn the first evening he'd kissed her, at the Brinksons' party, the pale, off-white satin neatly caressing her waist and nearly baring the slender curves of her shoulders, the just proper decolletage pleasingly hinting at those it hid. She was beautiful, he thought, and the contemplation of that beauty left him with a dull, hard lump in his chest.

203

"I suppose, after all, it was worth the wait, Abra," he told her with an appreciative smile. "You're quite nice to look at this evening."

She tossed her head as she turned away, without bothering to offer him a glance. "I didn't dress for you," she told him.

He reached out his hand and caught her arm. "If not for me, then whom?" he demanded softly.

Abra felt herself coloring as she finally looked up to face him. He was staring down at her, his eyes now pleasantly challenging, his smile apparently absolutely genuine for the first time in what seemed days. She found his expression entirely unsettling.

"Shall we stop this sparring now, Dash?" she asked softly. "Under the circumstances, can't we simply be friends?"

"It's one way to mend fences, I suppose," he agreed, starting to lower his face to hers. "But I can think of others far more pleasant."

It was tempting to simply stand there, to let his arms enfold her and let herself lose herself to the narcotic of his kiss. But that would be wrong, a voice inside her told her with unremitting logic. When this is done, he'll disappear, and the hurt will be all the greater if you let yourself love him.

She pushed against his chest and stepped back from him. "Perhaps," she told him primly. "But those are not the fences I want to mend just now."

He made no attempt to hold her, but let her draw away. He was disappointed, but he realized he would gain nothing with her if he were to force her. He pretended nonchalance.

"Then it's friends we're to be, Abra?" he asked, his tone slightly humorous, as if the thought brought him a good deal of amusement. "Brother and sister off on a honeymoon? Wouldn't that shock the good Mrs. Dewitte?"

She made an exasperated scowl and turned away toward the door.

"Cousins, then, if it will satisfy you and the good Mrs. Dewitte," she replied.

"Kissing cousins, Abra?" he pressed with a wide grin.

204

"No," she snapped, turning back to face him. "And I needn't remind you that this is not a honeymoon in any event, but a business venture. Or have you forgotten we are about the business of retrieving my father from the situation you've gotten him into?"

The accusation hurt him, more than he would have thought possible. All the banter and humor died within him. His expression hardened, granitelike, and he returned her angry stare.

"I haven't forgotten. Very well, Miss Beaumont. Business it is, and nothing more."

He strode to her, took her elbow firmly in his grasp, and directed her to the door.

It seemed that Abra was not to be allowed to let the matter end in their stateroom. As they entered the dining room, the maitre d' smiled at them, then motioned to the small string orchestra that played at the far side of the room. Suddenly the unmistakable strains of Wagner's "Bridal Chorus" from the opera *Lohengrin* filled the air, soon to be followed by a polite outbreak of applause.

Abra could feel the expected flush of red coloring her cheeks. "How could you?" she hissed under her breath to Dash. Despite her suspicion, however, it was immediately obvious to her that he was as much surprised and unsettled by the unexpected welcome as was she.

"For God's sake," he growled back to her. "You really don't think I'm responsible for this, do you?"

When they'd finally been shown to their table and the other diners had turned to their own meals, the embarrassment, at least, died. But not the charade. The six other passengers seated at their table were only too effusive with their congratulations. And she had no other choice but to smile and thank them, all the while returning Dash's warning looks with what were meant to pass as loving glances.


"I have never been so humiliated in my life," Abra fumed as she tore off her long kid gloves and threw them to the top of the dressing table.

"I told you I had nothing to do with any of that, Abra.

205

You can't think I planned it simply to embarrass you?"

Dash's mood had not been improved by the meal. It had, if anything, deteriorated as he'd watched Abra pick at the food that had been served her and tersely answer whatever questions had been asked of her by the others seated at the table. He'd seen her cringe when remarks were addressed to her as Mrs. Thorne. That she considered bearing his name so odious came as a mildly unpleasant shock to him.

"No," she replied in response. "I don't think you planned it. But you certainly enjoyed it, every minute of it, sitting there smugly and calling me "dear' in front of those people. You seemed quite comfortable with the charade." She narrowed her eyes and stared at him, contemplating. "But then, thieves are comfortable with lies, aren't they? They live lies. I suppose this isn't the first time you've played this particular game, calling some woman your wife."

His eyes grew hard, and whatever understanding had warmed them before completely vanished.

"That's enough, Abra," he said through tight lips.

"Is it?" she snapped back. She hadn't really thought of it before she'd uttered the words, but once they were said, the thought gnawed at her, that he'd presented other women as his wife, that perhaps the pretense had been complete, even when he'd been alone with them. Especially when he'd been alone with them.

"I suppose a convenience like a temporary wife makes life much simpler for you. People trust you. After all, a man wouldn't bring a wife along if his intent was larceny, now, would he?"

"I said that was enough, Abra!"

She could see the look of warning, but she was far too angry with him now to heed it.

"Or what?" she demanded. "You'll reveal to the other passengers that I'm not your wife, that we're bound together because you involved my father in some insane robbery and now his life is balanced on the chance that we can find a needle in a haystack and return it to some power-hungry sheik?" She laughed, a tight, unnatural laugh that seemed beyond her control.

206

"Damn it," he snarled, "I can think of other threats."

And he crossed the room to her. The laughter stopped abruptly.

"Touch me and I shall scream," she told him, taking a step backward, away from him.

He matched her step. "A young wife, on her honeymoon?" he asked her. "Anyone who heard would think them cries of pleasure." His eyes narrowed. "And that's what they'd be," he asserted as he took her arm and pulled her to him.

His kiss was angry and hard and seemed to travel from her lips all through her, filling her with the liquid warmth, making her mind reel. She tried to pull away, but his arms tightened around her, pulling her closer. She felt as though she were drowning in the pounding heat of his embrace, a heat she knew that they lit in each other.

The anger left his lips as he felt the warmth filling her, and his kisses trailed to her ear and neck. But he'd presumed too much, for she'd not yet given up.

"Thief," she whispered. "Would you steal that, too?"

The words had more power than she'd have thought possible. He released her, and drew back.

"Is that so terrible, Abra?" he asked her softly, and the question that he'd known all along that must be asked came to his lips. "Does it matter what I am, who I am?"

"Yes," she nearly shouted back, breathless now and panting.

"Your father was a thief," he reminded her needlessly.

Her eyes filled with hurt, and she turned away, not wanting him to see it.

"Perhaps that's why," she said softly. "It just matters."

He stood staring at her, his mind filled with the thought that if she loved him, it wouldn't. Nothing would matter except what she felt for him. The knowledge that she didn't love him enough to make what she thought him to be meaningless was bitter. He could taste it on his tongue.

He backed away from her, moving toward the door. As he passed it, his eyes scanned the bed.

"Go to bed, Abra," he told her with empty resignation. "You may consider it inviolate."

207

"Where are you going?" she ventured, wondering at the sudden change that had come over him.

He smiled at her grimly. "To the bar. I dare say they'll all think it a bridegroom's bit of courage."

"And later?"

His expression grew pained. "I already told you, your bed is inviolate, Abra," he retorted. "You know me to be a thief. I would not have you think me a rapist, as well."

Abra looked down to the bed for a moment, the bitterness she heard in his words eating into her, biting at her like corrosive acid.

But whatever words she thought to say, whatever compromise she might have offered, went unsaid, unoffered. When she looked up, he was already gone.

# Chapter Fourteen

They settled into a stiffly formal, but manageable truce. In public they maintained a posture of detached, apparently settled, devotion. Abra resigned herself to smilingly answering to the name of Mrs. Thorne when addressed by the other passengers and the crew of the *Arcadia*.

The first evening set the pattern for those following. Dash would go to the gentlemen's lounge for a late brandy, occasionally finding a game of poker to occupy him for an hour or two. On those occasions he would invariably win, never so great an amount as to raise any doubts in the minds of the other players that his fortune was excessive, even if they were apt to comment on his unfair position as a man lucky in love as well as in cards, comments made with more than a hint of envy, but without any real rancor. When made in his hearing, such comments were apt to elicit nothing more than a coldly indifferent glance from Dash. The other male passengers soon learned to keep such thoughts to themselves.

After he'd left them, however, someone was usually heard to comment drily that he hardly seemed the sort of man who would need a brandy before retiring to his bride's bed.

When he returned to the stateroom, Dash would find Abra already in bed, asleep, or at least pretending sleep. In either case, he would find himself relieved, for he would have found facing her under such intimate conditions far more trying than the silence that engulfed him as he lay, solitary and cramped, trying vainly to sleep on the

209

couch that lined the far wall of the stateroom.

When the captain announced, on the morning of the twelfth day, that the *Arcadia* would be docking in Lisbon within a few hours, both of them felt a decided flood of relief. The tense proximity had been a strain on the two of them, as had the formal politeness behind which they had unsuccessfully tried to hide their more volatile feelings.

Abra stood on the deck staring out into a mist-shrouded gloom, hoping for a glance of the port she assumed would offer some small refuge from the depressing feeling of futile longing that Dash's presence awakened in her. But there was little for her to see except the biting-cold drizzle, a thick, clotted mist that hung in the air, an expectant harbinger of foul weather to come. It unsettled her, for the coldly miserable weather reminded her that December was fast drawing to a close, and the time Sharify had allowed her to find the stone and return it to him was ticking remorselessly away.

"Nasty weather."

She looked up to find Dash at her side, his hand to the rail, as was hers, his eyes staring fixedly out to the misty emptiness around them. It occurred to her that despite his proximity, he nonetheless maintained a small distance from her, not letting his arm brush against her shoulder, nor his fingers touch hers where they grasped the brass fitting of the rail. She told herself that she was pleased with his reticence, but there was a small, biting discomfort within her that told her that she would welcome, no, more than that, that she *needed* some small gesture of comfort from him, and that she sorely regretted his aloofness.

"Do you think it will turn worse?" she asked timorously. "If the packet doesn't sail . . ."

Her words trailed off into the mist, but they were still there, if unspoken, between them. Each day that McErlaine evaded them made it that much more likely that he would already have disposed of the ruby by the time they found him. And if he managed to sell the stone, the possibility of their getting it back was reduced tremendously.

"He'll have the same problems with the weather we will, Abra," Dash told her, and for the first time in days she thought she heard a touch of real gentleness in his words.

"Not if he's already reached Marseilles," she replied.

"There's not much we can do about it in any event," he said. He turned to her then and put his hand to her arm. "You'd best come in out of this wet, Abra," he told her, once more acting the dutiful, if slightly distant, husband. "You don't want to catch a chill."

Patrick McErlaine stood on the small piazza that overlooked the bay. There was not really terribly much for him to see just then. Cap Ferrat dozed in the mist. The few boats that floated in the harbor were fishing boats, not the pleasure yachts that would come with the warmer months. It was an empty, almost bleak, view. But he found it pleased him, nonetheless.

He didn't regret having leased the house. The winter would be short there, far shorter than those he'd endured in New York at any rate, and the pleasanter seasons long and languorous. He looked forward to a genteel retirement.

The wind, he realized, was cold and wet, and he turned back to the interior of the house. As he entered, he began to laugh. He could not help but appreciate the irony of his situation. He'd been cheated of promotion for years because Vincent Beaumont had thought himself too smart to be outdone by a mere copper. But in the end, he'd won. If he hadn't gotten his promotion, if he'd been forced to leave his retirement behind him, he'd still come out far to the advantage. He had more money now than he'd ever dreamed of having, an amount that made the stipend he'd have received from the force to live out his life look like a pittance. In the end, he was the one to win, after all. And he had Vincent Beaumont to thank for his good fortune. That thought alone was enough to entertain him for months to come.

The sound of his laughter caught the attention of the old woman who cleaned, for she turned to him, wondering what it was that caused him to stand there, alone, laughter escaping from his lips like a furtive night prowler. He silenced it and made an effort not to scowl at her. If the estate manager had not insisted that she was part of the hire of the house, he'd have had her out before he'd walked in the door. But the agent had been firm, on direct instruction of the owner, he'd said, and it would have been foolish to pass up the house because of her even if he'd had other expectations of his new life.

The old woman, actually, was the one discordant element in the whole picture he saw of his new life. Sallow-cheeked, grey and ponderous, with heavy, sagging breasts and an ugly mole on her left cheek, she reminded him of everything he'd left behind him, everything dull and drab and ugly and poor. He'd envisioned himself employing a young girl, a pretty one, the sort of maid a rich man would have. But the old woman was part and parcel of the house, and the house, he'd decided, was reasonably priced and pleasant, even luxurious by his own standards. He'd tolerate the old woman, he told himself, and there'd be plenty of pretty young girls for him to look at in the town.

*"Il y a quelque chose que vous desirez, monsieur?"*

He hated the singsong of her voice, too high and too thin for a woman of her size. And even more, he hated her insistence on speaking to him in her own tongue.

"English," he growled at her. "Eng-lish!"

She drew back at his tone, and he was pleased that he could intimidate her so easily.

"There ees sometheeng you want?" she asked again, her pronunciation painful, trying to his ears.

"Bring me a beer," he told her. "No, a whiskey and soda," he amended. No more beer for him, he decided. He'd have whatever he wanted from now on. "And go to the kiosk and get the papers. The English papers. *London Times,* whatever."

The prospect of going out in the wet didn't please her, obviously, for she pursed her lips. Resigned, she turned away and set about her task of fixing his drink before she set out for the papers.

McErlaine watched her leave the room with a small feeling of triumph. She wouldn't stay long, he decided. Soon, she'll want to be let go. And then it would all be perfect.

It struck him that it had all been so improbably easy. Two days in Cannes and he'd sold the stone, for half of

212

what it was probably worth, of that he had little doubt, but still, he wasn't in a position to bargain, as he only knew of the one man who would care to take such a jewel, provenance unspecified. Anyway, it was enough for his needs, more than enough. And he'd found the house in an afternoon, settled himself in by sunset. Three days and his whole life had changed — he'd gone from servant to master. He quite liked the idea.

He closed his eyes. Perhaps he'd take the coach to Cannes the next day and do a bit of gambling at the casino. That was how gentlemen spent their evenings, he told himself. He smiled, and the laughter once more erupted, but this time a bit more discreetly so as not to divert the old woman from her task.

He was going to quite enjoy his new life, he decided. He wondered what Vincent Beaumont would think if he knew.


Abra looked up at the sign over the door and knew the address would not bring them face to face with McErlaine. For a moment she hoped they had made a mistake, that this was not the right place after all.

She turned to Dash. "Are you sure this is the right place? Maybe we have the wrong street," she suggested hopefully.

He handed her the slip of paper without a glance. "This is the right place," he told her grimly. "Nothing to do but get on with it."

He put his hand to the door, opening it to allow her to pass. Filled with omens of the worst, Abra stepped into the confines of Sancerre et Fils, Importateurs.

A harried-looking man in shirtsleeves looked up at them through the dim obscurity of the gold-framed glasses that perched on his nose. The cold breeze that had entered with them, more than the rattle of the bell, seemed to have roused him, for he shivered slightly.

*"Madame. Monsieur. Je peux vous aider?"*

His question was posed tentatively, as though he really doubted that he could be of any use to them, but was willing to make the offer in any event.

Abra looked around the dusty little storefront, with its

213

jumble of crates shoved in what appeared to be random order to the rear, the heavy rolltop desk where the man sat heaped with a disorderly mass of ledgers in varying stages of decay. She thought she agreed with his unspoken sentiment. How could they be such fools as to come to a place like this and expect to find a trace of McErlaine or the jewel?

*"J'espère que vous pouvez nous donner un peu d'information,"* she replied, the words coming to her awkwardly, with thought, her hesitancy caused more by the uneasiness she felt than by any lack of facility.

The man behind the desk stood, removing his jacket from the back of his chair and donning it as he approached them. He was tall, a good deal more so than he had seemed when he'd been seated, his long legs carrying him across the room quickly.

When he reached them, he put out his hand to Dash. "Charles Sancerre, one of the *fils,*" he said by way of introduction. His English was melodiously accented and his smile, when he offered it to Abra, made him look less like an owlishly bookish uncle and far more pleasant. "Information?" he asked. "What sort of information?" He seemed more curious than suspicious, and his manner gave the impression of a genuine willingness to help if he could.

"We're looking for a man," Dash broke in, his manner as easy as Abra's was tense. "A business associate. He planned to be traveling in the south here until he got settled, but he gave me this address and suggested you might know where we could find him. I believe you were to forward some of his belongings to him. His name is McErlaine, Patrick McErlaine."

Abra held her breath as she watched Sancerre's face. At first his expression was completely absent, and she thought that it was over, that the trail would end in that small shop in a dingy backstreet of Marseilles.

But then Sancerre smiled. "McErlaine. Of course. I only just received word of him yesterday." He turned an uneasy glance to the stack of papers that littered his desk. "I remember because I went to a good deal of trouble about it. Had to go to the shipping line myself, and all for one small trunk." He began to flip through the stack

214

of colored flimsies on the desk, all the while talking, more to himself, it seemed, than to either Abra or Dash. "The larger houses won't bother with this sort of business. Too much paperwork, and not enough profit for them, I suppose. But we've been taking small private shipments for years. It's worth it, if you're willing to take the extra effort. Ten francs a day storage, plus a commission on the shipping and handling. Ah, here it is." He pulled a sheet out from one of the piles. "He sent a wire yesterday asking that his trunk be forwarded to Les Pins, Cap Ferrat." He fell silent, his expression one of satisfaction that he'd proved himself so organized and useful.

"Cap Ferrat?" Abra queried Dash, never having heard of the place.

Only too glad to offer this information, too, Sancerre pointed to a navigation and shipping route map on his far wall. "It lies between Cannes and Monte Carlo, on the coast. In summer it's a pretty little resort town, for those who can't quite afford either of its neighbors. At this time of the year, it's pretty quiet, only the fishermen and a few retired folk, mostly English and Irish. They seem to like the climate, though God only knows why. It's as miserable on the Mediterranean as anywhere in the wintertime, chill and damp. But then," he added with a slight shrug, "France is heaven compared to the Isles, and even in the winter time it must seem pleasant to them."

Dash allowed himself a small smile. "And Les Pins?" he asked mildly. "A hotel, I suppose?"

"Oh, no, monsieur," Sancerre replied quickly. "There's but one hotel at Cap Ferrat, the Grand. It's probably one of those cottages that rent out for the season, I suppose. There'd be a good number of them, mostly vacant at this time of the year." He moved to the map and squinted slightly as he examined some lines of fine print. "If you're planning to visit, the easiest way is to take the packet to Cannes, then hire a coach. Unfortunately, there's no packet stop at Cap Ferrat from November through March. Not much call, I suppose." He looked thoughtful. "It's not quite pleasant on the water in December, I'm afraid," he added with a commiserating glance to Abra.

She thought of the trip from Lisbon, and paled. Another journey on the choppy water so soon was not really something she felt she could anticipate with anything other than a determined dread. But she managed a smile.

"You've been very kind, monsieur," she said.

"A great pleasure, madame," he replied with a small, formal bow, then turned his glance to Dash expectantly.

He was not disappointed. Dash, too, offered his thanks, as well as a more tangible reward, then he took Abra's arm and led her to the door.

"Tomorrow, then, to Cap Ferrat," Dash said with a slightly smug smile when they were once more out on the street.

Abra scowled. "And a little more intimate knowledge of the joys of sailing the Mediterranean."

He laughed at the misery he heard in her voice. "Perhaps we'd best forgo breakfast in the morning before leaving," he suggested. "In the name of discretion, not valor."

The Grand Hotel de Cap Ferrat may have been grand in the warmer months when the rich and almost rich fled the cities in the north to find the sun on the Côte D'Azure, but in late December its huge lobby, despite its gilded columns and velvet-upholstered banquettes, seemed more like a drafty cavern than a hall of opulence.

A few elderly women sat at the tables in the center of the lobby, sipping their late afternoon tea parsimoniously and listening to the tired refrains of a less-than-inspired string quartet. The waltzes they played seemed as flat and dull as the damp, chilled air.

A tentative fire sputtered and spit, valiantly making a small effort to attack the dampness in the air, but the exercise was futile. The huge carved fireplace was more decorative than functional, the few logs that smoldered there a hopeless wedge against the miserable weather. A pair of grey-haired, shrunken men huddled close to it, hoping for a little warmth and nursing solitary afternoon whiskeys. The Grand Hotel, it seemed, maintained its grandeur through the winter by catering to a few elderly with pensions enough to keep them there in relative comfort, but not enough to provide them with more pleasing an environment through the long, cold months.

It had been, Abra thought, one of the longest days of her life. First, the hours she'd spent on the packet, feeling the lurching, chopping waves beneath her, staring out the window at the rainfall with a dull disinterest, aware only of a horrifying feeling of nausea in her stomach and the growing misery that threatened to, but never quite did, erupt. Then, once the packet had docked and disgorged them, she'd been abandoned to the confines of a squat little tea house while Dash went about the business of hiring a coach. The smell of the place had been that of day-old croissants and damp wool, a not altogether pleasing aroma after the unpleasantness of the packet. She'd huddled over the warmth of a cup of tea, heating her hands with it, but scarcely daring to sip the dull amber liquid because of the lurching that remained in her stomach. And if that hadn't been torture enough, the only coach Dash was able to hire was ill kept, with hard, uncushioned springs that stabbed at her with each bump in the road. She was sore and tired, and wanted nothing more exotic than a hot bath and a warm, soft bed.

Dash, miraculously, seemed immune to the miseries that had plagued her. He'd smiled at her with a dimly commiserating look on the packet, but he was apparently without any sensitivity to the boat's movement. She'd known she hated him as she sat huddled in misery and watched him consume a hearty luncheon of ham and cheese sandwiches and beer, oblivious of the lurching movement of the waves.

Then, in Cannes, he'd seemed equally indifferent about the lacking comforts of the coach. His only words during the whole of the ride had come at the very start, as they'd passed the casino on their way through town. He'd looked at it with his concentrated, assessing stare.

"We'll have to spend an evening or two there, Abra," he'd told her, his tone dully determined. "We're almost without funds."

She'd been still too uncomfortable to do more than grunt a response, but the nausea had finally left her, and she'd had ample time to think on the tedious coach ride, think about the confident way he assumed he'd win at the gambling tables, the certainty he had that he could always find some money by using little more than the turn of a

217

card and his wits. His coolness, his absent acceptance of his abilities, somehow frightened her, and she was not really sure why.

They'd been shown to their rooms, and now she stood staring out through the window, peering into the heavy mist that filled the air to the rocky beach lining the harbor. For a resort, Cap Ferrat seemed terribly deserted and rather sad to her.

"It's pleasanter when there's some sunshine."

She hadn't heard Dash enter her room, and she turned to find him by the door, standing and staring at her. She wondered for a moment how he'd managed to read her thoughts. Then that thought was chased away by the realization that he'd entered without her knowledge.

"Don't you find it necessary to knock, Mr. Thorne, before entering another's room?" she asked with chilly animation as she moved across the room to the bed where she'd dropped her coat.

The accommodations, at least, were sufficient, unlike those of the small inn where they'd been forced to stay in Lisbon. The room was large and well appointed, and the bath huge and tiled in sparkling white, with enormous fluffy white towels warming themselves on a towel rack, all promising the simple animal comforts she so craved. Two such rooms could not be cheap, she realized. She assumed he expected to win handily when they finally found the opportunity to spend an evening at the casino.

"You won't need that while you bathe," he told her as he watched her pick up her coat and push her arms wearily into the sleeves.

She cocked her head. "Les Pins. Remember? We're going to find McErlaine," she protested.

Dash shook his head. "I'm going. You stay here."

She stared directly at him. "I'm going with you," she told him. "He's my father," she added, her justification coming automatically to her lips.

His eyes flared. "Not something I'm likely to forget as long as you're nearby to remind me, Abra," he retorted. "And while we are once more discussing the matter, I feel it time to tell you I've become heartily sick of your constant reminders that all this is my fault."

His sudden burst of anger surprised him almost more

than it unsettled her. He'd really not intended it, he knew, but somehow the tenseness of the past weeks, the strained uneasiness of their relationship, pushed him to say things and to act in ways he would not have considered in other circumstances. Trying to ignore her was more than hard enough, but the accusations were becoming intolerably painful to him.

"I'm going," she told him, her tone defiant and her eyes blazing. "If you don't take me, I'll go by myself."

She carefully buttoned up her coat and marched to the door. It was only then that she turned to face him.

"Well, Mr. Thorne?" she asked. "Do you take me with you or do I go on my own?"

"You are inflexible, stubborn, and opinionated, Abra," he told her. "Not to mention a bloody pain in the neck."

With that he crossed the room to her and pulled the door open to let her pass.


An unheard-of tip of twenty francs to the doorman had not only supplied them with a comfortable carriage, it also provided them with the precise directions to Les Pins. The rental cottages, it seemed, were all listed in a small directory at the hotel, directions at the ready for the convenience of summer visitors. The fact that the inquiry was more than a bit out of season did not seem to bother the man, especially as he contemplated the money he'd pocketed. He smiled as he read out the directions, then gave them once more to the carriage driver before helping Abra inside.

But now as she sat staring out the carriage window at the tidy little house with its winter-chilled rose garden behind a neat white picket fence, Abra knew that the ease with which they'd found McErlaine was really not going to do them very much good.

"He's sold it," she said flatly, and felt herself die a bit inside with the words. "The Tear is gone."

Dash leaned past her and stared out at the small cottage. Despite its size, it showed that a certain amount of care and expense had been given over to its maintenance. A simple comparison to the squalid rooms McErlaine had inhabited in New York was more than enough to tell him that the policeman was living a good deal beyond the means provided to him by the position he'd recently vacated.

"Then we find out who he sold it to," he said easily, trying to disguise the disappointment he, too, felt. He leaned past her, unlatching the carriage door and pushing it open.

The old woman who answered their knock was obviously preparing to leave herself, and was not at all happy to find visitors at the door. She listened disinterestedly to their request to see McErlaine as she finished buttoning her coat, pulling the straining fabric over her ample bosom and forcing the pieces of dark bone through the holes as if they were small enemies come to plague her.

*"Il n'est pas ici,"* she told them, her voice filled with disdain. *"Il est allé au casino. Comme hier soir. Comme chaque soir cette semaine."* She pulled a heavy dark shawl across her unruly mop of dark hair, and whispered under her breath, *"Nuit de Noël. Le païn."*

Then she darted out, pulling the door firmly closed behind her and locking it, then started off for the street without offering them another glance.

Abra stood numbly and stared after her. Dash waited a moment and then moved to her, putting his hand to her elbow.

"He's sold it," she said, not really to him, just verbalizing the thoughts that ran through her mind. "If he's had the money to be gambling, he's sold the ruby."

"As I said, Abra, we'll just have to find whom he sold it to," Dash told her calmly, nudging her forward to the waiting carriage none too gently.

"And then what do we do?" she demanded. "We don't have any money. How will we buy it back?"

He shrugged. "I suppose we steal it, Abra," he told her calmly as he opened the carriage door. "But for now, we can do nothing. We'll have to wait until tomorrow, until McErlaine returns."

Defeated, she climbed back into the carriage. Dash climbed in beside her, and the carriage lurched, then began to move.

Abra sat, still and distant in thought. Christmas Eve the old woman had said, *Nuit de Noël.* She hadn't even realized it was Christmas Eve. It seemed impossible to her. Christmas meant parties and shopping and the great tree in the front parlor. And her father. She'd never been away from Vincent on Christmas Eve before.

A heavy thickness seemed to form and then grow inside her, filling her with a miserable sense of loneliness and despair. She tried to force it away, but as the carriage made its way through the misty streets, she could not help but see the churches they passed, couldn't help but notice the candlelight or hear the sounds of carols drifting into the streets. The local working people would be in those churches, she thought, families, together. As it ought to be on Christmas Eve.

Dash hadn't meant to turn to stare at her. He'd taken on the habit of not looking at her when they were alone if it was at all possible. But as they neared a small stone church and he heard the unmistakable strains of "Silent Night" drifting through the moist evening air, he turned to her. She was staring straight ahead, and her cheeks were bright, shiny with her tears.

He was surprised at that, for she'd not made a sound. As he watched, another began a slow drifting trail across her cheek. She seemed not even to notice.

"Abra," he said softly.

"The old woman said it was Christmas Eve. I didn't even know until she said it," she told him, her face still fixed and composed, her tone distant. "We never forgot Christmas," she went on dully, as though the words meant nothing to her. "Even the year Mama died, Papa insisted. When I asked him why, he said because Christmas reminds us of our humanity, that we could never forget Christmas."

She turned to him then, and the composure left her, her face seeming to crumble as she fought to hold back the hurt. "I forgot. I didn't even know until the old woman told us."

She started to fall toward him, and he opened his arms for her, welcoming the opportunity with mixed feelings, anxious for the touch of her and yet knowing that it would hurt all the more when she once more regained her control and turned away from him. But for the moment he held her, letting her weep silently against his chest,

221

wishing he could ease the hurt for her.

"I miss him so much," she murmured. "And I'm so afraid I'll never see him again."

"We'll get him back," he told her softly, wishing he felt as much confidence as his tone implied. The truth was he felt as much at sea as she seemed to be. Holding her was the first thing he'd done in days that made him feel sure, confident. It was amazing, he thought, how the simple fact that she needed his comfort made him feel so sure of being able to protect her, to console her. Everything else in his life, it seemed, was far less certain.

They sank into an intimate silence. Slowly her tears ceased, but neither felt the need to move. Then the carriage drew to a halt and Dash knew they had returned to the hotel.

He couldn't see her simply going to her room, silent and alone, not on that night. He leaned out and called up to the driver to take them back to the small stone church they'd passed a few moments previous.

Abra collected herself, sitting upright and wiping her sleeve across her cheek absently.

"Where are we going?" she asked, curious but not aggressively so.

He offered her a crooked smile and his handkerchief. "To church, Abra. After all, it is Christmas Eve."

She blew her nose noisily, then sat silent, staring at him, apparently willing to accept his choice of destination without argument. When the carriage stopped once more, he climbed down, and then helped her out. For a moment they stood by the road, staring across a long stretch of wet grass at a simple, small Romanesque church. The windows seemed to pulse with the flickering candlelight within, and the sound of a boys' choir, high and sweet, filled the air.

"I'm not Catholic," she said softly as Dash began to guide her forward.

"Neither am I," he told her. "But I don't think anyone will mind. Certainly not tonight."

They walked to the door and slipped inside, finding two empty seats in a pew in the last row as the other occupants smilingly edged closer together to make room for the newcomers. They sat, and Abra stared into the

222

warmth of the place, her nose filling with the scent of incense, her mind still captive to the music.

Her hand crept out and took Dash's. Their hands lay, covered by the folds of fabric of her coat, tightly bound and close. There was an odd intimacy in that simple touch, she found, more than so chaste a contact ought to have. But it was warming to her, and, amidst all the strangeness that surrounded her, made her somehow feel as though she were not alone, after all. She looked up at the ornately decorated carved creche that nearly filled the apse of the church and drank in the scents and the music, grateful for the feeling of peaceful contentment that settled over her, the first such peace she'd felt since the whole madness had begun.

The service done, the echoes of the choir still filled the church, and smiling strangers turned to them with wishes of *"Joyeaux Noël."* Hands still clasped, they strolled slowly from the church.

"Not much chance of finding a carriage here," Dash mused as he looked out at the quiet street. "We'll have to walk."

"I don't mind," Abra told him, and she smiled. "This is really quite nice."

It was, she realized, very nice, walking through the cool, damp mist, her hand warm in his, the solid comfort of his body beside hers.

"Except there ought to be snow," he told her thoughtfully. "It doesn't feel quite like Christmas."

She stopped and looked up at him, her eyes wide and serious. "Thank you, Dash," she whispered when he, too, stopped and looked down to her.

He smiled at her, then lifted his hand to her cheek, rubbing it gently with his fingers, letting his thumb glide along the line of her jaw. Then he bent his head to hers and kissed her, a fleetingly soft kiss, on the lips. Just that one, gentle kiss, and he turned away, walking once more along the darkened, misty street with her at his side.

They traveled the remaining blocks in a peaceful, contented silence. When they reached the hotel, he walked her to her room, and she stood aside as he bent to unlock the door for her, then swung it open.

"Climb into a tub, Abra, and I'll order up some supper

223

for you, if you like. You look tired, and you've had nothing all day."

She considered his suggestion. "And you?" she asked finally, her fingers reaching automatically to the buttons of her coat.

He shrugged. "I suppose I'll do the same for myself," he told her thoughtfully, his eyes on hers.

She looked up at him. "You could eat here, with me," she suggested slowly, almost as if she weren't quite sure of what she was saying. "That is, if you'd like to." She looked down. "If you won't mind the company. One oughtn't to be alone at Christmas," she added softly.

"No, one oughtn't," he agreed with a slow deliberateness.


She'd meant only to stay in the bath a few moments, but the warm water was like a heady drink, easing away the hurt in her legs and shoulders, draining her of thought, save that she was comfortable for the first time in what seemed days. The knock at the bathroom door came as a bit of a surprise.

"Madame, your dinner awaits," Dash called in to her with mock subservience as he opened the door and peeped in at her. He smiled when he saw her still in the bubble-filled tub, even more when he saw her sink down into the mass of white until her shoulders were completely hidden.

"You ought to inform the servants when you plan to be late for dinner, madame," he went on, strolling easily into the room and lifting a huge bath towel from the rack. "We do get cranky when our preparations aren't received with due appreciation."

She stared up at him from the camouflage of the bubbles. "I'm sorry, Dash. I didn't mean to be so long. I won't be a moment."

If she'd expected him to drop the towel and leave, she was mistaken. He strode to the tub and held it opened wide for her. When she made no movement, he turned his head away with an exaggerated pretense of prudery.

When he spoke again, he managed to infuse his words with Hemmings's proper Bostonian intonation. "Surely

224

you wouldn't think the butler would consider peeping, madame?"

She giggled at his foolishness, then, with a single, fitful glance at his averted eyes, she stood and quickly took the towel from him, wrapping it around herself. But he made no move of backing away. Instead, he leaned toward her and swept her up, still dripping, in his arms.

"We pride ourselves on providing complete service, madame," he went on, still with Hemmings's sonorous tones.

"You'll get wet," she warned, but made no other effort to deter him as he carried her through the door and out into the bedroom.

"A sacrifice we are willing to make in the line of duty, madame," he said.

"And who is this regal we of whom you speak?" she asked as he set her down. "Oh, Dash," she went on before he could answer.

He'd done more than order a simple meal for them. A fire blazed in the marble-faced hearth, and two armchairs were drawn up to a small linen-covered table. A huge bowl of red roses decorated its center, and the table was set with the hotel's finest crystal, silver, and porcelain, all sparkling in the flickering light of the fire and of the two candles that formed erect sentinels to the bowl of flowers. From a nearby trolley came the blood-rich scent of roast, making her mouth water.

"If madame would care to sit?"

Dash pulled out a chair and lifted her napkin, flicking it to spread out the linen.

"I'm not quite dressed for dinner," she protested, hesitating.

He smiled a bit lecherously. "You look quite appetizing to me," he said, and this time there was no hint of the proper Hemmings about him.

For a moment she thought she ought to ask him to leave, or at least retire long enough for her to dress formally. For she'd little illusions about where he hoped the evening would lead after the wine and the roast, and she told herself that he had no right to expect her to be his dessert.

But then she realized that the desire was not all his, that she'd been forcing herself not to think of the way he

225

made her feel for fear of being hurt, and all the time she was succeeding only in hurting herself. If she could have him only for a while, she thought, then she might as well have the comfort, the pleasure, he could give her for that time. At least then she'd have a memory when he was gone. She needed him, she told herself, and by denying that need she was only making the loneliness, the hurt of Vincent's disappearance, that much harder to bear.

She stared at him wide-eyed, and it was as though words were only an impediment to the things she wanted to say to him. Instead, she moved to him, putting her hand to his chest and letting it run upward, to his shoulder and behind his neck. She pulled his head downward until his lips found hers, and then she kissed him. It was a kiss filled with longing, and with a taste of regret for the nights they'd wasted since they'd left New York, for the needless anger she'd let drift between them. It was a kiss of apology, and he accepted it willingly, the taste of her lips and tongue a honeyed offering of repentance.

Then she backed away from him, and sat obediently, looking up at him. He stared at her in silence for a moment, then bent forward and placed her napkin primly on her lap. Then he crossed to the other side of the table, leaning forward to pour the wine, silently removing the plates from the trolley and putting them on the table. Finally, he seated himself across from her.

She lifted the wine and stared into the rich, deep ruby glow that filtered through it from the candles between them.

"Has the butler gone?" she asked him softly as she lifted her eyes to his and found him gazing at her.

"I've given him the remainder of the evening off," he told her with a crooked smile.

"I'm glad," she told him as he lifted his glass to hers, touching rims.

They both drank, and Abra found the wine rich and flinty, a heady and old burgundy, one of the best she'd ever tasted.

"Why?" he asked her simply as he watched the flush of color the alcohol brought to her cheeks.

She shrugged, and the movement of her shoulders loosened the towel, letting it slip a bit to reveal the upper rounded curves of her breasts. She seemed not to notice.

"Because he seemed a bit of a prude," she said as she put her glass down and lifted her knife and fork. "And I think this evening I'd rather have some company that was just a bit more *sympathique*."

He watched her as she cut a bite of the meat on her plate, and he followed suit, eating several bites but all the while keeping his eyes on her.

She ate silently, hungrily, for a few moments, attacking her food with the empty hunger that follows a day of anxiety and fasting. But she'd eaten less than a third of the food on her plate when she put down her cutlery.

"Is something wrong, Abra?" he asked. "Dinner not to your liking?"

She shook her head, and lifted her wine glass once more. Do I really need courage to do this? she asked herself. She put the glass back down on the table decisively.

"I guess I'm just not as hungry as I thought I was, Dash," she said. She looked at him squarely in the eyes. "At least not for this."

He gazed at her silently for a moment, then put his own knife and fork down on his plate and lifted his napkin to his lips.

"Shall I leave you, then?" he asked her brusquely.

She shook her head in negation.

"No anger after, no regrets this time?"

"No anger," she assured him, her voice shrunk to a near whisper. "No regrets."

He pushed his chair back and sat, looking at her for a long moment more. Then he held his arms open to her.

She rose and went to him, lowering herself to his lap, feeling the warmth of his arms as they slipped around her, the heated strength of his hands as they snaked along her bare arms to her shoulders. The firelight danced over her hair and he lifted his hand to the pins that held it up, freeing it and letting it fall, heavy silken coils, down her back. Then he put his hands to her cheeks and pulled her to him.

She parted her lips to his tongue, tasting the wine he'd drunk along with the heady narcotic of the contact. She knew what would follow, the hot liquid yearning that

227

would fill her, but she was surprised at the speed of it, the way her blood seemed to pulse at his first touch.

He drew back from her and looked at her, thinking her beautiful, the most beautiful woman he'd ever seen, ever touched. He wanted, more than anything else, he realized, to please her.

He pulled her close once more, pressing his lips to the warm flesh of her neck, burying his hands in the thick silk of her hair as she leaned her head back and closed her eyes, riding the heated wave of pleasure that surged within her. The press of his lips traveled downward, to the rounded curve of her breasts, the towel falling away unheeded.

Abra wrapped her arms around his neck, losing herself to the pleasurable heat of his lips and tongue as they warmed her breasts. She felt her nipples grow hard with want and she leaned forward, bending her head over his, pressing her lips to his unruly dark curls. She was lost, adrift, floating on the waves of liquid heat that filled her. Her world was the fire that surrounded them, filled them both, and nothing else mattered, nothing else existed.

He put his hand to her arms and pushed her gently away. "You have me at a bit of a disadvantage, Abra," he told her softly, with his crooked smile.

"Have I?" she asked smilingly as she brought her hands to his necktie, pulling it loose and then moving to the buttons of his shirt. "Under the circumstances, I would say it is I who am at a disadvantage."

He laughed at that, and at the intense concentration she directed to the buttons, feeling the touch of her fingers against his flesh with sharp stabs of longing. He pressed his hands to her back, moving them downward slowly, to her hips and buttocks, caressing her as she freed him of his clothing, apparently pleased with her initiative.

When she'd bared his chest, she bent forward to him, pressing her lips to the thick dark curls. He leaned back in his chair, pulling her with him, feeling the waves of desire filling him.

And then he rose, holding her still in his arms and lifting her, and carried her to the bed. He set her down, quickly shrugged away his clothing, then followed her to the satin softness, splaying her hair with his fingers as his lips found hers.

She put her arms to his neck, pulling him close to her, her body straining to his. He slid inside her and Abra heard herself moan with pleasure. At that moment, she felt herself a part of him, and she realized that no matter what happened between them after, there would always be that tie now binding the two of them, as though she would leave a part of herself behind with him, and he with her. For a moment she pondered that feeling, wondering if he sensed it, too. Then, as she filled with the sensation of him moving inside her, she lost all thought, lost all sense of the guilt and loneliness that had haunted her since Vincent's disappearance. All there was for her was Dash. He filled her, emotionally, physically, he permeated her universe until there was room for nothing else.

He loved her slowly, gently, instinctively realizing that the act was more than one of physical need for her, drawing her to the edge of the precipice and willing her to plunge. And when he felt her body tremble and arch to his, he let himself fall, too. He wrapped his arms around her, holding her gently, and whispered softly to her, "I love you, Abra."

Her eyes focused, clearing as though she'd been looking through a mist at him but now could see him clearly. She shook her head slowly.

"No," she whispered and she put her fingers to his lips. "I've no need for that."

And she thought to herself, much as I want it, it's better to live without any pretense, without any lies.

Her words puzzled him, but he made no protest. If she wasn't ready for the words, he thought, there was still time.

Through the mist of the night came the muffled sound of church bells, proclaiming midnight and the start of Christmas Day, a joyous clamor to announce a birth that had changed the world. Inside his head, he heard a small prayer, that it might also mean the birth of something else, perhaps less earth-shattering, but momentous to his life, a love between the two of them.

229

Abra drowsed in his arms. He pulled the blanket around her shoulder and prepared himself, too, for sleep, but as he glanced around the room he spotted something dimly shining through the unclosed draperies at the window.

She seemed to sense his stiffening attention, for she stirred, and her eyes opened.

"What is it?" she demanded sleepily, her green eyes sparkling up at him, her lips smiling with a contented peacefulness.

"I don't know," he said, slipping his arm from beneath her and moving across the room to the large window that overlooked the bay. He stared out, expecting to see nothing more than the same mist that had filled the air all day, finding instead large, white flakes drifting lazily to the accepting warmth of the water below.

She threw off the blanket and crept up next to him, huddling close, until he realized she was there and put his arm around her to keep her warm. Then he turned to her and smiled.

"It's Christmas, after all, Abra," he told her softly.

She stood beside him and gazed out at the falling snow. The chilled night air would warm by the morning, she realized, and there would be little if any trace of the flakes remaining, but for now, there was indeed snow filling the air.

"A small Christmas gift for you?" she asked him, grinning, remembering his saying that it didn't feel like Christmas without snow.

"I'm sorry I have nothing for you," he said softly.

"Nor I for you," she replied.

He put his finger to her chin and pulled it up until she was staring up at him.

"You've already given me a gift I'll treasure all my life, Abra."

He leaned down to her and kissed her forehead, then turned and pulled her away from the window.

"You'll catch cold if you stay here naked," he warned her.

She ran quickly back to the bed. "It's warmer here," she told him, even though she made no movement to draw up the blankets to cover herself.

He stood and grinned at her, then moved to the table where the remains of their dinner lay. He lifted one of the wine glasses, filled it, and moved across the room to her, sliding his body beside hers. He looked at her with amusement, and sipped the wine.

"Dare I be presumptuous?" he asked as he offered her the glass.

She took it from him and brought it to her lips, inhaling the heady bouquet before she drank. "Presumptuous?" she asked.

"It is Christmas, after all," he replied.

She raised a suspiciously knowing brow. "A time for bestowing gifts?" she suggested.

He nodded in silence.

She smiled, then put the glass down on the bedside table, turning to him with a pleased grin.

"A mutually agreeable gift, perhaps?" she asked as she bent to him, her hair falling in a silken curtain that contained their faces as her lips met his.

## Chapter Fifteen

Abra watched Dash calmly apply *confiture de framboise* to his croissant. He was leaning forward slightly over the table, the hard muscles of his bare chest and shoulders oddly taut for so apparently relaxed a position.

She tore her eyes away from him, feeling as though there was something impure in the simple pleasure she took in the contemplation of his body. That was for men, she thought. They were the ones who were stirred by the sight of naked flesh. But still, she realized as she disciplined her glance and glued it firmly to the cup that held her café au lait, it pleased her simply to look at him.

"Perhaps I should dress, Abra."

She looked up to find his eyes on her. He was slightly amused, it seemed, and apparently completely aware of her thoughts. She felt a hot blush seep into her cheeks.

"A towel is hardly formal attire," he continued when he saw the red, motioning to the white terry that he'd wrapped around his waist.

"If it was formal enough for dinner, I suppose it ought to suit for breakfast," she replied, and finally smiled, too. "What do we do now?" she asked abruptly more than willing to change the subject. "Simply go back to Les Pins?"

He nodded. "And another pleasant little conversation with McErlaine's charming housekeeper. This time, hopefully, with a bit more result."

"And if he's still not there?"

232

He thought about that for a moment. "I suppose we have little choice but to wait here for him. In any case, we might make our own little trip to the casino. We've no money left. I gave my last sou to the collection plate in the church last evening."

"You're not serious?" she asked.

Again the crooked smile. "Not quite," he replied. "But almost. If we're to pay the bill here, I'll need to find some cash, and fairly quickly." He grinned then. "If I'd known we'd be sharing a single room last night, I'd have saved the cost of the second."

She blushed once more, then stood, wandering slowly to the window, carrying her coffee with her. The morning was grey, but dry, without the pervasive mist that had seemed to be an intrinsic part of the atmosphere the day before. A dull sun tried valiantly to cut through the haze. She sipped her coffee meditatively, regretting the fact that nothing remained of the snow of the night before.

She turned abruptly back to face him. "It's Christmas Day," she told him softly. "Will there be gambling to-day?"

He smiled at her as one would at a naive child. "Not everyone, Abra, is as pious as those fishermen and their families who shared their Mass with us last evening. Especially not in Cannes."

She sipped her coffee thoughtfully. "Well, then, I suppose we ought to be about our Christmas visits," she said absently, wondering what new disappointments the day would bring.

The first was that McErlaine had not yet returned from Cannes. The sour-faced old housekeeper seemed vindicated in her assessment of him by the defection, once more calling him heathen, as she had the day before, turning away from them and closing the door with a determined push, as though by asking for the recalcitrant McErlaine they had, in her eyes at least, allied themselves with him.

233

They returned to the hotel. Dash directed her to dress in evening clothes, the off-white satin, and then he left her to her toilette. When he returned to fetch her, he presented her with a mask of white feathers.

"What is this for?" she demanded.

"Tonight, it seems, is something special at the casino," he told her. "A *bal masque.*"

The ride that had seemed almost interminable the day before passed quickly. Almost suddenly, it seemed, Abra found herself standing in the enormous central hall of the casino, feeling a little unsure of herself and more than a little bewildered by her surroundings. If the feeling at Cap Ferrat was one of slightly pinched respectability, there was none of that here. The tall columns were gilded and topped with carved cupids, their not-quite-innocent faces peering down at the intrigues that were begun in their unblinking view.

Dash, too, seemed somehow less a known quantity to her, somehow more mysterious and far more dangerous once he'd added his black satin mask to his evening clothes. He took her arm and led her toward the long marble staircase.

"Stay close to me, Abra," he whispered to her. "I wouldn't want to lose you, certainly not here."

She needed little encouragement to put her hand to his arm and cling to it. Already she could feel strangers' eyes on her, evaluating eyes, wondering at the new prey that had fallen into their lair.

She felt herself staring at the spectacularly ornate hall, everything carved and gilded or covered with colored marbles, no surface, it seemed, left unadorned. She was not ordinarily impressed terribly by her surroundings and for a moment she wondered at her absorption, then realized it was simply that she did not want to see the people, as though by looking elsewhere, she could pretend they were not there at all. For a *bal masque,* she realized, at least this *bal masque,* was something more than a polite entertainment. It was for those who found life a bit boring, and who could afford to find whatever amusements they could, while still maintaining some

234

semblance of anonymity. As she climbed the stairs, Abra could not help but see two couples caressingly entwined, a strange double coupling in fancy dress. High-pitched, loud laughter came from the group as she and Dash turned away and entered the great ballroom.

Here everything seemed to glitter, the brilliantly lit chandeliers, the gilt decoration, the gold rope that edged the heavy silk draperies framing huge windows that fronted on the bay, and, most contrived to impress, the quantities of jewels that flashed from both the women and the men in the enormous room.

"I feel quite dowdy," Abra whispered into Dash's ear after a moment of this heady inspection.

He grinned good-naturedly. "There are some jewels that shine all the more brilliantly without undue adornment, Abra," he replied. "You are one of them."

"Such gallantry, Mr. Thorne. Should I dismiss it as abject flattery?"

He looked down at her, and his expression grew entirely serious. "You will do as you think fit, I've no doubt, Abra, despite my avowal that nothing insincere was spoken nor was it intended."

Abra felt her heart thump at his words. It seemed foolish to her that a few words could make her react so, but she could not dismiss the feeling, nor did she want to question it.

"A dance, perhaps, before the business of the evening?" he asked.

Without waiting for an answer, he took her arm, put his hand to her waist, and swept her onto the floor.

It was the first time she'd danced with him since that evening at the Brinksons', and she could not help but recall the feeling she'd had then, that he was quite good at it, an easy partner who guided her expertly with just the right pressure to her waist so that, despite the fact that they were not long-accustomed partners, there was no misstep, no small collision of foot or body. When she danced with him, she felt as if she had been born in his arms.

It was a lovely sensation, but one that was not fated to

last long. When they were in the center of the floor, Dash nodded to a pair of ornately gilded massive doors that half filled the opposite wall.

"The gaming rooms are there," he told her.

She considered his words with concentration. "You've been here before?"

He only smiled absently. "Once or twice," he said and it was apparent that he had no intention of saying anything more.

She didn't know why the fact of that small, evasive admission disturbed her. She would have liked to dismiss it simply as one more fact of his life that he'd managed to hide from her, just as he had hidden, she had little doubt, a great deal more. But it was more than that, she knew, the dim realization that a jewel thief would find the small strip of real estate between Cannes and Monte Carlo of the greatest interest, for it would have, she realized, the same sort of attraction as a big game hunter would find in Africa, or an archaeologist in the Valley of the Kings. This was his hunting territory, and his simple admission drove that fact home to her all too clearly.

"We ought to go there, then, I suppose. If he's here, he would most likely be there," she agreed with false enthusiasm.

He nodded, and directed them toward the doors. All the while, Abra regarded them with the sort of repugnance one would the doors to hell.


McErlaine saw that his hand shook slightly as he signed the chit. Ten thousand, his last ten thousand. He had to start winning, he told himself firmly, and start now.

Not that he really had any doubt but that his luck would change. Three days of heavy losses. It had to change now, go back to the way it had been that first night. He'd won then, and he remembered the feeling, the elation as he'd watched the stacks of chips being pushed across the table to him, the incredible feeling of control and the surprised sense of the ease of it.

236

That evening he'd even thought to take some of his winnings to the upper floors of the casino, where an introduction might be arranged, for an adequate price, an introduction to a handsome young woman who would be pleased to accompany a gentleman wherever he might choose to go for the evening. He'd even considered those other, smaller, more secretive rooms where one might obtain the use of a water pipe and a bit of hashish. Gentlemen, after all, were not stinting in their pleasures. And he had money now. He was a gentleman.

But then the table had turned against him, and he'd decided to put off his ventures into that hazily distant world, temporarily to be sure, until he was once more winning.

Only it hadn't gone quite the way he'd envisioned. His luck hadn't turned as he'd told himself it surely would, and each evening he'd lost, he'd known he'd have to return the next, to make up the money, to get back what had been his. After all, he'd told himself, luck did change. It couldn't continue to go against him for very much longer.

And now he was repeating the same litany to himself one last time, knowing that if it was not true now, there would be no other chance for him. But he didn't even think of that possibility as he watched the chips being slid across the table to him in return for his signature on the chit.

He pushed one chip to the center of the table as the first cards were dealt, turned up the two that had been dealt him, and nodded to the dealer.

"Card," he demanded and he could feel a slow glow of moisture appear on his brow and upper lip. He had to win this time, he told himself. His luck had to change.


Liveried servants, trained, apparently, to read the thoughts of those patrons whose minds were set on the pleasures of gambling, opened the doors as they approached. Abra looked in, at a room as large as the ballroom and as grandly decorated. But here the atmo-

237

sphere seemed tenser, more intent upon matters more pressing than the odd flirtation or late-night assignations being arranged in the ballroom. The air was filled with the heady atmosphere of men considering the gain or loss of money.

"Would you like to play a bit, Abra?" Dash asked her easily.

She turned and stared up at him, certain he wasn't being serious, or was, perhaps, drugged by the atmosphere.

"But what if I lose, Dash?" she asked him. "We have almost no money left."

He took her arm. "I have no doubt but that you'll do handsomely by us, Abra," he told her calmly as he led her to a roulette table.

The dozen or so players, all male, nodded to her and smiled as she approached, one rising to offer her his velvet-cushioned stool.

"Ah, a lovely lady to bring us some luck," he proclaimed to the rest as Abra seated herself. He smiled at her. "The wheel always turns when a beautiful woman plays," he told her.

"I'm not sure it will this time," she told him with an apologetic smile. "I don't know what to do."

"It's not so very difficult, Abra," Dash told her. "The betting's simple. Red or black, even money. The first, second, or third third of the table, two to one, the numbers, because the chance of a single number's coming up are less, are higher still, thirty-six to one." He handed her a small pile of chips. "Try your luck," he told her, then he backed away, apparently leaving her to her own devices.

She began hesitantly, placing a chip on the red, feeling the glow of delighted surprise as the croupier called, *"Rouge, vingt-et-un,"* and pushed another chip to hers. She left the two where they were, and once more won.

"You see how easy it is?" the man who had given her his seat asked her pleasantly.

"It is, isn't it?" she agreed. She put all four chips on the second third and won yet again.

Dash stood a bit apart, watching her play silently. He seemed to expect her to win, even to expect the other players at the table to begin to follow her bets, tentatively at first, then with greater confidence as she seemed to be able to outguess the vagaries of the wheel. But when the man who'd given up his seat to her began to follow her bets, pushing large stacks of chips to the croupier with the single word, *"Suivez,"* his attention grew more concentrated.

In about a quarter of an hour Abra had collected a substantial pile of chips in front of her, and the man who'd followed her with the large bets had a far larger one. More confident now, she placed a bet on the thirty-one, thirty-two, thirty-four, thirty-five corner, and yet again she won. Another large pile of chips was pushed to her.

"Becoming bored, my dear?" Dash asked, leaning forward to her as she placed another bet.

She turned to him, surprised by the bored, pedantic tone he'd used.

Dash watched as her fifty-franc bet was followed by a fifty-thousand-franc bet, the single word, *"Suivez,"* uttered as the chips were pushed forward.

And this time, Abra lost.

*"Zero, blanc,"* the croupier announced, sweeping up the chips that littered the table with his rake.

She watched the bits of ivory disappear feeling a bit bewildered.

"The wheel seems to have turned, my dear," Dash told her, and this time she realized his bored tone was a signal.

"So it has," she agreed, smiling and standing as he pushed a small pile of the chips to the croupier as a tip and then collected the rest.

"Perhaps madame would like to try again?" the croupier suggested hopefully, realizing he had made an error and aware that the realization came too late.

"Later, perhaps," Dash told him as he turned away.

The croupier shrugged, and pocketed his tip. The losses, after all, were not his.

"Will you please tell me what just happened?" Abra asked Dash as he put his hand to her elbow and led her away from the table.

"An old game, Abra," he explained easily. "A pretty young woman comes to a table where several men are playing without much interest. If she wins, they become more involved in the play and follow her bets. And later, when she starts to lose, they continue to follow her bets, more interested now in the lady than in their own losses."

She stared up at him, a bit dismayed.

"Then I didn't really win?"

"Oh, you won," he assured her. "These chips in my hands are material proof of that."

"But it was fixed. They gave me those passes so that the men would follow?"

"Precisely," he told her. "And as soon as a substantial bet was made to follow yours, you suddenly lose. And so did that kindly gentleman who gave you his seat. Fifty thousand francs, to be precise."

Abra gasped. "So much?"

Dash shrugged. "The croupier was not pleased when I suggested you leave." He smiled at her then. "Your admirer won more than fifty thousand on the preceding passes. If you'd played a few times more, then the table would have made a healthy profit. As it was, the croupier lost a bit for the house by your untimely departure from the table."

Abra shook her head, bewildered. "Isn't anything the way it seems?" she asked him.

He nodded toward a woman who approached half a dozen men at the table they passed. She stood, considering the stacks of chips they pushed forward to her, finally accepting the largest. The winner stood and took her arm. She smiled at him and then looked up, her eyes catching Dash's. She smiled then, her heavily painted face forming itself into a caricature of lustful invitation.

"Some things are entirely as they seem," Dash told Abra drily.

Abra looked, then turned away quickly, not wanting to see.

"She smiled at you," Abra whispered in dismay. "Even as she took another man's money."

"Be prepared for something even more distressing, my naive little Abra," Dash told her with a wry grin. "She is a he."

Abra's head turned back to the male whore, her amazement written plainly on her face. When he saw Abra's abrupt turn, he smiled at her, too, and blew her a kiss from red-painted lips. Abra blushed violently, and turned back to Dash. She realized that between the embarrassment and the bewilderment, she had never felt quite so ill at ease before in her life.

"What do we do now?" she asked in a shaky whisper.

Dash smiled and patted her hand complacently. "We find a friendly little game of *chemie,* or, better still, some good, old-fashioned American poker," he told her as he led her across the gaming room to several small rooms that had been partitioned off, the rooms where the real gambling was done.

Poker, it seemed, was not in the offing, but in one of the rooms several tables accommodated games of *chemin de fer,* and one sported an available chair. Dash headed for it.

"Don't wander, Abra," he warned her. "Stay close. This is not an entirely benign environment for a young woman of rather innocent mien."

"Innocent?" she countered. "I hadn't thought you found me so last night."

He lifted a corner of his mouth in amusement, but made no answer. Then he slid into the empty place, putting the stack of chips she'd won at the roulette game on the table in front of him.

Abra only half watched the play. Instead she was more fascinated by the speed with which Dash had turned her winnings into what appeared to be a small fortune, watching as the cards were pushed from the shiny brass and mahogany shoe, listening to the quietly spoken requests for "carte," the dull precision with which the paddle pushed the heavy ivory plackets with what seemed incredibly huge numbers imprinted on them.

241

There was no real reason for her attention to be drawn to the far side of the room. It was more the way the man pushed back his chair and stood that struck her. He had a kind of desperation about him that surprised her.

Everyone else she'd seen in the casino seemed to accept both winning and losing with an almost disinterested detachment. But this man's manner made it obvious that he was far from detached. He seemed to stumble to the door, his step looking almost as if he'd not make the distance safely, without mishap. And as she watched him with the feeling of pity growing inside her, Abra realized he was not the total stranger she'd originally thought him.

Despite the disguise afforded by the evening dress, she could not help but discern the heavy barrel chest. And even the near stumbling gait could not keep her from recognizing the underlying self-important amble she remembered. She was staring, she realized, at Patrick Daniel Francis McErlaine.

"Dash," she whispered hoarsely, putting her hand to his shoulder.

But his attention was riveted to the cards that lay on the table before him, and when Abra glanced down, she realized why. A huge stack of chips and bills lay in the center of the table. There was the nervous rustle of whispered speculation as those players who had dropped out contemplated the game. If she interrupted him now, they stood to lose a fortune, a fortune they would most likely need to ransom the Tear.

It took her only a second to decide to follow McErlaine herself. When the play was done, she knew, Dash would realize she was gone and follow. After all, it wouldn't be long, and McErlaine couldn't possibly go far.

She slipped away, following the big, dazed figure from the room. He made his way through the ballroom with what seemed tunnel vision, blind to everything except the door at the far side. Abra followed, fighting to keep her eyes on him in the crowd. I can't lose him, she thought desperately as she dodged groups of revellers.

"Not alone are we, love?"

A hand grasped her bare arm with an unpleasantly moist warmth. She tried to shrug it off, but it held tight, and she was forced to turn to face the owner of it, despite her reluctance to take her glance from McErlaine's retreating form. It was the man who'd given his stool to her at the roulette table.

"I thought that dull fellow would keep you chained to his side for the evening. This is a pleasant surprise."

"Please," Abra begged, putting her free hand to his and trying to push it away. "I have to leave."

She turned away from him, searching through the sea of bodies for McErlaine.

"Surely not so quickly. I haven't thanked you for winning all those passes for me. I dare say you would have continued to win had not your friend pulled you away so rudely." He smiled at her. "I'd be delighted to show my appreciation."

"I told you I have to leave," Abra replied.

"Then it would be a pleasure to take you wherever it is you wish to go," he suggested.

"I told you, no," Abra fairly shouted at him. She dug her fingers into his hand and the contact was apparently painful to him, for he released his hold of her arm.

"Only trying to be friendly, love," he told her, obviously a bit surprised and disconcerted by her manner.

But she wasn't listening. She was already starting after McErlaine, who had disappeared through the far door of the ballroom.

Dash smiled as the enormous pile of bills and chips was pushed to him. This was enough, he thought, enough to meet their immediate needs certainly, and a good amount more. There was no need to tempt the fates for too long or expect them to accompany one too far. Even one who knew the odds and played them very well lost from time to time, as he was only too painfully

243

aware.

He turned and looked up, expecting to find Abra standing behind him.

"Not looking for your good luck charm, are you?" asked a player across the table from him. Dash turned to face him. "She left a few minutes ago. It looked as though she'd seen someone she wanted to talk to."

Dash stood quickly. "You gentlemen will excuse me," he said as he distractedly scooped up his winnings.

"I don't blame him," the man who'd told him of Abra's departure stage whispered to the others at the table as he left. "It wouldn't be worth winning a fortune if that one got away during the play."

There was a round of knowing laughter. Then the shoe was passed, and Dash and Abra were quickly forgotten as all attention was returned to the game.


"And what have you done now, Patty Mac? You should know better than tryin' to live above yer station."

The words ran in his mind, his father's words, spoken in his father's voice, his father's all-knowing, all-important tones. His father, who always saw everything, heard everything, knew everything, disapproved of everything. The sanctimonious minister for whom nothing was ever quite good enough, at least nothing that Patty had ever done.

McErlaine wondered how that unwelcome spectre had appeared, now, when he was least able to cope with it.

"It's not my fault," he moaned, half aloud, just as he had done countless times as a child. Nothing was ever his fault. But somehow he'd always caught the blame anyway.

He put his hand to his forehead and felt the mask. It was damp with his perspiration, and he tore it off, dropping it to the moist ground. Then he pressed the heels of his palms into his eyes. That, at least, served to push away his father's condemning presence, the hateful expression that said he had never really expected anything better of such a worthless, godless son.

244

He's dead, McErlaine told himself, grasping desperately to a shred of rationality. And probably burning in hell.

But he could not as easily push away the realization of all that money, all those thousands. They had been his future, what there was left of it, his life. And now they were gone, along with the badge that had meant so much to him for more years than he wanted to think about, along with the image he'd had of himself as the incorruptible cop. He'd lost those when he'd taken the ruby, and now he'd lost the money for which he'd sold his conscience. He stared numbly down at his empty hands.

An irrational anger began to surge through him. If it hadn't been for Beaumont, he told himself, none of it would have happened. None of it. Not the stone, not the theft, not the horrendous losses at the tables. If it hadn't been for Beaumont, he'd still be what he had worked all his life to be, what he'd been meant to be. A cop. Maybe not liked, but he'd never really wanted that. But respected. Feared. That was what mattered. All but for Beaumont and his damned daughter.

And then there slipped through his mind the realization that there hadn't even been one girl. He'd had the money, and he'd never once had a pretty young girl, not even for a night. And now it was gone, it was too late to think there might ever be the chance again. That, in the end, was his greatest regret.

He put his hands to his empty pockets and stared out at the neatly manicured garden that fronted the casino, at the silent waters of the bay below, beyond the walled stretch of greenery and the sheer, steep drop. It all seemed filled with a hushed expectancy, a winter expectancy that spoke of things to come once the seasons changed and the earth warmed. It seemed unfair, that certainty of a lush life waiting beyond the winter, entirely unfair to McErlaine. After all, now there was nothing but an empty winter for him, for the remainder of his life, a dull, empty wintertime of regret.

And if it hadn't been for Beaumont, none of it would ever have happened.

There was a stir on the path behind him. He wasn't really listening for it, but the years of waiting for a sound, for a glimpse of something or someone, had sensitized him, so that the noise intruded on his thoughts enough so that he could not ignore it.

He turned, surprised at the flash of white satin that huddled close to the tree some twenty yards behind him. He didn't really understand why. No one would want to follow him, especially now, when he had nothing left worth the effort of stealing. But there was someone there, and he meant to find out who it was and why they were there.

It was a woman, he realized with a start as he crept silently back along the path, his bulky form surprisingly light and sure now that he'd determined not to make any noise, now that the old instincts had taken over his movements. A woman, he mused, crouching against a tree hoping she wouldn't be seen. And the thought came to him once again that he'd missed the opportunity, that he'd never once had the pleasure of a beautiful young woman.

He skirted the tree where she tried to hide, thinking how much smarter he was than she, how easy it was to catch her off guard. When he came up behind her, he watched her with a detached amusement, as she dared to look out at the path, expecting to see him still standing there.

"What are you doin', spyin' on me?" he demanded loudly as he grasped her arm and swung her around to face him.

She uttered a surprised cry, then fell silent, looking at him through the feathers of her mask, a hint of her panic glinting from her eyes. She tried to pull her arm from his grasp, but he caught her two hands in his and held them fast.

"I asked you a question, girl," he shouted at her.

She made no answer, just looked at him in numb terror.

He raised his hand to the white feathered mask, tearing it away and throwing it to the ground. Then he stared in amazement.

"Beaumont's daughter," he said slowly, the words bringing an unexpected taste of pleasure to him. His grasp on her wrists tightened and she uttered a small cry of pain.

"Let me go," she begged softly, as though she knew even before she spoke them that the words would do her no good.

"Beaumont's daughter," McErlaine repeated, and the thought returned to him once more, that he'd not yet had the pleasure of a beautiful young woman. "Beaumont's daughter," he whispered one last time, as though the words tasted good to him.

At least he wouldn't be cheated of everything, he told himself as he began to pull her off the path into the winter-deadened greenery of the garden.

## Chapter Sixteen

Dash scanned the gambling room quickly, but there was no sign of her white satin, no flash of reddish gold hair among the sedate black of the men's evening dress, the brilliantly colored silks and satins that the few female players wore. Not for them white, certainly. They had no reason to wish to paint a portrait of innocence. Certainly not here.

He stood at the entrance to the ballroom, once more scanning the crowd. Here it was harder to see, for the room was far more crowded. He felt a desperate fear that something terrible had happened to her, and it chilled him more completely than any cold he'd ever felt in his life.

"Looking for your little friend, are you?"

The words seemed disembodied at first. Dash turned to find a hazily familiar face, and then the memory, the one who had lost the fifty thousand at the roulette table.

"She left, rather abruptly," came the amused announcement as the man lifted the glass of champagne he held in his hand to his lips. "But then, if you leave them to their own devices, they always get away. There's always someone willing to pay just a bit more, I've found."

"Where did she go?" Dash demanded, the urgency he felt unmistakably finding its way to his expression.

This, too, seemed to amuse his companion. "As I said, she left. Through the doors and out, presumably into the night. Women are such fickle creatures, especially pretty women, don't you think?"

But Dash hadn't waited politely for the end of his small monologue, and there was no one left to answer him. He shrugged, then looked back to the roulette tables. Nothing better to do, he decided as he made his way to them.

Dash took the stairs in the great hall two at a time, his haste drawing a few curious glances, but little more.

At the front door, he turned to the liveried porter.

"A woman, dressed in white satin, a white feathered mask?"

The man nodded and smiled. He'd seen her, yes, just a few moments before. She'd left without her coat, and he'd thought that odd. It was, after all, not a warm night.

Dash put his hand to his pocket and drew out one of the large chips, dropping it into the man's hand in absent thanks as he ran down the front stairs to the carriage road. It was still and empty, and he stood, bewildered for a moment. Then he thought he caught a glimpse of something white across the road, on one of the garden paths. The light that shimmered from the casino picked it out indistinctly, but instinctively he knew it was not to be ignored.

He ran to the spot, bending to the gravel path, lifting up the white feathered mask. For God's sake, Abra, he thought miserably, where have you gotten to? And why?

It was then that he heard the noise, a muffled low thrashing in the shadows of the bushes. He turned to it, making his way through the prickly undergrowth. Beyond them he saw the black-dressed, bearlike figure of the man, the woman beneath him, thrashing wildly but unable to free herself from the frenzied grasp. Her cry was almost stifled by the hand to her mouth, his fingers viciously biting into her cheeks. He seemed oblivious to her struggle as he concerned himself with a frenzied groping with her skirts.

Dash threw himself on McErlaine, pulling him away from Abra and forcing him to the ground, his rage driving home the blow. Then he knelt over the man, his hand to McErlaine's throat, and he had but one emotion, of outrage and hatred, and he was governed by the sheer desire to kill. His fingers hardened on McErlaine's throat and the man's eyes widened, staring up at him in terror.

"No, Dash, don't!"

Abra had crawled to him. There was a dark purplish bruise already rising on her cheek and a long red scratch along her arm and leading down to her breast. The shoulder of her dress was torn.

He turned to her and stared at her, at the fear that lingered in her eyes, and listened to the panting breath she was trying desperately to control.

"We have to know," she whispered to him, her words nearly drowned by the pressure of imminent tears.

He nodded. The first, frightening rush of total rage was dimming and he realized he had almost killed a man. He turned to McErlaine, loosening his hold on his throat, and watched as the man gasped for air, coughing and straining as though he would never have enough.

"The stone," Dash hissed at him. "Where did you sell it?"

"To Bazetti," McErlaine gasped.

Dash released him completely and sat back on his knees, watching McErlaine pull away from him and rub his neck.

"Paulo Bazetti?" he asked.

McErlaine nodded, his hand still to his throat.

"And is he still here in Cannes, or has he gone back to Venice?"

McErlaine stared at him, numbly silent, unmoving.

"Damn you, man, I asked you a question. Has he gone back to Venice?"

Dash's voice was a low, cold threat. He moved toward McErlaine, his eyes blazing his rage.

McErlaine cringed, but he seemed to have found his tongue once more.

"He said he was returning to Venice."

Dash turned away from him, disgusted. He stood, moving quickly to Abra and helping her to her feet, holding her in his arms as she huddled to him. He removed his jacket and wrapped it around her, then lifted her into his arms as her trembling grew more pronounced, as the shock of what had nearly happened to her became more real to her.

"It's gone," McErlaine whimpered, turning his face up to them as though he expected their pity. He raised his hand and pointed a finger at Abra. "After what her father did to me, they owed me something, a life, something. And now the money's all gone."

Dash turned a cold glance to him. "You pathetic bastard," he said slowly.

Then he turned away, carrying Abra back to the bright glare of the brilliantly lit front of the casino. As he approached the steps, the porter he'd so handsomely tipped came rushing down the steps to him, hoping perhaps to provide some other small service and be equally well paid.

McErlaine watched them leave, and for the first time in his life he knew the meaning of real, invasive fear. They'll go to the police, he thought. Theft. Attempted rape. And I'll go to prison.

The thought petrified him more than anything he'd ever imagined. He knew what happened to rapists in prison, and to policemen. He told himself he could face living without the money, he could face anything but prison.

He staggered to his feet and made his way to the wall that marked the end of the garden, then stood staring, looking down at the rocky cliff beneath him and the water of the bay where it lapped easily against the stone.

Prison, he thought once more and shivered, not with cold but from the images that reeled through his mind at the thought.

And then, as though guided by some hand at his back, he climbed stiffly to the top of the wall. Once more he stood and looked down, oblivious of everything but the water and the rocks beneath him, oblivious of the cries he heard behind him from the steps of the casino where the porter who had come to help Dash and Abra now saw him, framed by a dull moon, standing on the wall. The water below seemed to beckon to him, welcoming him.

He closed his eyes and then he jumped.


"What happens now?" Abra asked.

Dash pressed a cold compress to the bruise on her cheek. He'd cleaned the blood from the scratch, and now all that remained was a long, red weal.

"Perhaps we should get a doctor to look at you, Abra," he told her gently.

She shook her head vehemently, rejecting the offer for the second time. "No. I couldn't stand a stranger to touch me," she whispered and shuddered, pressing her lips together, forcing herself to hold back the urge to cry. When she'd settled herself a bit, she looked up at him. "I'm all right, Dash. He didn't really hurt me."

She turned away, trying not to think what would have happened if Dash hadn't come when he had. She'd been a fool to go off after McErlaine alone, and she realized it all the more clearly because he'd refrained from telling her so. She told herself not to think of it, not any of it, most especially of the body lying on the rocks, still save for the movement the waves gave to it. McErlaine had paid dearly for the wrongs he'd done.

"Then you should sleep now."

But she shook her head again. She didn't want to sleep. The thought of being alone somehow frightened her. And so she asked him once more, "What do we do now?" more to keep him there, talking, close to her.

She forced herself to concentrate on his words, although they seemed distant and meaningless to her.

He sat beside her on the bed, looking down at her, wondering if she was really as unhurt as she claimed. Her eyes seemed a bit unfocused, a bit wild, and he realized she was still feeling the terror of those moments, still replaying it all in her mind.

He edged himself up to the head of the bed and leaned back, waiting for her to settle herself beside him, then put his arm gently around her shoulders. She seemed less tense that way, more at ease once he was holding her.

"If you're well enough tomorrow, I'll make arrange-

252

ments for us to take the train to Venice. We have to find Paulo Bazetti."

"You know this man?" she asked slowly.

He realized her words were a bit too precisely spoken. She was fighting for control of herself, forcing her concentration.

"I know of him," he replied softly, doubting that she'd remember much of the conversation but realizing she found his voice comforting. "He's a thief who fleeces other thieves, a trader in stolen jewels to those who don't know any better and have no other outlet." He looked down at her and smiled wryly. "He must have had quite a surprise when McErlaine brought the ruby to him. I'm sure he's never handled anything quite like it." He smiled once more. "It will give me the opportunity to show you Venice," he went on. "It's a beautiful city, a city I've always thought ought to be shared by lovers." The prospect pleased him and he smiled as he pictured it.

But Abra hadn't heard much of what he'd told her, after all. She lay, still and asleep, in his arms.

"You won't believe the Piazza San Marco, Abra," he continued softly, picturing the huge square in his mind and imagining her delight at the sight of it. "You can sit outdoors at a cafe and watch all the city pass, although I don't suppose the weather will be quite conducive to that. We'll take a hotel room overlooking the Grand Canal, at the Danielli or the Grand, and I'll show you a tiny *scuola,* a school whose walls Caravaggio saw fit to decorate with murals showing St. George slaying the dragon, no doubt for the edification of the school boys who aspired to grandeur."

He stopped then, and stared at her sleep-gentled features, wondering if there'd be the opportunity for them to do any of the things he'd mentioned, to behave like ordinary lovers, losing themselves to the Renaissance wonders of the city. Somehow, he very much doubted it.


The train ride had been dull and seemingly interminable. The short boat ride that followed, however, Abra actually found pleasant in the dimming sunlight.

The air that touched her lips was tinged with sea salt, almost brittle in its crispness. And she could only gaze in unbelieving awe at the profile of Venice as their boat worked its way along the Grand Canal.

Dash pointed out the graceful arches of the Doges' Palace, the stone turned a flickering, pale gold in the dimming glow of the setting sun, the Campanile beyond a sharp, pointed upright, speaking of solidity, of eternal power. And on the water, the scurrying movement of countless small boats, their sails glowing red in the waning light.

As he'd promised, Dash had obtained an opulent suite overlooking the canal, with a view of San Giorgio, the spires dim now in the near twilight, but mysteriously evocative. He'd disappeared, then, with instructions that she rest from the trip while he was gone, refusing to say anything more. Instead, she'd bathed, then passed the time staring out the window at the sweeping grandeur of the canal, intrigued by the sight of the gondolas that floated past with their cargoes of caped and furred passengers intent upon the imminent revels of the evening.

"I thought you were resting."

She swung around to find Dash at the door, his stare one of slight disapproval.

She smiled and crossed the room to him. "Impossible," she told him. "It's fairyland out there. One doesn't sleep in fairyland."

He smiled at that, then kissed her briskly on the lips.

"Where have you been?" she demanded as he removed his coat.

"Off finding the chief gnome in fairyland," he replied complacently.

"Bazetti?" she asked.

He nodded. "He dines tonight at Quadri, and, I think, so shall we."

She wanted to ask him how he knew about Bazetti, but she drew back from voicing the question. Of course, he'd know. He was a thief. He'd know who to go to, where to find the answers to whatever questions needed asking. As it had in the casino, the thought of who and what he was chilled her, reminding her that his life and

254

hers were only temporarily and loosely joined, that it would be over soon and forgotten, just one more episode of his life that he could turn his back on and leave behind.

She pushed the thought aside, telling herself that she need not torture herself with it, at least not just yet. When the time came, and it would be soon enough, there would be more than enough opportunity to contemplate who and what he was. For now, she would only think of him as the man she'd come to love.

She forced a smile to her lips. "And just how does one dress for dinner at Quadri? Especially for a gnome?" she asked, keeping her tone briskly cheerful.

He grinned at her. "Only the finest," he replied, loosening his tie and moving toward the bath. "By the way," he turned and asked when he'd reached the door, "Did you bring that brooch Sharify gave you?"

She stiffened at the mention of the sheik. "Yes," she told him. "I intend to return it to him." She offered him a challenging look. "Forcefully."

He laughed gently at her expression of distaste. "I'd be the last to try to dissuade you, Abra," he told her. "But for now, I think we might use it as bait to hook Bazetti. Wear it."

With that, he passed into the next room and closed the door behind him. Abra could dimly hear the sound of water running for his bath.


Quadri sported dark red brocade-covered walls, and the shimmering light of what seemed like hundreds of candles was reflected from the graceful arms of blown glass chandeliers and sconces.

Abra critically considered her reflection in the gilt-framed mirror as they entered. Her gown concealed all but the smallest edge of the angry red weal on her shoulder, and the powder she'd applied camouflaged the bruise on her cheek quite well, at least in the softly forgiving glow of candlelight. The mayhem outside the casino might have been a world away.

The headwaiter who greeted them inspected her as

well, appearing to be a good deal less critical in his evaluation. With an inviting smile, he led them to the small central dining room that overlooked the piazza. It was there that the richest and most powerful men took their dinners, and he was not oblivious of the fact that rich and powerful patrons were hardly immune to the enjoyment of gazing at a handsome young woman.

As they were seated, Abra found Dash whispering to the man, saw the smile and nod as the headwaiter discreetly motioned to a table nearby where a single man sat diminishing the contents of a plate of *scampi alla veneziana.*

She leaned across the table to Dash. "Bazetti?" she asked in a low whisper.

He nodded as he lifted the wine list that had been left at his place. "Now we see where Mr. Bazetti's weaknesses lie," he told her softly. "Perhaps with a bottle of excellent Serristori."

The captain, seeing he'd made his choice, approached, and Dash ordered two bottles, directing that one be sent to Bazetti's table with his compliments.

Abra obliquely watched Bazetti's face as the wine was brought to him, uncorked, and poured. She knew she ought not to show too much interest, but the man's face intrigued her, round and almost jolly, yet with an underlying hint of malice, like a not entirely benign *putto,* perfectly at home in the ornate surroundings of the room. He looked to where she and Dash sat as a glass was placed before him and the wine was poured. He lifted the goblet, his lips puckered in anticipation, then sipped. Only then did he smile, and he raised the glass to them in a gesture of thanks. He took one more swallow, then turned his glance entirely on Abra.

This time, when he smiled, it was only at her. She held his eyes with hers for a second, then smiled too.

Dash pushed her glass toward her. "It seems you've found another of Signore Bazetti's weaknesses, Abra," he told her evenly.

She turned her glance to him and cocked her head, not understanding.

"You," he explained with a slow smile. "But that's

really no surprise, now. The man would have to be blind and half dead not to notice you tonight."

She blushed as he knew she would at his words, and he grinned at her knowingly. "I dare say we will have a small visit of thanks paid us before the end of the meal."

He was right. Abra was addressing herself to a plate of *pernici arrosto* when Bazetti appeared beside their table. At first he seemed entirely involved with their dinner.

"Ah, the *pernici* are excellent here," he effused, his short, rounded body almost quivering with the contemplation of a dish he'd not included in his own meal. "You will enjoy it, I'm sure."

Abra looked up at him and smiled. "Yes, it's very good," she agreed.

"As was the Serristori," he replied with a smiling nod to Dash.

"Perhaps you would care to join us and have another glass?" Dash offered.

"Alas, I cannot," Bazetti moaned softly. "An untimely business engagement forces me to leave. But not without thanking you for your kind gesture." His expression grew pensive. "And admitting to you that I am led to wonder what prompted it."

Dash shrugged. "It was nothing. I'm delighted it pleased you." Then he looked up at Bazetti, his blue eyes turning hard and appraising. "Perhaps we might call on you sometime, with a small business matter of our own to discuss." He nodded toward Abra.

Bazetti turned his glance back to her just as Abra raised her fingers to the low decolletage of her dress where the diamond-encrusted brooch Sharify had given her nestled. For a moment she wondered if the gesture was too daring, for Bazetti's glance seemed more fixed on the incline of her cleavage than on the brooch.

But then he smiled, as though all was now clear to him, and turned back to Dash.

"But certainly," he replied. "It would be a pleasure to repay your kindness. I shall be home by midnight. Come then. You have only to tell your gondolier my name. Every one of them in the city knows where Bazetti lives."

With that he nodded to Dash in parting, then turned

257

his glance back to Abra.

"I look forward to seeing you once more," he said, and lifted her hand to his lips, leaving a moist imprint of them on her skin. Then he turned and made his way through the clutter of tables to the door.

Abra permitted herself a small sigh of relief. When he was gone, she lifted her napkin and wiped her hand decisively as Dash grinned at her.

"Well, that wasn't as horrible as I'd expected," she said.

Dash considered her for a moment before turning back to his dinner.

"But we've yet to face the gnome in his cave, Abra," he warned her before he lifted his fork to his mouth.


Cave was an apt description for the first glance they had of the interior of Bazetti's palace. The gondola left them at a set of stone stairs that led directly into the canal, and they stood with the water lapping almost to their feet until the door was opened to them by an enormous hulk of a man who stared out at them a moment, apparently deciding if they passed muster, before allowing them to enter.

The room into which they stepped was dimly lit by flickering candles, and dank. It was unfurnished and undecorated, save for a half-dozen marble busts placed in individual niches in the walls, imparting to the room a grimly mortuarial pallor. Apparently the waters rose from time to time and made their way into this level of the house. It seemed a fit habitation for a gnome.

But as they were led up a long flight on stone steps, the atmosphere changed markedly. Dark watered silk appeared on the walls, there were ornate carvings on the ceiling of the hallway overhead, and each door and window frame they passed was heavy with carved design and gilt.

They were finally shown into a small sitting room, almost claustrophobic with the press of ornamentation on walls and ceiling, a jumble of equally rococo furniture filling every available inch of wall, as well as much of the remaining floor space. An enormous carved stone fireplace filled one wall entirely, and a fire burned with an exuberant intensity, the heat of it more than compensating for any chill dampness the evening might have let stray into the room. The air had grown close and hot from it.

Bazetti looked up at them as they entered. He was seated in a darkly upholstered armchair by the fire, the black velvet of his smoking jacket dwarfing his bulk as it receded into the dark figured material of the upholstery.

"I'm delighted you've come," he nearly crooned, his round face bobbing pleasantly as he waved them to the chairs that circled the fireplace across from his. "Ugo," he called to the servant who had admitted them, "some champagne for my guests." Then he turned back to Abra and Dash. "A pleasant, star-studded evening, unusual for this time of the year. I hope you've been enjoying your visit to my lovely city?"

"It is incredibly beautiful," Abra agreed, wondering how long the prate of insincere pleasantries would continue and when the business at hand would be begun.

From the far side of the room was the sound of a cork being released from a champagne bottle, and she realized the servant was still there in the room with them. He'll chatter on at least until the servant has left the room, she told herself, and, aware of the attention Bazetti had turned to her, realized more was expected.

"I feel as though I've somehow stumbled into a fairy tale. The canals, the exotica of the houses," she waved her hand and looked around the room. "This magnificent house."

Apparently she'd said the right thing, because Bazetti's rounded chest seemed to swell a few inches more.

"This palazzo was built by Duke Alfonso Abrizzi in 1450. He spared no expense on it, and brought his new bride here soon after. But, alas, the young lady was not happy with a husband thirty years her senior, and she made the mistake of taking the duke's bastard son as her lover. They were both beheaded to salve the old man's wounded pride."

The story seemed to please Bazetti, for he smiled as he

259

told it, and only when he was done did he wave to Ugo to deliver the tall, elegant glasses of champagne.

Abra took hers with dampened enthusiasm. The story had not quite the same charm for her as it apparently had for Bazetti.

"And the duke. What happened to him?" she ventured softly.

Bazetti smiled once more. "It is said he lived on for five years after their deaths, but that his young wife and her lover haunted him and turned him mad. He is believed to have mutilated himself, and the palazzo was said to ring with the sounds of his cries for hours at a time in the night." He smiled at her with a bizarre delight. "I suppose that the story has a moral, that a man should never marry a much younger woman, at least if he has a bastard or two running free and capable of causing mischief. But such morals are hardly satisfying, and I don't know a single man who would not gladly offer himself up to madness if he could claim a beautiful young woman for his own." Once more he offered her his strangely intent smile, and then he lifted his glass in salute and finally raised it to his lips.

Abra sipped her wine tentatively, looking around the room as though the duke's ghost might spring out at any moment. With a start, she realized the servant Ugo had disappeared, and wondered how so large a man could move with such absolute silence.

Bazetti, too, noticed the unheralded exit, for he put his glass down on the table beside his chair and addressed himself to Dash.

"Now, there was that business matter you wished to discuss. You would like to dispose of a bit of jewelry?" he asked, turning his glance back to Abra and then lowering it to the place where the brooch nestled at her cleavage.

"Actually," Dash told him drily, drawing Bazetti's attention back to himself, "it was the matter of purchasing a jewel that has brought us, not disposing of one."

That seemed to pique Bazetti's interest, for he sat upright, resettling himself in his chair. "And just how can I help you in this endeavor?" he asked, his tone just a little too eager.

Dash sipped his wine in silent contentment for a moment, allowing Bazetti to stew. Then he smiled.

"I've had word that you might be able to put your hands on the particular jewel that interests us," he said slowly, swirling the remaining wine in his glass and staring into it as he spoke. Then he looked directly at Bazetti. "The jewel I speak of is a certain ruby, called the Tear of Allah."

Bazetti's dark, round eyes narrowed. "I have, of course, heard of this stone," he replied slowly. "But it is in the possession of the emir of Mukalla, and said to be held in almost mystical reverence by his people."

Dash grinned a humorless, crooked grin. "But word has reached me that the emir has recently been parted from the stone," he said.

Bazetti shrugged. "There are always rumors, of course. I had heard one such that the Tear had been stolen from the emir. But I have since learned that the sheik announced the stolen ruby was not the Tear at all, but a glass copy." He looked thoughtful, and took up his glass once more. "It would not do, of course, for him to be thought of as having lost so precious and holy an object."

"The sheik's political situation is, of course, distressing. But it is of no concern of mine. I am merely interested in the jewel."

Bazetti seemed to relax once more. He smiled. "And if I could locate such a ruby, what would you be willing to pay for it?" he asked. "Strictly conjecture, of course, as the Tear is safely in the emir's hands."

"Of course," Dash replied. "And the price would, naturally, depend upon the quality of the stone. What would you consider fair value?"

"Ah," Bazetti crooned, "who can place a value on something that holds not only aesthetic beauty in great measure, but is also the object of the religious zeal of a whole country?" Bazetti sipped his wine. "A small country," he conceded, "but a country nonetheless." He sipped once more, his expression thoughtful. "The man who holds such a jewel, whoever he may be, holds a

261

fortune in his hands."

Abra listened to the flow of words, and all she could hear were Bazetti's evasions. Had they come so far to be put off indefinitely by this horrid little man? she wondered. She put her wine glass down on the table with deliberate force, the small clatter echoing in the now still room.

Bazetti's greedy little eyes turned to her.

"Excuse me, Signore Bazetti," she interrupted. She noticed Dash send her a warning glance, but she ignored it. "We have no time for conjecture as to who has the jewel or where it might be. We know. We've spoken to the man who stole it, and before he killed himself he said he sold it to you. I must have it. My father's life depends upon it. So will you please tell us what you want for it so that we can get on to the business of ransoming him?"

Dash had looked displeased when she started to speak, but he made no move to interrupt. Instead, he sat and watched Bazetti's expression as the man listened to her words. The news of McErlaine's death did not seem to surprise him.

When she'd done, Bazetti pursed his lips. Then he smiled. "One million British pounds sterling," he said crisply.

Abra's eyes grew wide with disbelief. "A million pounds?" she repeated. "Surely you didn't pay McErlaine so great a sum?"

Dash grinned humorlessly. "Probably a tenth of that, Abra," he said, keeping his eyes on Bazetti. "But the price Signore Bazetti paid has little bearing on the price he's placed on the jewel, isn't that so, Bazetti?"

The round little man grinned. "Precisely. And as a matter of fact, I gave McErlaine a good deal less than the figure you mentioned. Some people were not meant to have money, after all. He is, ah, was, one of them. You said he killed himself?" His inquiry was made without any real interest.

Abra nodded. "He lost it all at the casino. Then he jumped to the rocks."

Bazetti shrugged. "A nasty death. But as I said, some people were not meant to have money. If there'd been

262

more, he'd doubtless have done equally badly with it. But that is of little consequence. My price for the stone is one million."

Abra felt numb. She'd never considered he would ask so great a sum. It dwarfed the amount Dash had won at the casino pitifully. Even if there were time, even if she could return to New York and persuade her father's solicitor to liquidate his holdings, everything, including the house, would not bring a million pounds.

Unlike her, Dash seemed unmoved by the enormity of the sum. "We would, of course, demand to examine the stone," he said evenly. "It would be a waste of our time to secure the funds and then find your goods inferior." He leveled a challenging glance at Bazetti.

The man seemed unused to such aspersions. "You may ask anyone who had dealt with me," he retorted with a hint of pique. "I have never dealt dishonestly with my buyers."

Dash considered him for a moment, apparently on the verge of contesting this assertion, but deciding it unwise. He shrugged. "Everyone makes mistakes from time to time, Signore Bazetti. Not even you, surely, are infallable."

Bazetti stared at him in angry silence a moment more, then seemed to resign himself to the inevitable. "Ugo," he called out, his irritation obvious in his tone.

The man appeared in the doorway nearly instantly. He bowed slightly. "Signore?" he asked.

"Go to the vault and bring me the ruby," Bazetti commanded. "My guests would like to assure themselves of its authenticity."

The man bowed once more and then disappeared as silently as he had come.

Abra sat in the silence that had fallen in the room, bewildered. Dash doubtless intended to do something, she realized, but she had no idea what. With the man Ugo in the house, the jewel was as secure as it would have been guarded by a small army. The man was a veritable army in himself.

Finally the servant returned, in his hands the pouch she recalled with such painful familiarity. She watched as

263

he brought it to Bazetti and dropped it into the little man's squat-fingered hands.

"Well," Bazetti announced, and he stood, crossing to Dash as he pulled the pouch open and let the stone fall into Dash's hands. "Have I your acceptance that the stone is genuine?"

Dash stared at it a moment, then stood and carried it to the side of the room where a large candelabra glowed with the light of a dozen candles. He held the stone up to the shimmer of the candlelight, then turned and returned to where Abra sat, dropping the stone nonchalantly into her hand. He stared at Bazetti complacently.

"A million pounds is a great deal to ask for a second-rate stone, and one that is stolen, to boot."

Bazetti bristled. "The sheik will pay that for it."

Dash shrugged. "I doubt it. After all, he is already in possession of the stone. This is just a glass copy."

"That's nonsense, and you know it," Bazetti retorted.

"Perhaps. But one the sheik must maintain if he is to hold on to his power."

"Then the rebels, they'll pay for it," Bazetti retorted.

"Perhaps they would, to force the sheik out. If they had the money, of course. But they don't." He looked thoughtful. "And I think the sheik might feel it necessary to eliminate anyone who gave out word he had the stone. It is not a very healthy bit of rock to have about."

"Do you mean to haggle with me?" Bazetti demanded. His face had grown red and blotchy and his eyes seemed to burst from their sockets.

Dash shook his head slowly. "Of course not. I would not insult either of us that way. I'm simply suggesting to you that you realize your market for this particular stone is quite small. In view of the limited demand, you might wish to reconsider the price you're asking."

Bazetti glared at him, then his glance fell once more to Abra. "It is your father who is in peril, or so you say. Perhaps you might wish to reconsider your companion's attitude," he suggested.

Before she could answer, Dash broke in. "I speak for the lady," he said flatly.

Bazetti didn't even glance up at him, but kept his eyes

on Abra's face. "So you may," he said. "But I find your manner offensive. Perhaps the lady's manners would please me more. Perhaps she and I could come to some mutually agreeable solution." He smiled. "In fact, I'm sure when you returned in the morning to fetch her, she and I could have settled the matter quite to everyone's satisfaction."

Abra felt a shiver of repugnance pass over her at Bazetti's words.

"The lady's evenings are not for sale, Bazetti," Dash snarled.

Abra hardly heard him. She lifted her hand to him and stared down at her other hand clutching the stone in her lap.

"We'll do as he asks, Dash," she heard herself saying. "Leave. I'll stay here with him."

Dash stared at her as if she'd spoken a foreign language. "You can't be serious, Abra," he said through clenched teeth.

She tore her eyes from the stone, up to his. "I don't see that I have much choice," she replied, then pulled her glance away, not liking what she saw in his. "I haven't a million pounds. And I will have my father back. So leave."

Bazetti glared at Dash with a look of triumph. "Ugo," he called.

The giant instantly appeared.

"You will show the gentleman to the door," he instructed. "And then lock up the house for the night and retire. The lady and I will not wish to be disturbed."

Dash didn't even look back to face her before leaving. Instead, he skirted her chair as though wanting to avoid coming close to her. Abra watched him leave followed by the servant, knowing the anger and disgust he was leveling at her. She considered herself with a stab of self-loathing, then told herself she had no choice, that there was nothing else she could do.

But Dash's image was quickly preempted by Bazetti's as the man's round face appeared before her, his thick, squat body leaning forward to her over the arm of her chair.

"And now, my dear," he said breathily, "shall we begin our negotiations?"

He lowered his face to hers.

*Chapter Seventeen*

Abra turned her face away.

"Perhaps we could finish our wine, Signore Bazetti?" she asked. She could hear her voice shake and knew Bazetti could hear it as well. "You'll excuse me, but I've not much experience in matters such as this."

He grinned then, and straightened up. "In few matters, my dear, is inexperience a greater asset than extensive knowledge," he said as he lifted her glass and handed it to her. "It is fortunate for us both that this is one of them."

Abra felt her hand tremble as she took the glass. A few drops of the wine spilled to her fingers.

Bazetti reached his hand to hers and steadied the glass, then he leaned forward and licked the drops from where they'd fallen on her fingers. She shuddered as she felt his tongue against her skin.

He apparently took her shudder to be the trembling of excitement, for he lifted his eyes to hers when he'd done, and smiled contentedly.

"Come, drink your wine, my dear. When you've done, I'll show you a bit more of this lovely palazzo of mine," He offered her a macabre grin. "I'm sure you will find the bedroom interesting."

He reached down to where her hand still grasped the stone, but she refused to loosen her hold on it.

"Might I keep it a while longer?" she asked, and then looked down at it, sensing the odd warmth that seemed to emanate from the ruby, feeling that it was Vincent's life she held in her hands.

Bazetti's hand reached down to hers and enclosed both her hand and the stone. He smiled. "Yes," he agreed willingly enough. "Keep it with you. It will remind you that it is to your benefit to please me." He drew back and straightened. "Now come, drink your wine. The night is not endless, after all."

Abra brought the glass to her lips and forced herself to swallow, telling herself that enough wine would numb her, that she'd not be able to feel a thing. She drained the glass quickly, and held it out to Bazetti.

"May I have some more?" she asked.

He brought the bottle to her and refilled her glass.

"It seems you need a bit of courage, my dear," he told her, but his smile told her more, that he enjoyed the prospect of her fear, that a partner who was not entirely willing was decidedly to his taste.

She shuddered at the thought of his touching her, but knew she had no choice now but to go through with it. She'd agreed to the bargain; now she must honor it.

She kept her eyes on him as she sipped the wine, trying to draw out the time, aware that he was growing impatient with her. She was not surprised when he put his own glass down.

"Enough of this," he said as he went to her, taking her arm in his hand and pulling her up from the chair. The glass fell from her hand, the remaining wine spilling on the marble floor, the crystal shattering. Neither she nor Bazetti paid any attention to the noise or the splatter of wet. Bazetti's hand grew tight on her arm and he drew her to him, his thick lips anxious as they buried themselves in the warm softness of her cleavage.

For a moment she stood immobile, telling herself she could endure whatever she must, that for Vincent's sake she must. But the feel of Bazetti's lips and of his hands pawing at her, pulling at the fabric of her gown in his haste to find her breast, sickened her.

She saw rather than felt her hand rise, noticed only the blood-red gleam of the Tear grasped in her hand, then felt the dull thud as she used it to strike the side of his head. He staggered a few feet away from her, then stared at her a moment in dull confusion before he fell to the floor in a thick heap.

She stood over him, staring with numb horror at what she'd done.

"Well, it seems the lady is not above reneging on her word. You quite shock me, Abra."

She started, looking up to find Dash standing in the ornate door frame, an air of pleased satisfaction about him.

"You didn't leave," she said stupidly, numb from the wine and the violence she'd done.

He stepped into the room, moving to her quickly. "I couldn't leave you here to give yourself to that lecherous cretin," he said matter-of-factly as he bent to Bazetti's side.

Abra looked down at the still body once more, horrified by the brilliant red gleam of blood that trickled from his temple.

"Have I killed him?" she asked softly, afraid that he might answer that she had.

But Dash smiled up at her. "You've given him a healthy respect for the abilities of a lady, no doubt, and a terrible headache when he comes to, but you've not killed him, Abra," he told her after he'd pressed his fingers to Bazetti's neck and found the man's pulse still even and strong. He stood and took her arm. "And now may I suggest that we leave before the trusting Signore Bazetti and his curious little friend Ugo wake from their dreams and decide that they're not quite pleased with the course of progress the evening has taken?"

"Ugo!"

He smiled at her. She'd apparently forgotten about the servant and now was reminding herself of his not particularly welcoming presence.

"Never fear, he's sleeping with much the same mien of comfort as his master. But I don't think he will for very long. We've got to get out of here. For that matter, we've got to get out of Venice. Signore Bazetti will not be pleased when he's found his fine ruby is missing, as well as the lady who was to warm his bed."

He gently pried the ruby from her grasp, then pushed her toward the door as he pocketed it.

"Wise of you to use what was at hand," he went on, talking to keep her calm, to keep her from stopping and thinking about what it was they were doing, what it was she had done. He snatched up her cloak from where she'd dropped it on a low chair when they'd entered the room as they passed, wrapping it around her shoulders and putting his arm around her waist to guide her.

"The first rule a thief must learn," he continued as he hurried her along the long corridor to the flight of steps that led to the door to the canal, "is to make do with whatever comes to hand. Shame Ugo wasn't aware of that fact," he added as they reached the foot of the stairs and found the servant's body lying limp on the cold stone, sprawled across the opening and nearly blocking their way. A small bust of a lady lay beside him, the old marble darkly veined and giving the face the image of hundreds of tiny, dark wrinkles, surprising age on the immutable features of youth carved in stone.

Dash leaped easily over the still body, then turned to Abra and lifted her over it. He started for the door, then seemed to change his mind, returning to lift the small bust from where it lay and replace it in the dark niche in the wall that it apparently occupied. He smiled at Abra when he'd completed the small chore and turned back to her.

"A gentleman never leaves a lady away from her home alone at night," he said by way of explanation, then he took Abra's hand and led her to the door.

The heavy, iron-bound door opened slightly to his push, and once more they were standing out in the darkness of the night. Abra was surprised to find a gondola tied up to the pole that marked the palazzo's door.

"Ugo was kind enough to summon him while I waited inside," Dash explained with an innocent smile as he helped her into the small open boat.

He settled himself beside her, then he looked up at the gondolier and smiled as the man took up his pole.

"The lady and I have the taste for a small adventure this evening," he said, pulling a handful of bills from his pocket and slipping them into the man's hand. "Have you a friend who owns a fishing boat and who might be willing to leave immediately on a short pleasure trip?" he asked. "For fair recompense, of course."

The gondolier's face wrinkled but immediately returned to its accustomed calm serenity when he'd examined and quickly pocketed the money Dash had given him.

"I know of someone who would be willing, I think, signore," he said with an equanimity that suggested that such requests came to him daily.

"Excellent." Dash smiled, then he leaned back into the velvet cushions that lined the carefully tended wooden seat. He turned to Abra, slipping his arm around her shoulders and pulling her close to him. "Look at those stars, Abra," he whispered into her ear and pointed up at the shimmering dots in the dark velvet of the night sky. "What man could ask for more magnificent jewels than those?"

Abra shivered as she stood on the dock and watched Dash talk to the fisherman. He seemed far more dubious than the gondolier had been, but the instant Dash drew out the wad of bills he'd readied in his pocket, the man's expression became less reluctant and far more agreeable. When he finally turned to Abra, he made a clumsy attempt at gallantry, bowing low and making a sweeping movement with his arm, motioning her aboard the *Mala Femmina* as if it were a pleasure yacht.

*Mala Femmina* was an apt name for the vessel, Abra thought. She had the air of an elderly streetwalker, down at her heels and not very clean, past all thought of the impression she made, intent only on her survival, however miserable it might be. And everywhere was the pervasive stench of rotting fish.

271

"Shame we hadn't time to return to the hotel to change," Dash told Abra easily as he took her arm to help her aboard. "I must admit we're just a trifle bit overdressed for the surroundings."

He leaped the gunnels, then turned, put his hands to her waist, and lifted her onto the deck. He looked around quickly, and an expression of distaste spread over his face.

"If I'd known you intended to lightfinger the good Bazetti's stone this evening, Abra, I'd have made some more agreeable arrangements. And I'd have seen that our belongings accompanied us." He stared at her with an expression of regret. "Damn, my best boots are lying abandoned back at the Danielli." He heaved a theatrical sigh. "A true adventurer, I suppose, must learn to take these disappointments in stride and with good grace," he added with a crooked grin, hoping to ease the tight, uncertain expression he saw on her face.

"But what could Bazetti do to us, Dash?' she asked him thoughtfully. "After all, he could hardly report us to the police for stealing what was already a stolen jewel."

He shook his head as though disappointed by her simplicity. "I don't suppose you noticed the good and faithful Ugo?" he asked. "I can assure you he'd delight in tearing me limb from limb about now, slowly, if he could to make it all the more painful. As for you, modesty prevents, but you might use your imagination. And aside from the distasteful possibilities of a little private vengeance, I'm sure Signore Bazetti has the local *carabinieri* in his hip pocket. After all, this is his home ground. And if they really needed one, he could always give them the grounds of assault to arrest us. Or have you forgotten that you coshed the repulsive little gnome quite professionally and left him sprawled rather ungracefully on his shiny marble floor?"

Abra shook her head and laughed softly. Now that the shock of what she'd done had begun to wear off, she felt herself beginning to take a bit of perverse pride in having bested Bazetti. She knew she ought to feel guilty, that she had committed an illegal act. But some-

272

how she could not feel as though taking the stone from the horrid little man had really been an immoral act, or even a crime. After all, Bazetti was a criminal himself, a trafficker in stolen goods. She quashed down the voice of her conscience as it was about to tell her that a crime is a crime, that the character of the victim did not change that fact.

She felt a sudden rush of excitement, a feeling that quite mystified her, and she smiled brightly at Dash.

"I did do a fairly good job of it, didn't I?" she preened.

He stared at her, then broke into a loud laugh. "You little hypocrite," he accused. "You enjoyed it."

She sobered quickly. "Well, not at the time, I didn't."

"No matter," he replied. "I suppose it's in the blood, and bound to come out sooner or later."

She turned quickly cold. "Well, if I inherited my larcenous inclination from my father," she retorted, suddenly angry with him that he had reminded her of the fact of Vincent's past, "then I've nothing for which to apologize. Most certainly not to you."

He lost whatever sense of amusement he had felt. "No," he told her with an edge of bitterness, "you've nothing for which to apologize to me."

Abra was shocked by the hurt she saw in his eyes, and wished she could call back the words. The anger was gone now, as quickly as it had come, and she wished she could call that back, too, wished that it had never been.

"Where are they taking us?" she asked him, wanting to get away from the edge of the precipice between them, knowing she must avoid the subject of his life, his future, if she wanted to maintain the tenuous harmony that had grown up between them. She interested herself purposefully in the movements of the boat's captain and mate as they set the sails.

"To Tunis, if this tub will go that far," he told her, as anxious to avoid the subject that divided them as was she. "Then, I suppose, we'll have to find our way overland to Mukalla. After all, the emir is expecting us for a visit. It wouldn't do to disappoint so illustrious a

273

personage."

Then he put his arm around her, and the two of them stood by the rail, watching as the *Mala Femmina* cast off and the intriguing lights of Venice slowly began to recede into the night mist.

When Dash had suggested she try to rest below, she'd ventured down to the cabin, but she reappeared on deck almost immediately. If the *Mala Femmina* had a decidedly pungent aura out in the open air, below, where the smell was closed in, it was magnified a hundred times more. One decent breath of it made her gag, and she welcomed the bit of the air on the deck above, despite the night damp and cold.

The captain of the trawler, one Jacopo Pascone by name, divided his time between the contemplation of his unprecedented passengers and the navigation of his ship. From time to time he called out a hoarse order to his mate, a small monkey of a man who climbed through the rigging with a facility that astonished Abra. But the remainder of the time he stared at her and Dash with a guarded curiosity.

Eventually Dash pushed a large coil of rope to a sheltered spot away from the sea spray, and settled himself there with Abra in his arms. She dosed fitfully, huddled close to him, sharing the warmth of her cloak and their bodies.

Eventually the sun rose, bringing with it a brittle, cold dawn that gradually mellowed into a briskly chilly morning.

"The winds are good," Pascone assured them as he offered them a morning meal of bitter coffee and limp bread. "We should reach the Tunisian coast by nightfall, assuming the authorities do not take it into their dim minds to patrol for smugglers. They make sweeps occasionally, to keep their superiors happy."

Dash eyed the man evenly. There was that about his manner that told him Pascone was not entirely the innocent fisherman, that he had personal knowledge of the authorities and sweeps for smugglers, and that he wanted to avoid them at any cost.

"What has that to do with us?" he asked, his voice casual. "We're not smuggling. We're simply on a pleasure cruise."

Pascone seemed to consider his words with interest, and then dismiss them.

"I think not, signore," he replied. "I think you left Venice because you had to, not to simply enjoy the night airs at sea. Your business is your own. But in any event, I think it will suit us both best if I deliver you and the lady somewhere on the coast a few miles from the city. That way we will both be able to evade the police."

Then, without waiting for a response, he turned away, back to his wheel, and proceeded to ignore his passengers' presence entirely.

The coast seemed to draw closer, a dark, muted presence appearing out of the horizon and grew steadily larger. Abra stared at it as a hungry man stares at a loaf of bread, with an expectant hunger that only seems to grow more insistently pressing with each passing moment. If her two trips on the packets, from Lisbon to Marseilles, then from Marseilles to Cannes, had not proven to her that she was not well equipped to travel in a small craft on rough waters, the hours she'd spent on the *Mala Femmina* had. She never again wanted to see more water in one place than could be conveniently held by a large bathtub. Not ever.

But finally the solidity that had been mistily distant grew so close she felt she could reach out and touch it with her hands. The mate busied himself putting down the trawler's single lifeboat, letting it land with a smacking splash on the surface and then settling into the rhythmic sway of the waves.

Pascone approached Dash and smiled. "It seems that we must part here. Tunis is to the east, not more than two miles." He held out a thick hand in expectation.

Dash's left hand moved to his pocket and drew out a thick wad of bills, which he dropped into the waiting

275

palm. "I wish I could say it's been a pleasure, captain," he muttered. He, like Abra, was chill and damp, uncomfortable in the wrinkled evening clothes he'd worn continuously for too many hours. The prospect of a long walk did not entirely please him.

But none of that seemed to bother Pascone. He smiled with toothy exuberance and slipped the bills into his pocket without even bothering to count them.

"I think, signore, in view of the risks I have taken to bring you here, your passage should be a bit higher."

Dash was unruffled. "Five million lire. It seemed more than fair to me." he replied.

"But that was before I had the time to consider your desire to leave Venice in such haste, signore. Now that I have had the opportunity, it seems to me only fair that you double that amount."

He raised a speculative brow, and brought his hand meaningfully to a heavily bladed knife that he wore sheathed at his belt.

"Come, signore. You are obviously not a poor man. It would not be a great hardship on you, especially when you consider the profit you will take from whatever business it is that brings you here."

"And that will satisfy you, five thousand more lire?" Dash's voice hinted at something akin to amusement, but his expression was fixed.

Instead it was Pascone who smiled. He shrugged thick shoulders as he slowly drew out the knife.

"Perhaps not, signore. Perhaps it would be best to take all you have. If you give it up without argument, I will not be forced to slit your throat and that of the pretty lady, something I would surely regret." He smiled at Abra pleasantly. "Most decidedly, in the lady's case."

"I should not want to force you to some action of which you would have need of making repentance," Dash told him. Then he smiled, but there was no warmth in it, more threat than anything else. He moved so that Abra was behind him, out of the range of whatever Pascone intended to do with the knife.

"Under the circumstances, I have little choice," he said, and once more his left hand slipped into his pocket.

Pascone's eyes followed the movement, greedily hungry for what Dash would extract, involved enough so that he did not notice Dash's right hand as it, too, moved to a pocket.

"This will have to satisfy you," Dash said as he drew out another wad of bills, this one a good deal smaller than the first. "Two thousand." He dropped it into Pascone's waiting palm. "And if it seems insufficient to you, I can offer you a taste of this."

His right hand flashed into sight, a small, shiny pistol held firmly in it, already cocked and pointed directly at Pascone's heart.

The burly man grimaced, then smiled, as though he had been treated to a joke he had found extremely amusing.

"You do not have the look of one who keeps such playthings about you, signore," Pascone muttered, waving absently to the now wrinkled evening clothes.

"If you think you need to have me prove to you that I know how to use it, captain, I'll be glad to oblige," Dash offered amiably.

Pascone shook his head. "No, no, signore. I will take your word."

"Then I will ask you to have the kindness of moving to the bow before the lady and I leave this floating pile of rot." Dash grinned crookedly. "No offense intended."

"And none taken, signore," Pascone assured him as he backed away, nearly tripping over the pile of rope that had served as Dash and Abra's makeshift bed the evening before. This, too, seemed to amuse him, because he smiled once more at his clumsiness.

"We part friends, then?" Dash asked pleasantly as he helped Abra over the gunnels with one arm and kept the pistol firmly aimed at Pascone's retreating figure. She grabbed the line that held the boat and lowered herself to it.

The captain looked up at Dash and grinned. "As long as you are in possession of the pistol, signore, I would not think of suggesting otherwise."

"Good," Dash told him, then he swung one leg over

277

the gunnel, grabbing the line with his free hand. "*Arrivederci,* and many thanks for a delightful journey," he said.

With that he swung himself down to the lifeboat and seated himself in the stern at Abra's side. The mate scrambled down after them, quickly taking up the oars.

Fifteen minutes later, they were standing on the rocky shale of the beach and watching the *Mala Femmina* silently slipping away into the mist of the night.

"Where did you get that thing?" Abra demanded as Dash slipped the pistol back into his pocket.

He took her hand and urged her away from the water's edge.

"Lucky I had it, don't you think?" he asked. "Never does to go into a pit of vipers without a bit of venom of one's own."

She pulled away from him. "Have you been carrying a weapon all this time?" she demanded.

"Under the circumstances, I don't suppose you care to complain, do you, Abra? Or do you fancy having your throat slit by the likes of one such as the good captain?"

She shook her head, but turned away quickly. It frightened her to think that he was prepared for fatal violence, even more when she realized that he was quite obviously capable of committing it. She began to trudge silently at his side, wondering what other secrets she had yet to discover about him.


Abra was so exhausted, she was barely awake when Dash led her into the small inn, and completely oblivious of the puzzled glances of the innkeeper as he inspected their rumpled, formal attire. As soon as they were shown into the spare little room she fell into the bed, cold, wet, wanting only to sleep. She was unprotesting as Dash pulled off her sodden clothing and removed her ruined evening shoes, then pulled a blanket over her. Before he bent to kiss her forehead, she was already asleep.

She didn't wake until the following afternoon, and

278

found herself feverish and dizzy. She sat up for a moment, lifting the note Dash had left on the table beside the bed for her, then sank back to the pillows, too ill to read it.

He's gone off somewhere and left me here to die, she thought miserably, feeling a dull, irrational panic that that was indeed what he'd done. He's taken the stone and left me, she thought as the little of her strength she'd managed to muster swiftly faded away.

But her eyelids drooped closed once more before she could manage to force her thoughts to consider the unpleasant prospect more intensely, and she was unable to open them again. She drifted off, the crumpled piece of paper grasped tightly in her hand.

When she woke again, the heated dizziness was gone, but she felt drained and weak. She lay still, staring up at the ceiling through sleep-blurred eyes as she gathered her energies.

"Well, my lady finally awakens."

She managed to move her head to the side and found Dash sitting in a chair beside the bed, leaning toward her and putting a cool hand to her temples.

"That feels good," she murmured softly, and smiled up at him. Then, "Am I sick?"

He grinned at that. "Let's just say that a day on the water followed by a brisk walk in the night air didn't do you any good. How do you feel?"

She groaned softly. "Like something the cat dragged about for a good while before deciding to gnaw on it." She considered for a moment. "And thirsty."

He stood, went to a table by the far wall, and lifted a glass and a pitcher. "I'll see to getting you something to eat," he told her as he poured some water for her and then returned to the bedside. "You must be hungry." He watched her struggle to sit up, then put down the glass, lifted her easily, plumped the pillows behind her, and pushed her back into them.

"You do that quite well," she said as he handed her the glass of water.

"I thought I might turn to nursing when I get too old to steal jewels," he told her easily. "Always seems

279

wise to have something to fall back on."

She drank the water greedily, wondering how it could possibly taste so good, and stared at the bright morning sunlight that streamed in through the window.

"Have I slept a whole day away?" she asked.

He took the glass from her and casually wiped away a drop she'd spilled on her chin with his finger.

"Not one. Three. That first morning I thought you were just tired, and I went off to do a bit of looking around. I was rather dismayed to return to find you still asleep, even more to find you clutching my note telling you I'd be back in an hour or two. That was when I realized you were ill. I couldn't imagine you clinging to my words so tenaciously if you were well." He grinned at her smugly.

"Three days?" she asked, ignoring his manner, bewildered at how so much time could have passed without her knowing.

He nodded to her. "You missed New Year's Eve entirely. I was forced to celebrate without you."

She scowled at him, then paid some attention to the rumbling she felt in her stomach.

"You did mention breakfast?"

He grinned his crooked grin and went off to find her some food, while she contemplated the fact that she had somehow managed to become clothed in a man's shirt. One of his, she mused, and wondered where it had come from.

When he returned with a porter bearing a loaded tray, she studied him. He was wearing a clean white linen shirt, khaki trousers, and high leather boots. She wondered where it had all come from even as she realized with a small internal lurch that she thought he looked terribly handsome.

When the porter had laid out the food and left, Dash brought her a bowl of fresh figs and cream and a cup of thick, sweet coffee. She sniffed it contentedly before she sipped.

"Was I really ill for three days?" she demanded.

He nodded as he poured himself some coffee. "You had me quite worried for a while."

280

He didn't say more. But there was a great deal that passed through his mind. The memory of returning from his solitary shopping jaunt, when he'd intended merely to find them both some suitable clothing, came back to him, bringing with it the dull feeling of panic he'd felt as he'd found her flushed and limp with fever, stricken by the thought that he would lose her, not to another man, not to another life, but to a solitary death in a miserable little room a world away from her own. And despite the assurances of the doctor the inn-keeper had summoned for him, despite the concerned nursing the innkeeper's wife had voluntarily provided, he'd stayed with her the whole of the time, feeling helpless as he pressed cold compresses to her forehead and found himself shocked by the heat that seemed to radiate from her body. It was only the night before that the fear had left him, when he'd realized the fever was nearly gone and that she would, indeed, recover. And now he knew he could tell her none of it, only stare at her and be thankful to find her slightly bemused, wan, but almost back to normal.

"But that means it's the second day of January," she mused aloud. "We've little more than four weeks to reach Mukalla."

Dash looked at her reassuringly. "No problem there. I've found us a guide. He'll have seen to hiring whatever livestock we'll need and to purchasing supplies by the end of the week. It shouldn't take more than nine or ten days of travel. We'll be there well before Sharify's deadline." He smiled encouragingly. "Vincent is virtually home now, Abra. Don't worry about him." He pointed to the bowl of fruit that lay still untouched in her hands. "Now eat something. You look like a poor little beggar waif who hasn't eaten a decent meal in days."

She scowled at him, then lifted her spoon and attacked the figs with surprising gusto.

But even as she chewed the first sweet bite, she couldn't help but allow her attention to wander, couldn't help but wonder if it would really all go as easily as Dash said it would. Somehow, she couldn't

281

help but think that something unpleasant lay still ahead of them. The sweet, rich taste of the figs and cream turned bitter in her mouth. Whatever it was that was out there waiting for them, she instinctively knew it wouldn't let them escape all that easily.

## Chapter Eighteen

Three days later Abra found herself walking past the stalls in the *souk,* inhaling the odors of spices and fresh-roasted coffee lightly tinged with the less pleasant ones of animal excrement and rotted vegetables. She found it an entirely pleasant outing, feeling the warmth of bright sunshine on her head and shoulders, eyeing the endless flow of children that darted about, occasionally begging a dinar from Dash before they disappeared into the maze of stalls, trying not to stare at the exotically robed women, their faces veiled as they went about the business of their daily marketing, the burnoosed men who sat at cafés and drank their small cups of aromatic coffee while they considered the passing crowds with suspicious indifference.

"This way, Abra."

Dash took her arm and led her along a narrow street, then into the dimness of a small café. She stood there momentarily blinded by the near absence of light after the brilliance of the glare outside. When her vision cleared, it was to see a tall, wiry man in a striped burnoose and with a turbaned head, his long, dark-complected, wiry, bearded face seemingly slashed vertically by a large, narrow, hooked nose and punctuated by two glittering dark eyes.

"Salaam aleechum," he said softly, lifting his hand to his chest and forehead in a swift, fluid motion.

"Aleechum salaam," Dash replied easily, as if the greeting were almost second nature to him.

The stranger darted a look at Abra and a flash of

283

what looked like distaste passed over his features. It apparently disturbed him that Dash would show the bad manners of bringing along a woman on a matter of business. But whatever his judgment of that matter, he forced it away quickly, and Dash made the obligatory introductions.

"Abra, this is Ajib Rajeek. Rajeek, my wife, Mrs. Thorne."

Abra barely blinked as Dash introduced her to the man. They'd been through it before they'd left the inn.

"A woman does not travel in North Africa in the company of any but her father or her husband," he'd said, waiting for the expected outburst of protest and hoping to stifle it before it could begin. "And as I don't think even a fool would mistake me for your father, Abra, it seems evident that you are once again Mrs. Thorne, at least for a while."

She remembered feeling a stab of regret as he'd said the last words, feeling oddly bereft at the loss of that name before the time came for her once again to give it up—for that matter, before she ever had any right to claim it. But then she reminded herself that it was all just some sort of a game to him, a pretense, and that if there would be any regret when the pretense was done, it would be all hers.

Now she turned her thoughts to the heavily robed and veiled women in the market stalls, and to Rajeek's momentarily open look of distaste at her presence. She realized he had been right, that here a woman's place was firmly defined, and certainly not one of independence.

Rajeek looked at her now as if he were considering an animal he was contemplating acquiring in the marketplace.

"I would suggest that Mrs. Thorne might consider covering her head once we are begun traveling," he told Dash. "Not every place is quite so civilized as we are here in Tunis, Mukalla most especially." He pointed to her hair. "And that alone would bring a small fortune. A great temptation to the bandits who inhabit the hills between here and your destination."

Abra shrank back from the man, shocked by his

words, but even more so by the evaluating way he considered her.

Dash merely nodded and said, "If you think it wise," then followed Rajeek to a table in the rear of the café. Abra mutely followed.

A waiter appeared immediately and Rajeek ordered in Arabic, then the three of them sat silent until the tray was brought, a large, round brass tray neatly set with three small cups and an ornately chased brass pot from which emanated the now familiar bouquet of the thick, sweet coffee Abra had found so warmingly satisfying that morning when she'd awakened after her days of illness. Now she found the pot placed in front of her, and the waiter quickly departed. It was, she realized, assumed that the woman at the table would serve the men.

Dash offered her a quick, brow-raised glance. Dutifully, she lifted the pot, pouring out the three cups as Rajeek and Dash remained silent and waiting. Then she presented the men with their cups, offering Dash a quick smirk with his. He pretended he had not noticed.

When Rajeek had taken a sip of the coffee, he obviously considered the pleasantries concluded. He put down his cup and looked at Dash with his oddly glittering black eyes.

"You did not mention what it is that takes you to Mukalla," he said with no effort to hide his curiosity.

"We go there for business," Dash replied, making it evident he intended to make no further explanation.

Rajeek continued his inspection a few seconds longer, then realized he would get no further. "I have seen to the horses and the supplies. All will be ready for departure in the morning. It would be best to get away early, not waste the morning hours. And I will need four hundred dinar more. The horses proved more expensive than I had anticipated." His litany completed, he once more picked up his cup and drank the remainder of his coffee.

Dash drew out the amount he had demanded without comment, laying it on the table between them.

"Sunrise tomorrow, then," he said.

Rajeek nodded. "Sunrise," he agreed.

Then he stood abruptly, picked up and pocketed the bills, turned, and left the café.

Abra watched his departure with a feeling of unpleasant foreboding. "I don't like that man," she said softly.

Dash nodded his agreement. "Neither do I. But he seemed the least dishonest of the lot I could find. Unfortunately, I'm not exactly well versed in the terrain here. We need a guide. I'll keep an eye on him, and that, I'm afraid, will have to do."

Abra looked down into the cup of dark, sweet liquid, suddenly aware of how vulnerable they were in this foreign setting. It was not exactly a comforting thought.

"Do you think there really are bandits in the hills?" she asked.

Dash looked around the dim café slowly, then turned back to face her. "I wouldn't be at all surprised, Abra," he said as he lifted his cup.

Morning found them riding out of the city. Abra stared in bewildered awe as they passed the ruins of the ancient city of Carthage, unbelieving as Rajeek gave them a quick history of the city's ruin by the Roman legions nearly two thousand years before. But there was no time to explore the fallen columns and rocky slopes that bore the imprint of brick streets beneath the rubble. They were not, after all, following ancient footsteps, but making their own.

Slowly the scenery changed from the lush greenery of the coast, where groves of orange and fig trees lined their way, to a more parched countryside. Rajeek reminded them as they made their first evening's camp by a small, trickling stream that they would soon reach the desert. The sight of flowing water, Abra realized, would soon become a longed-for memory.

That evening Dash and Rajeek pitched their two tents, and then the guide prepared their dinner over an open fire, a simple meal consisting of a stew flavored with olives and raisins, flat bread, and wine they'd brought from the *souk* in Tunis. After they had eaten, Rajeek cleared away the remains of their meal and then made a show of retiring and leaving them to their own

286

devices for the evening.

"I think he intends to watch us," Dash said to Abra as the guide disappeared into the smaller of the two tents.

"But why would he do that?" Abra demanded. "For all he knows, we are simply a boringly wed man and wife."

Dash shrugged. "To see what our habits are, to find the weaknesses," he muttered softly. He took another swallow from his cup and emptied the last of his wine into the fire. He turned to her, taking her arm. "It's time, I think, Mrs. Thorne, that we retired."

They entered their tent and Dash pulled down the flap behind them. Abra removed her boots and jacket and shook out the folded blanket that lay on her small cot.

"Not quite the Ritz," she murmured.

Dash offered her a crooked grin. "That's just as well, I think," he replied as he lay, fully clothed, on his own cot. "You're too tempting to resist, and under other circumstances I'd be hard put even to try. But I think that tonight I don't want to sleep very soundly." Then, meaningfully, he laid his pistol in easy reach.

Abra stared at him silently for a moment, then finished undressing and lay down to sleep.

They awoke to the scent of coffee and the vision of a dim light just starting to appear on the eastern horizon. Abra groaned as she stood and peeped out of the tent.

"It's not yet full dawn," she moaned softly, but knew it was useless to protest.

Dash only offered her a small chuckle, then left her to sort through the pile of her clothing in the dim light.

By the time the sun had fully risen, they'd eaten their morning meal and were ready to set out.

"Today we will reach the desert," Rajeek told them as they climbed into their saddles. "Three days more and we should reach the border of Mukalla. Then four days of sand and we will be at the capital, by the great oasis at Tahaf."

To Abra's ears, the itinerary sounded endless.

The succeeding days seemed to melt, one into the next, the afternoons long and dry and filled with the taste of hot sand, the nights surprisingly cold once the sun had set. Rajeek led them from oasis to oasis, tiny islands of greenery in the thick golden haze of the desert, the date palms and wild tamarisk trees an anomaly rising out of the sands. And then, on the fifth day, as the last images of the Adrar Abbes Oasis disappeared behind them, Rajeek announced that they had passed into Mukalla.

Nothing seemed outwardly changed. But in the evening, when they drew close to the tiny oasis where they would camp, they noticed that the Bedouins who had come there with their flocks seemed somehow more diffident than the others they'd seen, more suspicious and even a bit angry. The men made no effort to speak with them as the nomads of Tunisia had, showed no curiosity about the foreigners. Instead, they stared at them with ill-guarded hostility and waved their women and children to their tents, as if they feared exposure might contaminate them.

Abra watched as one wide-eyed skinny little boy was harshly scolded and sent off to his mother. In the difficult life to which these people had been born, they seemed to be on the losing side of the battle.

"It is not well here," Rajeek told them absently, then he turned away to make their camp.

That night the air seemed especially cold. For the first time since they'd set out, Abra was grateful for the great hooded cloak Rajeek had suggested she wear. She huddled into the wool, glad of the warmth and the anonymity she felt it gave her. The night seemed to her to be filled with angry, suspicious eyes.

As they ate their evening meal, Abra was sure she heard noises in the darkness around them, noises that were unlike the sounds she'd heard in the past evenings, stealthy, human noises.

"Why are these people so angry?" she asked Dash, feeling sure he would not know but voicing the question anyway, as if the words might scare away the unpleasant feelings that had been growing on her since

288

they'd made their camp.

He surprised her. "Westerners have come here, Abra, Frenchmen, Englishmen, Americans. Their geologists have found rich oil deposits in this otherwise desolate landscape. And so a small country that has been virtually ignored, valueless to the industrial nations, suddenly becomes quite valuable. Sheik Sharify bargains with his people's heritage for the most money he can. And all his people see is that their land is being stolen from them, what little they have is being trampled under the feet of foreigners. You really can't blame them for hating us."

She watched him, surprised at his knowledge of the country and the people.

"But we have nothing to do with any of that," she insisted. "And besides, if there is oil here, it could bring prosperity to these people."

Dash smiled at her with the sort of condescending smile one offers a pleasing but not terribly bright child. "Do you really think they will ever see any of that money, Abra?" he asked her softly. "Do you really think Sharify would share all that wealth with these people?" He made a wide, expansive movement with his arm, motioning to the area behind their camp where the nomad tents were. "Do you really think he would give up the money and the power?"

He was right, she mused, as she listened to his words. Sharify was not the sort of man to care for anything but his own wants. He would have no concern for the misery of his people.

"And there is no one to resist him?" she demanded.

"Ah, yes, lady, there are rebels," Rajeek interrupted with surprising vehemence. "But they can not rouse the people to revolt against the ruler. After all, Allah has given the sheik to them. They do not question Allah's choice. And so they live as they can, and stare their hatred at foreigners like you."

He spoke with unexpected force, and Abra wondered where his sympathies lay, this oddly cold man who seemed immune to the vagaries of any life but his own, any thoughts but his own.

"And you, Ajib Rajeek, do you side with the rebels?"

she asked him curiously.

He laughed. It was the first time Abra had heard his laughter and it surprised her. She thought it filled with a near malicious contempt.

"Ajib Rajeek sides with Ajib Rajeek," he told her. Then he turned his eyes to the fire and kept them fixed there.

Later, when they were alone in their tent, Abra sat on her cot and watched Dash settle himself on his for the night, the pistol at his side as it had been the previous nights, his thoughts obviously far from her.

"Those things you told me at dinner, they're true?" she asked him.

He turned his glance lazily toward her. "Do you think I would lie to you about such matters, Abra?" he demanded.

She shook her head thoughtfully. "And that's why Sharify needs the stone, isn't it? To keep the hold he has on these people?"

His eyes narrowed as he stared at her and Abra felt a fiery flush of pleasure as she read acceptance in them.

"To these people the Tear is holy, Abra. They believe anyone who holds it has the acceptance of Allah. Allah, after all, would not allow an unworthy man to gain possession of his Tear."

No wonder Sharify was willing to kill for it, she thought. And then, suddenly, something else seemed entirely obvious to her, something she'd not thought of before.

"You wanted to take it so that his people would revolt against him, didn't you?" she asked him softly. "It wasn't just for the money it would bring, but something more, something you felt during those miner's strikes, that the rich and powerful ought not to be allowed to control the lives of others simply because their money can buy them the power to dominate."

He stared at her a moment and felt the urge to say to her, yes, Abra, that's why I wanted to take the stone, to help these poor people. But the words died before he could speak them. It was far too much like buying her acceptance, her love. If she needed a reason, an excuse, then it wasn't what he wanted from her.

He turned away from her abruptly. "I am what I am, Abra. Don't try to make me into something more noble than a thief," he told her softly.

She watched his fixed expression for what seemed an eternity to her, hoping to see it crumble, to see some of the rigidity leave. But it didn't. She lay back finally on her cot, telling herself she ought to sleep. But sleep was in no hurry to bring her an escape from her thoughts, and her thoughts seemed destined to bring her only hurt.

The next morning started much the same as those preceding it, with a breakfast of flat bread and Rajeek's almost painfully strong coffee, eaten in the dim glow of light that slowly turned into dawn. Abra stared at the sky as she had each morning since they'd reached the desert, wondering how the colors that filled it managed to form in an air that would all too soon be empty and solid, a featureless blue dome to cover the dull gold of the sand. But as the sun rose there was a riot of rosy, vivid fingers that lifted upward and filled the sky, and she watched them fade with a surprisingly strong regret at their loss.

Rajeek went off to fill the water bags and allow the horses one long, last drink before the start of their day's trek, while Dash and Abra drank the remains of their coffee. When he returned, there were four filled skins hanging from each mount's saddle.

"So much water?" Abra asked as Dash helped her into the saddle.

Rajeek only shrugged. "There will be no oasis to-night," he told them. "We need to bring enough for our needs as well as for the horses."

With that he turned away, swinging himself into the saddle with a wiry, indifferent grace, and set out, expecting them to follow.

The day passed as those before it had, hot and dry and tinged with the bitter, gritty taste of sand. But that evening there was nothing green to ease the scenery when they made their camp as there had been on preceding evenings, no sweetening of the air by the proximity of even a small pool of water.

Abra watched as Rajeek fed and watered the horses, drinking a cup of the flat, warm liquid herself, and knowing even before she asked that there would be none to waste on such extravagances as washing. She ate little of her dinner, feeling grimy and unkempt as well as achy and uncomfortable. As she excused herself and went to the tent she would share once more with Dash, she wondered how long it would take before her body acclimated itself to the rigors of a day spent in the saddle. Until that moment, she hadn't realized how comforting the small pleasures of soap and water could be after a wearing day.

She fell asleep before Dash joined her in the still, stuffy little tent, aware only of a nagging feeling of incipient self pity.

She awoke to the sound of a shot. She didn't know it was a shot, of course, only that there'd been a noise, sharp and loud, that had roused her. But in the absolute stillness that followed there was a pregnant feeling of disaster.

She sat up, staring at Dash's empty cot numbly for a moment before she ran outside.

She was entirely unprepared for what she found there. A few yards from their tent, Dash lay facedown on the ground, a bright red, growing blossom sending long tendrils of color into the white linen of his shirt. Only yards away, Rajeek busied himself saddling the horses, his manner unconcerned, as if this were only another morning like all the rest, as if the blood-red fingers of the dawn that filled the sky did not echo the blood dripping slowly into the sand.

Abra uttered a miserable cry and ran to where Dash lay, throwing herself to the sand beside him. Rajeek turned at the sound, and smiled at her as though in greeting.

"Good," he said. "I will not have to wake you." Then he turned back to finish his task.

He's done this, Abra thought with sick panic as she tried to turn Dash over.

But Rajeek was beside her before she'd managed, pulling at her shoulder.

"Dress yourself," he ordered her. "We've a long ride today."

Abra pulled herself away, grabbing desperately for the pistol that Dash had kept in the pocket of his jacket, which lay crumpled at his side.

"I said, get yourself dressed, woman," Rajeek snarled at her, pulling her back, away from Dash.

She turned quickly, the pistol in her shaking hands.

"You killed him," she screamed as the first sickening waves of loss tumbled over her. She pulled the trigger.

The bullet was wide, and Rajeek ran toward her, kicking outward before she realized what had happened, his booted foot coming in painful contact with her hand and sending the pistol flying. Then, as though to prove his new position of authority over her, he kicked again, his carefully aimed blow landing in the flat of her stomach, sending her sprawling backward with the hurt and the force of it.

"I told you to get dressed," he roared at her. "Do it."

She lay panting for a moment, staring numbly up at him, until he strode to her and grabbed her roughly by the arm, pulling her to her feet. She flailed at him, scratching his face with her nails until he grabbed her hands and held them firm as he pulled a piece of rope from his belt and tied her wrists, tight, in front of her. Then he pulled her back to the tent, grabbing up the hooded cloak where she'd left it at the foot of her cot, and throwing it around her.

He shouted at her, "Be quiet."

Until that moment she had not realized she was sobbing, that she was moaning with a mournful, keening wail of loss. His words focused her to the sound, and suddenly she could hear it echo around her.

Rajeek pulled her back out of the tent and she stared numbly at Dash's still body lying on the ground.

"You can't just leave him there," she pleaded softly, knowing even as she uttered the words that it would do little good, but unable to keep herself from trying.

Rajeek pushed her roughly away, toward the horses. "Why not?" he snarled at her. "If he's not dead yet, he will be soon enough, more than a day from any water. Let the desert bury him." He turned then, and sneered

293

at Dash. "I told him he was a fool to bring a woman like you into the desert," he said, as if the warning had been vindication of what he had done.

Then he lifted Abra and seated her roughly in the saddle, taking her horse's reins and tying them to the pommel of his own saddle. Abra sat, numb and filled with an aching hurt, as he led her away from the grim picture of the small camp, deserted save for the still man lying on the sand, his life slowly flowing with his blood into the desert.

They rode without stopping that day, and all that night. If Abra had not been numb with the grief of loss, she would most probably have felt sick with exhaustion. As it was, she felt nothing, neither the heat of the afternoon sun nor the chill of evening, not even thirst, although she drank what Rajeek gave her in a numbed state of oblivion. All she could see when she closed her eyes was Dash lying on the sand, the bright red fingers of his blood leaking from his back. And so she chose not to close her eyes, but kept them absently fixed on the back of the man who led her. She did not even have the energy to wonder to what it was he was taking her.

Late on the second afternoon Rajeek drew in the horses, but did not dismount for the short rest periods he had so far allowed them. Instead, he backed his horse to hers, and she found herself staring at bright white towers, three of them, startling in the lowering sunlight. Around them were the walls of a fortified city. From where they were, on a rise above the level of the town below, she could just discern the bright green of foliage, the tops of a few tall trees. This was an oasis, she realized, a sizable one if it could support a fair-sized population like that of the town.

"Tahaf," Rajeek told her as if he could read her thoughts. "Those towers mark the emir's palace." He fished about in his saddlebags for a second and drew out a thick scarf. "It wouldn't do for you to disturb the peace of the local peasantry."

With that, he leaned toward her and used the scarf

to gag her, tying it tight and then drawing up the hood of her cloak to hide her face. A few moments later she realized she was crying, not from the hurt where the cloth dug into her cheeks, but from the realization that she had been too numbed to think to fight him.

They rode on, entering Tahaf through wide gates. From what Abra could see through the limited view the hood afforded her, they were soon in a warren of narrow streets, dusty, dun-colored houses lining either side and seeming to tumble one into the next.

Eventually Rajeek stopped the horses before a wrought iron gate, dismounted, and rang a sharp-sounding bell. Immediately a boy appeared, stared out at him, and then unlocked the gate and threw it open. Rajeek walked in, leading the horses. Only when the gate clanged shut behind them did he lift Abra down from the saddle.

"I would see your master," he told the boy sharply. "I have business to discuss with him."

The boy nodded, obviously not unused to similar demands or the sight of a bound woman. He darted off, returning only a moment later to lead them into the cool of the house. Rajeek took Abra's arm and pulled her roughly along.

"What is this you have brought me, Ajib Rajeek?"

Abra's eyes had barely time to adjust to the dimly soft light that filtered through fretwork window screens, but she saw plainly the huge man who sat on a mound of pillows, a bowl of fruit and a ewer of wine beside him ready to appease a stealthy attack of hunger. His dark eyes darted from Rajeek to her, curious, greedy to see what lay beneath the heavy woolen cloak.

"Refreshment?" he offered Rajeek, pointing to the fruit and wine.

"Business first," Rajeek told him, making no effort to draw away even the hood from Abra's head. "This one is of great value."

"They are all of great value," the fat man told him with a wave of his hand. "Two thousand dinar."

Rajeek smiled. "Not two thousand, Hazig. Not twenty thousand." And he pulled the hood away from Abra's face.

The big man looked at her and smiled, then got clumsily to his feet and walked with a rolling gait across the room to them. "Let me see her face," he said to Rajeek as he untied the gag.

As the scarf fell away, Abra began to scream, but the two men simply stood, silently smiling at her. After a moment, she, too, fell into silence, already knowing what it was he was going to say before Hazig told her, "Cry out if you like, little one. But I warn you, it will do you no good. No one will hear you." He smiled. "And even if they did, they would not come."

Somehow Abra knew he was telling her the truth. She closed her eyes, cringing away from him as he put his hand to her cheek. And when she did, the image of Dash's still body appeared before her. Somehow nothing else seemed to matter.

"Fifty thousand dinar," Hazig said to Rajeek, but the guide only shook his head.

"I could bring her to the emir myself and get more than that."

Hazig nodded. "You could. And perhaps he would pay you. Or perhaps he would simply cut your throat. You may try if you like."

Rajeek did not respond, and the fat man slowly drew away the cloak. Abra stood staring at him, clad only in her shift. And then Hazig put his hand to the thin linen and tore that away, too.

"You should not have done this to her," the big man told Rajeek. "It will lower her price." And he pointed to the dark bruise on her stomach where Rajeek had kicked her, several marks on her arms where he'd handled her roughly, and the welts at her wrists and her cheeks from the rope and the gag. Then he turned to Rajeek. "We can both of us profit from this one," he said evenly. "We will hold an auction. Let the emir have some competition for her."

"And my share?" Rajeek demanded.

"One half," the fat man told him. "After all, I bear the burden of the arrangements and the expense. But I can promise you, you will not find yourself with less than seventy-five thousand." He fingered a lock of Abra's hair as he looked down at the bruises on her body once more. "It would be best if we waited for a few days. Until the bruises have healed."

Rajeek shrugged. "It makes no matter," he replied. "I'm in no hurry."

The slave trader smiled. "Good. For this one may make us both our fortunes." He turned his attentions to the rope that bound Abra's wrists, untying it and letting it fall to the floor, looking disdainfully at the welts it had raised. "You ought not to have done that," he muttered to Rajeek. "It may leave a scar."

Abra slowly backed away from the two men as they spoke, hoping their involvement in their conversation would keep their attention from her. When she'd retreated a few feet, she turned and started to run to the door.

Despite his size, Hazig was fast. He caught one of her arms just as Rajeek caught the other.

The guide raised a hand to her.

"You need a lesson, woman," he snarled at her.

But the fat man caught his hand before it fell. "If you have no thought to your profits, I have," he said sharply. Then he lifted the cloak from where it had fallen on the floor and wrapped it around Abra's shoulders. "Eight days, perhaps ten, for the bruises to heal. And then we shall both be rich men."

Rajeek's dark eyes peered intently at Abra for a moment, and then he smiled, the first time she had seen him smile. It sent a shiver of fear through her.

"I think I will like being rich," he said softly.


The room they had brought her to was small, but not uncomfortable. Had it not been for the bars at the single window and the heavy click of the lock at the door, it would not have been that very different from the room in the inn she'd shared with Dash.

Dash. The thought of him brought her a new wave of misery. She threw herself on the bed and began to sob, inconsolably and without reservation. It was as though she'd just seen the body, only a moment before, as though the shock and the loss were completely new to her.

But she was not alone long. The door was opened and an elderly woman stepped through, behind her two boys carrying a heavy brass tub. She did not hesitate, but walked immediately to where Abra lay on the bed.

"Tears will do you no good now," she said, not ungently, but with little nonsense about her manner.

"Leave me be," Abra snarled at her, but she did not back away.

"If you do not do as I direct, Hazig will send servants to help me. You will not like their manners at all," she warned.

Aware that resistance would do her little good, and too numb to really care, Abra allowed the old woman to lead her to the tub and wash her, then to help her dress in a simple white cotton robe. After that, a tray was brought to her with food and wine.

"*Yakul,*" the old woman said. "Eat."

But despite the woman's insistence, Abra could not. She shook her head and pushed away the offered tray.

"At least some of the wine," the woman urged. "It will ease the hurt."

And so she drank from the cup the woman handed to her, willing to lose herself to the forgetfulness of alcohol. It was only after she had drunk a long swallow and found her senses begin to dim that she realized it had been drugged. She fell back, sinking into oblivion.

## *Chapter Nineteen*

Dash opened his eyes slowly. He was stiff and it hurt when he breathed, but he was dimly aware that the pain meant he was still alive.

"It is time you awoke. I was beginning to think I was too rash when I'd decided I'd saved you."

Dash looked up at the tall, dark-haired man standing beside the bed. His face was more than a little familiar.

"Sharify?" he asked bewildered.

The man smiled. "I see you have met my brother the sheik. I am Salim Sharify," he said. "And if your sympathies lie with Shahab, I fear I may regret not having allowed you to bleed to death in the desert."

"No," Dash told him forcefully, shaking his head and attempting to sit up. "I have no love for the emir."

Salim put a hand to his chest and pushed him gently back down to the pillows. "Do not try to move much yet. The bullet missed your spine and your lungs, but it still did a good bit of damage. It will take time for you to heal."

Dash's eyes narrowed. "You seem to know a good deal about medicine," he said.

Salim smiled. "For a simple, ignorant Arab, you mean?"

"I didn't say that," Dash replied quickly.

"No, you didn't and I apologize. As for the medicine, when I was younger and more idealistic, I thought I could help my people best by healing them. I've had the best education that money and enthusiasm, if not genius, could buy, London School of Medicine, no less." His tone turned bitter. "I didn't realize then that my people needed freedom more than they needed pills."

Dash considered his words a moment, and then realized why Salim's face had seemed so familiar to him. It was more than just the resemblance to his older brother. He'd been shown a photograph of this man, it seemed years ago, by Charles Nevin.

"You're the leader of the rebels," he said flatly.

Salim grinned wryly at that. "As the fact does not seem to send you into paroxysms of fear, I will assume you were not lying when you said your sympathies are not with Shahab. May I ask you why you were lying out in the desert, alone, bleeding to death? Just idle curiosity, of course. You need not answer if it doesn't suit you."

"Alone? You don't have Abra as well?" Once more Dash struggled forward, only to collapse back into the bed in exhaustion.

"Abra?" Salim asked. "A woman?"

Dash nodded.

"Not, I suppose, an exceptionally handsome one, with reddish golden hair?"

"Then you do have her?" Dash asked thankfully.

Salim shook his head. "No, but I know where she is," he said slowly.

"Where?" Dash demanded. "Damn it, what's happened to her?"

"A slave trader, on Mohammed Hazig by name, has put out word that he intends to hold an auction soon, only to very wealthy buyers who can afford such exotica as a foreign woman with pale skin like cream and hair the color of red-burnished gold."

"My God," Dash muttered. "I've got to help her."

Salim looked at him doubtfully. "You are not in the condition to help anyone just now, I think. Relax. They won't hurt her, for that would lower her price on the block. And there are a few days still before the auction.

Let me see if I can't think of a way."

Dash watched as he turned and left. Salim was right, he realized. He was in no position to do anyone any good yet. He would simply have to believe, as the rebel leader said, that Abra would not be harmed, and pray that Salim would find a way to get her away from Hazig.

My God, he wondered, how have we gotten ourselves involved with this insanity?

Abra allowed herself to be led into the same room she'd been brought to the first evening. Not that she had much choice in the matter, for two burly servants marshaled her with unremitting attention. But she'd grown almost indifferent to these daily inspections, being led into Hazig's presence and left with him and the old woman. The woman would draw back her robe and Hazig would stare at her, at the now faded bruises on her stomach and arms, at the shrinking welts on her wrists. Twice he'd instructed the old woman to put some salve on the welts, but this day he seemed pleased with the progress of her minor wounds and made no such demands.

"Two more days and there will be no sign of the damage Rajeek did," he told her, obviously pleased. "You should thank me. Left to that fool's supervision, there is no telling what harm he might have done you."

"Why is it I cannot find your kindness altogether without self-interest on your part?" she asked with an angry sneer.

She pulled away from him and closed the robe, her fingers fastening the buttons with steady fingers.

He watched her progress, and then turned to the old woman. "You have not been seeing to her diet," he accused, pointing to the ease with which her fingers fastened the buttons, the lack of trembling, the absolute control.

"She's refused to eat yesterday and today," the woman

301

whined, defending herself.

Abra glared at him. "That's right. I won't touch any more of your drugged food or wine," she told him.

For a second she thought of what was happening to her, where the will to resist him had come from. For the first few days she'd felt nothing but lethargy, cared nothing for what happened to her, could think of nothing when she was clear enough of the drugs to think but of Dash. But the previous day she'd realized that giving in to Hazig, docilely allowing him to keep her drugged and quiet, would not bring Dash back to her. And it would not bring her any closer to repaying Rajeek for what he'd done.

For that was what she had to do, she realized, see that Rajeek paid for Dash's death. Even if it meant her own, she swore, she would somehow find a way to see that Rajeek paid for the life he had taken.

Hazig turned back to her and smiled. "No matter. Your bruises are almost healed. The auction is arranged for the day after tomorrow. And in the meantime you will be locked securely in your room."

He motioned to one of the servants to take her back to her room. As the man put his hand to her arm, Abra turned back to Hazig.

"You'll pay for this," she told him softly. "One way or another, you'll pay."

He grinned at her maliciously. "Perhaps. But the emir will pay first, and heavily," he told her.

"I know Shahab," she said, her tone cold and even. "And if I ask it of him, he'll have your head in a basket."

For a moment Hazig stared at her, and she saw a shadow of fear pass across his expression. Then he seemed to shake it off, and he laughed.

"I almost believe you," he said as she was being led away, back to her private prison.


"There's no drug in it."

302

Abra stared at the old woman's face. "If there isn't, you eat some of it," she replied.

The woman stared at the bowl of couscous and turned away.

"You can take it with you," Abra called after her. "I won't eat it."

But the woman disappeared, leaving the food behind. Abra sniffed at the bowl. She was hungry, she realized, and the fact surprised her. Could her body have stopped mourning so quickly? A few days before the thought of food was repellent to her, and now her stomach groaned with emptiness. She closed her eyes and thought of Dash, but the image of his dead body had faded. Somehow her mind rejected that. Instead he was standing before her, smiling at her, his hair windblown as it had been that first time she'd seen him on the wharf in New York. It all seemed so long ago, another lifetime almost. And yet now, when she thought of him, he was alive, and she was glad to think of him that way.

But the memory of his smiling face didn't send away the emptiness in her stomach, and she knew she couldn't eat the food the old woman had left for her, counting on her hunger to persuade her. She took the bowl and climbed up on her bed until she could just reach the barred window. The bowl barely fit in the space between the bars, but she managed to force it through and heave it, throwing it into what she had come to realize was Hazig's private garden below. She firmly wished he was under the window and had the good fortune to be struck by her falling missile.

She put her hands to the bars and pulled herself up, staring up into the darkening sky. Two days more she would remain in this room, and then what? To Sharify's harem, or some other? And what would happen now to Vincent? After all that she and Dash had gone through, it seemed so unfair. Surely all three of them deserved better than the end fate was offering them.

She lay down on the bed and thought. If it was Sharify who bought her, perhaps she could convince him

303

that she had brought the jewel. She wondered if he would believe her, if he would go out into the desert and help her find Dash's body. For the stone would still be there, she realized, in the bag that held Dash's belongings. Rajeek had not known what treasure it held, and she was sure he hadn't touched it. Perhaps it was not too late to salvage Vincent's life, at least. That was something for which she still could hope.

She ought to sleep, she told herself. It would be better than lying there, wondering, thinking about things over which she had no control. A cup of goat's milk remained on the tray, and she wondered idly if it, too, would be drugged. Then she sat up, lifted the mug and took a single, small sip. Enough, she told herself, to give her sleep.

There was the sound of scuffling in the hall, and a woman's shout. At first Abra was confused. She had heard no other sounds in the house since she'd been brought there, except the occasional noise of footfalls in the hall. And then there was a muffled cry, a woman's cry, she felt sure, and she decided that Hazig had found another victim for his greed.

She felt a momentary wave of pity for the newcomer, wondering what horrors had brought her into Hazig's hands.

The scuffling sounds continued for a while longer, and then there was silence once more, followed a few moments later by the pad of booted feet against the stone floor. She looked up to the window and saw it was pitch darkness outside. Night. As the sound of the key being turned in the lock of her door came to her, she wondered why Hazig would send for her so late, the puzzle turning into fear as she gave the question the only solution that came to mind, that the slave trader had decided to give her a taste of what her new life was to be like.

She scrambled to her feet and ran to the side of the

room, lifting a small ceramic vase of flowers, determined to fight, at least, and not submit like a sheep at the slaughter.

The door opened and swung inward, and a tall, burnoosed figure entered. She took aim, and let the vase fly, delighted when she saw it strike him on the shoulder. He staggered backward and she was struck with an almost alien surge of hope. She darted toward the door.

He was not so badly hurt as she had thought him to be, however, for he caught her arm. She turned on him, hands flailing, striking out at him until he pushed her to the ground and pinned her there.

"Be still, Abra," he hissed at her.

She stopped struggling, surprised at his use of her name, and stared up at him. But the face that looked down at hers bewildered her.

"Shahab?" she asked, fitting the features she made out in the dim light to a name, wondering even as she asked what he was doing there, what has happening. But then she realized it was not Sharify, although there seemed to be an almost uncanny resemblance.

"She's not in the room next door."

The voice was too familiar to be real, and before Abra had a chance to think that she'd heard a ghost, a tall form appeared in the doorway.

"Abra?"

Salim rolled off her and she scrambled to her feet, telling herself it was a dream and she didn't care, as long as she didn't have to waken from it.

"Dash," she cried, throwing herself into his arms, not believing it until she felt the warmth of his arms around her, heard his voice whispering her name. She turned her face up to his, and was rewarded with a hard, searching kiss.

"Your woman is a hellion, Thorne," Salim said with a laugh as he got to his feet. "It would have served Hazig right if she'd done this to him, but me, I am innocent of any wrongdoing, and look how she has treated me." He rubbed his shoulder and scowled.

305

But neither Dash nor Abra were paying him any attention.

"I can't believe it," she murmured to him. "I saw you on the ground. I thought you were dead."

"I nearly was," he told her.

"But what happened?" she demanded. "How did you find me?"

"There'll be time enough for explanations later," Salim interrupted before Dash could answer. "Right now, I think it would be safest for all of us if we were away from here and out of Tahaf."

Dash nodded, and then he and Abra followed Salim from the room. They ran down the corridor and into the large room that now had become so familiar to Abra. This time, however, Hazig was not sitting on his pillowed divan waiting for her. This time he was stretched out on the floor, and it was evident from the amount of blood that surrounded his body and the two others that flanked his, that Hazig and his servants were dead. Their throats had been cut.

Abra turned away from the gore, sickened by the sight of it. A half-dozen men, Salim's apparently, came to abrupt attention as he entered.

"It was necessary," one of them said. "They would not cooperate."

None of them looked as though they much regretted the act they'd committed.

Salim nodded to the old woman who stood trembling in the corner. It seemed she expected to meet the same fate as her master, and the thought had little appeal to her.

Salim stepped toward her, and she cringed away. But the rebel leader made no outwardly threatening move.

"Tell them this is the end of all those who would steal my people's freedom," he said, waving his arm toward the bodies. Then he motioned to his men to follow, and they closed around Dash and Abra, sweeping them forward into the darkness of the night, their footsteps followed by the old woman's wails of relief.

There were horses in the courtyard waiting, stamping their impatience. Without a word, the men mounted, Dash drawing Abra up to the saddle in front of him. She leaned back to him as they started to move through the gates, out into the narrow street, feeling his warmth close to her, assuring her that he was indeed still alive, that he was there, that it wasn't some wishful dream from which she would soon awaken.

The rebel camp was just a few dozen tents huddled together between two huge dunes. When Abra looked up, all she could see was sand surrounding them, and the glint of early morning sunlight off the sentries' weapons.

"We move soon," Salim told them as he ushered them into his tent. "Soon it will no longer be safe here, especially after tonight's activities."

The tent was enormous compared with the tiny one Abra had shared with Dash while they had traveled, and decidedly luxurious. Thick, colorful rugs covered the ground beneath their feet, brass lanterns glowed softly, and there was almost a feeling of domesticity about the space. As they walked in, a woman stepped out from a partitioned-off area toward the rear of the tent.

Compared to the women she had so far encountered since she'd stepped foot in Tunis, this woman looked completely Europeanized to Abra. Dressed simply in a long, soft gown of pale blue, with her thick, dark hair worn in a chignon at the nape of her neck, Abra thought she seemed more mirage than real. Her manner, too, was unlike those of the meekly subservient women Abra had seen. She walked quickly to Salim, offered a cheek to be kissed, then turned to Dash.

"Mr. Thorne," she said with a wide smile. "I am delighted to see you have returned safely." She turned to Abra with a welcoming gesture. "And this must be the missing Mrs. Thorne."

"This is my home," Salim told Abra with a smile,

"and my wife, Shaida."

Abra greeted her, then turned to Dash for some sign of how she should act with these people, what she should tell them of their errand. But those questions fled quickly from her as she looked at his face.

"Dash," she said as she moved to him.

She was a moment too late. He'd already fallen when she reached him.

Salim moved to him, and, like Abra, knelt at his side. "I knew I shouldn't have let him come with us," he said to Abra. "But he wouldn't let us leave him. He had to make sure we did not come back without you."

Abra took Dash's hand and pressed it to her cheek, then turned worried eyes to Salim. "What's happened?" she asked, almost afraid to hear the answer.

Salim shrugged. "The wound's probably reopened." He turned to his wife. "Shaida, get my bag."

Then he stood and lifted Dash, holding his arm around his own neck. Abra helped, putting her arm around Dash's waist.

"There," Salim directed, motioning to an area toward the rear of the tent partitioned off with a large sheet of decoratively embroidered material. "We'll see what we can do for him."

Once they'd settled him on a divan, Abra helped Salim strip Dash to the waist. She was sickened by the gory hole in his back, which, indeed, was leaking blood.

Shaida brought in a black doctor's bag. Salim took it, opened it, and drew out ointment and some fresh bandaging. When he'd cleaned the wound and rebandaged it, he turned to Abra. Her fear and concern were more than obvious. He could read them on her face.

"He can't die," she said numbly. "I thought he was dead once. I can't face that again."

But Salim was calmly assuring. "He won't die," he told her. "I'm too good a doctor for that. All he needs is a few days' rest." He smiled at her. "And having you to nurse him."

Then he stood and left them, aware that there was

nothing left for him to say.

Abra was almost unaware that he'd gone. All her attention was centered on Dash, on his motionless expression, on his face that had grown suddenly so pale. She crept silently to where he lay, and once more took his hand and pressed it to her cheek, remembering how his touch felt, feeling as though she would never feel alive again without it.

"You can't die, Dash," she told him softly. "I won't let you. Not again. I couldn't face that again."


Salim was right. He was too good a doctor to allow Dash to die.

Early the next morning Dash opened his eyes to find Abra sitting beside him, her worried attention attesting to the hours she'd spent at his side. He looked up at her and smiled crookedly.

"I thought you might use some practice with your nursing skills," he told her.

"Well, the next time you make a similar decision," she told him as she put her hand to his cheek and stroked it, "please remember to inform me that it's merely a drill. I've been just a little bit concerned."

"Just a bit?" he asked as he reached up to her. "I thought that when you looked up and saw me back there in Tahaf, you were, well, overjoyed."

She scowled at his look of amused triumph. "It was simply the shock of seeing a man who'd risen from the dead. I'm sure Lazarus drew a similar response as he swaggered about town."

"You're lying, and we both know it," he told her. "Why is it so hard for you to admit that you're in love with me? That the thought of my having been killed meant a bit more to you than a passing inconvenience?"

She stared at him a moment, searching the endless blue of his eyes, and knew she couldn't go on with the game any longer. He was right, the thought that he had been dead had devastated her, had numbed every

309

thought, except the wish for revenge against the man she'd thought his killer. She didn't have anywhere to hide any longer.

"All right," she said softly. "I love you. When I thought you were dead, I felt dead inside myself. Does that satisfy you?"

He grinned as he looked up at her, then put his hand to the heavy golden silk that framed her face. She felt his fingers in her hair, felt the tingle of fire that passed through her at his touch. But most of all she saw his eyes, the look of satisfied triumph that filled them.

"Not by half," he told her softly as he wound his fingers in her hair and pulled her gently down to him, hungry for the taste of her lips.

His kiss was long and searching, and Abra surrendered to it just as she'd surrendered to him with her words. Whatever the future held for her, whatever Dash chose to do with his life once they'd ransomed Vincent, even if it meant his abandonment of her, she found she didn't care. It was like casting off a heavy weight to say the words to him, to allow herself to admit to him that she cared. The way she'd felt when she'd thought him dead had convinced her that she could not simply go on without him, coolly self-assured, afraid to say the words because they might mean she would be vulnerable to his whims. Just as she had surrendered to him with her body in Cap Ferrat, now she surrendered to him with her heart, and prayed he would not use his power over her unfairly.

He held her tight for a moment, and then his arms fell to his sides. She looked at his face, and saw in his eyes evidence of the pain the effort had cost him.

"I'll fetch Salim" she told him. "He'll give you something for the pain."

But he caught her arm and kept her from turning away. "All I need is you, here, beside me," he said softly.

"I am, Dash, here, always," she told him as she watched his eyes slowly drift closed.

*"Balid!* Stupid fool!"

Sheik Shahab Sharify was displeased, and he made no effort to disguise the fact.

"You were instructed to wait in Tunis for the appearance of a woman, a particular woman, and then guide her here, to me. And what do you do, you greedy pig? You kill the man who accompanies her and you take her to a slave trader!"

"You made no mention of the man," Rajeek protested.

"And all you could think was that Hazig would offer you a few more dinar than I had promised you. Fool. Did you think I wouldn't hear what you and Hazig were doing, finding a few more buyers to raise the price of the goods? Your greed has ruined it for the both of us. You are left without any money, and I without the woman."

He turned and glared at Rajeek, then moved slowly across the room to where the guide stood, held to attention by two burly guards. He calmly drew back his hand and slapped him, viciously, across the face.

"I did not know that the rebels would choose that moment to make an example of Hazig," Rajeek mumbled through the blood in his mouth.

"Idiot. Do you think it is as simple as that?"

Sharify considered the guide's face for a moment, saw the fear that flickered in his evasive, dark eyes. Could he have found the Tear after all? he wondered idly, then chased the thought from his mind. No, they would never have told him of it, and he would have been far too anxious to get away with the woman to think of searching through their belongings for something he did not know was there. It was still out there in the desert, with the man's body. There was still the chance he might retrieve it.

"Do you think often of death, Rajeek?" he asked softly, moving to the guide's side as he pulled a jewelhilted knife from his belt. He pressed the blade to the soft skin of Rajeek's neck, allowing the sharp steel to prick the flesh and sprout a thin line of red in its wake. He could smell the man's fear. "Do you?"

Rajeek shook his head, a short, lurching movement actually, rather than a real negation, but enough to convey his meaning. And when Sharify saw it, he smiled.

"If I were you, I would think about it a great deal from now on. Because if I have cause to be disappointed in you once more, you will not have the means for thought. Do I make myself clear to you? Do you understand me?"

"Yes," Rajeek croaked.

"Good," Sharify replied. "Now, I will tell you what you will do, Rajeek. You will take Amad to the place in the desert where you left the man. A simple enough chore, don't you agree?" He let the knife fall away from Rajeek's neck, and motioned to the two guards to release him.

"Yes, Excellency," Rajeek agreed, completely cowed now. He rubbed his arms where the guard's grip had bitten into the flesh of his arm.

"Now get out of here and clean that blood from yourself. The sight of you disgusts me."

Rajeek bowed and backed away, thankful for so easy a release and not at all sure why he had been let off without worse punishment. He murmured a small prayer of thanks beneath his breath as he reached the door.

When he'd gone, Sharify turned to his white-robed lieutenant.

"When he's shown you the place, search it, search it well. And then kill him. The desert can swallow two bodies as easily as one."


Four days more and Dash was up and about, stiff, but apparently on his way to being healed. Which was well, as Salim had ordered the camp struck and moved.

312

Another valley in the dunes was found. And it was none too soon. Word soon reached them that the sheik's troops had found the old camp only a day after they had left it.

"Salim asked again today what our plans are once you're able to leave," Abra told Dash softly that evening as she settled herself beside him, ready for sleep.

"And you told him what?" Dash asked.

She could feel him tense at her side. "Just what we've both told him the last several days. That we have to return to Tahaf and free my father. And do it soon," she added. "We have only eight days more," she added, a hint of worry creeping into her tone.

Dash was silent for a moment. When he spoke, he sounded thoughtful. "He knows we haven't told him the whole truth. But he seems to trust us, at least where it comes to our dislike for his brother."

"And you're sure he has no idea you have the stone?" she asked him.

He shrugged. "I can't believe he didn't go through our belongings when he brought them back with me to his camp. But it's still there, in my bag, and he's not made any mention of it."

Abra sighed audibly. "I wish we could give it to him. He's honest and fair and he genuinely wants to help his people. If there were some way of getting Papa back without it . . ."

"I know how you feel, Abra. But there's nothing we can do about it. We have to return the stone to Sharify if we're to get Vincent out of Tahaf alive."

She nodded in the darkness. "I know. But I hate the thought of Shahab going on as he has, doing as he wishes with no thought to the hurt he does to other people's lives."

"Perhaps Allah will see him fairly rewarded for the evil he does."

She snorted. "Allah needs a bit of help, the way I see it."

"And someday perhaps Salim will give it to him. In

313

the meantime, I suggest we concentrate on Vincent."

"You're right," she agreed. "But I don't have to like the way things have turned out," she told him before she turned over and willed herself to sleep.

She liked it even less two days later when she and Dash rode out of the camp, supposedly for a short ride and a bit of exercise. Abra waved gaily to the sentries as they passed them, and was rewarded with tolerant nods. It was evident that they thought the foreigners a bit mad to be taking a pleasure ride through the desert.

But once they were out of sight of the camp, she sobered, and any evidence of ebullience drained away from her expression.

"I hated lying to Salim and Shaida," she told Dash. She threw him an accusing look. The lie had been his idea, and it seemed to have had absolutely no negative effect on his conscience.

"I thought we'd agreed Salim wouldn't simply let us try to storm the palace alone. And without telling him we have the stone, I can't see any other way to explain what we're doing."

"Then perhaps we should have told him we have the Tear," she said thoughtfully. "He'd have understood. I know he would. And he'd have offered to help us."

"Perhaps. But his perspective is different from ours. Weighed against the possibility of being able to engineer a popular uprising, I'm sure he'd count Vincent's life an unfortunate, but necessary, sacrifice. He'd never have let us leave with the stone."

They'd already argued the matter twice before, and both times she'd been persuaded by Dash's insistent logic. She really didn't know why she couldn't simply let it go and get on with what she knew they had to do. But something inside her could not help shouting at her that it was wrong to return a tangible symbol of power to a man who would, she knew, misuse it.

"Perhaps, once we've gotten Papa out, we might try to

314

get it back," she suggested hopefully.

Dash threw her an amused glance. "You mean, we might ply the trade of jewel thief?" he asked, not without a hint of humor. "Intriguing idea. Our finances could certainly use the infusion."

"Not for that," she shot back at him. "For Salim and his people." She grew angry with him. "Or haven't you any motivations beyond simple greed?"

His eyes narrowed as he returned her stare. "The simplest motives are the strongest, Abra, and usually the most honest," he told her softly. "And after all, I am a thief."

She drew back from his tone and his eyes, not wanting to see them, not wanting to recognize what she read in them. He was reminding her of who and what he was, letting her know that he traveled through his life unencumbered, without any values but those he defined for himself, without any ties but those he placed upon himself.

No wonder he'd felt no remorse at having lied to Salim, she told herself. Even after the man had saved his life. And close on the heels of that thought was another: How could she have fallen in love with such a man?

They reached Tahaf late in the afternoon as the sun was lowering, setting the bare white stones aflame with the reflected colors of the sky. The palace seemed to shimmer before them, afire with a rosy glow.

The guards who stopped them at the gate seemed unabashed at the sudden appearance of foreigners proclaiming they had urgent business with the emir. They eyed Dash and Abra coolly before allowing them to pass into a courtyard where they were instructed to wait in the still, hot, fading sunshine.

Abra looked around at the embellished inner walls of the courtyard as she absently wiped the dust and sand from her hands and face. If the palace had seemed

315

bleakly fortlike from its bare exterior, it was dizzyingly ornamented once one passed into the interior. And this, she realized, was not even the true interior, but only the fringes, where guards and the household servants went about their business.

"Something catch your eye?" Dash asked her idly.

She nodded. "I was just thinking that I might have spent the rest of my life here. Both Hazig and Rajeek thought the sheik would buy me."

He seemed unsurprised at this information. "It wasn't an unlikely expectation, Abra," he told her absently. "Fair women are considered prizes here, but the sheik's predilection for them is well known, almost an obsession."

His words startled her. "Well known here, perhaps, but how do you know of it?" she demanded.

He turned cool blue eyes to her, but didn't answer.

"You knew that all along," she said slowly. "From the very start. That's why you weren't surprised when he asked to see me in New York, when he paid me court. It was what you wanted, so you'd be able to get to the yacht, to the stone. You knew it before you and Papa began the whole thing. You planned it, intending to use me from the very beginning."

He arched a brow. "I told Vincent about it at the start, Abra," he told her evenly. "We both agreed it was the easiest way. Neither of us thought it would go as far as it did." He looked at her, almost accusing her. "And it wouldn't have, if you hadn't let it." His tone was as heated as hers had been.

"Would you have come to Papa for help if he hadn't had a blond-haired daughter?" she demanded. "Or would you have found another old man, looking for a bit of excitement to brighten his last years?"

He turned away, apparently done with the discussion. But she was not. "It was all a game to you," she said slowly, the realization hurting her as much as his indifference to Salim's cause had. "You're as bad as he is."

"Abra," he said finally, reaching out for her arm.

316

But she shrugged away. And before he had the chance to pursue the matter, a guard approached them.

"The emir will see you," he informed them with an air that said all too plainly that they ought to be appreciative of the honor. He turned, motioned to them, and moved briskly toward a brightly painted decorated arch that led to the interior of the palace.

Without a glance at Dash, Abra followed.

## Chapter Twenty

"And so you've come to me after all. I was beginning
to think you wouldn't." Sharify smiled. "I expected you
weeks ago."

Abra was a bit shocked by the room. She had by no
means expected to find Sharify living a spartan existence, but the enormity of the room, the figured mosaics
on the walls, the multicolored marble that sheathed
pillars and floor, the sheer extravagance of it seemed
malign, almost vicious, after the poverty in which she'd
seen the common people living.

"It took a bit of time to locate your stone, Shahab,"
she told him. "And steal it."

He seemed more amused than not by the sharpness of
her tone, for he smiled at her as he rose and crossed to
them.

"So you didn't have it, after all," he said, a bit
surprised. "Vincent told me you hadn't stolen it, but I
must confess I really didn't believe it." He turned to
Dash. "And this is?" he asked.

"A thief," Abra replied sharply. "I needed the services
of a thief to get your stone for you."

Dash ignored her, as did Sharify. The two men eyed
each other, evaluating.

"Dashiel Thorne," he said finally, and, reluctantly it
seemed, gave his hand to Sharify's offered one.

"Ah, yes, Mr. Thorne. It seems to me I heard some
rumor that you'd met an unfortunate end." His lips

formed an unpleasant grin. "An unpleasant exaggeration, it seems."

"You knew about his being shot and my being taken to a slave trader?" Abra gasped, shocked. "Is there no law at all here?"

"But of course there is, Abra. The man Rajeek was brought in and questioned. But in the absence of a corpse, there was no proof of foul play. Except, of course, in the case of the unfortunate Hazig. I don't suppose I should lay any of that at your door, Mr. Thorne?" But without waiting for Dash to respond, he went on, answering his own question and offering Dash a smug smile. "Ah, that, of course, is foolish. The old woman said it was the rebels. She is not shrewd enough to lie." He shook his head. "It seems my unfortunate brother has stepped beyond the bounds of reason. I'm afraid I shall have to see him executed once he is caught."

"Hazig bought and sold women like cattle," Abra fumed at him. "He was an animal."

"Ah, I think you are too harsh in your judgments, my dear Abra," Sharify countered mildly, apparently unconcerned with her wrath. "A woman must have a protector. If she has no father or husband, someone must see to making provision for her. And in return for the service, he seeks a fair fee."

"He sold women," she repeated obstinately.

"We didn't come here to discuss morals with you," Dash interrupted, putting his hand to Abra's arm before she could go on, aware that Sharify was not as calmly unperturbed as he pretended to be and not wanting to push him too far. "We have something you want. And you have Vincent. Shall we get about our business?"

Abra turned to him and thought, business, that's all it is to him, just business.

Sharify looked at him and smiled with false pleasantness.

"The Tear?" he asked, holding out his hand.

"When we've seen Vincent," Dash replied.

Sharify's eyes narrowed. "I could have it taken from

319

you, you know."

"Assuming I had it on my person," Dash replied.

"Ah, but you must. You wouldn't leave it in the town, it wouldn't be safe. And certainly not in the desert. But no matter. Vincent is well, and I am more than willing to reunite him with his daughter."

With that he called out, and a servant appeared at the far end of the room, bowed after Sharify had directed him to bring Vincent, then disappeared.

"In the meantime, will you rest yourselves, have some wine?" He smiled in invitation and motioned to the divan.

"We didn't come for a taste of your hospitality," Dash replied.

Sharify turned to him, pretending surprise. "But of course, you will not refuse it," he said. "At least, for a day or two. I would not think of sending you off without seeing that you've first enjoyed the small pleasures my humble home can offer you," he said with his eyes firmly settled on Abra. "Besides, I consider it my duty to make up to you for the unpleasantness to which I've unintentionally put you."

Abra turned her eyes to his and felt herself shiver with the sudden intensity of his gaze. She turned away, refusing to let herself be drawn in by those strangely powerful eyes, remembering the effect they had had on her in the past.

"I only want to be away from here with my father," she told him. "And to give you this." She put her hand to her pocket and fumbled a moment, then finally drew out the lamb-shaped brooch he'd given her, the only remnant of her evening with Bazetti that she'd salvaged after her night on the *Mala Femmina*. She held it out to him, glittering on her palm.

He looked down at it and frowned, then shook his head. "I have no wish to see it returned, Abra," he said to her.

"You said it was a token of friendship," she reminded him. "After what you've done, I want none of your friendship."

320

Still he made no move to take it from her hand, and she let it fall to the marble floor, making a small clatter as it touched the stone.

But Sharify was apparently not aware of her gesture, for at that moment he looked up to the door. "Ah, Vincent. You have a most welcome visitor."

Abra spun around. "Papa?"

The tall man who approached sported a grey silk robe edged in black and crimson piping, an unlikely costume for the father she'd always found the epitome of quiet Bond Street good taste. But it was, indeed, Vincent.

"Papa!" she cried once more as she ran across the room to his open arms, heaving a long sigh of relief as she felt them close around her, as she heard the familiar sound of his voice.

"My God, Abra, you didn't try to come for me without the stone? You shouldn't have. You and Dash will only end up hurt as well."

And suddenly words and tears started simultaneously. "No, we have it. McErlaine had stolen it. He went to Cannes and sold it to a man named Bazetti and he killed himself and Dash and I followed Bazetti to Venice and we had to steal it from him and, and . . ." Her words faded away. "Oh, Papa," she whispered, then buried her face against his chest.

Dash approached them slowly, smiling at Vincent. "You look no worse for wear, Vincent," he said as he motioned to the luxurious silk clothing. "And I quite like the transformation. You look like a pasha."

"Why shouldn't he look well?" Sharify demanded abruptly, with false joviality. "I'm not a monster, after all. And my ladies quite enjoyed entertaining him."

"Papa!" Abra exclaimed, a bit appalled.

Vincent tried to look repentant, but didn't succeed. "A man who thinks he may die soon, my dear, is prone to inexplicable weaknesses," he told her with a smile. Then he turned to Dash, just as Sharify did. "You brought the stone?" he asked.

Dash nodded and quickly produced it, handing it to the sheik with apparent disinterest.

"So it was the policeman who took it, after all," Sharify mused as he stared into the glowing red of the stone. "I'd never have thought he had the courage or the imagination." He shrugged dismissively. "Well, it seems I misjudged him." He turned and smiled at Abra and Vincent. "Just as I misjudged the both of you," he admitted. "I hope you'll allow me somehow to make amends."

Abra spun around to face him, wiping away the tears that lingered on her cheek with her hand. "You have what you wanted. Now we want to leave. There's nothing you can do that will ever compensate for what you've already done to me and my father."

"But do be reasonable, Abra. It was a grievous error, one I heartily regret having made. But it's done and I can not remake the past. After all, no harm's been done. You and Vincent are both well, and reunited. Surely you'll allow me to extend my hospitality to you." He smiled expansively. "Besides, it's nearly evening. I wouldn't think of allowing road-weary travelers such as yourself and Mr. Thorne to leave without spending the night."

Vincent put his hand to Abra's arm, preventing her further protest. "It's all right, Abra," he said gently as he stared fixedly at Sharify. "Shahab has excellent cooks. And a night will make no difference."

"Excellent," Sharify exclaimed with a grin. He leveled his gaze once more at Abra. "Perhaps you will enjoy the hospitality so well, you will choose to stay."

She backed away, seeing something in his look that told her his words were not those of simple invitation, but something far more sinister.


In all honesty, Abra could find no fault with the accommodations. She was shown to an enormous room lavish with silk on the huge draped bed, and filled with furniture that had obviously been at home in a great house in Paris in the days before the Revolution. She could only wonder at the cost of finding the dressing table, the chaises covered with tapestry, and the magnificent inlaid tall chest, and bringing them here, to this unlikely place in the middle of a desert. Tall fretwork doors opened onto a charming small garden, headily fragrant with heliotrope and white jasmine, cool and pleasant in the near twilight. From a half-dozen ornate bird cages came the fluttering music of songbirds who stretched their brightly colored wings and hopped from bar to bar as she passed.

By the time she'd finished her exploration, she found that a bath had been readied for her, an enormous tiled tub filled with warm flower-scented water. A half-dozen unblemished gardenias floated on the water's surface.

She stripped off her clothing, suddenly aware how unpleasantly travelworn she must appear, the khaki riding skirt and linen blouse Dash had bought for her in Tunis no longer seeming adventurous, but merely wearily limp. She hardly noticed when a servant appeared to spirit them away, for she was reveling in the decadence of the sweetly scented water. She closed her eyes and let herself grow limp, feeling the warmth and comfort steal away her resistance, leaving only a languorous feeling of abandonment behind.

When she finally managed to remove herself from the water, she found the servant had miraculously reappeared once more, this time bearing a huge towel and a silk robe. Abra dried herself briskly, telling herself she was a fool to allow herself to be so easily seduced by Sharify's luxurious hospitality, wondering once more why she had been given a room apart, away from her father and Dash. She wondered, if she were to wander through the maze of the palace, how long it would take her to find their quarters.

It had grown late, and when she peered out the window, she realized the sun had set long before, and that the night had already grown dark. The servant urged her to dress quickly, and she turned to the bed expecting to find the travelworn skirt and blouse, aired perhaps, but in much the same condition they had been when she had shed them.

323

Instead there was a beautiful flowing silk gown, the fabric iridescent, of a shimmery blue-green color that constantly seemed to change as she touched it. Of eastern design, the dress was simply draped, and when she had put it on, she found the abundance of soft silk seemed to float around her, revealing soft curves as she moved and yet appearing completely demure in that it made no daring revelations. It was, she realized, somehow far more suggestive even than the deep decollete of the gown that had so fascinated the lecherous jewel merchant Bazetti.

When she'd completed her toilette, she was led to a dining room—another surprise, it was furnished in dark mahogany; Georgian antiques. Silver epergnes glittered on the shiny surface of the huge table, their burdens of fruit and sweetmeats looking like still life sculptures in the flicker of candlelight.

Sharify was sitting at the head of the long table, and he was alone. Abra hesitated as she entered the room, not quite sure she wanted to face him without Dash and Vincent.

But he seemed more than delighted at the prospect. He rose and walked the length of the long table to her, his eyes on her in such a way as to make her wish she were still wearing the crumpled and stained traveling clothes.

He smiled at her. "You look absolutely beautiful, Abra. I knew that color would suit you. When I saw the silk in the marketplace, I could only think of you."

She was intrigued by his admission. "You purchased the silk?" she asked, surprised he'd admitted to such an act of domesticity.

He nodded. "And had the dress made for you."

"But how is that possible? I've been here only a few hours."

"But I've been expecting you for weeks, Abra. I knew you'd come for Vincent. And I had preparations made for your visit, the room, dresses, anything you might need. And now that you've brought it back to me, I'm not sure which pleases me more, to have the Tear once more, or to have you here with me."

She backed away from him. "I'm not here with you. I came to give you your stone to buy my father's freedom. And for no other reason."

He looked entirely bewildered. "Were you not pleased with your quarters?" he asked. "The garden, the servants? Did something dissatisfy you?" He seemed almost laughably concerned, like a small boy who has tried to please an elder and found his efforts all futile.

"No, no," she assured him quickly, ashamed she'd attacked without provocation. "It's all quite lovely. In fact, it's the most beautiful bedroom I've ever seen."

He smiled with obvious relief. "Then I am satisfied. But there is one thing more."

He strode to the handsome Georgian sideboard that ran half the length of the side wall, and took from it a long, narrow box. Then he turned back to her.

"This belongs with that silk," he told her as he returned to her. He opened the box and drew out a necklace of huge aquamarines and diamonds. The precious stones shimmered in the candlelight.

She took a step backward, away from him. "I don't want your jewels, Shahab," she told him evenly. "I thought I made that understood. And I have no intention of allowing you to buy me."

"Buy you? Is that what I'm doing?" he asked her softly.

"Isn't it?" she demanded.

He looked at her thoughtfully, apparently considering. "Perhaps it is, Abra," he told her finally. "Or perhaps I'm just trying to show you how much I love you."

"You love no one but yourself," she retorted angrily. "If you had even the smallest grain of feeling for me, you would never have put me through all this, made me believe you'd have Papa killed."

"But it worked, didn't it? It brought you here," he said evenly.

She considered him in silence for a moment. "That's all that matters to you, that you got what you wanted. It's like a game, someone wins, someone loses. And you don't really care."

"Oh, but I do care," he replied with a tolerant smile. "I want very much to win."

"Those aren't the kinds of games I play, Shahab," she told him softly.

He didn't seem very put out by her refusal, almost as if he'd expected it. "Wouldn't you wear the necklace tonight, at least?" he asked. "Would it hurt you so badly to allow me the small pleasure of seeing it around your neck?"

She didn't answer, but he moved to her side and draped the necklace around her neck. She stood, frozen, afraid to move, aware of the touch of his fingers close to her skin. But once he'd fastened the clasp, he moved back, away from her, as though he wanted to prove to her the complete innocence of his intentions.

They stood, a tense silence growing between them as he stared at her. As she had that evening when she'd stood with him alone on the deck of the yacht, Abra felt a fear nagging at her, something she could not quite define, but she knew that at the bottom of it was the thought that he might somehow manage to persuade her, to seduce her despite the fact that she knew that his words of kindness were all lies, that his pledges of devotion meant nothing.

"Ah, Vincent. We've been waiting for you."

Abra turned, relieved to see her father at the room's entrance, feeling as though she'd been reprieved. With an unexpected stab of disappointment, she realized he was alone.

"Where's Dash?" she demanded.

But Vincent only shrugged. "I'd thought he was with you," he said.

"Ah, the many-lived Mr. Thorne?" Sharify asked. "Why, he was being entertained by two of my ladies. He sent word an hour or so ago that he was tired and wished to be excused from the formalities of dinner." He smiled mildly at Abra. "No wonder you hired him to help you steal the Tear, Abra. If he pursues his vocation of thief with as much enthusiasm as he pursues his

326

pleasures, he must be quite adept at it."

Abra felt as though he'd stabbed her with a blade through the heart. It's done then, she thought. Dash has done what he promised he would do, and now that Papa's safe, he's ready to wash his hands of me. He could have thought of a less callous way to do it, she mused. He could have told me himself.

"Abra, my dear. I haven't said anything that disturbs you, have I?" Sharify asked as he noticed the look that passed over her face. "I often forget that American women are so easily shocked by the mention of sex."

"No," she snapped back. "Why should I be upset? What Mr. Thorne does is no matter to me."

Sharify grinned. "That's just as well. Then we won't miss him at dinner. I hope you're hungry." He took her arm and led her along the length of the table to where three places were set at the head. "I've instructed my cooks to prepare something extraordinary for you this evening. After all, it is my fondest desire to impress and please you."


"This is Sharify's personal wing of the palace," Vincent told Abra evenly as a servant showed them back to Abra's quarters. "My rooms are at the other end, in adequate, but far less exalted, a location."

His tone was guarded, and Abra realized that he wanted to say something more, but chose not to in the presence of the servant.

"But you've had the liberty of the palace?" she asked, pretending only passing interest.

"Oh, yes," he replied. "I've been a virtual guest, roaming about at my will, allowing my curiosity to take me where it would. Of course," he added drily, "on the occasion it attempted to take me outside the palace, I was given to understand that such actions would be highly frowned upon."

Abra scowled at his words. She'd tried to keep her attention on the turnings they'd taken as they walked through what seemed an endless series of corridors, but, just as she had when she had been brought to the dining room earlier, she realized that she was completely confused. The palace seemed a maze, and she had no doubt but that unguided she would have become completely lost within minutes.

Just as she was about to decide she'd never find her way, the servant led them around a corner, stopped before a large, carved door, and offered her a deep bow. Then he pulled the door open for her to pass.

"I'll stay a while and talk with my daughter," Vincent told him. "You needn't wait for me. I'll find my own way back to my quarters."

He ushered Abra into the room, then turned and waited for the door to be closed behind them.

"He'll still be there," he told her once they were alone. "I'd be willing to put money on it."

"Are they watching you so closely as that?" Abra asked him.

He nodded. "Today they started again, for the first time in weeks." He stared at her with a fixed contemplative expression. "I almost wish you hadn't come, Abra," he told her. "Much as I would hate to have died without seeing you one last time, I would have preferred you weren't mixed up in any of this."

"Papa!"

"Sharify is up to something, Abra. Something that I have no doubt will be quite nasty. I just don't know what it is."

"Well, it doesn't concern us," she told him. "Tomorrow we'll be away from here."

Vincent raised a doubting brow. "I hope so, Abra."

"What does that mean?" she demanded.

But he waved a hand in dismissal, then looked around the room, strolling to the garden doors and peering out. She followed at his side.

"A rather nice little prison he's prepared for you here."

"Prison?"

"Damn it, Abra, don't be so obtuse. Surely you realize he has no intention of allowing you to leave here."

"But he promised, tomorrow. . . ." she protested.

"There'll be some reason why we can't. A skirmish on the border that makes traveling too dangerous, an outbreak of plague, I don't know, but he'll have some reason."

Abra shook her head. "Don't be silly, Papa. Why should he want to keep us? He has his stone."

"For no more reason than that he's accustomed to having what he wants. And at the moment, my lovely daughter, he wants you."

He stared at her intently, and Abra could not simply dismiss his words.

"You're serious, aren't you?" she asked softly.

"Entirely," he told her.

"Then what do we do?"

"I suppose tomorrow we find Dash and find a way out of this place." He didn't look hopeful. "Though for the last several weeks, I've been trying to do little else, with not much result."

But Abra didn't hear the last words. She felt a sudden rise of anger at the mention of Dash's name. "I dare say Mr. Thorne may very well be just as happy if we left without him. Besides," she added, turning away, knowing he would see the lie in her eyes, "he's no concern of ours now."

Vincent took her arm and pulled her back until she faced him.

"No concern of ours, Abra?" he asked her softly. "No concern when you're in love with him?"

"I'm not," she cried, even as the tears began to form in her eyes.

He simply stared down at her, and she found she could no longer pretend in the face of his knowing expression, found that it commanded the truth of her just as it had all her life.

"He doesn't want me, Papa," she said as she hid her face against his chest. "He did this because he felt guilty, responsible. But now it's done. He's a jewel thief. And all he wants is to go back to his old life, a life that has no place for a wife or a home."

329

He patted her shoulder softly. "Jewel thieves have been known to reform, Abra," he reminded her.

She looked up at him, her eyes blurry with tears. "Not him," she said, but still there was a gentle surge of hope within her at his words.

He smiled down at her complacently, then wiped away her tears with his sleeve. "Don't give up so easily, Abra. I never thought you were a quitter."

She sniffed. "Well, at least he owes me an honest, face-to-face good-bye."

Vincent pursed his lips and nodded. "At the least," he agreed. "Now, get some sleep. Shall we see if my shepherd is waiting for me?" he asked as he led her to the door and pulled it open.

Just as he had predicted, the man was still standing there, waiting for him. Vincent turned back to her and kissed her on the forehead.

"Tomorrow we'll have a long talk," he told her softly. Then he backed away from her a step, smiled, and turned to the servant. "Well, since you're still here, I always do appreciate a little company during a late-night amble. Do you suppose you might have time for a game of gin back at my room?" He turned quickly and winked at Abra. She laughed softly and watched him turn away before she closed the door.

She stood silently staring at the carved wood for a moment before turning back to the room. Then she roamed idly back to the garden door and stood, silent, inhaling the sweet night perfume of the flowers and listening to the darkness. She was not expecting movement in the garden, and so when she noticed the shadow moving in the dimness, she told herself it was her imagination. But the stir in the air beside her that followed was unmistakable. Startled, she turned to it.

A woman stepped into the circle of light that fell from the room until she was only steps from where Abra stood. She moved with a slow deliberateness toward Abra, her look almost mesmerizing in its intensity and terrifying in its implications. For there was hatred written on her features, cold, determined hatred, and she

330

made no effort to conceal it.

Abra stepped back. "Who are you? What do you want?"

But even before she looked down to see the blade of a knife in the woman's hands, even before she spoke, Abra knew. It was there, written in the woman's eyes, in the way she stared, unblinking at her. This stranger had come to kill her.

# Chapter Twenty-one

"Well, Thorne, do you find the accommodations to
your liking?"

Dash managed to sit up on his cot and look around
the bare, bleak cell. Except for a few spots where the
wall had become discolored by a splash of his own
blood, it was an unmarred white.

"I find your taste in decor a bit boring, Sharify," he
managed to mumble through lips that were swollen and
cut. "But I hardly expected anything more from you."

Sharify smiled. "Still willing to play games, are you,
Thorne? Perhaps another taste of Amad's skills would
dampen your enthusiasm."

Dash shrugged painfully, but he managed to smile. "If
your man Amad were so fine a pugilist, Sharify, he
wouldn't need the advantage of my arms being bound
and held."

"Ah, but were it otherwise, then you would not be
quite so impressed with the fact that I mean to have
answers to my questions, Mr. Thorne," Sharify told him
amiably.

"And just what questions are those?" Dash asked.
"I'm afraid I've become a bit muddled in the past few
hours. No doubt, thanks to your friend Amad."

He darted a glance to where Amad stood in the far
corner of the cell, beside the door, like a dog waiting for
his master's leave before he charged.

"Then I will be delighted to remind you," Sharify told

him. "You will tell me where my brother Salim has taken his ragtag little band now. His meddling tires me, and I have decided to put an end to it."

"Ah, yes, Salim the rebel," Dash mused aloud as he leaned back against the hard wall behind his cot. "What makes you think I know where, or even who, he is?"

"Let us not play any more games, Thorne. Salim found you in the desert, and after tending to the wounds Rajeek gave you, he did you the further favor of killing Hazig and reuniting you with Miss Beaumont. It does make one wonder, doesn't it? Why would he go to so much trouble for you, a foreigner, someone who could do him or his cause absolutely no good?"

"Perhaps he's just a benevolent fellow?" Dash suggested. "And speaking of Ajib Rajeek, I don't suppose he could be a friend of yours? Something about his morals reminds me of you."

"Your astuteness astounds me, Thorne," Sharify replied slowly. "And Rajeek was a greedy, stupid fool. But he no longer interests me. I want to know what relationship you share with Salim? Why did he trust you? Why did he allow you and Miss Beaumont to bring the stone back to me? But most of all, I want to know where he is and what he intends."

Dash offered him a crooked grin made macabre by his swollen and bruised lips and cheek. "I'm afraid you'll have to ask your questions of him, Sharify. I have no answers for you."

Sharify strode toward Dash until he stood over him, looking down at him. He slapped him, hard, and Dash's head fell back against the hard wall.

"You will, Thorne."

Dash lunged forward toward him. But even as his fist came into contact with Sharify's stomach, Amad was there, the heavy metal rod he wielded landing forcefully against Dash's ribs. He fell back to the bed and stared up at Sharify, panting, fighting for his breath. When the first wave of pain had passed, he put his hand to his chin and wiped away a trickle of blood.

"You will give Abra my best, won't you?" he asked

333

slowly. "I don't suppose I'll have an opportunity to say good-bye to her tomorrow before she and Vincent leave?"

"In all honesty, I don't think she has much interest in your good wishes," Sharify told him with a satisfied grin. "After I told her you'd decided to retire to pursue the more hedonistic pleasures my hospitality offers, she declined further conversation about you. I think she was rather shocked by your immoral behavior."

Dash smiled painfully. "No doubt. But she won't remain mute on the subject forever. Sooner or later she'll want to see me, if only to vent a bit of her temper. What will you tell her then?"

"Why, that you've left, of course. Besides, I intend to introduce her to a bit of hedonism myself quite soon. She won't have any time or energy for thoughts of the likes of you." He turned to the door. "Think about my questions, Thorne. Perhaps something will come to you. Soon." He lifted the small jug of water that stood on the table by the door. "Until you manage to remember what I want to know, I'm afraid you'll simply have to do without this." He smiled as he emptied the jug onto the earthen floor. The water spread out and disappeared quickly. "Until the morning, Thorne," Sharify said. "Perhaps you'll be thirsty enough by then to find your memories."

Then, motioning to Amad, he stepped out of the cell. The servant followed, slamming the iron door closed behind him and locking it with a loud, final-sounding thud.

"Who are you? What do you want?"

Abra felt like a fool asking the questions again, but she could think of nothing else. She tried to keep her eyes on the woman's face, telling herself it was madness to stare at the blade.

She was handsome, Abra realized, or would have been if her attention had not been so fixed, with striking, dark eyes, a mass of thick, curly hair, and cleanly regular features. And she was not a servant, of that Abra was sure. She was dressed richly, in silk, and wore jewels at her neck, her wrists, and on her fingers and earlobes. It all seemed incongruous, all that elegance combined with the look of cold hatred and the sharp glint of the knife.

"I've not decided," the woman told her. "Perhaps to take your life. Perhaps to give you your freedom. Shall we sit and discuss the matter?"

She motioned with the blade and Abra complied, backing into the room and sitting, nervously perching at the edge of the seat of one of the antique French *fauteuils*.

"Good," the woman said as she seated herself facing Abra. "Are you comfortable, Miss Beaumont?"

"No," Abra told her evenly. "Who are you?"

"My name is Raisa. I am his first wife. My son will succeed him. Do you understand?"

Abra shook her head. "No," she replied softly. "Why do you come here to me, like this? I do not understand at all."

"Because he pursues you," Raisa burst out vehemently. "Because you are a threat to my son's future."

Abra shook her head. "Your son's future. How can I threaten your child? You are speaking in riddles."

Raisa's eyes narrowed and she peered at Abra intently. "You really don't understand, do you?" she asked slowly, the possibility seeming to surprise her. She didn't wait for Abra to answer, but went on, her tone slowly pedantic, as though she were lecturing to a pupil, teaching an important lesson. "He's never gone to so much trouble for a woman before. He intends you to be his queen, to take my place, to make your child his heir, if that is the price you demand to come to him willingly."

"But I want none of that," Abra burst out. "I told him that. I came here only for my father."

Raisa shrugged. "Perhaps," she said. "But more than one woman has been enticed by the lure of a crown." She stared at Abra evenly. "I was."

"And you would kill me to keep it?" Abra asked her

335

slowly.

She shook her head. "No. I would kill you to keep him," she said. "The others, they mean nothing to him, not really. But he's infected with you, like a sickness. I can see it in his eyes."

Abra leaned forward, closer to her, ignoring the weapon in Raisa's hand. "I don't want your husband, or your crown. I only want to get away from here with my father."

Raisa stared at her a long moment, considering, and then she leaned forward and dropped the knife to the table between them. "I believe you. I don't know why, but I believe you. It is as Vincent said."

"You've spoken to my father?"

Raisa smiled. "I know everything and everyone in the palace. There are no secrets that can be kept from me here. But when I learned of the necklace, and when I saw you just now, wearing it, I thought I had been misinformed."

Abra put her hand to the jewels at her neck, then moved them to the nape, to find the clasp.

"No," Raisa told her, raising her hand. "Don't take it off. You must keep it. Shahab was always generous with his women. It will pique him to think that one woman finally took his gifts and spurned his advances. He will think he is growing old." She smiled with a near malicious expression at the prospect.

"I don't want it," Abra told her decisively. She unclasped the necklace and dropped it to the table beside the blade.

The two women sat in silence for a moment longer, considering each other. Abra, surprisingly, found herself pitying the other woman. She could only imagine what heartbreak she had felt when Sharify had first begun to grow tired of her, when he'd brought other women to replace her in his bed. And she tried to see herself as Raisa saw her, a woman at least ten years her junior, a foreign woman at that, who she thought ready not only to steal away what little of his affections she still held, but to supplant her child's birthright, as well.

336

"He doesn't deserve your love," she said softly.

Raisa's expression grew hard. "Perhaps not. But it is all I have left to cling to."

Abra straightened. "You said you brought either my death or my freedom. Have I convinced you to give me the latter?"

Raisa nodded and then stood, motioning to Abra to do the same. "And it must be now. The longer you are here, the harder it will become."

"And my father?" Abra asked as she, too, rose.

"Yes, we will go to him."

Abra started to the door, but Raisa caught her arm. "No, this way. Follow me. And be silent."

She led the way back to the dark garden, across it to what Abra had thought was a solid wall. But once they reached it, she realized that there was a door, obscured by a heavy trumpet vine. They slipped behind the foliage and through the gate, silently shutting it behind them.

Abra found herself in a small courtyard, dimly lit and ajumble with gardening tools, rakes and hoes grown into macabre shapes in the deep shadows. Of course, she thought, there would need to be some way for the gardener to enter the small, private Eden, to silently and invisibly keep the neat beds of flowers, the elegantly draping vines all perfectly groomed. And that would mean that at the far side of the courtyard there would be access to the servants' sections of the palace.

She was right. Raisa led her across the courtyard to another entrance to the interior of the palace. The corridor they entered here was dark and dimly lit, not at all like those she had seen on her travels to Sharify's dining room and back. She followed close at Raisa's heels, heeding the older woman's warnings for silence. Twice the two of them turned into crossing corridors and hid themselves as the sound of voices warned them they might be discovered. But it had grown late, and the passages were mostly deserted. Within fifteen minutes Abra found herself staring at her father's very surprised face.

"Abra?" he asked, bewildered. He turned to the woman at Abra's side and his confusion grew. "Lady Raisa?"

"Your daughter has told me that you and she wish only to leave here," Raisa told him in a brisk tone. "Is this true?"

"You will help us?" Vincent asked, still perplexed, but starting to understand what was happening.

"I have horses waiting for you both. Come." She turned back toward the door.

But Vincent shook his head. "Not without Mr. Thorne."

Raisa turned back to face them slowly. "That will not be quite so easy," she told them thoughtfully.

There was something about the other woman's expression that startled Abra. "Why not?" she asked suspiciously. "Surely the entertainment the emir has given him is not so unique he could not find it elsewhere," she added drily.

Raisa arched a brow. "I very much doubt that he would look for it elsewhere. He's being held in the cells below."

"Imprisoned?" Vincent demanded. "Why?"

"Because Shahab found it far too coincidental that the rebels would help him, free your daughter from Hazig, and then allow them both to come here with the Tear. He wants to know what Salim is up to, and he thinks your Mr. Thorne can tell him."

"But that's nonsense," Abra burst out.

"I think not," Raisa said, her tone cool and even. "I cannot help him. I would not, even if I could."

"I won't leave without him," Abra told her.

"It is impossible," Raisa told them, then raised her eyes to Vincent's as though looking for some words of reason from him, at least.

But Vincent was as determined as Abra. "You want to be rid of us, Raisa," he told her. "Neither you nor your son want us to stay here."

"There'll be a guard," Raisa countered, trying to make them understand. "We have no weapon."

338

"The knife you left in my room," Abra suggested.

Raisa felt a stab of panic. The knife, she thought. How could she have been so foolish as to leave the knife? He'd find it and he'd know.

There was no way she could go back for it now, she realized, not without running the risk of finding him there, of exposing herself even further. But then she steadied herself, telling herself that he would not remember the dagger, that it had been years since he'd seen it. Surely, he wouldn't remember.

Raisa shook her head and looked at Abra. "He'll be there," she said. "We can't go back for it."

Abra understood: that he was Sharify, that he intended to pay her a late-night visit, and that this one, finally, was not to end with his allowing her to slip through his fingers as she had before.

"If not now, soon," Raisa continued. "And when he finds you gone . . ." She glared angrily at Abra. "You must go, now, before it's too late."

"Not without Dash."

Raisa's eyes narrowed. "I should have killed you and been done with you," she hissed.

"He'd have killed *you*," Vincent told her flatly. "You and your son. You know it. Your only hope is to get us away from here."

"But we have no weapon," Raisa insisted, hoping he would see reason.

Vincent strode across the room to a table bearing a plate of fruit, a ewer of wine, and a goblet and a plate of small cakes. Beside the fruit was a small knife. He took it and held it aloft. "We have a weapon," he said with a wry smile.

Raisa scowled. "A paring knife. You're insane. You would face knives and pistols with a paring knife?"

Vincent grinned at her warmly. "But we have truth and justice with us," he averred. "How can we know anything else but victory?"

Raisa led them once more through the dim corridors

339

and out into another courtyard. This time, however, the courtyard led them not to a garden, but to a steep flight of stairs. A few smoky lanterns held the darkness at bay. Otherwise, there was no light, not even a window giving view of the stars.

"There," Raisa whispered when they'd come to a landing. She pointed to a white-clad guard with the memorable crimson sash, the hilt of a dagger prominently tucked into the red.

He seemed intent on the consumption of his dinner, but a pistol was laid handy beside his plate, attesting to his vigilance. The scent of lamb and spices slowly floated to their nostrils as they watched him.

Vincent clutched Abra's shoulder, pulling her back into the shadows as she leaned forward to see. "Raisa is right," he murmured softly. "We can't get by him."

Abra looked at him with disbelief. "I won't leave Dash here," she told him.

Then, before he could stop her, she stepped out into the light and walked directly toward the guard.

It took a few seconds, for her sandled feet were silent on the stone floor, but eventually the guard noticed the change in the light as she passed through the lamp's path and cast a shadow on him. He looked up at her, his hand reaching automatically for the pistol.

She smiled at him, straining for the few words of Arabic she'd heard Rajeek utter. *"Salaam aleechum,"* she said softly.

He stared at her, not quite sure he believed what he saw, his eyes straying downward, over the length of her body, and back very slowly to her face.

*"Aleechum salaam,"* he said finally. He stood, evidently relaxing a bit, for his hand left the pistol and rested itself instead casually on the hilt of the knife as he watched her approach, turning to keep his dark eyes on her as she moved around the table and behind his chair. He pushed it away.

*"Gulli ismak eh,"* she said softly, and hoped she had asked for his name and not offered him some great insult.

340

But his dark eyes glittered as she drew closer to him. "Yvsuf," he replied as he let his hand fall away from the knife hilt.

She put her hand to his cheek and he reached out for her waist.

*"Kuwayes,"* he murmured. "Beautiful."

It was his last word before the blow fell and he sank into darkness. Abra's eyes watched him fall, then looked up to where Vincent stood, the heavy piece of rock he'd grabbed to hit the guard still in his hand.

"That was foolish, Abra," he scolded as he knelt and quickly removed the guard's sash, using it to gag and tie his hands behind him. "Poor sot. Someone should have told him that a beautiful woman is as like as not to be a man's undoing," he said as he finished and stood.

Abra grinned at him.

"Quickly," Raisa told them, passing by them to a long corridor behind the guard's post.

She began to peek into the cells through the small windows at each door. Abra and Vincent followed, and did as she did, peering into the dark cells, meeting the frightened eyes of the prisoners.

Abra almost didn't recognize him when she saw him. His face was swollen and bruised and there was a long line of dried blood on his cheek.

"Here, Papa," she cried, her voice echoing the sudden fear that had arisen at the sight of him, the same pain she'd felt the night she'd spent by his bed at the rebel camp when she thought he might die.

Vincent hurried to her, drawing back the bolt that held the door. She ran through without waiting for him to follow.

"Abra?"

Dash's confusion was even more pronounced than Vincent's had been. He simply sat, staring up at her.

She knelt in front of him, reaching tentatively up to him, her fingers shaking as she surveyed the trail of bruises and cuts on his face and torso.

"My God, Dash, what has he done to you?"

He smiled his crooked smile. "This is his idea of

341

conversation, Abra," he said as he reached out for her, putting his hand to her head and drawing her close to him. He closed his eyes and simply held her, as though her presence could heal him, as though she were all the release he needed. Then he opened his eyes abruptly.

"What are you doing here?" he demanded.

"We're getting away, Dash. Now." She drew back and stood. "Can you walk?" she demanded, offering him her arm.

He grinned once more. "Just try and stop me," he said as he got painfully to his feet. Then he looked up and saw Vincent standing at the door. "Evening, Vincent," he said casually. "Pleasant evening for an outing, I trust?"

Abra put her arm around his waist and he draped his around her shoulder. They made their way fairly well to the door.

Vincent nodded. "Shall we get on with it, then?"

They returned to the guard's post and found Raisa waiting for them. "We must hurry," she told them angrily, and Abra realized now that she was afraid, that soon Sharify would know of her disappearance, and would start a search.

Vincent gathered up the guard's knife and pistol as they passed the place where he lay, tied and silent, on the floor, then he hurried after the others, back up the stone steps.

They emerged into the moonlight, surprisingly bright after the smoky dimness below.

Raisa motioned them to follow, her agitation quite apparent now. They skirted the edge of the courtyard, keeping to the shadows, until she stopped them before another door.

"There," she said, pointing. "The tunnel will take you to the oasis. There are two horses waiting. Go quickly." She pulled aside the wood bar, pushed open the door, and stood aside so that they could pass.

Abra peered into what seemed an endless blackness. She couldn't believe that they were to go blindly into this unlit hole.

"You aren't coming with us?" she asked.

"I've done all I can for you," Raisa told her. "Now hurry."

Abra stared at her eyes a moment, wondering if the woman had her own surprise planned, one even more devious than that Sharify had planned for them.

"We have no choice, Abra," Dash whispered to her softly as he stepped through the door, pulling her along with him.

Vincent followed, and Raisa closed the door behind them. There was a soft thud as the wooden bar was replaced, effectively sealing them off from the courtyard behind.

Abra felt as though they had been swallowed by the darkness.


Sharify nodded to the guard who stood at the side of Abra's door. He bowed and opened it, then stood back and allowed the emir to pass.

From the moment he stepped inside her room, Sharify knew something was wrong. An oil lamp glowed with a hazy, warm light that shimmered from the silken pillows, the intricately woven rugs, the polished carved furniture. For a second he thought only of the elegance of the room, how it must have pleased her. And then it occurred to him that it was silent, too silent.

He turned to the alcove that housed the enormous bed, expecting to see her lying there, and was greeted only by the sight of the untouched and empty bed.

He ran back to the door, pulling it open angrily, his eyes finding the surprised ones of the guard.

"Where is she?" he demanded, his voice a low, tight rumble that promised trouble.

"But she has not left, Excellency," the guard replied.

"She's gone," Sharify shouted at him. "Fool," he cried. "Incapable of watching a woman. Call out the guard. Find her."

The guard bowed low, then, shaking, ran off, grateful to have escaped.

Sharify wandered back into the room, moving first to the dressing table and lifting the combs he found there, then dropping them, turning back to the garden doors. He moved toward them, then stopped, his eyes caught by the glint of something bright on the table by the chairs grouped near the doors. He lifted it, watching the jewels sparkle in the dim light, and then his glance fell and his hand followed it to the blade, touching it gingerly with his fingers, looking out into the darkness of the garden as he thought. How had she gotten a knife, he wondered, and what was it doing here? He stared at the ornately chased hilt, wondering where he had seen it before, sure it was familiar. It was there, nagging the edge of his memory, but he could not place it.

He dropped it back to the table's surface, telling himself there were other matters to attend to. She would have gone first to find Vincent, he told himself as he strode from the room. Without a guide to show her the way through the palace, she would not find him easily. He would be there when she arrived.

But he'd barely reached Vincent's room when two of his guards appeared. They bowed to him nervously, their agitation apparent.

"Well?" he demanded.

"The American," the guard replied. "He's gone."

Sharify clenched his fists with fury and his face grew white.

"Have the gates closed," he ordered. "And I want every man out looking for them. They haven't had time to get far." He stared at the guard. "The man who finds them lives."

Sharify watched them as they backed away from him, then he thought once more of the knife he'd found in Abra's room. She couldn't have done this alone, he told himself. She's had help from someone in the palace. And whoever it had been, he swore, he'd see that man's head on a platter before he was done.


Abra felt as though it had been hours that they had

344

been stumbling forward in the darkness. The walls of the long corridor seemed to close in on them. Even though she'd kept one hand to the wall to guide her, she'd stumbled twice, nearly falling. Only Dash's hand on her shoulder had kept her on her feet. And she tried not to think what it was that she touched when she felt movement beneath her fingers as she put them to the wall. Things lurked there, in the dark, and the realization sickened her, and set her imagination reeling.

It was the darkness, she told herself, just an irrational fear of the darkness. However logical, the thought did little to dispense the terror she felt. She shuddered with revulsion each time she touched the wall.

Dash sensed her fear, for he pressed his hand where he held her shoulder, holding her closer.

"We'll be fine, Abra," he whispered to her gently.

"Yes," she murmured, nodding in the darkness, grateful that he seemed to be walking more steadily, knowing that if he stumbled she would not be able to offer him any real help.

Something brushed against her cheek, and she uttered a surprised squeal, pressing herself closer to Dash.

"Cobwebs," he told her, encouraging her to move forward. "Just cobwebs."

She hastened her step a bit, telling herself she was behaving like a silly little fool, but she could not dismiss the thought that all spiders were not benign, that they were helpless in the darkness if they couldn't even see the things.

Vincent had no way of knowing that the corridor had ended. When he walked into the door, the cold impact was more surprising than painful.

"I think we've arrived," he said drily, and Abra and Dash stopped just behind him.

He felt around in the inky blackness, his hands finally finding the heavy bar that kept the thick iron door bolted. He pushed against it, but it didn't move.

"Damn," he said. "The thing's too heavy. I can't budge it."

For a minute the three of them stood in the darkness,

the same thought gripping them all. This was a trap. Raisa had sent them down into this hole to die.

"No," Abra cried softly. "I won't die here in the darkness."

She stepped forward, like Vincent groping for the bar in the darkness. She pulled at it frantically, scraping the skin from her fingers and palms.

Dash moved up beside her. "Let's do this logically," he said softly, putting his hands to hers. "The three of us together."

The three of them stood close and grasped the rough bottom edge of the bar.

"Ready?" Vincent asked before he slowly counted to three, and then all of them pulled up.

Abra could hear Dash's muffled groan and knew the effort must have cost him pain.

"Dash," she murmured, and started to turn to him.

But he cut off her words of sympathy with a harshly muttered, "Pull, damn it, Abra."

She turned back to the door, feeling his tensed muscles close to her, almost tasting his hurt.

"It's no good," Vincent said, dropping his hands to his sides. "It must have rusted shut."

Dash and Abra stopped, and Dash leaned against the door to rest. "We'll have to go back," he said when he'd caught his breath.

"No," Abra said firmly into the darkness. "You can't go back. And I won't."

"Be reasonable, Abra," Dash said to her softly, his hand reaching out to find her cheek. "At least you and Vincent will have another chance to get away."

"And you?" she asked. "Would you have left me to Hazig and gotten away?"

She didn't wait for him to answer, but turned to where she presumed Vincent stood. "Papa, do you still have that paring knife?" she asked.

"A small blade won't do much good against an iron door, Abra," he told her with a shade of sadness.

"But it might," she insisted. "I can feel the brackets that hold the bar. That's where it must be rusted. If we scrape a bit . . ."

"Excellent idea," Vincent agreed. "I'm ashamed I didn't think of it myself."

He found her hand with his in the darkness, and then handed her the knife. Abra turned back to the door, her fingers eagerly finding the bracket. For a moment there was only the scritch-scritch sound as she scraped, and then Vincent turned to the second bracket that held the bar to the wall.

"Can't be outdone by a child, and mine at that," he murmured as he took the second knife, the one he'd taken from the guard, and he, too, scraped.

They worked in silence for a while until Vincent suggested they try to lift the bar once more. Abra was a bit relieved. She'd scraped her knuckles badly against the metal and her fingers ached from holding the knife. At least she'd have the opportunity to uncramp her hands, she thought.

But to her surprise, this time when they all pulled against it the bar began to move with a rough scraping sound, then finally slid free.

They stood in the darkness an instant longer, panting with the effort, and then they pushed the door open. At their feet was the open water of the oasis pool, a round circle of the moon's reflection floating on it like a huge golden water lily. It was the most welcome sight Abra had ever seen. Beyond were the still streets of Tahaf.

Dash turned back, glancing up at the walls of the palace behind him. "I'll be damned," he mused aloud as he moved to the water's edge. "She didn't lie." He fell to his knees and drank.

"Yes, she did," Vincent told him sadly as he and Abra also knelt to the water. "There are no horses waiting as she promised. She meant for us to die in there, in the darkness."

"And I, for one, am delighted to disappoint her," Dash replied. He splashed some water on his face and chest, reveling in the feel of it, wondering why, as he took one more handful to his mouth, it tasted quite so good. Then he stood and moved back to the door, swinging it closed behind them and carefully noting its location with respect to the towers.

"What are you doing?" Abra demanded when she turned to him and saw what it was he was doing.

He grinned. "I think we owe the emir another visit, don't you, Vincent?" he said, almost jovially. "And sometimes a visit is best begun through the back door."

Vincent looked at him intently before he answered. "I know my way around the palace fairly well," he said softly. "Especially the location of the treasury. I must admit, it fascinated me."

"You two can't be serious," Abra gasped. "Raisa bolted the door at the other end of the tunnel. I heard it."

"That was a wooden door, Abra," Dash told her with a smile, "and not a close-fitting one, at that. A few minutes with a long blade," he snapped his fingers, "no impediment at all to someone with a thief's talents."

"You're mad," she insisted. "We can't go back inside there."

"We can't go alone," Dash agreed with a nod. "But I think I know where we might be able to find a few friends for company."

"Salim?"

"Precisely," he told her.

"Now I know you're mad, Dash. We lied to him. He won't believe you now."

Dash looked up at the dark star-studded sky. "I don't see that we have much choice in the matter, Abra. Without horses we can't get away from here. And Salim is our only chance to find help in getting out of Mukalla. So that means we have to find him and convince him we intend to help him, that is if we ever want to get out of this damned sandbox alive." He started to move off. "Come on. It'll be light in a few hours. I don't want to be walking around the desert in the middle of the afternoon."

Abra scrambled to her feet, then helped Vincent up. "Papa, you've got to stop, him," she begged.

But Vincent only shook his head. "He's right, Abra.

348

We may be out of the palace, but without the rebels' help, how long do you think it will be until Sharify finds us? We haven't any choice in the matter."

Together the three of them slipped through the still, quiet streets and out of Tahaf. The desert in front of them looked terrifyingly wide and empty.

Salim's men found them a few hours after dawn. Their manner spoke more plainly than any words could of precisely what they would face when they were finally brought to him.

He didn't disappoint them. "I don't suppose you could give me even one reason why I ought not to have you killed?" he asked. "Although by the looks of you, Shahab has already made a small beginning in that direction."

"I should think that ought to be a good enough reason in itself," Dash told him with a grin.

"You've given him the stone, I suppose?" Salim asked, almost indifferently, as though he were already aware of the answer.

"I'm afraid we had to," Dash admitted.

"You knew we had it?" Abra gasped.

Salim turned to her, his dark eyes glittering. "Please do not take me for a fool, Miss Beaumont. I am many things, but not a fool. At least I didn't think I was, until I realized how wrong I was in trusting you."

"But why did you let us leave in the first place?" she demanded. "Why didn't you hold us here?"

Salim turned to Dash. "Because I trusted you. Because your government has sent me word that they were to provide me with some aid. And for some bizarre reason, I assumed you were part of it. Obviously, I was wrong." He shrugged, as though with indifference, although Abra doubted he felt anything like indifferent.

A thick, uncomfortable silence fell over them as Salim considered the three of them. Vincent broke it.

"We can get the stone back for you," he told Salim softly. "As well as the remaining contents of the trea-

349

sury. Would that mitigate my daughter's and her friend's sins?"

Salim peered at him intently. "You're serious?"

"Quite."

"There's no way to get through the palace gates unseen," Salim said flatly. "I know. I lived in the palace as a child."

"Not through the gates," Dash agreed. "But there's another way."

Salim shook his head. "No. No, there's not."

"We got out," Dash told him reasonably. "Can you trust us? It costs you nothing now. And believe me, I've a few little matters of my own to settle with the emir." He motioned to the bruises on his chest beneath the torn remnants of his shirt.

Salim considered him a moment. "I think I am a fool, after all," he said, then shrugged in resignation. "When?"

"Tomorrow, at dawn."

"Then you'll want to bathe and rest for a few hours." He motioned to Dash's torso. "Do you need any treatment?"

Dash shook his head. "I'm sore as hell, but I think a tub of hot water should serve."

Salim smiled a bit sardonically. "You ask for a lot in the middle of a desert," he replied. "But I'll see what I can do for you. Then I'll look at you. You might have a few cracked ribs." He turned away, and lowered his voice before he went on. "I hope for your sake that you're not lying, my friend. Because if you are, I promise you, what Shahab did to you will seem a romp in the woods compared to what I will have done to the three of you." He turned back to Dash and smiled humorlessly. "I don't take well to being treated as a fool."

Then he called for one of his men to take them to a tent and provide them with whatever they required.

The white tape that bound Dash's cracked ribs looked inordinately bright against the dark discolorations of his

350

bruised skin. But bathed and rested, he seemed in excellent humor, even if his movements were a bit stiff from pain.

"You're sure you can get into the treasury?" he asked Vincent as he scooped some *mechouia* onto a piece of flat bread and ate it hungrily.

Vincent nodded as he, too, swallowed. "Child's play. I could do it with a hair pin." He turned his eyes to Abra who sat beside Dash picking at her food. "Shame you lost all yours," he said with a smile, motioning to the thick folds of her hair that fell, a bit wildly but not unbecomingly, down her back. "But I suppose I shouldn't be surprised, considering the way you've chosen to dress of late."

She barely looked down at the cotton trousers and shirt she'd managed to convince Salim's wife to find for her in exchange for the elegant silk gown. It was more than obvious that she found no humor in their situation. Instead, she turned her glance to him, not bothering to repeat the words she'd already voiced, that she wished they'd reconsider, that they could still flee. But the words were there, if unspoken, in her eyes.

"You shouldn't come with us, Abra," he told her.

She only shook her head. "If you're going to get yourselves killed, I want to be there, to say I told you," she replied. She turned away and put her bowl down abruptly, standing a bit stiffly. "I'm exhausted," she said as she moved to the makeshift bed at the side of the tent. "I'm going to sleep."

Dash watched her as she fell onto the pillows, silently finishing his meal. He felt she had grown distant from him, and he couldn't quite put his finger on the reason why.

"We ought to leave her," he said softly to Vincent when she seemed to have fallen asleep.

"We ought to, but she'll just follow when she finds we're gone. It'll be safer for her if we can keep our eyes on her."

The two fell silent once more, each lost in their own thoughts, until Vincent turned to Dash. "Have you told

351

her the truth?" he asked.

"No," Dash replied. "There didn't seem to be the right moment. And I don't want her going to Salim."

Vincent pondered Dash's absent expression, then turned away, wiping the last of his eggplant salad from his plate with a bit of bread and then eating it with thoughtful intentness.

"She's in love with you, you know."

Dash looked up at him, his expression startled. "I thought she was," he said slowly. "But now I'm not so sure."

"You ought to tell her," Vincent said with a tone of finality as he got to his feet. He clasped his hand to Dash's shoulder. "I think I'll get some sleep, too. You should do the same."

Dash nodded, but made no move. He lifted the cup of wine at his side and sipped it silently, staring at Abra's still form. It would all be settled in a few hours, he told himself. One way or another, it would soon be over.

The words drifted into Abra's sleep-dulled mind.

"Have you told her the truth?"

"No, there didn't seem to be the right moment. And I don't want her going to Salim."

And although she tried not to think at all, the words stayed with her.

They could mean only one thing, she told herself. Her father and Dash intended to double-cross Salim after all, and take the ruby for themselves. She hated them, she told herself. She hated them for the good they chose not to do, for ignoring the things Salim was trying to do for his people, for giving themselves up to simple greed. And most of all, she hated Dash and what he had made her father become. Whatever he had done in the past, she knew, Vincent had never taken from those in need. And now that was what they intended, for by stealing the Tear, they were stealing a whole people's future. If they were going to risk their lives, she told herself, they should be doing it for a real reason, not avarice. She couldn't understand how they could be so blind.

And there was nothing she could do. There was no way she could stop them. Going to Salim would mean their deaths, and she would die first before being party to that. She had no choice but to go along with them, to allow herself to become a part of it. But if she ever got home again, she swore to herself, she'd cut off her hand before she'd let herself be seduced again by Dashiel Thorne. And if it meant spending the remainder of her life on her knees scrubbing floors, she'd never accept a cent of the proceeds of this foolish, heartless venture.

She felt a tear cross her cheek, and she brushed it away and buried her face into the pillows, telling herself she had no strength for tears. Then she forced herself to sleep, hating the inevitable that the dawn would bring.

# Chapter Twenty-two

Abra was the first to stir, startled into wakefulness by the movement of one of Salim's men come to alert them that they would leave camp within the hour. She stood and stretched, feeling achy and as tired as she had been when she'd gone to sleep.

She watched as Vincent lit a lamp, then poured some water and splashed it onto her face. She found she couldn't bear to look at either her father or Dash.

A simple meal of flat bread and goat cheese was brought to them, but none of them could eat. As Abra tied back her hair, she silently watched Dash leave to talk with Salim. She wondered how he could seem so calm, knowing what he intended to do, how he could lie so easily.

It must be easy for him, she told herself, just as it was easy for him to lie with his hands and his lips when he made love to her. She wondered how she would get through the day.

An hour more found them riding amidst a group of ten of Salim's men, their hoods drawn over their heads and scarves protecting their faces from the sand. A heavy wind had blown up during the night, causing the sand to swirl and writhe, filling the air like angry wraiths. Salim told them that this was good, that it would cover their approach to Tahaf and the palace. Abra could think only that it burned her eyes and bit into what skin it could find unprotected. It seeped through the scarf at her mouth, leaving her with the taste of bitter grit on her tongue.

They seemed to stumble upon Tahaf. The towers of the palace emerged out of a whirlwind of the sand like improbable monsters out of a dream. They dismounted, leaving the horses and a man to guard them, and continued on in the near darkness of dawn on foot, slipping into the town silently, thieves giving no warning.

The streets were silent and empty, shrouded in the gloom of the sandstorm and mute with the earliness of the day that had not yet been fully born. Like shadows themselves, they moved in silence and left the air undisturbed in their wake.

Dash led Salim to the edge of the water hole, to the empty, tall, unbroken wall of the palace.

"There," he whispered as he pointed to the iron door set into the stone of the wall.

"Fool," Salim hissed, his anger obvious that he had brought his men into danger for nothing. "That door has been bolted shut for generations. There's no way in."

"It's unbolted now," Dash whispered back as he edged his way to the door, then pushed it open.

Salim stared at him, surprised, then passed into the dark corridor without saying a word, and peered into the gloom. He reappeared a moment later and motioned to his men that it was safe to proceed.

Dash put his hand to where his belt held a long, thin blade, assuring himself that it was still safely there, then took the lead, entering the blackness of the tunnel first. Vincent and Abra followed, and behind them Salim and his men. As soon as the door was swung shut to hide their entry, one of the men lit a torch, its light first a dull flicker and then a smoky glow that illuminated the dry, crumbling walls and filled them with shadows.

Abra immediately drew closer to Vincent. The place was filled with spiders and a horde of other insects she couldn't identify at first glance. Nor did she want to.

355

She felt sick to think that she had doubtless touched some of the things on their first trip through the tunnel the night before. The darkness, it seemed, had been more merciful than otherwise, despite the fear it had generated in her. If she had thought she was trapped with the swarms of the scurrying, darting things, she would doubtless have given herself over to hysteria. As it was, this second trip through the tunnel set her stomach lurching. She was grateful for her empty stomach, sure she would have spilled its contents had she eaten before they left the camp.

She concentrated on the sounds they made, or the lack of them. She was surprised that the whole of the group somehow managed to move with such silent stealth. All she could discern was the dim echo of the men behind her breathing softly. The noise was less loud to her than the thudding of her own heart.

The tunnel seemed much shorter this second time they traveled it, perhaps because they moved much more quickly with the advantage of the smoky light the torch provided. It seemed only moments before Dash put up his hand, signaling those behind him to stop. Then he knelt before the wooden door that led to the servants' courtyard from which Raisa had sent them into the tunnel hoping they'd find their doom. A thin line of dim light entered the tunnel from the edge of the door. Abra could see now what Dash had intended when he'd told her it would not prove an obstacle to them.

He drew the thin blade from his belt and slipped it into the narrow opening. Slowly, he forced it upward, then gave it a hard push when it had encountered the wooden bar that held the door shut. It seemed to lift without any great impediment.

Dash waved them all back as he opened the door a few inches and stared out into the courtyard. Apparently it was still quiet, and he pushed the door all the way open, slipping out and motioning the others to follow him.

Once they were all in the courtyard, Salim showed

his men to a small storeroom as Dash reclosed and barred the door to the tunnel. Then he followed the rest to the storeroom where they waited in hushed, nervous silence.

"Give us thirty minutes before you set your diversion," Dash told Salim in a hoarse whisper. "Just make sure it's loud. And then get yourselves out of here. We'll meet you back at your camp. Don't wait for us. We'll need you to draw away the sheik's soldiers. When it's safe, we'll bring the stone to you."

Salim's eyes narrowed at Dash's last words. "I hope I'm not simply helping you fill your pockets, Thorne," he said softly, and Abra could hear the unvoiced threat behind the words.

Dash only smiled. "I'd like to get out of this hell hole," he said easily, as though that were assurance enough that his intentions were no different from his words. "Thirty minutes," he repeated as he began to move away, motioning Vincent and Abra to follow him.

The three of them edged their way back into the still quiet courtyard.

"Which way?" Dash asked Vincent.

Vincent nodded. "Through there," he said, indicating an open arch leading to a narrow flight of stairs. He smiled, obviously pleased with himself. "Wonderful what a bit of reconnoitering and an excellent memory can do for you." He sounded delighted that the talents of his youth had not rusted in their years of disuse.

They crept up the stairs in silence, keeping close together, Dash in the lead and Abra sandwiched between him and Vincent. She was amazed at how calm they both seemed. She felt her hand shaking and her legs unsteady, and knew she would have become ungainly with her own fear had she not determined that she'd not act the fool before them after insisting they bring her with them.

She peered out a narrow window as they climbed, keeping her eyes on the narrow slit and watching the sky color with the golden hues of dawn as the sun rose and the wind slowly died. She forced herself to keep her mind on the unlikely beauties of nature, lest it wander to the insanity they were intending. And somehow they made it to the top of the flight of stairs without incident.

Now Vincent took the lead, motioning them first to silence. They followed him along a seemingly endless corridor. From the servants' quarters below, Abra could hear the sounds of morning activity. The household servants were rising and beginning to prepare breakfast. Soon the corridors would be filled with them as they went about their daily duties, and the tramp of guards would echo in the long empty corridors as they took their turn at post.

"Here," Vincent hissed, and he motioned them to an offshooting arch. Abra could make out the change in the decor beyond, where the bare white walls changed to a mosaic of beautifully colored tiles, and the floor from plain brown tile to marble. They were entering the emir's personal domain.

Now they moved a bit more slowly, and with even more caution, ducking into a recessed doorway at the slightest sound of activity, twice hearing the passage of feet as they stood pressed against the cool of the tiles. Both times Dash covered Abra's body with his own, and the press of him close to her combined with the fear of discovery made her heart pound furiously. She wondered that it didn't echo through the length of the corridor, and she half expected Sharify's men to appear before them, summoned by the sound.

And then, finally, Vincent stopped them and pointed to an intersecting corridor. Abra nodded, understanding. She pulled the hood away from her head and freed her hair from the bit of wool she'd used to tie it back, all the while aware that, despite their inclination, she could not allow her fingers to begin to shake. There's nothing to fear, she told herself. One guard, Papa had seen one guard there only, and he would not hurt her, it would be Sharify's orders that she not be harmed in any way.

She nodded to Vincent and Dash, then stepped forward, into the corridor, into the full view of the guard. Funny, she mused as she took the few steps, she'd done almost the same thing to free Dash, drawn the attention of a guard. The only difference was she'd felt no fear then, except fear for him. This time it was different, this time she was terrified. And as she looked down the length of the short corridor, she realized she had good cause. There wasn't one guard there, but three.

She had little choice, she realized. If she were simply to lure them out after her as they had planned, Dash and her father would be caught, unprepared for the three of them. She would have to do something more than stand there and smile.

Raisa woke with the feeling of something sharp pressed against her neck. Her eyes still closed, still drugged with sleep, she raised her hand to the small hurt, to push it away, and was rewarded with a far greater one.

Her eyes popped open and she looked up to Sharify's angry glare, then down to the blood on her fingers.

She didn't have to look down to the hilt to know what blade he held to her neck. She didn't have to hear his words to know he knew what she'd done.

"Where is she?" he snarled at her. "What have you done with her?"

She pressed back against the pillows, trying vainly to draw herself away from the blade.

"You are sick with her," she told him. "Can't you see she wants no part of you?"

He pushed the blade a bit closer, and she could feel it bite into her flesh, could feel the warm drip and the slight bite as the blade opened the first layer of her skin. She dared not breathe, but stared at him in mute terror. Then she lifted her cut fingers and stared at her own blood for a moment, as though to convince herself that he would actually do this thing to her. Then she turned the bloodied fingers to his face, a visible sign of the suffering he had caused her, a small token of the hundred hurts he'd dealt her through the years.

But he seemed oblivious. "Where is she?" he hissed at her. "Or I swear to you, it will be more than a scratch."

She looked up at him, but held her silence, wondering if he would dare, if he could forget the times when she had been all he'd thought of, all he'd hungered for.

"Where is she?" he screamed at her, and she knew it was useless, that he was lost to her.

"She's here, in the palace. They're all here."

The words were a bare whisper. She hardly recognized the sound of her own voice. He stood and dropped the knife, letting it lie on her pillow, close to her. She breathed then, what seemed the first breath she'd taken in hours. She stared up at his face and thought of how much she had once loved him.

"Where?"

His eyes tore into her like knives.

"I locked them into the old tunnel through the walls," she told him. "They have to be there still. The far end is sealed, and the servants won't touch the gate on the inside. They believe it unholy." It *was* unholy. In the past it had been used to seal up a transgressor who had especially displeased the emir, to leave the miserable sinner to starve or be poisoned to death by the venom of the bites of the tiny creatures that lived there in the darkness. The words had been hard for her to force out, but now that they were said, she smiled. Perhaps the woman was already dead, she thought. If I must die, too, at least it would please me to know she was already dead.

He stared at her in a dark silence for a moment, then he slapped her, hard, across the face.

"I'll deal with you later," he promised as he turned and left her.

The guards were just starting to leave their quarters

360

as he entered the courtyard, and in the air there was the smell of food being cooked. He ignored the surprised stares of the servants he passed, yelling out to a half-dressed guard to fetch a lantern and to follow him. The man spurted into a run as though he had been woken from a daze, calling out for a light as he pulled his arms through the sleeves of his shirt.

The guard was only a few feet behind him when Sharify reached the door to the tunnel. He pulled away the bolting bar and flung it open as though he expected to see Abra tumble out and into his arms. When only the stillness met him, he grabbed the lantern from the guard's hand and entered.

He ran the distance to the far wall, only then admitting that the tunnel was empty. He'd turned, ready to return to Raisa, to deal with her, when he realized that the door was not bolted. He turned back and stared at it numbly, feeling a sickening awareness fill him. Then he turned on his heel, pushing the guard aside.

"Hurry, you fool," he shouted as he began to race back to the courtyard. "To the treasury."


The three guards stared at her as though she were an alien creature, not merely a woman. Abra walked forward, trying to smile at them. Behind her, Vincent grabbed Dash's arm, the two of them not understanding what she was doing, why she was not drawing the guard back to them as they had instructed her.

"My, three of you," Abra said gaily, her words for Dash and Vincent, knowing the guards could understand none of it. "I don't suppose Shahab put you here and told you to wait for me, did he?" she asked as she moved toward them.

They seemed to stiffen at the mention of the emir's name. Then one of them, the first to realize who she was, spoke rapidly to the others, then moved forward to her, putting his hand to her arm.

She made no protest, did not try to draw back, but instead nodded at him as though she were back in

361

New York, accepting a young man's invitation to dance. He seemed disarmed by that, and his manner softened, enough so that he did not notice her hand moving to his waist, or realize she was drawing his dagger from its place at his sash, until she had grasped it firmly and pulled it free in her hand.

He stood still, as though dazed by the fact that she'd disarmed him, even as the two others moved forward to her.

"Stop," she cried, brandishing the knife. "All of you."

But either they didn't understand what she meant or didn't care. The guard from whom she'd taken the knife lunged toward her, and in terror she pressed the blade to him, not really understanding anything in her panic until he gasped and she saw him fall.

The two others were on her now, but Dash and Vincent leaped out to meet them, and they, too, acted with the dulled responses of surprise. The scuffle was nearly silent as Dash leaped forward, pulling the first away from Abra and silencing him with a quick blow to the chin. Then he turned to the second as the guard pulled his knife from his sash and advanced on Vincent. He pulled his own blade to meet the guard's and the two struggled hand to hand for a few tense seconds. And then Dash raised his knee and kicked, hard, the blow landing in a pain-filled second of surprised agony, and the guard dropped his knife and fell to the floor, clutching himself as the explosion of pain filled him.

Dash leaned down, kicking the knife away from his grasp, and planted one more swift kick, leaving the guard senseless and still.

"Where did you learn to fight like that?" Vincent asked him with undisguised admiration.

"Harvard," Dash told him dully. "No one ever fought clean there."

He turned to Vincent as he knelt by the still guard, assuring himself that the man was quite incapacitated.

"You said it was child's play," he said, nodding to

362

the wrought iron gate that fronted the treasury. "It's time to prove it."

Vincent smiled and moved to the gate, kneeling and addressing himself to the lock. He had it opened in a matter of seconds.

Dash dragged the three guards' limp bodies inside, behind the gate, quickly tying and gagging the unconscious men with their sashes, ignoring the third, the dead one. It wasn't until he'd done that that he noticed Abra standing and staring at the small pool of blood that lay on the floor where the guard she'd stabbed had lain.

He went to her, moving slowly, as though he were afraid she might bolt at a sudden movement.

He put his arms around her. "You didn't have much choice," he told her softly. "And if you'd done otherwise, it could have cost both Vincent's and my life."

She let herself fall against him, wondering how she had come to this point, how she had actually used a knife and killed a man.

Dash wanted to comfort her, to hold her close and try to make her forget everything that had happened in the last days, but she wouldn't let him. She pulled away from him, her body growing rigid at his caress.

His eyes found hers for an instant, perplexed, wondering what it was she thought as she stood and stared at him. She seemed to have become a stranger to him, and he realized that whoever it was who stared out at him through her eyes looked on him as something alien and untrustworthy.

"I've got it."

They both turned to watch Vincent pull open the vaultlike inner door of the treasury. Behind the door was what appeared to be a huge closet, its shelves laden with strongboxes.

Vincent moved inside, scanning the shelves, and Dash and Abra followed him. She watched numbly as Dash began to rifle through the boxes. Vincent, however, seemed to know where the stone was kept, as if he was drawn to it. He moved to the far wall of the

363

closet, to a shelf with a single small jeweled casket in its center. This he lifted down and opened with a marked respect.

"The Tear," he said softly as he drew the stone out.

Dash took it in his hand and stared at it a second, then turned back to the door. "Let's get out of . . ." He stopped, silenced by what he saw.

"Abra? What are you doing?" Vincent demanded as he, too, turned to face her.

She stood and stared at them, her face white and strained, the knife she'd taken from the floor where the last guard had dropped it held firmly and threateningly in her hands.

"I want it, Papa," she explained with rash forcefulness. "I won't let you steal it. It belongs to Salim, for his cause, for his people."

"Damn it, Abra," Dash began, but she cut him off.

"Don't try to lie to me, Dash," she shouted at him. "I know what you intended to do. And I won't let you. My mind's made up."

"Listen to me, Abra. It's not what you think, none of it has ever been what you've thought."

"No," she shouted at him. "I won't listen. I won't let you make me believe any more lies." But she backed away from him, for he was moving slowly forward, toward her, and she was terrified that he would force her to use the knife.

"Abra, listen to him. You're wrong. It's not what you think."

"No, Papa. It's not just a game any more. It's the future of a whole country. He can't have blinded you to that, you've got to see."

"Oh, I'm sure they see, my dear. I'm sure they both see."

Dash looked up to someone behind her, and his expression changed to one of complete hatred.

Abra knew, even before she turned. She knew by the voice. She felt herself filling with a sickening feeling of terror as she turned and faced Sharify. The pistol he held in his hand was pointed directly at Dash's heart.

364

"I'm so glad you've decided to return to me, Abra, my dear," Sharify said with a satisfied drawl. "And, this time, I can assure you, there will be no more foolish attempts at running away. That was really rather childish of you, don't you think?"

The corridor behind him filled with his soldiers, and Sharify moved forward to her, wresting the knife from her grasp with a quick, jerking motion even as he kept the pistol pointed squarely at Dash.

"As for you, Thorne, I think I will make an example of you, one that Salim and his foolish band will not soon forget, one that will give them nightmares in the weeks to come."

"Let Abra and Vincent leave, Sharify," Dash said slowly, his voice low. "They're neither of them a real part of any of this."

"Aren't they?" Sharify asked with a humorless smile. "I think Vincent is not quite so innocent as you would have me think. And as for the lovely Abra, well, I don't really care whether she is or she isn't. I've made a few plans regarding her, and I have no intention of seeing them disrupted any further than they already have been."

He motioned to the guards and they moved forward, surrounding Dash and Vincent and quickly removing their weapons and restraining them. Then Sharify stepped forward.

"I'll relieve you of the responsibility of that," he said as he took the Tear. "I'm sure you will feel relieved to be well out of the grips of temptation."

Then he motioned to the guards once more. "Take them both to the cells. And this time, see that there are no escapes."

Abra watched, dazed, as Vincent and Dash were led away.

"You've been a fool, Abra," Dash said to her as he passed, and his words bit into her like knives, leaving hurtful bleeding wounds behind. She followed him with

365

her eyes, too numb to speak, barely noticing Sharify's hand on her arm until he pulled her roughly around to face him.

"And now that we've done with the preliminaries, my dear, I think it about time we got down to the business at hand." He pushed her against the wall, his body pressing close to hers, his hands holding her arms tight to her sides. "And if you ever want to see your father alive again, I suggest that you make a great deal of effort to please me."

He lowered his lips to hers.

# Chapter Twenty-three

Dash and Vincent, surrounded by a ridiculously large phalanx of guards, had reached the courtyard when the explosion tore through the palace armory and the guards' barracks next to it. The deep, low rumble and the shuddering impact that followed it sent the soldiers who were still inside stumbling out, some helping the wounded, most with bloody gashes evident. But the initial explosion was insignificant compared with the one that followed. As the heat reached the stored munitions, they, too, ignited, and within seconds of the first explosion came the second, the force of it shaking the ground and splitting walls, sending bricks and rubble flying.

When Dash managed to get back to his feet, he grabbed Vincent and pulled him up. The guards were in confusion, and seemed more interested in determining if they were still relatively whole than keeping close watch. Dash ran to the cover of the corridor they'd just left before any attention could be redirected in their direction, pulling Vincent along with him.

When they were out of plain sight, Vincent stood, leaning against the wall for a moment, his hand pressed to his chest. Dash peered out at the courtyard, assuring himself that the confusion persisted, that they hadn't been followed.

"They're still numb," he whispered, although the tone

was really unnecessary, as the courtyard was filled with the sounds of men shouting and pushing in a dazed attempt at flight. He turned to Vincent. "Your heart," he said as he helped the older man to sit. "Are you all right?"

Vincent looked up at him and offered him a smile of absolute glee. He nodded, then breathed deeply twice. "Just a bit old for this sort of thing, I'm sorry to admit," he said. "Salim really knows how to grab a bit of attention when he tries, doesn't he?" He put his hand on Dash's arm, then got back to his feet.

"We've got to get Abra out of here," Dash said, staring at the stairs. A long crack had appeared on the facing wall. "Do you think that is safe?"

Vincent shrugged. "This place is a fort. It would take fifty explosions like Salim's little diversion to do any real damage."

They climbed upward, Dash leading, and raced back to the treasury. The air was filled with the babble of the panic from below, as men raced to the fire that now flared brilliantly in the courtyard, engulfing the armory and the guards' barracks. And they nearly tripped as they encountered Sharify, his attention occupied with dragging Abra along with him, as he ran to the courtyard to discover what had happened.

All four of them stopped for a moment, both pairs dazed by the sudden appearance of the other. Then Sharify released Abra, pushing her aside, and his hand fell to the hilt of the blade at his waist.

"So it's come to this, has it, Thorne?" he said as he drew the knife. "Just the two of us. Shall we see if I can't find the end of this rather extended streak of luck you've been having?"

Dash smiled as his hand found the blade he'd managed to grab on his scramble from the courtyard. He motioned to Vincent to back away.

"I'd prefer to think of it as skill, Sharify," he replied with a note of derision. "I've always found a man makes his own luck."

"As you like, Thorne," Sharify responded, dismissing him with a nod. "Whatever it is, it ends now."

With those words, he lunged forward, the blade extended. But Dash anticipated him, sidestepping the blow and deflecting the sheik's arm with his own. They grappled, hand to hand, each man holding off the other's knife, pitting his strength against the other.

Abra stood, staring wide-eyed at the struggle, her wits dulled by her fear for Dash's life. But then she remembered the pistol, Sharify's weapon. He'd dropped it in the corridor by the treasury when he'd grabbed her. And it would be there still, she realized.

She turned and raced back, but when she turned the corner, she found the floor shining and empty save for the blood of the guard she'd stabbed. He lay, still and pale, his eyes peering up at her as though with mute accusation. She started to move to the body, thinking to take the blade that still protruded from his chest, but found she couldn't touch it. Her stomach heaved and she turned away, sickened at the thought.

But then she realized the double gates to the treasury were still open, that the guards, distracted by the explosion and the fire below, had not come back to relock and secure them. She dashed inside, easily found the Tear, and dropped it into her pocket. Then she grabbed one of the brass-trimmed mahogany boxes from a shelf. She hefted it, and realized it was more than heavy enough to make an effective weapon. She wrapped her arms around it and hurried back around the corner to where Dash and Sharify still struggled.

She'd been gone only a moment, but the fight had become more unbalanced. Sharify was larger and heavier, and that, combined with the injuries Dash had suffered while he'd been imprisoned, was weighting the fight in the sheik's direction. Dash had been forced backward, almost to the wall, and Sharify advanced on him with the intent assurance of victory.

Abra raised the chest, aimed it, and threw.

She swore as it missed its mark, hitting the wall a good half foot from Sharify's head.

But the impact was loud and startling, enough to break Sharify's concentration. He turned to stare at the fallen box, its lock popped open and a scattering of precious stones dropped to the floor.

It was the chance Dash needed. He twisted aside,

away from Sharify's grasp, and then, both hands grasped into a tight ball, lowered them with all his might into the back of the sheik's neck.

Sharify went limp, then fell to the floor. Dash stood over him a moment, panting. Then he turned to Abra and smiled.

"Excellent idea," he said with a lopsided grin. "I couldn't have done better myself."

He knelt, pushed most of the stones back into the box, then closed it, lifting it as he stood.

"The Tear?" he asked, and she nodded numbly, patting her pocket where she'd put the incredible ruby. He grabbed her arm. "Then I think it's time we left the good emir to his own devices."

They turned away, more than ready to flee, only to find themselves face to face with Raisa.

She stared at them wildly. "You've killed him," she screamed, and raised her hands to them.

She was holding Sharify's missing pistol.

Dash shook his head.

"No," he said gently. "We didn't come here to kill. If his people still want him, he will continue as he has. If not, then Salim will deal with him."

But Raisa shook her head. She hadn't really heard his words, for her attention was centered on Sharify. She stared at his still body numbly, as though she were seeing him for the first time, seeing him as he really was. Then she lifted her eyes to Abra.

"This is all your fault," she cried, and there was no mistaking the anguish in her eyes. "If you hadn't come here . . ." Her words trailed off and her eyes drifted back to where Sharify lay.

Abra stepped forward toward her. "Let us go, Raisa," she begged softly. "We didn't want to come here. We didn't want any of this. He did it to himself."

Sharify groaned and began to stir. Abra knew that if they didn't leave quickly, they would have no other chance.

"Please, Raisa," she begged.

"Go. Get out of here before I change my mind," Raisa shouted at them without even lifting her eyes from Sharify.

Abra breathed a sigh of relief, and then Dash's hand was once more at her arm, drawing her away. She looked back just once, to see Sharify turn onto his back and stare up at his wife. Then she darted along with Vincent and Dash, not wanting to know what would happen.

Even when the sound of two shots followed them, echoing through the long corridor, she told herself that she did not want to know.

They couldn't go back the way they had come. The fire and confusion in the servants' courtyard would have started to abate, and the guards would be hunting there for them, with the taste for blood.

But Vincent had other plans for their exit. He led them through the long, empty palace halls to the front gate. Here, too, there was confusion, but it was less organized, far more bewildered.

"Fire," Dash shouted from behind the cover of a pillar. "At the armory. Every man is needed."

No one seemed to be concerned that the issuer of the orders did not show himself. Trained to follow directions, they rushed past.

Dash motioned to Abra and Vincent to pull their hoods over their heads, then they simply melted into the flow of men, drifting toward the palace gate and eventually out through it.

The town of Tahaf, wakened to the smell of smoke in the early morning air, flooded into the streets in curiosity. Despite the fact that the three walked with an odd purposefulness amidst the generally milling populace, no one paid them much attention. Within a matter of moments they had slipped through the city gates, leaving Tahaf unchallenged.

They walked then in intent silence, looking very much like three desert nomads leaving the luxury of Tahaf for the harsher, purer life of the desert. They strode through the shifting sand, eventually coming to the high dune at whose opposite side they'd left their horses.

Dash hefted the strongbox, and suddenly he began to

laugh. It was a low, soft rumble at first, but it grew, deeper and louder, until both Vincent and Abra were contaminated and joined him. The sound of their laughter seemed to shimmer around them in the bright morning sunshine.

"Your daughter appears to be the greatest thief of the three of us," Dash told Vincent when his laughter died enough to allow him to speak. "She stole not one jewel, but a whole strongbox full."

Vincent sobered. "But she's not trusted either of us with the Tear," he said.

Dash stopped, and his laughter died as he stared at Abra with hard blue eyes. He set the box down on the sand at his feet.

"That's true," he said, suddenly very sober. "Well, Abra, what is it to be? You pointed a weapon at me not an hour ago and informed me that you couldn't trust me. Can you trust me now?"

Abra peered up at him, his features bright and hard in the clear sunlight. She'd nearly gotten all of them killed, and yet he was still asking her to trust him.

With sickening awareness, she realized nothing mattered to her more than being with him, that losing him was worse to her than her own death. She'd fought against it, harder than she'd ever fought against anything in her life, but now the fight was gone. He was her life, and if he chose to live in a manner she would not have chosen, she'd simply have to abandon her scruples. It was not a matter of choice for her actually, because she couldn't willingly abandon him. It was physically impossible for her.

She put her hand into her pocket and drew out the Tear. She stood still and silent as she held it out to him.

He took it from her, and without bothering even to look at it, tossed the stone to Vincent as if it were nothing more than glass.

"Does this mean you've decided to accept me as I am, Abra?" he asked her slowly. He put his hands to her arms and inched slowly closer to her. "Does this mean you're willing to let me decide what to do with that piece of rock?"

She nodded, still silent. Then she licked her lips, as though looking for the strength to speak.

"Yes," she said softly.

A look of decided pleasure filled his face. He leaned toward her and kissed her, his lips finding hers with a knowing, possessive certainty. She accepted them, surrendering herself to him just as she had surrendered the stone.

"I hope for your sake you've chosen to act nobly, Thorne. I would hate to be forced to have you killed."

They turned to the ridge of the dune and saw Salim staring down at them, smiling a hard, humorless smile. The rifle he held in his hands was pointed down, toward them. With an abrupt movement, he motioned for them to join him.

Dash turned to Abra, his glance hard and distant. "Well, it would seem you get your wish, Abra," he said through tight lips as he knelt and retrieved the strongbox from where it lay on the ground by his feet. "I don't suppose Salim's gracious display of trust was in any way due to your intervention, was it?"

She started to protest her innocence to him, to swear that she'd said nothing to Salim. But then she stopped, even before the words were formed in her mind. She'd done nothing for which she had any need to apologize to him, she thought. And his manner told her more plainly than words that she had been wrong to offer him her trust in the first place.

The three of them climbed the remaining distance to the top of the dune. They stood there and peered down to the far side, to where Salim's men stood, stiff and tense, expecting the emir's soldiers to appear at any moment, waiting for the order to mount.

Salim squinted into the bright sunlight, staring back towards Tahaf. The gates to the city remained open but empty, the pursuing force he seemed to expect to stream from it failing to appear.

"I see our little noise was enough for your purposes. But I wonder what keeps my brother from the chase. It is unlike him to let an insult pass so easily. Especially so great an insult as we have done to him this day."

"I don't think the sheik will be coming, Salim," Dash

373

told him as he handed the box to him.

Salim's eyes narrowed. "That was not a part of the bargain," he said. "Just the jewel. He's my brother."

Vincent moved forward and offered the Tear to his waiting hand. "It was not our doing," he told the rebel leader. "It was Raisa."

Salim took the stone and stood staring into its fiery center as he contemplated this unexpected bit of news.

"It was never my intent to take power by killing," he said slowly. "There has been too much of that already here. My people must learn other ways, ways more fitting to the world we now inhabit."

"They will learn them," Abra told him softly. "With you to show them, they can't help but learn."

Salim's grip tightened on the Tear. "And with this to guide me, I suppose they can't help but follow." He looked up at Abra, his dark eyes intense. "After all," he murmured, "it is the will of Allah."

Salim's men gave them safe passage back to Tunis. After the long, hot days in the saddle, Abra was more than willing to call the whole adventure simply a bad dream, to immerse herself in a huge tub of warm water and tell herself none of it had really ever happened.

But Dash directed them first to the American consulate.

"Why here?" Abra demanded crossly as she read the brass-lettered plaque at the door and saw the uniformed guards.

"Lest you forget, Abra, our papers were left in Venice. And Vincent was smuggled without benefit of any at all. If we intend to go home, we'll need passports."

"Can't those things wait?" she begged. "All I want to do is take a bath."

"No."

That was all, no other explanation. Just no. He'd treated her with the same distant bare tolerance all the way from Mukalla. And during those days she'd come to resign herself to the fact that her final submission to him, that small show of faith when she'd given the stone over to him, had simply not been enough. Not that she blamed him, not after what she'd done. She supposed he'd leave her and Vincent once the matter of papers and passage had been attended to, his final obligation to them before he left. There was, after all, nothing left to hold him.

Dash and Vincent climbed the first few steps, then paused and turned, waiting for her to follow. She gritted her teeth. If she must go through with this, she told herself, she would do it with a modicum of good grace if it killed her.

She climbed the steps to join them. Dash took her arm, guiding her up the last of the steps and to the front desk where an officious-looking man inspected their travel-worn appearance with obvious displeasure.

But Dash ignored his manner.

"We'd like to see Charles Nevin. He's expecting me. Dashiel Thorne."

The receptionist seemed a bit unsettled, and he stood.

"Wait here," he said, nodding toward a wooden bench against the wall. "I'll see if Mr. Nevin can see you now."

Then he turned away and disappeared through a door to the rear of the reception hall.

"Who is this Charles Nevin?" Abra demanded suspiciously as Dash led her to the bench. "And why should he be expecting to see you?"

Dash only shrugged. "If you don't act as though you're more important than these petty officials, Abra, you spend a great deal of time waiting. I'm too damned tired and sore to wait around here all day."

Then he sat on the bare wooden bench, his long legs extended in front of him and gave absolutely no indication that he intended to say another word.

Abra turned to her father, but Vincent, too, seemed to have decided that her questions were not worth further conversation. He sat down beside Dash and busied himself with a concerted consideration of his fingernails.

Abra stood and fumed at the two of them in silence. They gave absolutely no indication of being even remotely aware of her presence.

375

"It seems Mr. Nevin is available to see you now." The superior expression had crumbled just the slightest bit, and the receptionist's manner now seemed almost deferential as he showed them through the cool, quiet marble halls. He pulled open a shiny dark door and stood back, letting them pass through to the office beyond.

A small man looked up to them and rose, smiling profusely.

"Damn it, Dash, I don't quite believe it, but you've done it."

Dash cut off his flow of words with a wave of his hand. "It seems that the three of us find ourselves without necessary travel documents. I assume the consulate can arrange to have them prepared, Mr. Nevin?"

Nevin's smile vanished at Dash's abrupt manner.

"Certainly, but . . ."

Once more Dash interrupted. "And we'll have need of an official who is empowered to perform a marriage. Immediately."

"Marriage?" Abra and Nevin, both wide-eyed with surprise, queried simultaneously.

Dash turned to her, putting his hand to her shoulder. "You and Salim have seen to it that I'm to live the remainder of my life in near penury, Abra. I expect you'll have the good grace to offer to share it with me. Besides," he added with a grin, "I expect you to make an honest man of me."

Abra only stared at him with open-mouthed disbelief.

"Well, Abra," he asked, softly now as he drew her close to him. "What is it to be? Living in some dim little cottage somewhere with an ex-thief? Or do you go back to New York and the likes of Freddy Westmore?"

A slow grin worked its way to Abra's lips. "Well," she replied thoughtfully, putting her hands to Dash's shoulders, "given the choice, I think I'd prefer poverty to Freddy."

"And marriage is what people become involved with when they're in love," Dash continued. "You are in love with me, aren't you, Miss Beaumont?" he asked with a wrily knowing smile.

She returned the smile with an equally knowing one of her own. "I suppose I am, Mr. Thorne," she told

376

him.

He lowered his lips to hers, and Abra accepted his kiss, knowing that it was what she wanted more than anything else, feeling for the first time since the whole insane adventure had begun that she was sure of herself, sure of where her life was leading her. She would go with him, she told herself, gladly even live in the poverty he had promised her. As long as he was there, it didn't really matter to her.

"Then say it, Abra," he whispered. "Say you love me."

She looked up into his icy blue eyes and willingly admitted it. "I love you, Dashiel Thorne."

Dash turned to Nevin. "I think we'd like that wedding ceremony as soon as possible, Charles," he told the short man, then turned back to Abra's welcoming smile. "I don't want the future Mrs. Thorne to have any time for second thoughts. It wouldn't do to have her change her mind.

Nevin beamed at them with an owlish smile. "Certainly, Dash. I'm sure matters can be arranged." He removed his glasses and nervously polished them. "But this matter of poverty really isn't neccesary, you know. My, ah, superiors are delighted with the way matters have worked out. They're more than willing to reimburse you for the expenses you've been to, as well as a reasonable fee for your time and effort."

Dash tore his eyes from Abra's. "Do you think they might manage to finance a few days at the bridal suite of the best hotel in town, Charles?" he demanded with a grin. "After all, we have to stay somewhere while you arrange passage back home."

Nevin returned his spectacles to his nose and rifled through some papers, obviously embarrassed at the sight of Abra throwing her arms around Dash's neck and pressing a decidedly enthusiastic kiss to his lips.

"I'm sure that can be arranged," he replied in a hoarse murmur.

"Then see to it, Charles," Dash told him without turning his glance away from Abra. "I'm not sure we can either of us wait very much longer."

Then he swept her up into his arms and carried her

377

out of the room, leaving the two older men to stare after them, one with apparent shock, the other with pleased amusement.

"A glass of bubbly, Mrs. Thorne?"

Abra neatened the rumpled sheets around her and peered out at him through the white film of the bed netting. She smiled as he approached, and she reached up and accepted the offered wine.

"Certainly, Mr. Thorne," she replied quite soberly. "I make it a habit of never rejecting an offer from a naked man carrying a heavy bottle."

"Hmm," Dash mused. He set the bottle down on the bedside table and rejoined her on the bed. "Have there been a great many of those in your decidedly checkered past?"

Abra sipped her wine thoughtfully, then shook her head. "Only one who made any lasting impression on me," she replied with a smile. She stared at him for a moment and her smile disappeared. "You promised me some explanations, Dash. I think it's time."

He leaned to her and nibbled at her shoulder. "I thought we agreed that could wait until more pressing matters were dispensed with, Abra," he said with a lecherous grin.

She giggled, then pulled away. "You said you were exhausted," she taunted.

"Never so exhausted as that," he countered.

"Well, I haven't finished my champagne."

He leaned back. "All right. What do you want to know?"

Abra faced him expectantly. "All of it. First of all, who is Charles Nevin?"

"I thought that was made amply apparent by the fact that he was graced with office space at the embassy, Abra," Dash replied evasively. "He works for the government."

"But how do you know him? What has he got to do with the Tear?"

Dash drained his glass, his expression thoughtful. Then he leaned to the bedside table, retrieved the bottle of champagne, and refilled it.

"I suppose you want it all, then. From the start?"

Abra scowled. "I thought I made that entirely clear."

He grinned. "All right," he agreed. Then he refilled her glass as well and returned the bottle to the table.

Abra watched him, her impatience growing more apparent with each passing second.

Dash resettled himself, then took one more sip of his wine, apparently relishing her intolerant expression.

"I think you might prefer the version you already know, where I'm simply a greed-driven thief. But if you want the truth, here it is. I'm a lawyer, not a thief, not a professional one, anyway. The only real burglary I ever pulled before this started was the one I told you about, the one with your father's friend, James Sutton."

"So you did know the doctor?" she asked.

Dash grinned. "All my life. He was my mother's brother. A decided black sheep of the family, but an endearing one. And he's the reason Nevin came to me when his oft-mentioned superiors decided the Tear must be taken. I was a favorite nephew of Uncle James, and he'd given me a few lessons, as well as a wealth of information. If I couldn't get it myself, I would know who to go to for help. And that, of course, was your father."

"And Papa knew about this all along?" she asked, dismayed.

He shook his head. "Not at first. In fact, my instructions were to convince him I was absolutely genuine. Nevin even had worked out a plan for me to steal the Dewitte diamonds if necessary to insure that Vincent was convinced he was dealing with James Sutton's protegé. But as soon as I realized that Vincent was only interested in seeing if it could be done, not in having the Tear or the money it would bring, I confided in him. He's a hard man to lie to."

"Unlike his daughter," she accused.

He turned to her and his eyes grew liquid. "At first, Abra, we thought it was safest for you if you didn't know. We thought you'd be more cautious if you thought we were about to commit a robbery, not go

379

about some bizarre governmental acquisition. And then," he shrugged, "then I realized I needed to know you loved me, regardless of what I was, who I was."

"You're a bit mad, you know," she said softly, staring into his eyes and feeling herself drowning in them.

He grinned gently. "So I've been told."

"But why would the government want the Tear stolen?"

"I thought that was obvious. They wanted Salim in power, not his brother."

Abra smiled pleasantly. "Because Salim would bring a more liberal government, one fairer to the people."

Dash grew sober. "It would be nice if that were so, Abra. And I swear to you, if I hadn't been convinced that Salim would change things in his country, I wouldn't have gotten involved with any of it. But even if he were the same sort of despot that his brother was, they'd still have wanted him in control."

Abra shook her head, confused. "Why? I don't understand."

"Oil, Abra," he told her. "There's a great deal of it in Mukalla. And Salim has promised to make a favorable arrangement with our oil companies. Shahab was holding out, blackmailing not only the United States, but England and France as well, looking for the biggest plum he could pluck."

Abra fell back against the pillows and stared up at the crown that held the netting to the ceiling. "So all this has been about money after all, nothing but money."

"I told you you wouldn't like it," he reminded her.

"Papa was right," she said bitterly. "They're all thieves. Some of them just have the sanction of the law."

"It's over, Abra," he told her, turning to her and putting her hand to her cheek, forcing her eyes to meet his. "And a good deal of good came out of it. Salim will make sweeping reforms. And, more important for us, I found you."

She smiled at that. "And you don't need reforming after all," she replied.

He took her glass from her hand and put both of

380

them on the bedside table.

"I wouldn't be so sure of that, Mrs. Thorne," he told her as he pulled her down on top of him. His hand slowly caressed her naked back and haunches. "I should think a strong guiding hand would be helpful for two such ne'er-do-wells as we."

She splayed her fingers through the wiry hair on his chest. "What sort of a guiding hand?" she asked as she teasingly circled his nipple with the tips of her fingers, then leaned forward to his chest and repeated the motion with her lips and tongue.

He grinned. "I hadn't thought you'd need lessons any longer, Mrs. Thorne," he chided as he pulled her body close to his. "You seemed such an adept pupil all evening, I thought by now you'd have progressed to a few variations of your own."

"Like this?" she asked mischievously, her hand trailing along the hard muscles of his chest, to his abdomen and downward.

"You're becoming quite accomplished," he whispered as he reached up to her hair, and pulled her face to his, his lips finding hers with pleased ardor.

He was lost, he realized, the first time she'd smiled at him. He wondered why it had taken so long for them both to realize that some fates can not be denied.

For a second his glance strayed to the small leather pouch that lay on his dresser across the room. Inside it was a handsome ruby, not nearly so incredible or large as the Tear, of course, but still a fine stone. Salim had called it a memento when he had taken it from the chest of stones they'd brought to him, and Dash had taken it, not sure if Charles Nevin would prove as persuasive with his superiors as he'd promised to be. But now, it seemed, he wouldn't have to sell the ruby, after all. He'd have it made into a wedding ring for her, he decided, and maybe, just maybe, he'd let her think he'd stolen it. After all, it was to a thief she'd said "I do!" that afternoon. Maybe she loved that part of him more than she was willing to admit, even to herself.

Abra laughed softly, a low, throaty laugh, and Dash's thoughts left the ruby for the far more important matter at hand.

"I love you, Mrs. Thorne," he whispered as he pulled her body to his and slid inside her. Then he wound his hands in her hair, hungry for the taste of her lips as he stared up at her.

And Abra smiled.

## TURN TO CATHERINE CREEL—THE REAL THING—FOR THE FINEST IN HEART-SOARING ROMANCE!

**CAPTIVE FLAME** (2401, $3.95)
Meghan Kearney was grateful to American Devlin Montague for rescuing her from the gang of Bahamian cutthroats. But soon the handsome yet arrogant island planter insisted she serve his baser needs—and Meghan wondered if she'd merely traded one kind of imprisonment for another!

**TEXAS SPITFIRE** (2225, $3.95)
If fiery Dallas Brown failed to marry overbearing Ross Kincaid, she would lose her family inheritance. But though Dallas saw Kincaid as a low-down, shifty opportunist, the strong-willed beauty could not deny that he made her pulse race with an inexplicable flaming desire!

**SCOUNDREL'S BRIDE** (2062, $3.95)
Though filled with disgust for the seamen overrunning her island home, innocent Hillary Reynolds was overwhelmed by the tanned, masculine physique of dashing Ryan Gallagher. Until, in a moment of wild abandon, she offered herself like a purring tiger to his passionate, insistent caress!

*Available wherever paperbacks are sold, or order direct from the Publisher. Send cover price plus 50¢ per copy for mailing and handling to Zebra Books, Dept. 2613, 475 Park Avenue South, New York, N.Y. 10016. Residents of New York, New Jersey and Pennsylvania must include sales tax. DO NOT SEND CASH.*